AFTER DARK
WARRIOR SERIES

Also by Melanie P. Smith

<u>Warrior Series</u>

Dusk

Serendipity (Anthology)

Dawn

Shadows

<u>Novels</u>

Hidden Lakes

AFTER DARK

Warrior Series

Book Two

---

by:
Melanie P. Smith

MPSmith Publishing

Dedication:

To the Survivors

Chapter One

Ariel sat perched on a large chair in front of the bank of security monitors. She was studying them for movement. At least when Dimitri did something, he did it right. If someone was in the forest, she would see them. Montgomery Incorporated was the best security company around. Installing cameras right into the trees had been brilliant. Nobody could come within 200 yards of the cabin without being recorded. It was twilight now, but with the sun falling below the horizon it was only a matter of minutes before darkness would settle over the entire area. Ariel glanced around the small security room. She'd left all the interior lights off when she entered the cabin. She didn't want whoever or whatever was out there to know where she was hiding. She'd only caught a glimpse of movement as she exited her car, but that was enough to put her on alert. The security room had a small window, but the blinds were shut. Very little light seeped into the room. It was going to be dark soon. Ariel hated small dark rooms. They reminded her of that room, the terrible cold room so long ago. She checked the monitors again, watching closely for the slightest movement. There it was again. A white streak ran across the screen. They couldn't be vampires, could they? Another light figure flew across the edge of the monitor. It was moving too fast to determine its identity. Could it be a vampire? Vampires couldn't go out in the sun, they would eventually burn to death if they tried. Ariel's gaze moved to the steel door, it was bolted shut. She should be safe here. The metal door would keep intruders at bay, too bad it couldn't lock out memories of her past. She'd just have to concentrate on something else.

Ariel remembered hearing about a group of vampires that tried to go out on an overcast day. They were fine as long as the sun didn't peak through the clouds. Direct sunlight would kill them. It would burn them to death, but not instantly. She'd heard it was a slow painful death. That experiment had been centuries ago. As far as she knew, nobody had tried it since. The consequence of failure was too severe. Would the shadows from the trees protect a vampire if they wanted to hide in the forest? Had Radek, the vampire king, become so desperate he was now sending his vampires out during the day? Ariel hoped that wasn't the case. It was bad enough fighting them after dark. But if those things in the forest weren't vampires, what were they?

Movement crossed two separate monitors at the same time. So whatever was out there, it wasn't alone. She could be facing multiple attackers, again. The fear of the unknown was causing her imagination to kick into overdrive. It would be different this time, she had powers now. Ariel stood and began to pace the room. She had to keep moving. The memories were starting to flood her mind. She didn't want to relive that awful incident again. Not tonight. Not out here in this cabin in the middle of nowhere. She closed her eyes and began counting to ten. Bad idea, she could still see the dirty, grungy men standing over her naked body. The smell of whiskey was strong on their breath. "No," she said aloud. She wouldn't go back there. It had happened so long ago. You would think the memory would fade with time and eventually go away completely. She owed her life to Dimitri. She'd been nineteen; young and vulnerable. He'd shown up in the nick of time. If he'd been just a moment later, that day would have been so much worse.

Now centuries later she was hiding away in this safe room Dimitri had built for Alex, the love of his life. Ariel stood next to the chair and prayed she really was safe. She hoped this room could withstand any attack from anyone. In a way, maybe Dimitri was saving her all over again. She wondered if she should call him. Should she tell him what was happening? She knew if she called, he would rush over. Or, he would send a couple of the warriors. She took several slow, deep breaths. She was starting to panic, but was it from old memories or her current situation? She would not pull Dimitri away from Alex for old memories. He was enjoying a rare night off. She knew Alex would understand, but then she'd have to explain why she freaked out. She didn't want to talk about that time in her life. Eventually she would tell Alex about it. They had already become such good friends. But she hated to relive those memories. She wasn't ready to talk about them again. The only one that knew about the incident besides her parents and Dimitri, was her best friend Breena.

Ariel took a deep breath. She'd be okay if Breena were here. Breena always knew how to calm her down. She glanced back at the monitors. Yeah, they were still there. She closed her eyes and tried to concentrate on other things. Breena and Orin would be home soon. "Try to think about that," she told herself. Ariel began to feel nauseous. No matter how hard she tried to forget, the musty stench of that rickety old house kept coming back to her. The ugly laughter that followed the crewed comments of those drunken men rang in her ears. She could hear them arguing as if they were here in this room, at this very moment. The Robert guy was yelling at the other three men. He insisted once they were finished with her, she would have to die. They couldn't let her live, she would run to the police. He was afraid she could identify every one of them. Ariel had been so frightened and cold that morning. She just kept praying that somehow, someone would help her. To this day she still didn't know what happened to those men. Dimitri wouldn't tell her.

Ariel slumped down against the wall. She began to weep. She felt like such a coward. Why couldn't she forget those awful memories? She'd been terrified and abused, but Dimitri had saved her in time. Why after all these years, all her training, could she still be drawn back to that awful time in an instant? How could she be this weak? Put her up against ten vampires, no problem. With just a small group of eight, they had battled hundreds of vampires on Bree and Orin's front lawn. But put her in a small dark space to face the unknown, and she relived the horrors of her youth.

Ariel realized she was shaking. She felt so cold and alone, tears were running down her face. She picked up her phone again, debating. She really didn't want to bother Dimitri tonight. She started to slide the phone back into her pocket when it rang. Ariel looked at the display and sighed with relief. It was Dimitri, or Alex.

"Hello," Ariel said, trying to sound casual like she wasn't in a panic about to crumble into a million pieces.

"What's wrong?" Dimitri demanded, clearly worried.

Ariel smiled a little. She never could fool Dimitri. "I'm okay. Really. I guess I'm just a big coward. You know how I get sometimes when I'm alone and I get nervous or frightened. I'm just over reacting again."

"Ariel, tell me what's frightened you," Dimitri said. Compassion and understanding in his voice.

"It's probably nothing. I'm sure I'm just jumpy because of everything that's happened the past few months. But there's something out in the forest," Ariel admitted.

"What do you mean something is out in the forest? Have you checked the monitors? Where are you?" Dimitri was on alert. He was a born leader. It was so like him to immediately take charge.

"I'm in this world class panic room you and Ty built. Perfect description I guess. Once I got in here, I pretty much panicked. Anyway, I have checked the monitors. There is definitely something out in the forest, I just can't tell what it is. There are big white or gray figures flying across the screen too fast to identify. At first I only saw one at a time. Now I can tell there are at least two of them. It's still light outside. You don't think they could be vampires do you?"

"I doubt it. Radek is desperate, but I don't think he would risk sending vampires out during the day. Not even in the forest. Thomas is working tonight. He should be close to the cabin. I'm sending him over immediately. Don't leave that room for anything. Thomas can get in on his own. He still has a key to the cabin and he has the code for the safe room. You're lucky your landlord's working in the area. It's going to take longer for me and Alex to get there."

After Dark

"Dimitri," Ariel interrupted. "I don't want you and Alex ruining your night off together. Don't drive all the way out here just to check on me. Thomas can handle whatever is going on here. Promise me you won't come out unless Thomas calls for backup after he arrives and checks things out."

Dimitri sighed. "Do you know when Breena and Orin will be home?"

"Not exactly," Ariel admitted. "They haven't had a real night out in months. I didn't press, they deserve this time alone together. Things have been difficult for them for a while. I'm not sure Alex knows what a great thing she did that night when she healed Breena. Those two can finally have the relationship they've always deserved. Between you and me, I was starting to worry about Orin. He was spending more time drinking at some club than was healthy."

"You sound a little better. Are you going to be okay until Thomas gets there?" Dimitri asked sincerely worried about her.

"I think I will be now. Thanks Dimitri. You're probably the only person who truly understands what I'm going through. You always know how to calm me down. I'm sorry I've been such a basket case about this for the last what... 357 years? I'm a lot better than I used to be. I haven't had one of these attacks for decades," she paused. "I always knew I owed you my life. Now I realize I also owe you my sanity." Ariel was embarrassed, but knew Dimitri understood.

"You don't owe me anything," Dimitri said soberly. "You're not the only one who's had nightmares about that incident. Things could have been so much worse. Try to remember that. You survived. You're strong and brave. Don't ever think you're a coward, Ariel. Anyone in that situation would have been shaken. I'm going to call Thomas now. Stay locked in that room until he gets there. It shouldn't take him long but if you need to, call me back. I'll talk to you until he arrives."

"Thank you for everything, Dimitri. I'll be fine until Thomas gets here. Sorry for all the trouble. The last thing you and Alex need is me interrupting one of the few nights you have together. You're supposed to be planning your wedding. Hey, by the way, why did you call me?" Ariel asked.

"I'm not sure. I just had this feeling I should check on you. It was something I couldn't shake, so I finally made the call," Dimitri admitted.

"Don't tell me the mighty warrior leader has gone psychic. Queen superstar's in for a challenge. Speaking of the queen, will you apologize to Alex for me?" Ariel said regretfully.

"Not psychic, just in tune with those I care about. There's no apology necessary. I've got to call Thomas now. We need to know what's going on in that forest. Hang in there for just a little longer," Dimitri hung up.

Ariel stayed on the floor. She could still see the monitors from her location and she just didn't have the energy to get up. The gray figures, whatever they were, flew across the screen again. She wiped the moisture from her eyes and leaned her head against the wall. She was so lucky to have Dimitri in her life. They were close. She thought of him more as a brother than a friend. He'd always been there for her, no matter what. She'd looked up to him as a child and then loved and respected him once she became an adult.

After Dark

Thank goodness she and Alex were such good friends. She would have been devastated if Alex had put a stop to her relationship with Dimitri. He'd been a part of her life for too many years. She was truly happy for Alex and Dimitri. They were so perfect for each other. Some of the women Dimitri had dated in the past became jealous of his friendship with her. Not Alex, she accepted Ariel completely. Ariel didn't feel like she was losing Dimitri, she felt like she was gaining a sister. Maybe Alex understood the bond her and Dimitri shared because Alex and Thomas were so close. They weren't related by blood, either. Thomas' dad had married Alex's mother when they were children. Whatever the reason, Ariel was grateful for them both. If she could just hold on a few more minutes, Thomas would be here and everything would be okay.

* * * *

Victor set down his pen and rolled his shoulders. He'd just finished the club's payroll for the month. He was actually caught up on all his paperwork. He was grateful to Dimitri for giving him an extra night off. Things had been so busy the past couple months. He'd been relying on his staff too heavily. The little things were piling up. Jack, his manager, had come in last night sick as a dog. Victor was lucky to have someone that dedicated working for him. He immediately called Dimitri and explained the situation. Dimitri didn't hesitate, he gave Victor the night off and then offered an additional night if needed. The extra night gave Victor time to catch up on paperwork and complete payroll. No matter what happened he was now covered for at least two weeks; three if he needed it. All the warriors were hoping things would stay quiet for a little longer, but unfortunately you just never knew what was coming. It was a relief to know the club would be covered no matter what came his way.

Victor loved this club. He slowly stood and walked out of his serene office into the noise and lights of Bojan Taverns. As usual, it was packed. It felt good to create something that gave pleasure to so many people. The club was a huge success and had been for years. Victor knew how to create an atmosphere that allowed his patrons to relax, forget their troubles and have a good time. He couldn't have a better staff. Victor learned long ago if you took care of your people, they would take care of you. He casually glanced around the room taking in the scene before him. He grinned when he spotted Thomas sitting at the bar chatting with Rocky, Victor's best bartender. All the warriors stopped by frequently. They got along with most of his crew so it gave them a place to unwind. Everyone got along with Rocky. "Sorry, been waiting long?" Victor asked as he casually pulled Thomas' tab out from under his glass and tossed it in the garbage.

"Hey! I told you already, I pay my own way." Thomas started for the garbage can.

"And I told you, none of the warriors pay for drinks in my club. Now, sit down before I sick Rocky on you." He shot the bartender a conspiratorial smile. "Anyone steps behind that yellow line and Rocky will kick their ass. Including you, hotshot." Victor gave Thomas a playful shove. Thomas lost his balance and fell back onto the stool laughing.

"Fine. But before we head out, I'm finishing my drink. Free beer always tastes better somehow." Thomas jabbed Victor in the ribs with his elbow still laughing. "Thanks Vic, I appreciate the hospitality."

After Dark

"No problem. I drink enough at your house to make things even," Victor admitted.

Just then Thomas' phone rang. He looked at the display and then up at Victor. "This can't be good. It's Dimitri," Thomas opened his phone. "Hello?"

"Thomas," Dimitri started.

"You'll have to speak up," Thomas yelled. "We're still at Victor's club and it's pretty wild tonight. Well okay, it's pretty wild every night but tonight it's exceptionally loud. The live band is amazing."

"Go outside," Dimitri yelled impatiently into the phone. Alex laughed in the background. They all knew Dimitri hated talking to the warriors when they were hanging out at Victor's place.

"Okay. I can probably hear you now," Thomas said after a few seconds of silence. "What's up?" He was now standing just outside the club's back door. The night was cool, but pleasant.

"I need you to get over to the cabin as fast as you can. Ariel's there alone. There's someone or something in the forest. She said she can't tell what it is from the images on the monitors. They're large white or gray figures running through the woods. There are at least two of them. She's pretty freaked out so be gentle with her when you get there," Dimitri finished hesitantly.

"I'll take care of it. I'll call you back when I have more information. She's lucky we haven't left Victor's yet. We're pretty close to the cabin. It shouldn't take more than a half hour to get there." Thomas hung up and turned around.

Victor was standing behind him. He'd pulled on his leather jacket and was waiting for answers. "What's up?"

"I'm not sure. Ariel's at the cabin alone. Dimitri says she can see something in the forest from the monitors in the safe room. Sounds like she's kind of freaked out about it. We need to get over there right away. I don't think they could be vampires. It's just starting to get dark. They wouldn't have had enough time to get from their caves to the cabin already. What do you think it could be?" Thomas asked, truly perplexed.

"I have no idea. I can't think of any animal that could run fast enough those monitors wouldn't pick it up. Do you mind driving? I'm on the bike," Victor said apologetically.

"I don't mind. I'll get there faster than you anyway," Thomas smirked.

Victor laughed out loud. "Do I drive too slow for you, Thomas? Good to know. Next time I'll make sure I speed it up a little."

"Sorry I said anything," Thomas groaned. "You already think your Mario Andretti." Thomas jumped in the car and started the engine. "If you go any faster, we'll be dead for sure."

Chapter Two

Thomas and Victor arrived at the cabin. They rushed into the house and straight up to the safe room. "Ariel, it's Thomas. I'm going to unlock the door," he called out as he punched in the code.

Victor followed Thomas into the room and saw Ariel sitting on the floor, leaning against the wall. He was shocked. She was clearly upset and looked like she'd been crying. Thomas was crouched on the floor in front of her. Good, Thomas could handle her. Victor wanted to know what was in the forest. He walked to the monitors and studied them for movement.

"You okay?" Thomas asked gently.

"Much better now," Ariel gave a weak smile. She started to get up. Thomas reached out to help her. He put an arm around her in comfort as they walked over to join Victor.

"So describe to us what you saw," Victor said. He couldn't believe this was the same woman he had fought vampires with in that back alleyway just a few weeks ago. She couldn't be this upset over what she saw on the monitors. Something else was going on here. Ariel was strong and courageous, not the type of woman to hide out in a room terrified of her own shadow.

"There," she pointed to the monitor. "That's one of them."

Thomas and Victor had seen the figure. She was right, it was moving too fast to determine what it was. They were also crossing the lower edge of the monitor so the entire being wasn't visible. "Thomas?" Victor inquired.

"Yeah," Thomas answered, not taking his eyes off the monitor.

"Can you stop one of the recordings? Then play it back on the monitor and freeze the image so we can try to see what it is?" Victor asked.

"Good idea," Thomas answered, pushing Victor away and sitting in the empty chair in front of the monitor.

Victor glanced back over at Ariel. She looked a lot better now, but he thought she could still use more color in her face. Maybe a stiff drink would help. He looked around the room for the second chair. He knew there was one in here somewhere. He'd spent the night in this room not that long ago monitoring the area for vampires. He finally spotted a chair in the corner and pushed it behind Ariel. "Here, have a seat."

Ariel looked behind her and then up at Victor. She was tall, five eight, but Victor was really tall; maybe six four or five. all the warriors were large in stature, but she was pretty sure Victor was the tallest of them all. She also thought he was the hottest. "Thanks, but I think I'm going to sit over there on the bed for a minute. You take the chair. I've watched them for over an hour now and I can't figure out what they are. Maybe the two of you will have more luck." She turned and headed for the bed.

Victor was surprised. He followed her over to the bed and sat down next to her. "You sat in here watching those things for an hour without calling for help?" he asked. "Why?" He realized he was angry with her, but wasn't sure why. If she wanted to risk her own life, what was it to him?

Ariel looked at Victor for a moment and then looked away, embarrassed. "I saw movement out there and kind of panicked. That's when I came up to this room and locked the door. Once inside I knew I was safe, so I watched the monitors for a while. I thought maybe I could figure out what it was. I hoped it was nothing, just some kind of animal wandering around in the forest. Then I saw two of them and they seemed to be running the perimeter. Like they were looking for a weak spot or something. That's when I started to wonder if they could be vampires. But it was still daytime, so that theory didn't make sense to me either. I guess I let my imagination get the best of me and I started to panic again. I was just regaining my composure, getting ready to call Dimitri, when he called me. Then, he called Thomas." Ariel shrugged like this was a perfectly acceptable explanation.

"An hour? You think it's reasonable for you to sit out here alone, possibly in danger for a full hour before you decided to call for help? You didn't even call for help, Dimitri just happened to call you. How much longer would you have waited? Another hour? Two?" Victor didn't know what was in the forest, but the possibility of what could have happened to Ariel infuriated him.

Ariel was surprised at Victor's anger. She really didn't know him that well. Why was he so upset she had put herself in danger? "I told you, I was just getting ready to call Dimitri when he called me." She looked away from Victor's demanding gaze. "Do you think it's safe to go downstairs? I could really use a drink," Ariel told Thomas, still not looking at Victor.

"I'll get it. What do you want?" Victor grumbled, standing and starting toward the door.

"Just a coke would be nice. There should be plenty in the fridge. Help yourself to whatever you want while you're there." Ariel saw that Thomas had isolated a figure. He had it positioned in the middle of one of the monitors. He was playing with keys, trying to get it into focus.

"Hey, grab me a coke while you're down there will you?" Thomas called. "Then come and look at this. It should be clear by then and I want your opinion."

Victor opened the fridge and pulled out three cokes. Why was he so upset with Ariel? If she wanted to be reckless with her own life, why did he care? Yeah, she was hot and he'd known for a long time he was attracted to her. But so what? It's not like he was looking for anything lasting. If she wanted to risk her own safety that was her business, not his. Women couldn't be trusted. Hadn't he learned that lesson a long time ago? And then again five years ago? So why did he have this desire to protect her? It almost broke his heart when he walked in and saw her sitting there on the floor, distraught and afraid. He wanted to pull her into his arms and comfort her. He could honestly say he'd never felt that way for a woman before. He'd comforted plenty of women in his lifetime. He had always felt protective of women and children, but he'd never had this feeling in his gut. The need to hold her close until everything was all right. Why now? He was 547 years old. "Just ignore it," he told himself. He'd learned his lesson. Women could not be trusted. He would not open himself up again. He'd already been disappointed and betrayed enough for one lifetime. Look at his father if that wasn't proof enough, what was? He'd deal with the situation tonight and avoid Ariel from now on. That should be easy, they didn't exactly run with the same crowd. Other than the warriors that is. With this new vampire threat and the possibility of war, he'd seen Ariel too much for comfort the past couple months.

He closed the fridge and headed back upstairs. Thomas had isolated one of those things on the monitor. Forget about Ariel. They needed to concentrate on the mystery in the woods. As he entered the room, he saw Ariel had moved again. She was now standing behind Thomas. Victor handed them each a coke and took a drink from his bottle. He looked down at the monitor. "That's a wolf," he said confidently. "So, no big deal, we have a couple wolves in the backyard."

"There are no wolves in The Gunk," Thomas said flatly. "There are coyotes and red fox, a few black bear, but there are no wolves here."

Victor took another look. All the locals called the Shawangunk Mountain Range 'The Gunk.' He'd never heard of wolves in there either but there had to be. "Well, apparently there are because that is a wolf. It's too big to be a coyote. It's clearly a wolf. Don't coyotes and wolves hang out in the same type of terrain? Maybe they migrated down from Canada or something."

Thomas looked up at Victor. "I realize it looks like a wolf, but there is another possibility." He knew the instant Victor understood.

Victor's face went hard. He looked at the picture a little closer now. "If that's a shifter, there's no way to know the difference unless it reveals itself. Let's just walk outside and call to it. Tell them we know they're out there and if they want to live, they better come out immediately."

"You want to just walk out into the yard and yell at the wolves?" Thomas asked.

"Sure, why not. We have that electrical fence. If it's a real wolf that will scare it away. If it's a shifter," Victor shrugged. "We ask them what they want and send 'em on their way. Problem solved." He looked around the room and was puzzled by the look Thomas and Ariel was giving him. "What?" he said defensively.

Thomas and Ariel sat in silence for half a second, then they both stood and headed for the door.

"So, I guess this means you're just a little slow and you've both recognized the brilliance of my plan?" he said as he followed them down the stairs and out the door. "That's okay, I forgive you. No apology necessary," Victor said sarcastically.

Thomas was smiling as he marched purposefully out the front door. Victor was definitely one of a kind. He stopped about half way into the yard and called to the woods. "Hey, we know you're out there. If you're up to something, I guarantee you won't get passed our security. If you're not, show yourself. We want to talk to you." The three of them waited.

Within seconds two men surfaced from the woods. "We aren't up to anything," one of the shifters answered. "My name is Morrigan and this is my friend, Austin. He's injured. We got into a fight with a group of vampires we were tracking. They took off that way," Morrigan pointed in the opposite direction of the cabin. "We came this way thinking maybe we could find help for Austin. I hope we haven't caused any problems. We didn't want to approach the house until we were sure the people inside were friendly." Morrigan was supporting his friend. Austin looked like his injuries were pretty severe.

Ariel watched the two men surface from the forest. They were both extremely handsome. They weren't as large as the warriors, but they were built! Neither man wore a shirt. They stood there, in jeans and sneakers. One was blonde, your typical Hollywood heart throb with a pretty boy face and a sexy smile. His hair was tasseled and he had such big, bright eyes. The second one, the one that was injured, was just as sexy but his hair was light brown. He had a thin mustache and that unshaven look that, on the right face, made the guy look ruggedly sexy. The look was perfect for Austin. Ariel took a couple steps forward trying to get a better look. She could see blood all over Austin's pant leg and his side was swollen and bloody. Obviously he needed help. She quickly turned and ran to the front of the house. She switched off the electrical fence and ran back to stand beside Thomas and Victor. "Bring him in. He looks pretty bad. I turned off the fence, nothing will stop you from entering the yard now."

Victor glared at Ariel. How did she know this wasn't some kind of trap? Lilith said Hector was going to get others to help. Victor had dealt with shifters before, well were-panthers anyway. They were a type of shifter. They just couldn't shift into anything but a panther. Anyway his experience with shifters told him they would say or do anything to get what they wanted, or to save their own hide.

They all turned when they heard a car coming up the drive. Ariel spoke first, "That's Breena and Orin," she turned back to study Austin. "You're in luck. Breena is the best at curing what ails you. She'll know what to do for these wounds." She put an arm around Austin and directed him toward the house.

Thomas and Victor looked at each other. They were both skeptical of these two men. With a sigh, they followed Ariel to the house. If it was a trap, they needed to be close by when it sprang. Breena exited the car and hurried to Austin's side. The two women ushered the men into the house. Orin stepped onto the porch behind Thomas and Victor. "Who are they?" he asked.

"Shifters. Morrigan and the injured one is Austin," Victor answered. "They claim they got into a fight with vampires and that's how Austin was injured."

"You don't believe them?" Orin asked.

"We're not sure," Thomas admitted. "Austin looks injured. But Lilith did say they were recruiting others. We're just being cautious. What if this is some kind of trap?"

"It's always good to be prepared," Victor put in as he held the door open. They all entered the cabin.

Austin was lying on the couch. Breena was studying the wound on his leg. Ariel was standing behind her waiting to see if she could help. Morrigan was pacing in front of the big window. Orin quickly moved to Breena's side. He wanted to be close if this was some kind of ploy. The two warriors leaned against the wall close to the door. Thomas reached over, locked the door and reset the security. If this was a trick, nobody else was getting inside the cabin. These two guys were on their own.

After Dark

"So," Victor began. "How did the two of you end up in a fight with a group of vampires?" His tone spoke volumes. It was clear he was skeptical and untrusting.

Morrigan stopped pacing and looked up. He took a deep breath. "My father is our pack leader. Last night, in the middle of the night, a group of vampires broke into our house and abducted my sister, Abby. Father immediately split the pack into groups of two and sent us into the forest to search for her. Austin and I searched an entire day before we came across the scent from a group of vampires. We followed it and walked right into a large cluster of them. We honestly weren't expecting that many and there was no sign of Abby. Austin was injured early on in the fight. We eventually escaped into the forest. I thought the vampires would follow us, but they lost interest after a short time and went the other way. I figure it was almost daylight, so they headed back to their hide-e-hole. Wherever that is.

We were really far out in the wilderness by then. It took us most of the day to get here. When I saw the cabin, I circled your property for a while looking for a way in. Austin is wiped out, but he forced himself to help. We planned on monitoring the area until nightfall to see what happened. This place seemed too secure and protected to be a vampire hideout, but we just couldn't take the risk." Morrigan studied Victor's cold hard stare. "I can see you're still skeptical and obviously you don't trust us. That makes me even more grateful for your willingness to help Austin," he paused. "But I have to ask one more favor," he looked to Orin and Breena.

"I've got to get back out there. My sister is missing. Every minute I stay here could be a minute too long. We don't know why the vampires took her. Do they want something from us or do they just plan to kill her? Maybe they already have," he said quietly.

"Until I have proof to the contrary I have to believe she's still alive, scared and in need of rescue. I need to get back out there tonight. I have to find my sister."

"The vampires haven't made any demands?" Thomas asked.

"No," Morrigan answered. "I wish they had. At least then we'd know why they took Abby. We don't even know if she was target specific or if they were just looking for someone to grab."

"I'm sure she was target specific," Victor stated flatly.

Morrigan looked at him sharply. "Do you know something I don't? Do you know why my sister was abducted?"

"Maybe. I don't know for sure, but I have a theory." Victor gave Morrigan a long, hard stare. He couldn't decide if the man was telling the truth or if there was more to the story. He looked over to Thomas. Thomas gave him a subtle nod. "Do you know who Radek is?" Victor asked.

"Yes. He's the vampire leader, or king," Morrigan answered.

"Right. Well, he has an associate named Lilith," Victor began.

"I'm familiar with Lilith," Morrigan answered. "She's an evil woman. She may even be worse than Radek."

"We're on the same page so far," Thomas cut in.

Victor nodded. "A while back myself, Ariel and another friend got involved in a battle with several new vampires and Lilith. She made the comment that Hector, Radek's first lieutenant, was gathering an army. When the others arrived and joined up with the vampires, Lilith was certain the fae would lose this fight. Once this final battle was over, Lilith and Radek would rule the world. I can only assume the shifters are the others Lilith talked about."

"You think the shifters have joined the vampires to fight against the fae? That's absurd," Morrigan demanded, obviously offended by the suggestion.

"Probably not willingly," Thomas answered quickly. "I think that's why they have your sister, leverage. You fight with us, we'll give your loved one back. It's not a coincidence that the daughter of the pack leader was taken. Like Victor said, she was definitely target specific."

Ariel was furious at Thomas and Victor, mostly Victor. They were being rude. These two men were injured and frightened for the life of their pack member and the warriors were treating them like they were the enemy. "I'm sorry," she interrupted. "You'll have to excuse Victor. He doesn't get out much during the day so his manners leave a lot to be desired. He tends to stick to the club scene. You know, loud music and wild women. Having a civilized conversation seems to be beyond his capabilities." She gave Morrigan her friendliest, most sincere smile. Ariel saw Victor lean in and whisper something to Thomas. Then he turned, disengaged the security and walked out the front door.

Thomas was furious. "You are out of line, Ariel. Victor and I have every right to question these two strangers. They just happened to show up on your doorstep shortly before dark. That's a little suspicious. I realize you're staying here, but this is still my cabin. No one will disrespect Victor that way in my home." The two of them glared at each other for a long moment. Then, Thomas turned to the shifters and continued. "So I'm going to ask you again, have the vampires made any demands? Have they struck any deals with your pack for the safe return of your sister?"

Morrigan studied Thomas. He looked over to Austin. Could this really be the reason the vampires had taken Abby? There was no way the shifters would join forces with the vampires. Not even to save Abby. Father wouldn't consider such a ridiculous demand. He was about to say as much when Austin began to speak.

"Thank you," Austin said sincerely. "You didn't have to provide us with that insight. I think the information might help us deal with Abby's abduction. I also understand why you were so suspicious and unfriendly at our arrival. If the tables were turned, I'm not sure I would have allowed the two of you into my home. Again, thank you for your kindness. I realize there's no reason to believe me, but the shifters would never join forces with the vampires to fight the fae. I don't care who they abduct. Mason and Jackie, Morrigan's parents, would not be manipulated that way. They would not agree to fight the fae, not even for the safe return of their daughter."

Victor blocked out the rest of the conversation. Thomas could deal with the shifters. He knew he was bias toward them. He'd trust whatever decision Thomas made on this. He communicated that to Thomas before he left. If Thomas felt they were telling the truth, they would all head out in the morning to find the missing girl. Victor knew Thomas had good instincts. He'd been helping Luke deal with people and business negotiations for years.

Victor sat on the long bench that stretched across the patio. Why had Ariel's assessment bothered him so much? Hadn't he spent most of his life using that facade to shelter himself? He'd learned pretty early on that good, decent women weren't interested in what they considered players or womanizers. It had been easy to gain that reputation. Even easier to keep the image alive. Initially, that was the reason he'd opened the club. It was another stigma he could attach to himself to keep desirable women away. Surprisingly, he'd grown to love Bojan Taverns. He now thought of it as an extension of himself. He closed his eyes and leaned his head against the cabin wall. Women were definitely Victor's weakness. He'd spent his entire life building a wall to protect himself from them. For more than five hundred years he'd been able to walk away, avoid any woman that raised the slightest interest. Then he met Lakeisha. She was so full of life. He had decided to open up a little and allowed himself to care. That had certainly ended in disaster.

Now, he could feel himself falling for Ariel. He couldn't allow it. The attraction was so much stronger than it had been with Lakeisha. That meant the fall would be harder too. He promised himself a long time ago, he would not follow in his father's footsteps. He would not spend his life as a recluse, locked away on a lonely farm because his heart had been broken. Ariel could definitely break his heart. It wasn't just the physical attraction, although she was beautiful and athletic, he also respected her. He stood back watching her battle the vampires in that dark alley. She was strong, courageous and smart. It would be easy to fall for her. He had to get away. Hopefully, he and Thomas would be heading into the wilderness tomorrow. He'd put this craziness behind him once and for all. When they got back, he'd just avoid her. He had plenty of work to occupy his time.

Victor looked up when he heard the front door open and close. He expected to see Thomas, but Ariel stood there watching him. She slowly walked over and sat next to him on the bench. "I think I owe you an apology," she began, looking out into the darkness.

"For what?" Victor tried to act casual.

She turned and looked at him. It was difficult to see through the nonchalant attitude he always tried to portray. She watched him for a full minute in silence. "Does that usually work?" She finally asked.

Victor was confused. He wasn't sure what she was getting at. "Does what work?" he asked finally turning to look at her.

"Look, I can see the image you want to project to the community. That, 'I'm a lazy surfer dude without a care in the world' persona you perpetuate. Then throw in the leather jacket, a big Harley and some attitude and I suspect most people run the other way. Most people don't take the time to look passed the surface at the real you. Am I right? Does the flippant attitude usually work for you?" she asked quizzically.

He watched her for a minute. "What makes you think it's a persona? Maybe that's the real me," Victor said seriously. Why wouldn't this woman go away and leave him alone? She was sitting so close. All he wanted to do was grab her and press his mouth to those soft irresistible lips of hers, but he had to push her away.

Ariel smiled a humorless smile. "I've seen the real you. It's the little things that give you away. I watched you the night Alex was injured, the first time I met you. You stood back, let Thomas and Dimitri fuss until they were confident she would be okay. Then, you stepped in. You brought her tea and made sure she was comfortable. Like I said, the little things. Alex was completely out that night. I don't think she knows how concerned you were, but I do. You also came to the cabin that night after the battle at Breena's for the sole purpose of protecting us, all of us. You monitored security so the other warriors could get some rest. Then, there was that night in the alley. You rushed to my side, supported me until I got my footing. If you didn't care, you would have rushed in and fought off the vamps until I pulled myself off the ground, but you wouldn't have supported me. You wouldn't have cared if I fell.

No matter how hard you try to come across as uncaring and aloof, you can't hide the real you. Oh, maybe you're successful with the casual observer. But anyone that takes about half a second and even less effort can see through the facade pretty quickly. I'd lay odds that not one of the warriors believe all that crap people say about you. I don't, neither do Alex, Breena or Orin."

Ariel smiled at the shocked look on Victor's face. "Yeah, we've talked about you. Most of us don't get it. We don't understand why you embrace the bad image. Until recently I didn't know you and Orin were so close. Orin, Breena and I have been living in pretty small quarters lately. It's given us a chance to talk. I have to admit that's been nice," she paused. "The last few years we've all been too busy with our lives to spend quality time together talking and catching up. I know you've been there for Orin while he tried to cope with Breena's disease." She smiled and shrugged. "See, goes back to the little things. You just can't help yourself. Deep down you're truly a good, caring soul. So back to my original reason for being out here, I'm sorry for those things I said in there. Thomas was right, it was disrespectful. Plus I don't believe any of it, I was just angry with you for being rude to our guests," Ariel confessed.

"It's been my experience that a woman is most honest when she's angry," Victor said soberly.

Ariel looked at him, frowning. "Is that true? Is that really your experience?"

Victor silently watched her, wondering why she looked so appalled by his comment.

"Well," Ariel finally broke the silence. "If that's true, I think that's pretty sad. I also think you need to re-evaluate the type of women you associate with. For the record, when I'm angry you should ignore anything I say." She smiled at him. "I have this competitive streak. I'm working on it, but for me a verbal fight is the same as a battle. No rules. Anything's fair play. Even stupid rumors that have no substance. It's a flaw, I know, but there it is." She sat back and stared into the darkness. She'd expected some kind of response, but Victor was just sitting there silently. Ariel wondered if she had blown it. She'd felt his interest before tonight. Experience told her he was just as attracted to her as she was to him. Now sitting here in the silence, she wasn't sure how he felt. Maybe her comments had offended him to the point he was no longer interested. That would be unfortunate. She'd lived a long time and her heart had never done that little flip before, the way it did when Victor smiled at her.

Victor finally broke the silence. "It's getting late." They both stood at the same time and bumped into each other.

Ariel placed her hands on Victor's chest for balance. When she looked into his eyes, she couldn't help herself, she leaned in and pressed her lips to his.

Victor froze and closed his eyes. He had to maintain control. He could not act on his emotions. He could not let Ariel know how much he wanted to pull her in and deepen that kiss. If she thought he didn't want her, maybe she would avoid him. Problem solved.

Ariel pulled back. She felt humiliated. So, she had ruined things. She had to act casual, like it was no big deal. "Sorry, my bad. I'm usually more astute than that. I'd gotten the impression you were interested in me, too. I guess I'm just a little off lately. Don't worry, that won't happen again." She turned and headed for the door.

Victor tried to stop himself. He told himself to let her go. Let her think he wasn't interested. Let her walk away. But he couldn't ignore that flicker of disappointment, of sadness he'd seen in her eyes when she pulled away. He spoke before he could stop himself. "Ariel?"

Ariel stopped at the sound of her name. She slowly turned around and was surprised to find Victor standing directly behind her. He leaned down and pressed his lips to hers. What did this mean? Maybe she hadn't ruined everything after all. Victor placed his hand behind her neck and pulled her in closer, deepening the kiss. He slowly released her and took a step back, leaning against the wooden rail. He didn't say a word, just studied her quietly.

"Or maybe I wasn't completely wrong," she said slowly, smiling at him. "Goodnight Victor."

"Goodnight Ariel," Victor answered.

Ariel turned and walked into the cabin. Victor turned around and pressed his elbows on the railing. He laid his face in his hands and groaned. What was he doing? He'd had the perfect escape and he'd blown it. Maybe he could still get his head straight if he and Thomas left first thing in the morning. If they left early enough, he could get out of the cabin before Ariel woke up. His mind kept wandering back to that kiss. It had been explosive. It left him wanting more. How was he going to deal with this? The wall he tried to build to keep Ariel out had been obliterated with just one kiss. He was so deep in thought he didn't hear Thomas walk out of the cabin and onto the porch.

As Thomas stepped into the darkness, he spotted Victor. He looked stressed. Had Ariel said something else to upset him? If so, he and Ariel were going to have words. He knew Victor could take care of himself, but Thomas still felt protective. His friend had suffered through so many tragedies. Victor wanted everyone to believe he was a tough guy that didn't care about anything, but deep down Victor was vulnerable. He was caring and giving to a fault. He just hid it well, or thought he did anyway. All the warriors knew the real man, the man Victor tried to hide. Thomas would not tolerate anyone bad-mouthing or disrespecting Victor in any way. He stepped up to the rail and leaned against the big post. "Rough night?" he asked casually.

Victor jumped a little and straightened. "I've had better. What's the verdict with our new friends in there? Do we leave in the morning?" Victor turned and leaned against the other post so he was facing Thomas.

"I think I talked Morrigan into waiting until morning. He's anxious to head out, but I tried to explain why that doesn't make sense. It would be much safer in the morning and with your tracking skills, I think we can find his sister pretty quickly. He was hesitant and never did give me his word he'd wait. But I think between myself and Austin he may stay put for the night," Thomas said exasperated. "That boy is stubborn though. I won't be surprised if we wake up and find him missing."

"We better plan on an early morning then," Victor suggested. "If he's that anxious, he won't wait for us."

After Dark

"I agree," Thomas answered. "I already talked to Dimitri. He and Alex are going to start out just before sunrise. He figures if he gets an early start, maybe we can talk Morrigan into having breakfast to stall him until Alex can heal Austin. He agrees we should try to help Morrigan locate his sister. Morrigan, Austin, you and I will leave as soon as Alex is finished with Austin."

"Good plan," Victor said. Relieved he would be leaving this cabin and Ariel along with it. A few days in the wilderness would help him get that distance back between them.

Thomas sighed. "Dimitri is worried that Hector isn't only holding Abby for leverage. Nobody has seen Hector for weeks. He has to be feeding on something or someone. Dimitri suggested Hector might be feeding on his hostage. If that's the case, she may not have a lot of time. Even if he's careful about his intake, losing that much blood day after day is going to take its toll. When we find her, if she's alive, she might be extremely weak."

"We'll have to plan for that," Victor said thoughtfully. "I don't think shifters have any special item that helps them get their strength back. We have blood, the fae use tea. I think shifters just use food. It takes a lot of energy to shift and I know they need a high protein diet to keep up their strength. Maybe we should tell Dimitri to stop and pick up some of those protein shakes on his way."

"Good idea," Thomas admitted. "Maybe with a couple of shakes, she can regain enough strength to get her back to her people. Once we turn her over, they can worry about her recovery."

"It's late. Let's get to bed. We're going to have an early morning and a long day ahead of us. We'll both need our rest." Victor opened the door and held it for Thomas. "Thanks for standing up for me in there. I know my rep and I can handle the gossip, but it meant a lot to me that you were willing to stand up for my honor." He slapped Thomas on the back as he walked into the cabin. "See you in the morning."

The two men silently slipped through the dimly lit kitchen and headed for bed.

* * * *

Ariel sat in a comfortable lounge chair on the front porch. It was still dark outside, she guessed it was around three in the morning. She couldn't sleep. She had too many things running through her head. Victor and that kiss were foremost on her mind. But she was also worried about Morrigan and his sister. She took another sip of her tea. She had hoped drinking a cup would calm her enough to get some sleep. So far it wasn't working. She was more restless now than when she'd gotten out of bed. Victor was a complex individual. She'd been so sure he was interested in her. After her kiss, she'd been sure he wasn't. Then, he surprised her again by pulling her in for that mind blowing encore. Her emotions felt like they'd just gone on the mother of all roller coaster rides.

Ariel didn't understand why he was so closed off. Why was he such a contradiction? She knew she was right when she told him the aloof attitude was just a facade. What she didn't understand was why. Why did he want people to believe those things about him? Ariel overheard three friends talking to a group of girls the other day at lunch. They were going on and on about the night they'd spent with Victor. Ariel immediately knew they were lying. The night they claimed to have a wild passionate interlude, was the very night they had battled the vampires at Breena and Orin's house. Victor had been busy all night relocating council members. Once that was finished, he showed up at the cabin to monitor security so the rest of them could get a good night's rest. He certainly hadn't been entertaining three friends in the penthouse of the finest hotel in town. So, why did Victor encourage those stories?

The front door slowly creaked open. Ariel watched as Morrigan tried to silently close the door behind him. He was obviously trying to sneak away. "You do realize that by sneaking away like a thief in the night, you look suspicious and extremely guilty," Ariel said casually taking another sip of her tea.

Morrigan jumped. He hadn't realized anyone was up. "I can't help the way things look. I tried to take Thomas' advice and wait until morning, but I can't. I can't sleep knowing Abby is out there. She's got to be terrified and she may be injured. Knowing that, I can't sleep peacefully in a comfortable bed until morning. I have to go search for her now."

Ariel stood and set her cup on the small patio table. "I can understand that, but you can't go out there alone. I know all about Hector. He's bad news. He's more cunning than most vampires. He has to be very old to control himself so completely. Most vampires can't do that. We're pretty sure Hector is behind this. Even if you miraculously find your sister, how are you going to get passed all those vampires to save her? If you get killed, where does that leave Abby?" Ariel said soberly.

"I honestly haven't figured that part out yet. I just know I have to leave. I have to get out there and find her. Not knowing her condition is driving me insane. If you don't have siblings, you can't understand what I'm going through. I'm sorry I can't explain it. I just have to go." Morrigan took another step toward the front yard.

"I don't have any blood siblings, but Dimitri is like a brother to me. I understand how you feel. If Dimitri was missing, I'd do whatever it took to find and rescue him. He'd do the same for me. We all understand what you're going through, but you still can't go alone. Give me ten minutes. I'll go with you," Ariel turned toward the house.

"I can't let you do that. Like you said, it's dangerous out there. There's no way of knowing how many vampires we might come across before we find Abby. I can't put you at risk that way," Morrigan argued.

Ariel laughed. "I'd wager, whatever you want, that I have more experience battling vampires than you do. I also have a few tricks that will help us both survive in the wilderness and fight off the vampires. Ten minutes isn't going to hurt you. I need to grab a bag with a few things and leave the guys a note. I don't want them jumping to the wrong conclusion when they wake up and find both of us gone. If they think you kidnaped me, your life will be in danger. So would Austin's. Ten minutes. Promise you'll wait for me," Ariel pressed.

Morrigan took a deep breath. He knew if he left her, she would just follow. If they were together, he could keep an eye out for her. If she followed behind him, she might get in over her head. "Ten minutes, but not a second longer. If you're coming, you'd better hurry!"

* * * *

Victor woke early. He was having a hard time sleeping. His dreams were full of Ariel and that monumentally stupid kiss. How could he get her out of his system now? Just the thought of kissing her again was driving him insane. He took a quick shower and headed downstairs. Maybe after a cup of coffee, Dimitri and Alex would be here. He could head into the wilderness and focus on work instead of on women, or more to the point one particular woman. Victor entered the kitchen and switched on the light. The cabin was silent. He must be the only one up. He started the coffee and turned toward the refrigerator when he spotted the folded piece of paper on the table. "This can't be good," he thought to himself as he slowly opened the note and began to read.

Victor had just finished reading when Thomas walked through the kitchen door. Thomas froze at the look on Victor's face. "What's wrong now?" he asked. "Is the coffee ready? I need at least one cup before I hear the bad news."

Victor had forgotten the coffee. He walked over and poured two cups. "Read the note on the table. Then one of us will have to call Dimitri and it's going to be ugly." Victor handed Thomas a cup of coffee and sat down at the table. He wasn't sure who he was more angry with, Morrigan or Ariel.

Victor hung up with Dimitri and turned to Thomas. "They should be here shortly. They got an earlier start than we planned. Alex insisted they had to leave early. She was certain Morrigan wouldn't stay until morning. She told Dimitri she wouldn't wait if you had been abducted. She was also certain you wouldn't be sitting around a comfortable cabin waiting for daylight if she were abducted and held captive by vampires."

"That's true," Thomas admitted.

Victor stood. "I'll go wake Orin and Breena. We're going to need those packs right away. The sooner we head out, the better." He walked through the door leaving Thomas fuming in the kitchen.

* * * *

Dimitri knocked on the big wooden door. Oberon was going to be upset. Dimitri knew he wouldn't be surprised. Ariel was extremely independent and used to venturing out on her own. This wasn't the first time she'd gone off and done something dangerous. But, she wasn't usually this reckless. How was he going to convince Oberon he shouldn't worry when he was so worried himself? The big door opened and Mara stood there smiling. Dimitri took a deep breath. He was in for a long, difficult morning.

Oberon was relaxing in the family room. He spotted Dimitri and stood. "Hey son, what brings you out this morning?" Once he saw Dimitri's face, he sobered. Something was up and it wasn't good. "Mara, would you mind getting us all some coffee. I need a little time with Dimitri alone." Mara left the room. "What is it? I can tell something's wrong."

"I don't want you to worry," Dimitri started. "It's kind of a long story, so just let me get through it all before you ask any questions."

"Okay," Oberon sat back down in the large chair. He motioned to the other chair inviting Dimitri to sit.

"Yesterday, early in the evening, a couple shifters were located at the cabin. Initially, Ariel was concerned because she didn't know what they were. They arrived in the form of a wolf and didn't show up that clearly on the monitors. I sent Thomas and Victor to the cabin to check things out. That's when they discovered the shifters. One of them, Morrigan, is the son of their pack leader. He said a group of vampires had abducted his sister. The pack split into pairs and headed into the forest to try and track down Abby, the missing girl. Long story short, Morrigan and his partner Austin got into a fight with a group of vampires and Austin was injured. That's when they came across the cabin.

We thought we had a plan. Breena worked last night to get Austin back on his feet. Alex and I went out early this morning to see if Alex could heal him. We were going to send Thomas and Victor into the forest with the shifters to see if they could locate the vampire's hideaway and rescue the girl. By the description Morrigan gave us, we are pretty sure Hector is behind this. When you put this latest development together with the conversation Alex had with Lilith a few weeks ago, it all makes sense. Lilith was confident Hector's plan would work and they wouldn't have to wait until they turned more vampires before they could lodge another attack. Remember, she said the others would help them. We think Hector abducted Abby in an attempt to force the shifters into the fight."

"You said you thought you had a plan. What happened?" Oberon said soberly.

"Morrigan was impatient. He wanted to get started back out right away. We thought we had him convinced it would be better to spend the night at the cabin and let Alex heal Austin. Then they could head out first thing in the morning. When Alex and I got there, Morrigan was gone and Ariel went with him. They apparently took off last night after everyone went to bed. Ariel left a note explaining that Morrigan was leaving by himself. She felt she had to join him. She didn't think it was safe for him to wander around in the woods alone in case he encountered more vampires."

Oberon stood. How had he raised such an independent, stubborn daughter? Once she got something into her mind, there was no changing it. It was just like her to wander off with a shifter in the middle of the night. Oberon stood in front of the window. He was worried about Ariel. Finally, he turned back to Dimitri. "I'm going after her. I can't allow her to wander around the forest, possibly in search of Hector of all people. She's in danger. If she's not smart enough to realize that, I do."

Dimitri was still sitting in the chair, he shifted to look at Oberon. "I understand your need to search for Ariel," he began.

"But you don't think I should," Oberon finished. "Do you think I'm too old?"

"No," Dimitri stated flatly. "I don't think you're too old. I think you're the chairman of the council and we need you here. Now is not the time to be wandering off, out of touch. If something big happens, we need you here to help make decisions." Dimitri saw Oberon was about to interrupt. "Just hear me out. We believe Hector abducted the Pack Masters' daughter in an attempt to force their pack into the fight. As misguided as it was, Ariel running off with Morrigan to find his sister actually helps our situation." Oberon's face hardened. "I know, don't get mad at me. You know I'm just pointing out the obvious. I never said I thought it was a good idea. I think it was a terrible idea. When Ariel gets back, I'm going to throttle her myself," Dimitri said angrily.

Oberon grinned. "Okay, so we're on the same page with that one. I keep forgetting you're just as protective of her as I am. I think I follow you though. You believe I can use this to create allies with this shifter pack. My daughter is out there with your son, risking her life to try to save your daughter..." he trailed off.

"Exactly," Dimitri nodded. "It's a terrible situation, but I think we should use it to our advantage. We need you here to handle it. You know I'm not a politician. I'm a warrior, sometimes I'm less than tactful."

Oberon laughed. "That's certainly putting it mildly," he paused. "I don't know this pack, but if they are allies with the were-panthers, this might not work."

They were both silent. Neither man wanted to get into that conversation.

Oberon finally spoke again. "Okay, so hypothetically if I agree to stay and negotiate with the shifter pack, where does that leave Ariel? I'm not leaving her out there alone. Hector is dangerous." Oberon walked back over and sat down.

"I sent Thomas and Victor after her already. Luckily Orin and Breena like to backpack. When we cleaned out their house, they brought all their stuff to the cabin. Thomas and Victor have their packs, sleeping bags, and Breena sent along some tea and other herbs just in case they run into problems. They're prepared for the elements. Now they just need to find Ariel."

"You sent Thomas and Victor? Are they going to stay out there until they locate Ariel?" Oberon asked, clearly worried. Both men had responsibilities, businesses to run.

"Look, Oberon. I know Victor doesn't have the best reputation among the council members or the fae community. But I'm the warrior leader and I say he's the best man for this job. He's experienced in the wilderness and he's good at dealing with injuries. Plus, he's the best tracker alive. It was convenient that he was already at the cabin, but if all of my warriors were standing in a line and I had to choose two of them to go on this mission, Victor would have been one of them." Dimitri took a deep breath.

"Hold on a minute Dimitri," Oberon interrupted. "I never said I had a problem with Victor going on this mission. In fact, I happen to know Victor is a good man and I know he's good in the wilderness. He may not have a good rep with some of the community, but he does with me. Other than you, there's nobody I trust more with my daughter's life."

Dimitri was taken by surprise. He and Oberon had never talked about Victor, but Dimitri knew Oberon was on the council when Victor was suspended. "I'm glad to hear that. I feel the same way. Ariel couldn't be in better hands," Dimitri said sincerely.

"I've surprised you," Oberon stated studying Dimitri.

"A little. I've never talked to you about what happened five years ago. I didn't think it was my place. I guess I just assumed you believed Victor was guilty like everyone else seems to," Dimitri admitted.

Oberon sat forward in his chair and studied Dimitri. "I have never talked to you, or anyone else for that matter, about Victor's situation because I felt doing so would violate the oath I took when I became a council member. I'm going to talk to you now because you're the warrior leader and there are some things you should probably know. I've served on the council for a lot of years, too many to count. There are only two times I've felt like the council has failed, that justice wasn't served. Actually, I will go one step further, I believe in these two instances a great injustice occurred.

After Dark

One was five years ago with Victor. One was several hundred years ago with Victor's father, Atticus. I know Victor is damaged. I also know, without a doubt, the council holds the blame for at least part of that. We have done too much harm to that family." Oberon ran his hands through his hair and sat back.

"I tried, I honestly don't know what I could have done differently with Victor. I even followed him out to Pennsylvania, to Atticus' farm to try to get support from his father. I practically begged him to confide in me. I was sure I could help him if he would just let me try. There is no doubt in my mind that Victor was innocent. The problem is, Victor wouldn't tell us anything. He wouldn't trust the council, he wouldn't trust me. He just shut down completely." Oberon stared absently out the window. "Victor was protecting someone. I just don't know who. Lakeisha and her family were at the hearing demanding Victor accept responsibility for that girl's pregnancy. They mainly wanted financial support, but the amount they were asking was astronomical. We all thought it was unreasonable. Victor wouldn't budge. The only thing he would say is the child wasn't his. He refused to support it in any way. The family brought in witnesses to testify that Victor and Lakeisha had basically been living together for months. Lakeisha testified. She swore the child was Victors. She claimed there was no possibility someone else fathered that baby. I didn't believe her. That girl was lying through her teeth. I know Victor knew something. He might even know who the real father is. He just wouldn't say anything," Oberon sighed. "Everyone on the council decided he was guilty. I was the only one who demanded an investigation. I was overruled and Victor was suspended from the warriors for a year."

"I think that was the worst punishment you could have given him," Dimitri said soberly. "Oh, he tried to pretend it was no big deal. He was going to travel the country on his bike. I think it almost killed him. I worried every day he was gone, wondering if he would come back to us. I don't know who fathered that child, but it was not Victor. It couldn't have been Victor." Now Dimitri stared out the window. He wasn't sure he should tell Oberon how he knew that, but he trusted Oberon. He was like a father to him. Oberon had just trusted him. Dimitri looked back and realized he was being watched.

"What I'm going to tell you, I'm not telling you warrior to council leader," Dimitri began. "I'm telling you father to son. I know you're not my father, but all my life you've been like a second father to me. Since dad died, I feel like you've stepped into that role in my life. I'm going to trust you with something that I'm not sure I have a right to share." Dimitri took a deep breath.

"Dimitri, you can trust me. No matter what you tell me, I will not betray that trust. Not with anyone for any reason," Oberon promised.

Dimitri hesitated a few more seconds then began. "I was hanging out with Victor one night at his club. I'd just broken up with some girl. I can't even remember her name now. We were drunk and I was pretty down on women at the time. I said something about giving up. I was tired of the games and manipulation. Before Alex I was never really serious about anyone I dated. Most of the women were just after my money. Anyway, Victor said something about how deceitful women were and he wasn't sure they were even capable of love. Like you said, Victor is damaged emotionally. I'm not sure you realize just how much. This thing with Lakeisha messed him up, but he was already messed up. He won't talk about it, but I think it goes back to his childhood."

"I think you're right," Oberon agreed.

After Dark

"Anyway I confided in Victor that this girl, the one I'd just dumped, was trying to get pregnant. She wanted to force me into marriage for my money. She thought I'd marry her if she was having my child. To this day I'm not sure Victor remembers our conversation that night. We've never discussed it again. We were both drunk, but he was worse than me. He told me I should get a vasectomy, that way no woman could manipulate me into marriage with pregnancy. I remember exactly what he said that night, 'I had one several years ago. Women can't be trusted. They will manipulate you, deceive you and then betray you. It's not worth the risk.' I don't know who got that girl pregnant, but it wasn't Victor. Victor could not be the father of that child." He looked into Oberon's eyes. "We had that conversation more than ten years ago."

Oberon closed his eyes. Why hadn't Victor told the council it was impossible for him to get Lakeisha pregnant? Had what they'd done to his father made him so mistrusting? Why did he choose punishment for a crime he hadn't committed over truth? It didn't make sense. Oberon and Dimitri sat in silence for a long time. They were both so deep in thought they didn't notice when Mara walked in with a tray of coffee. She silently slipped back out without a word.

Finally, Oberon spoke. "What do you know about Victor's father?"

"Not a lot. I know he lives in Pennsylvania on a farm. I also know he never leaves, I guess he's sort of a recluse and Victor tries to visit as often as he can. I also know Victor feels guilty because he doesn't get up there more frequently. Dad also mentioned him a couple times, so I think they used to be friends. In fact, I believe dad went to visit Atticus in Pennsylvania a few times before he died. Why?" Dimitri asked.

"Atticus was a warrior," Oberon began. "He was one of the best men I ever knew. He loved being a warrior. He lived for it and he excelled at it. He was married to a fae named Dannica. I remember when he met her, he fell head over hills in love. They only courted a short time before they got married. Not too long afterwards, she was pregnant with Victor. Atticus was the proudest father you could ever meet. The warriors had to leave home a lot in those days. It was exceptionally hard on Atticus. People were spread out more and there was danger everywhere. A small group of warriors would be sent on a road trip for days. Then, they'd have several days off when they returned. I know it was hard on family life. Most of the warrior's wives had a very difficult time with the schedule. Atticus missed Dannica, but he really missed Victor. He felt he was missing out on the little things. On Victor's childhood."

"I remember mom being depressed a lot. Then everything was okay again when dad got home," Dimitri said reminiscing.

"I know. That was pretty normal at the time. Anyway, Dannica tried to talk Atticus into quitting. She hated the fact that he was a warrior. When Atticus wouldn't give up his lifestyle for her, she hated the job even more. Maybe I shouldn't say this, but I don't think that woman was quite right in the head. I personally witnessed a couple things that made me wonder about her mental stability. Nothing big though and Atticus always made excuses for her. He blew it off as her being tired or not feeling well. Every family has their secrets, but I believe Victor and his father's secrets are darker than most and Dannica is at the center. I could never get anyone to tell me what was going on in that family, but I believe the other warriors knew something about that night. The night Atticus killed Dannica."

"That was the other time you're talking about, the other time you feel the council failed?" Dimitri asked.

"Yes," Oberon confided. "Atticus left on a road trip, but the warriors returned home after only a couple days. They weren't expected for at least another week. I remember seeing Atticus, your father and Charlie arrive in town. They were all so excited to be home. They were thrilled with the prospect of surprising their loved ones with an early return. I distinctly remember thinking Atticus looked relieved. Later that night, the council was informed Atticus had killed Dannica. He was going to stand trial for murder." Oberon was silent for a minute. "Don't get me wrong. I'm not disputing that Atticus killed her. I think he did. He said he did, I have no reason to doubt him. I just don't think it was murder. Just like Victor, Atticus wouldn't say anything. No explanation. He just said he didn't have a choice. We couldn't get him to elaborate. The council voted eight to one against Atticus. He was suspended from the warriors for 30 years and banished from the community. He was also told he could not have any contact with his fellow warriors for the entire sentence."

"I assume you were the one?" Dimitri asked.

"Yes," Oberon said simply. "That sentence almost killed him. I often wonder if a death sentence would have been more kind. He's never been the same. The honest, caring, fun loving man I used to know died that day. He became a complete recluse. That's when he got into farming. He just packed up his things and left that night. We were all living in Dublin at the time. He moved to a big spread on the outskirts of town. Eventually most of our community moved to America. I think he moved to the farm in Lancaster, Pennsylvania for Victor. He wanted his son to be close to the rest of the warriors. Atticus loved being a warrior. He wasn't just good, he thrived when he went on those trips. The rest of the warriors loved and respected him. He was so proud of who he was and the fact that his son would follow in his footsteps. Atticus was banished that day, but basically so was Victor. He was only twelve years old at the time. For thirty years the only contact Victor had with the fae community was when the warriors went to visit. Victor wouldn't leave that farm until Atticus's sentence was over.

The council ordered the warriors to stay away, but they refused of course. Every one of them stood by Atticus, openly declaring his innocence. They still do. I knew your dad and Jake went out there at least once a week. All the warriors did. The council was furious, but there was nothing they could do about it. If they punished one, they would have to punish them all. We couldn't afford to suspend all the warriors. Who would protect the community? Your dad went to see Atticus every weekend until the day he died. I think Jake and Charlie still go out pretty regularly. Atticus still hasn't left that farm. I heard he's started to do his own shopping, but he won't even come here to visit his own son. A part of his soul died back then. Not only because he lost his standing as a warrior, but because he lost the woman he loved. Atticus did love Dannica with all his heart. You could see it in his eyes. He would light up whenever she walked into the room. He didn't murder that woman. I don't know what happened that night, but Atticus never would have killed her in cold blood the way the council believed he did. The way Foster, Dannica's brother, claimed he did.

I don't know if all the warriors knew what happened that night, but I know your dad did. Years after all this happened, Dylan and I had a lengthy conversation about that time. We talked about Atticus and the whole tragedy. Your dad told me the council got it all wrong. He said Atticus did kill Dannica, but he didn't have a choice. I asked him to explain, but he just said it wasn't his secret to tell. If

Atticus wanted anyone to know, he would have to tell them himself. Dylan took that secret to his grave. Atticus could have gone back to being a warrior after the thirty years were over. The warriors wanted him back, they begged him to come back, but his heart wasn't in it anymore. He lost so much. That loss had to have had an impact on Victor, like I said, he was only twelve at the time his mother died.

To be honest, I was surprised when Victor walked into our council meeting and declared he was there to accept his responsibility as a warrior. He's a better man than I am. I don't think I'd give all Victor has given to a community that caused him and his father so much pain." Oberon had been staring into space as he recounted the story. Now he looked back at Dimitri. "I am grateful that someone who has that much character, that much honor, is willing to go out in the wilderness and search for my daughter. I'm part of the enemy. I was on the council when he was suspended and I was on the council during the incident with his father. Yet, he is risking his life to help my family. I've lived a long time, Dimitri. I've known a lot of men. I can honestly say I have never met anyone as selfless and altruistic as Victor Keisser."

Dimitri didn't know what to say. He had been furious when the council suspended Victor. He came close to quitting and telling Victor he'd go on that road trip with him. His father had talked him out of it. Hearing what the council had done to Victor's father, Atticus Keisser, made him more than furious. He'd often wondered why Victor's dad was the way he was. Now, Dimitri didn't blame him. Society had turned their back on him, why would he continue to embrace society. "I know you've told me a lot of things tonight you probably shouldn't have. I have to be honest with you, it doesn't make me like the council any more than I did before. In fact, the opposite is true. Since Victor's suspension, I haven't had a lot of faith in your group. Hearing about Atticus deepens my distrust. Not in you personally, but in the council as a whole." He looked up at Oberon and noticed he was frowning. "I guess I probably shouldn't have told you that," Dimitri admitted.

"Dimitri, I understand why you might feel that way. Like me, you know without a doubt that Victor was innocent. Yet, he was punished. I hope you will think about this some more, when you can be more objective. When you're not so angry at the injustice of it all. Yes, the council made a mistake with each of the Keisser's. Monumental mistakes as far as I'm concerned. But, Victor and Atticus do hold some of the responsibility for this. In both cases, there was additional information, information that would have allowed the council to make a better decision. Both of these individuals chose to withhold that information. They chose to go before the council but refused to present a defense. The council only got one side of the story and they were forced to make a ruling on the facts presented. It wasn't fair, but it wasn't our choice. Victor and Atticus made the choice for us."

"I understand," Dimitri admitted. "And I guarantee you, I will be thinking about both situations for a very long time. Speaking of injustices, I think you should know Ariel had another one of her panic attacks, or memory flashes, last night when the shifters were outside the cabin. She said she hasn't had one in years, is that true?" Dimitri asked.

Oberon closed his eyes and ran his hands through his hair. "I wish there was something I could do to help her get passed that terrible time. I'm glad she has you, Dimitri. I think you're the only one that really helps her get through those episodes. Yes, I believe she was telling the truth. She's pretty open with me about her nightmares and those memory flashes. She tends to keep it from her mother, but she still seems comfortable telling me when she has an episode. I've been worried the events of the past couple months might be a trigger for her. Dahl's kidnaping, Marlena's death, the threats to abduct Alex, it all hits too close to home. They have to find her. I can't even imagine what life would be like if we lost her. What was she thinking when she took off with that shifter? She knows she has a hard time sleeping in strange places. How is she going to get through this alone?"

"I know," Dimitri soothed. "I just keep telling myself if anyone can find her, Thomas and Victor can. You have to believe in that. Trust them. It's all we can do right now."

Dimitri walked over to Oberon and they embraced. Oberon smiled at him. "Dimitri, I know I'm not your father. Dylan was the best friend a man could have. He was also the best father a boy could ask for. I would never try to take his place. But, I'm grateful you're comfortable coming to me, talking to me, confiding in me. I love you like a son," he paused. "I am so proud of you. I know I don't tell you that often enough but I want to thank you and Alex for everything you've done, and continue to do, for this community. We all owe both of you, and the rest of the warriors a great debt. Next time you see them, will you pass along my gratitude? My daughter couldn't be in better hands. That will bring me comfort while I wait. Please keep me updated on any developments."

"I will. I'm afraid it might be awhile before we hear anything though. They're going deep into the Gunk. I doubt there is cell phone coverage out there. Have faith, our boys will get her home safe. If you need anything, I'm only a phone call away." Dimitri turned and headed for the door.

Chapter Three

Thomas and Victor approached the cave cautiously. There was no way to know what they would find inside. It had been easy to follow Morrigan and Ariel's trail from the cabin at first. They'd lost it for a while, but Victor figured Morrigan would stay close to the river for the water. He'd been right, it wasn't long after they lost the trail that they picked it back up again. The problem was, the trail was now splattered with blood. Victor was certain it was fae blood, which meant Ariel's blood. The blood trail led them straight to this cave. How sloppy could Morrigan be? Once they determined Ariel's condition, Victor was going to have to go back out and dispose of the trail. When night fell vampires would swarm the cave, the fae blood would be like a beacon in the night.

Thomas looked at Victor. It was now or never. They had to go in. They both hoped Morrigan and Ariel were alone, but the cave could be full of vampires or shifters. Both warriors took another deep breath and simultaneously shook their heads. Neither of them could detect the smell of vampire inside. That was a good sign. Hopefully, Morrigan and Ariel had come here on their own seeking shelter from the night. Victor held up three fingers. He slowly lowered one, then the other. He took a deep breath and motioned to the opening with his index finger. He and Thomas entered the cave at the same time.

Morrigan was on the attack. He was in the form of a wolf again. Thomas was trying to hold him back, but Morrigan was fighting hard. He obviously didn't recognize them. Victor got behind Morrigan and was able to get an arm around his neck. He called Morrigan's name, then he called it again. "It's Thomas and Victor. Stop fighting so we can let you go," Victor yelled. Morrigan finally calmed and Victor released his hold. He scanned the cave and spotted Ariel. She was lying on a blanket, but she wasn't moving. Had she passed out, or was she dead? Victor's heart sank. He spun to look at Morrigan who had turned back into a man.

"What happened to her?" Victor demanded. He quickly went to Ariel and knelt down beside her. She had a thin blanket covering her, but she was shivering. He glared at Morrigan. "What happened?" he demanded, a little more forceful this time.

Morrigan looked at Victor, anguish in his eyes. "Everything was going fine when we left the cabin. We were on alert, expecting to run into vampires. When we came to a fork in the road, we followed the trail that stayed close to the river. We couldn't see any sign indicating which way the vampires went. I wanted to make sure we had plenty of water," Morrigan hesitated.

"The vampires went the other direction," Victor said flatly. "Tell me what's wrong with Ariel."

Morrigan closed his eyes. How had he missed that? "We came around a bend and ran into some kind of animal. I have no idea what it was. I've never seen anything like it before!" Morrigan became excited as he looked up at Victor, then to Thomas. "It was similar to a coyote, but it was bigger, more muscular. Its teeth were razor sharp and it was strong. It was so strong and fast. I shifted to a wolf, thinking that was the best form to fight this thing but I soon realized that wasn't going to help. Ariel started throwing fire. That was a shock too. I've never seen anything like her before. She was fast and accurate. Ariel finally hit the animal hard enough with a fire ball to stun it. I jumped in and stabbed it through the heart. I was just pulling my knife out when another one flew into the clearing. Before I could get to Ariel, it had grabbed onto her calf. She was able to hit it in the face with a fire ball. It was so stunned and in pain it let go of her instantly. I rushed to her side and plunged my knife into that one too. It died instantly."

Victor pulled the cover off Ariel. He studied her lower leg. It was swollen severely and crusted over with blood. He couldn't tell how badly it had been damaged. There was too much blood and dirt covering the injury. Obviously pretty bad if she was unconscious. He pressed a hand to her forehead, she was burning up. Ariel needed help and fast. "Did you give her any tea?" he glowered at Morrigan.

"Not yet. I got Ariel to this cave and she was mumbling something about tea, but then she just passed out. I had just gathered the firewood and returned from the river with fresh water when I heard the two of you. I pulled that stuff out of her pack, but I have no idea what I'm doing. She didn't have a chance to tell me if I was supposed to mix it all together or what. I'm really glad you got here. I'm out of my element. I don't know anything about fae, or their tea." Morrigan slumped against the wall.

After Dark

Victor walked over to him. "Maybe you should have thought about that before you snuck off in the middle of the night with one in tow." Victor wasn't fazed by the guilty, sorrowful look on Morrigan's face.

"Cut him a little slack, Victor. I would have done the same thing if Alex was missing," Thomas chastised.

Victor was still scowling at Morrigan. "What did you do with the animals you killed?" he demanded.

"Nothing yet," Morrigan answered. "My first priority was to get Ariel to safety. Once I got her settled and figured out that tea, I planned to go back, dispose of the bodies and try to do something about that blood trail."

"Ariel's wound is that recent?" Victor said surprised. "How long ago did you have that fight with the animals?" Victor knew he wasn't going to like Morrigan's answer.

"Thirty to forty minutes, maybe. She got bit, then it took us a few minutes to finish the thing off. I immediately helped her up and started this way. The trail leading to this cave was overgrown and didn't look like it had been traveled much. I decided to follow it and got lucky. As you noticed, the trail dead ends here at the cave." He looked over at Thomas who motioned for him to continue. "Anyway, I found the blankets in Ariel's bags and got her settled. I pulled out that tea stuff, but didn't have any idea what to do with it. I decided to gather the wood and fetch water, then try to work on the tea. Like I said, I'd just gotten back when the two of you arrived. That whole process couldn't have taken more than forty minutes. I'd guess more like thirty to thirty-five."

"Shit," Victor muttered under his breath.

"What?" Thomas asked.

"Ariel shouldn't be this bad off yet. I'm worried about what that animal is. If I'm right, Morrigan is going to have to go back to the cabin tonight. We don't have anything that will help Ariel. I think Breena will need Oberon's help to save her. Let's just hope I'm wrong about this." He took a deep breath then walked over to Morrigan.

"I can't go back to the cabin," Morrigan argued. "I have to keep looking for my sister."

Victor gave him a long, cold stare. He wasn't going to argue about this. Ariel's life might depend on it.

Morrigan backed down. "Let's figure out what's going on here, then we can decide what to do about it. Do you want me to take you to the animals we killed?"

"Yes. I need to see what we're dealing with," Victor looked over to Thomas.

"I'll stay here and take care of Ariel," Thomas decided. "Have Morrigan take you to the animals. I wouldn't know what they were anyway." He reached into his pocket and pulled out his phone. "This doesn't work out here, we can't get service. Take it. Use the camera to take pictures just in case you need to send them back to Oberon. I'll get the fire going and get some tea into her. Even if it doesn't help much, it won't hurt." He handed his phone to Victor. "Do you know how to operate the camera?"

"Yeah, good idea," he turned to Morrigan. "Let's go."

After Dark

Victor followed Morrigan as he backtracked down the trail. They reached another intersection that led toward the river, or back toward the main trail. Morrigan took the modest trail heading toward the river. It didn't take long before they were in a small clearing. Victor held out an arm to block Morrigan from continuing. Morrigan instantly looked over at Victor, wondering if he'd missed something.

"There's nothing to worry about, I just don't want you to touch those things. What did you do with the knife you used to kill them?" he asked as he slowly moved toward the dead bodies.

"I left it in the cave. After the reaction Ariel had to that bite, I didn't want to use it until I cleaned it thoroughly." Morrigan watched as Victor crouched down beside one of the animals. He studied it for a minute then looked back at Morrigan. Victor slowly stood and walked to the other animal. This one was positioned in the sunlight. It wasn't shadowed by the trees like the first one. Victor pulled out the camera and began to take pictures. His face was grim and he was obviously concerned.

"So, what are they?" Morrigan finally asked.

At first Victor didn't say anything. Morrigan thought he was going to ignore him when he finally spoke. "My father told me about an experiment Radek's father, Balthazar, conducted. It was before I was born, but Oberon will be able to confirm my suspicions. I think Hector or Radek may be trying the same experiment. I can't understand why they would though. It went horribly wrong the first time around." Victor was obviously perplexed.

Morrigan began to interrupt. He still didn't understand and needed clarification. Victor spun on him. His look was not friendly.

"Look," Morrigan began quickly. "You haven't liked me from the moment I arrived at the cabin. I know that. I don't know if it's because you don't trust me or because you think I'm after Ariel." Morrigan laughed at the look on Victor's face. "I don't know what your relationship is with Ariel, but I'm a shifter I can feel the animalistic tension between the two of you. You are protective of her and for lack of a better word, territorial. I get it. You have nothing to worry about with me. Ariel and I are just friends. That's all we would ever be. The chemistry just isn't there for either one of us."

Victor sighed. "Ariel and I don't exactly have a relationship," he paused, deciding to start again. This wasn't about his feelings for Ariel. "I don't dislike you, personally. You're right, I didn't trust you at first. I was also pretty pissed at you this morning when I found out you let Ariel accompany you on this quest to find your sister. The two of you ran off into the forest, where you know there are vampires, in the middle of the night. However, my tension and frustration right now is not with you." He watched Morrigan intently. "I'm not sure Ariel is going to survive that bite. How am I going to tell her father I couldn't save her? I promised Dimitri I'd bring her back alive. If I can't keep my promise both of them are going to be devastated." Victor closed his eyes.

Morrigan laid a hand on Victor's shoulder. "I understand where you're coming from. I made the same promise to my father. A promise I don't know if I can keep. Sometimes it just feels like the weight of the entire world has settled on your shoulders, doesn't it?"

"Yeah," Victor admitted. "Sorry I've made you feel like the enemy. At first, I wasn't sure you weren't the enemy. Now, I know you're not. I'm just pissed off and frustrated and I guess you've been a handy punching bag. To be honest, I think you're all right Morrigan. If we make it through this, come to my club anytime. I'll even buy you a drink." He smiled and went back to the dead animals.

Morrigan followed. He was surprised at the abrupt change in Victor's attitude. When he first met Victor, he had disliked him instantly. Now, he realized the attitude was all for show. Given time, he thought they could actually become friends.

"So as I was saying," Victor continued. "Back in Balthazar's time, he decided to turn dogs into vampires. He thought they would make better guards. He gathered the biggest, meanest dogs he could find. The experiment went terribly wrong. Animals don't turn. The dogs my father described to me were a lot like these coyotes. They went wild, almost rabid and they were strong and fast. Their venom is very poisonous. If I'm right, you're extremely lucky you're not lying on that blanket in the cave with Ariel. Make sure you don't touch anything that has fluid on it. I would sterilize that knife of yours in the fire as soon as we get back, too. Saliva, blood, urine, any liquid that comes from this thing is toxic." Victor picked up a large stick and pushed it into the animal's mouth.

Morrigan walked over and took it from him. "Let me hold that while you get pictures."

Victor snapped the shot and stood. "We need to bury these things and get back to the cave." The two of them went to work digging a deep hole. They carefully placed the animals inside making sure they didn't touch them with their bare hands. Then they quickly buried the hole and headed back to the cave. "I need to check on Ariel and get a few shots of her injury for Oberon." Victor paused and looked at Morrigan. "I know what I'm going to ask of you will be difficult, but I need to ask it anyway."

Morrigan looked over at Victor. "You want me to go back to the cabin tonight?" he asked, already knowing the answer.

"Yes," Victor answered. "I need you to go back to the cabin tonight. If I'm right, we don't have much time. Breena can make whatever potion or medicine Ariel will need, but Oberon is going to have to help her. The venom from that bite will act quickly. I'm not going to sugarcoat it. If we don't get Ariel help within the next 24 hours or so, she's going to die."

Morrigan took a deep breath. He was in an impossible situation. "I feel like I'm being forced to choose between Ariel and Abby. If I go after Abby, Ariel could die. If I help Ariel, Abby could die. How am I supposed to make that choice?"

Victor studied Morrigan. He really was a good man. He was truly suffering with the choice he thought he was being forced to make. "I don't think you have to make the choice of who lives and who dies," Victor answered. "The choice you have to make is probably just as difficult though. I'm asking you to save Ariel's life. In return, I will do everything I can to save Abby's life. If you can trust me, I promise you we will locate your sister. I've never met a better tracker than myself. It's just a gift I have. I know the vampires went the other direction at that intersection in the trail. There's a pretty big cave up that way. It would be the perfect hideout for Hector. I realize you don't know me very well so this is all going to be done on trust. Trust in a stranger. You trust me to find Hector and Abby and I'll trust you to save Ariel." They walked in silence for a short time.

After Dark

Morrigan thought about Victor's words. He was right, they had to depend on each other. Was it possible to save both women? If there was a chance, Morrigan had to try. He knew Ariel was still alive, barely. As hard as it was to admit, he didn't know the same about Abby. He didn't know Victor, but he wasn't exactly a stranger either. In the short time Morrigan had known him one thing was obvious, Victor took his duty seriously. He was cautious and Morrigan believed he was an honest man. If Victor said he could find Abby, Morrigan believed he probably could. Maybe if he took this leap of faith, they could save both women and improve relations. If their pack and the fae became allies, both groups would benefit from the arrangement. Morrigan closed his eyes and hoped he was making the right decision. "Okay, I'll go back to the cabin. I think I should leave right away so tell me what you need from me."

Victor was grateful for Morrigan's sacrifice. He wouldn't forget it. "You can travel at night, right? You can turn into an eagle or something that will be safe? I don't want you putting your life at risk for this."

"I can get there safely. If I have to, I can shift into different animals to escape danger. However, I think the wolf is my best bet. I can travel quickly and it will be easier to carry that phone you're taking pictures with," Morrigan answered.

"Right. The phone could be a problem. I hadn't thought of that," Victor paused for a minute. "Thomas has Dimitri's number programmed in the contact list. Once you reach the bridge you should have service again. Call Dimitri. Tell him what's going on and have him get Oberon to the cabin immediately. Breena is a master with herbs but she's not old enough to know about these things. Oberon will have to confirm we're dealing with a vampiric animal. He can help Breena come up with a cure for Ariel," Victor paused. "Austin should be healed by now. If he is, bring him back with you. We'll need all the help we can get if we end up in a battle to save your sister."

"Do you think there are more of these things? Is Hector using them as guards like Balthazar tried to?" Morrigan asked.

"There may be more of them, but they won't be guards. The experiment didn't work. They ended up killing most of the vampires stationed at Balthazar's headquarters. That's why I can't understand them trying it again. They're trying to build an army, any loss is one too many. You would think they'd have learned from their history." Victor was honestly perplexed at Hector's reasoning. Hector was smart and cautious. Maybe this wasn't Hector's doing. Radek seemed to be making every mistake his father had made. Maybe Radek was the one trying to turn animals into vampires.

They arrived back at the cave to see Thomas giving Ariel the last of her tea. He looked up in question when they walked in.

"I think Hector or Radek tried to turn at least a couple of coyotes into vampires. It didn't work but if I'm right Ariel's life is in danger," Victor supplied. "Morrigan has agreed to return to the cabin with your phone to get help. He's leaving as soon as I get a couple pictures of Ariel's wound." Victor circled Ariel, trying to get the best angle with the most lighting to take the pictures.

Morrigan was sterilizing his knife over the fire. As the hot flame hit dark liquid that had dried on the blade, it popped and sparked. It was another sign they were dealing with something toxic.

Thomas walked to Morrigan. "Thank you," he said sincerely. "I know how hard this must be for you. I promise, we will do everything in our power to find Abby. This trip is going to take you all night. Then, it will probably take all day tomorrow before you return. We'll start tracking first thing in the morning. By the time you get back, I'm sure we'll know where your sister is being held." Thomas was trying to encourage Morrigan, but could see he was failing.

Victor walked to Morrigan. "Thomas is right. I'll spend all day tomorrow tracking. Trust me. I will find your sister. There's one more thing I need to tell you. I know you've considered the possibility your sister is no longer alive." Morrigan winced but Victor continued. "Dimitri suggested Hector could be feeding off her," he paused as Morrigan went visibly pale. "I know, it's not a great thought. There is a silver lining to that theory though. If he's using her to feed, she's probably still alive. Anyway, we don't know your kind well enough to know what will help her if she's weak. If he feeds on her every day, the loss of blood could take its toll. She may not be strong enough to travel. We brought a couple protein shakes with us, but if there is something that will work better, get it while you're at the cabin. We need to be prepared for anything." Victor held out his hand. "Good luck and be careful."

"Thanks. I'll see you sometime tomorrow. We'll be back before dark." Morrigan turned and headed out of the cave.

* * * *

Once Morrigan left, Victor returned to Ariel. He felt her forehead again and frowned. "Her fever is getting worse."

"Do you think more tea would help?" Thomas asked.

"I doubt it. Can you handle things here? Get everything ready for tonight?" Victor asked.

"Sure," Thomas said immediately. "Is there anything special you need done other than the obvious, gathering wood, preparing the cave?"

"I need to take Ariel up to that river. Morrigan said there's a spot above us that has a waterfall running into a small pond where the water's pretty calm. I want to try to get her fever down as well as clean up that wound. That's going to take a while in her condition. We really need to get rid of that blood trail before dark." Victor paused to remove the blanket covering Ariel. "Did Breena send a canteen of lemon juice with you too, or do I have the only one in my pack?" he asked Thomas as he rummaged through his things pulling out the items he needed.

"I haven't noticed one in the stuff she sent with me. I'll double check, if not I'll grab yours and take care of the trail. I'll also gather up enough wood to keep the fire going all night. That should help keep her warm. Breena sent the cave covering. It's a great idea, with that hung across the door the vampires won't be able to see the fire. You should try to get back before dark though. Once I hang the cover, it's going to be hard to find the opening." Thomas moved to his backpack to search for a canteen.

Victor slung a small pack over his shoulder and lifted Ariel into his arms. "I'll be back as soon as I can." He gently walked out of the cave and down the trail.

Thomas found the canteen stored in Victors pack. He was surprised but delighted to find a small eyedropper among his medical supplies. Perfect, that was going to make things easier. He exited the cave and searched for the first splatter of blood. He quickly poured lemon juice into the metal cup and secured the canteen over his shoulder. One drop of lemon juice over the blood and it dissipated immediately. This task was going to be tedious, but it was necessary. Once he finished with the lemon juice, he'd flood the area with water to eliminate the lemony smell. Most of the vampires wouldn't suspect a thing if they smelled lemon juice. Thomas was worried about Hector. He would know to follow the smell if he came across it. Hector had assassinated his mother, Marlena, using St. John's Wort and lemon juice. Luckily they didn't have to worry about wasting water. He had access to all he needed in the nearby river.

Victor climbed over the large rock formation and found himself on the edge of a serene pond. It was a beautiful, tranquil area. If he wasn't so worried about Ariel, he would have enjoyed the peace and solitude of the scene before him. The small waterfall cascaded down three subtle tiers and flowed into an emerald green pond surrounded by large rocks. The massive boulders were strategically placed to make this small oasis. Victor could almost imagine ancient giants creating the secluded area as a swimming hole or a place to bathe. He knew better, giants were a figment of the human's imagination. This beautiful area was created by nature, but it was entertaining to envision giants hauling large rocks through the forest to create a little piece of paradise.

Victor gently set Ariel on the bank of the pond. He stripped off his clothes and then turned to face her. He hoped she wasn't one of those modest fanatics. If she got upset when she found out he'd bathed her, he'd deal with that later. Right now, he needed to cool her down. Victor quickly undressed Ariel then carefully cradled her in his arms and slid into the pond. Breena had covered everything. She'd sent some kind of herbal soap that wouldn't harm the plant life or animals. He was glad. It was too tranquil here to disrupt the natural ecosystem.

Victor strode over to the waterfall. Luckily the water was cool, but not cold. It was actually perfect for Ariel. Hopefully, the cool water would bring down her fever. He gently positioned her next to the waterfall. There was a small, natural rock outcropping that he could use as a seat. He steadied Ariel on the base and washed her hair. To rinse out the soap, he cradled her head and shifted her underneath the waterfall. This might be easier than he thought it would be. He gently soaped her down then propped her against a large rock formation to soak. It worked perfectly. She was almost completely emerged in cool water. He just hoped this helped with her fever.

Victor quickly washed himself then returned to Ariel. He needed to do something about her leg. The blood and dirt were gone now. He could clearly see where the animal had sunk its teeth into her calf. There was something that looked like puss seeping out of the wound. Maybe that was why it looked so swollen. Victor checked to make sure Ariel was steady and then walked over to his pack and removed his knife. He'd have to slice the wound open and try to force the puss out. Maybe some of the poison would leave with it.

Victor positioned himself to the left of Ariel's leg. He made sure that as the liquid came out, it would flow away from their bodies and down river. He thought the toxins in the venom would be diluted enough in the water that it wouldn't cause any harm. He hoped so anyway. He didn't have any other option. Victor hesitated for only a moment and then made one quick slice across Ariel's leg. White liquid began to flow out of the wound. Victor pushed directly on her calf forcing the liquid out. His fingers started to burn, but he had to continue. If he could get enough of the venom out, Ariel might have a chance. The liquid began to clog the slice he'd made with the knife. He wiped it away with his left palm as he continued to press on her leg with his right hand. Both hands were starting to burn now. Just a little longer and he'd be done.

Victor pressed hard on Ariel's leg until nothing more would come out. He'd done as much as he could for her. Now, it was up to Ariel and Breena. He'd get her back to the cave, force more tea down her and do his best to keep her warm tonight. His hands were still burning, so he soaped them as thoroughly as he could then rinsed them in the cool water. Hopefully, that would be enough.

Victor carried Ariel to shore, dried her off and dressed her in one of his t-shirts and clean underwear. He smiled. This was a new experience for him. He'd undressed plenty of women, but he'd never dressed one before. He paused to admire her figure. She was so beautiful. He was afraid he'd already fallen for her. No matter what happened from here on out, he was going to get hurt. There was no preventing it. Victor ran his fingers through Ariel's wet hair. He gently brushed his thumb across her cheekbone. He would do everything in his power to help her survive. Victor knew his personal price would be high. Caring for her this way felt intimate somehow. It was becoming more and more difficult to shield himself from his own emotions. Had he fallen in love with her already? The thought terrified him. He took a deep breath, pulled on his jeans then gently cradled Ariel in his arms. He leaned down, picked up the backpack and headed for the cave.

He arrived back just before sunset. Thomas had done a great job getting rid of the blood trail. Victor knew it was there, but still couldn't find any sign of blood. He could smell the slightest hint of lemon, but Thomas had even eliminated most of that from the area.

He entered the cave amazed at the work Thomas had completed in such a short amount of time. The fire was burning bright, but Breena's cave covering blocked out all indication of light from the outside world. Victor was confident they would go undetected tonight. Wood was piled next to the fire pit. It would last at least a couple nights, probably more. He walked to the sleeping bag next to the fire and gently set Ariel on top of it. As he stood, he turned to face his friend. "You are a miracle worker, Thomas."

Thomas was lying on top of the other sleeping bag positioned on the opposite side of the fire. He leaned up on one elbow. "I have tea in the pot warming on the fire. I thought Ariel should have one more cup before we went to bed. I also heated some stew. I've already eaten. After all that work I was famished." Thomas stood and peeled off his shirt. "I'm going to sleep. If you tell me where that pond is, I think I'll take a bath as soon as the sun comes up." Thomas stripped off his pants and climbed into the sleeping bag. "Goodnight Victor. Wake me if you need help with anything."

Victor poured a cup of tea and sat next to Ariel. He gently lifted her head and poured a few drops in her mouth. Then, he tipped her head back slowly until the hot liquid slid down her throat. He continued this process until the entire mug was gone. It took a long time, but she needed the strength. He slowly looked around the cave. He hated places like this. They were always so dark and cool. Not cold, just cool and uncomfortable. It reminded him of the cellar. The one his mother had locked him in when he was a child. He covered Ariel with the small blanket and moved to the fire. He was starved. He grabbed a spoon and ate the stew straight from the pan. Fewer dishes to clean that way.

Once the dishes were washed, Victor added a couple more logs to the fire, just to make sure it lasted throughout the night. He unzipped the sleeping bag and slid Ariel inside. Victor quickly slid his jeans off and climbed into the sleeping bag next to Ariel. After zipping the bag closed, he pulled Ariel into his arms and tried to get some sleep. Yeah, right. This was going to be a very long night. Victor pressed his lips to Ariel's temple. "Hold on my sleeping beauty. Morrigan will be here tomorrow with medicine. You just need to hold out a little longer." He tightened his hold on her and closed his eyes.

Victor woke with a start. He'd been dreaming about that wretched cellar again. It must be the cave. He hadn't had those nightmares for centuries. He thought he had put all that behind him. He sat up and checked on Ariel. She was still unconscious, but the fever wasn't as bad as yesterday. He quietly climbed out of the sleeping bag and pulled on his jeans. He rummaged through his pack and found a clean t-shirt. The fire wasn't burning anymore, but there were plenty of red hot coals. Good, that would be perfect to start the coffee and heat water for Ariel's tea.

He looked at his hands. They were still burning and they felt raw. He'd have to find that cream Breena sent and see if it helped sooth the pain a little. Once the coffee was on, he looked up and saw Thomas watching him.

"What's wrong with your hands?" Thomas asked.

"They're okay," Victor replied, trying to act like it was no big deal.

Thomas climbed out of his sleeping bag, pulled on his jeans and walked over to Victor. He grabbed one of his hands and studied it. "They're not fine. They look like you picked up a couple of those hot coals. What happened to them?" Thomas insisted.

"After I got Ariel bathed, I started to tend to her wound. I could see it was swollen and white liquid was seeping out of it. I decided to drain it the best I could. Unfortunately, it was impossible to drain the venom without getting some on my hands. Don't worry about it. They'll be fine. They're just tender and sore this morning. I was actually looking for that cream Breena sent. I thought it might help. Do you know what happened to it?" Victor turned from his bag and looked over at Thomas.

Thomas walked to his bag and pulled out a container of cream. He then grabbed a metal thermos and walked over to Victor. "Cream first, but then you're drinking this." He held the thermos out to Victor.

"No. That's for emergencies," Victor protested.

"And this is an emergency," Thomas said calmly. "You're not having coffee until you drink this blood. I'm sure your body is trying to fight off the effects of that poison. You're using up a lot of your own blood supply. You need this to replenish your system."

"Fine," Victor relented. Thomas was probably right. "But that's it. I won't wipe out our entire supply of blood for this. I can handle a little pain. It really isn't that bad."

Thomas rolled his eyes. "Whatever." He walked to the other side of the cave and started pulling out clothing. "I'm going to the pond. Is it easy to find or will I need directions?"

Victor gave Thomas directions to the pond then paused. "I need to go tracking today." He poured Ariel a mug of tea. "I'll take care of this tea and breakfast will be on when you get back, but then I need to take off." He glanced over his shoulder at Thomas.

After Dark

"I don't think it's a good idea for you to go out there by yourself," Thomas countered. "It won't take me long to clean up, then I'll go with you."

Victor set down the tea and stood up. "If it wasn't for Ariel and her current condition, I would agree with you," Victor paused. "I thought a lot about this last night and I couldn't come up with a solution to keep her safe while the two of us went tracking for the day. She's just too vulnerable while she's unconscious."

"True," Thomas conceded. "But there could be more of those things out there. I also think we need to watch your hands. That venom is toxic. We don't know what kind of damage it can cause."

"I've had the blood and I'll take the cream with me. It seems to help with the burning. I'll be okay, Thomas. Trust me. Morrigan is counting on us to find his sister. I can't let him down. He didn't have to return to the cabin last night, but he did for us and for Ariel. Now it's my turn to sacrifice for him. You know Ariel can't stay here by herself and we can't haul her through the forest all day. The best solution is for me to track while you stay here and take care of her." Victor was watching Thomas closely. He really couldn't think of another solution.

"Okay. I'll agree to this arrangement on one condition," Thomas paused.

"What's that?" Victor asked.

"You have to promise you will be back before nightfall. It's too dangerous for you to be out after dark in your condition. You can't fight with those wounds on your hands," Thomas stood, unwavering.

"I plan to be back before dark, or right at dark at the latest. I need to do two things, try to track the vampires to their hideout and see if I can find a cave for us to move to. If the vampires are in the large cave where I think they are, there used to be a small cave not too far from there. I want to check that out and make sure it's still habitable, then I'll come back. I promise I will be careful and I'll be back as soon as I can. Morrigan and Austin should be here later this afternoon. I expect a nice dinner when I return," Victor said with a smile.

"Just be careful. I don't like this, but I realize it's the only way. Hopefully, Morrigan will have a miracle cure for Ariel and she'll be awake by the time you get back," Thomas said optimistically.

"That would be nice," Victor answered. "Now, go take that bath, you're starting to stink up my cave."

Thomas smiled and headed outside.

* * * *

Morrigan paced the small living room of the cabin. It had been light for over an hour. He was anxious to get started. Victor was right, Austin was completely healed. Morrigan was amazed. Befriending the fae had come in handy. Alex could heal and Ariel threw fire. He wondered what the rest of them could do. Obviously Breena was a master with herbs, kind of like a medicine man he supposed. He looked over at Oberon. "What's taking so long?" he asked impatiently.

Oberon glared at him. He was growing tired of this shifter's impatience. "We will take as long as we need to ensure the health of my daughter. If that means three more hours, that's how long we are going to take. If it means three more days, we'll take three days."

Morrigan wanted to argue, to remind Oberon his daughter didn't have three days and neither did Abby, but he could tell he was already pushing it. "I'm sorry. I know you're worried about your daughter. I'm just as worried about my sister though. I know we need to work together here. I didn't mean to annoy you."

Oberon took a deep breath. "I'm sorry, too. We're all on edge right now. I think Breena is almost finished. I keep remembering the painful way our people died last time the vampires tried this moronic stunt. Knowing I could lose my daughter that way is making me a little crazy," Oberon paused. "I've tried to convince Dimitri I should go with you, but deep down I know I have to stay here." He watched out the window for a minute. "So far, I haven't been able to get in touch with your father. Do you have any suggestions? I think we should try to meet and see if we can work together during this difficult time," Oberon stated.

Morrigan pulled a letter from his pocket and handed it to Oberon. "I agree. I think our people need to meet. This is a letter to my father explaining our situation. On the back are contact numbers for dad. It would be best if you called him this morning, as soon as I leave. Try to schedule a meeting with him today. If you tell him I sent you, he'll meet with you right away. I'm not sure how things work with your community. I know you're the council leader, but you also have a queen and then Dimitri is the warrior leader. If you guys are right, we need to start making preparations for war. I don't know what the situation is going to be when we find Abby. There may be too many vampires for us to handle. It would be nice to know we had backup waiting if we can get back here to the cabin. Whoever can make those decisions needs to go with you to meet my father," Morrigan paused. "Dad is big on efficiency. If you don't show up with the right decision makers, he will be less than cooperative and question any alliance between our people."

"I understand. Thank you. This will help prepare the way," he held up the letter. "Dimitri and I will be able to handle the meeting with your father," Oberon answered.

Morrigan watched Oberon as the older man turned to stare out the window. He could see the weariness in his eyes. Worrying about his daughter was beginning to take a toll on this ancient man. Morrigan wondered when Oberon had last slept. He also suspected his parents were at home feeling just as tired and helpless with Abby missing. He moved in beside Oberon and took a deep breath. "I know this is hard on you. Like you said, we are all under a lot of stress. You strike me as an honorable man. I think you're struggling with the same thing I was before I returned to the cabin. Your duty is pulling you in two separate directions. You feel like you have a duty to your daughter and your family. However, you also have a duty to your community and your people, right?"

"Exactly," Oberon admitted. "I can't take care of my daughter and take care of my community. I feel like I have to abandon one to save the other."

Morrigan laid a hand on Oberon's shoulder. "I was feeling exactly the same way. Victor asked me to come back here to get medicine to save Ariel. I felt like if I saved Ariel, I could lose Abby. Conversely, if I abandoned Ariel and went searching for Abby, Ariel could be lost. How could I decide whose life to save?"

Oberon looked at Morrigan with sincere gratitude and surprise. "You chose my daughter?"

After Dark

"Not exactly," Morrigan admitted. "Victor helped me to understand I didn't have to make that choice. I was the best man to return to the cabin. I can travel at night with very little risk. Victor was the best choice to track my sister. I'm told he's the best tracker in the universe," Morrigan smiled.

Oberon smiled too. He really did like this kid. "I think I understand where you're going with this."

"Victor helped me to understand I only had to choose whether I trusted him or not. Now, you have the same decision to make. Can you trust me and the warriors to take care of your daughter while you and my father take care of our communities? We are the best ones for the job, taking care of your daughter that is. You and my father are the only ones for the job of protecting and rallying our communities. Nobody else can do that. If we work together and trust each other, I think we can all get through this terrible time," Morrigan finished.

Oberon turned back to the window. Morrigan was right. Victor was right. It was difficult, but he had to put his daughter's life in the hands of these shifters and the warriors. He had to negotiate and prepare for war. He was the only one that could do that. To be honest, there was nothing he could do for Ariel that Victor and Thomas wouldn't do. He told Dimitri he trusted Victor with his daughter's life. Now it was time to prove it. "You're right. I trust you and the warriors to care for Ariel. You can trust me and your father to have things ready when you get back here. We'll be prepared for the worst and hope for the best." He turned to Morrigan and placed a hand on his shoulder. "Thank you for reminding me I don't have to do this alone. I'm surrounded by good, capable men. I constantly ask my people to trust me. As difficult as it is, I also have to trust my people."

Morrigan gave him one quick nod and turned toward the kitchen. "I'm going to check on Breena. Don't worry, I won't pester. I just want to see how much longer."

Morrigan met Breena at the kitchen door. "Oh, good. I was just coming to find you. I think we're ready." She turned back and handed him a large pack. "It's early so you shouldn't have to shift before you reach the cave. I tried to keep it as light as I could, but everything in there is essential."

Morrigan looked at the pack and blinked. It was huge. "Everything in that pack is essential?"

Breena laughed, he looked so flabbergasted. "Yes. You guys are going back into the wilderness. It's not feasible for you to return to the cabin every time you have a problem. We are basically dealing with three species. Each one has their own special needs. I've tried to prepare you for any possibility." She handed Morrigan a piece of paper. "I've written down everything you need to know. There are directions for taking care of Ariel. I've also included instructions on what to do if any of the warriors get infected by that venom. The cream and powder I made for the warriors should also work for shifters. The powder can be mixed with anything, but it's going to taste terrible. Look that over and let me know if you have any questions. I have also sent another sleeping bag for Ariel. I assume you're more comfortable shifting into a polar bear or something to stay warm."

Morrigan laughed. "Yes. However, I don't think I've ever taken the form of a polar bear. Did you include plenty of food in here for us? You got the jerky and the nuts?"

After Dark

"It's all in there." Breena hugged Morrigan and then stepped back. "Be careful. And take care of my friends. We'll be praying for you."

* * * *

Victor crouched behind a large tree. It was surrounded by brush and created a great hiding place. He'd almost been caught. Maybe getting within feet of that cave wasn't such a great idea. He'd had a close call, but everything was fine now. The risk had paid off. He was sure Abby was inside that cave. They would need to move to the smaller cave as soon as possible. From there, they could do surveillance and determine the best way to rescue Abby. He was waiting for a large group of vampires to pass him by, then he needed to get away from here as quickly as possible. There were too many vampires wandering around in the woods. Once the coast was clear, he could silently make his way back to Ariel and the others. He figured the cave couldn't be too much further now. Hopefully Ariel would be awake by the time he got back.

His hands were on fire. Breena's cream had helped initially. Unfortunately the last time he applied it, he hadn't felt any relief. He decided to save the rest for later. There was no use wasting medication if it wasn't helping anyway. Victor could hear vampires crashing through the forest. They didn't seem to care about the noise. Once they were out of sight, Victor started to stand. He stumbled and had to hold onto the tree trunk for support. The pain he felt as his hand pressed against the rough bark shocked him. His hands were so raw and they continued to burn intensely. The weakness and dizziness were also getting worse. If he could just get back to the cave and get more blood, he would be okay. Thomas had been right. His body was using up his own blood supply in an attempt to counteract the damage the venom was causing. So far, the venom was winning. Now, he was weak, dizzy and running low on blood. His body was starting to ache from the loss. He had to get back to the cave.

Darkness was just starting to fall when he had left the secluded area he was crouched in near his enemy's lair, but large groups of vampires had already started to disperse. They were like ants scattering from their hole to roam the forest in search of food. Now there were hordes of them wandering around the forest. If he took much longer, Thomas would panic and come looking for him. He didn't want anyone else outside and vulnerable with all these vampires on the loose. He was surprised Hector had such a large group housed out here in the wilderness. Victor took a couple long, deep breaths. Once he steadied himself, he quietly slipped through the trees making his way through the monsters' playground.

Victor finally reached the intersection that led to the cave. He was so close. He didn't want to stop, but he could hear vampires closing in on him. He wasn't going to make it. If he tried, he would just be leading the enemy into their camp. He refused to take that risk. He studied his surroundings. There was a large section of foliage just ahead. He'd have to hide and wait for them to pass. Victor crouched on the ground but lost his balance and fell onto his side. He laid there, trying to fight the blackness. If he didn't get to the cave soon, he was going to pass out. Suddenly, two figures crouched beside him. He tried to jump up, but the two men held him down. Morrigan leaned forward and whispered in his ear. "Calm down. It's Morrigan and Austin," Victor relaxed. If they remained quiet, the vampires would pass and they'd be in the cave in no time.

After Dark

Moments later the two men helped Victor to his feet. They were shocked to see his condition. He was pale and could barely walk. Morrigan was sure Victor had faded in and out of consciousness several times before they reached the cave. As they slid through the opening Thomas jumped up. "What happened to him? I knew I should have gone with you."

"We don't know. We found him hiding in the bushes not too far from here. We had to wait for a group of vampires to pass by. I think it might be serious. He's passed out a couple times," Morrigan supplied. "It wouldn't have made any difference if you had gone, Thomas. We found him this way. You know it's safer for Austin and me to travel after dark."

Ariel was now awake. Once Thomas gave her the new tea and rubbed some salve on her leg it had only taken an hour for her to wake up. Her leg was still terribly sore and she was a little weak, but all things considered she felt pretty good. She stumbled over to Victor. He looked awful. "Get him over to this sleeping bag. He needs to lie down," she directed.

Victor groaned. Thomas quickly jumped on the opportunity. "Are you injured, or is this still a result of your hands?"

"Hands," Victor croaked and then passed out again.

"What happened to his hands?" Ariel said as she looked down at them in shock. He looked like he had third degree burns covering the entire surface of both of them. She swung back around to look at Thomas. "Was he injured like this before he left this morning?"

"He was injured but it wasn't this bad," Thomas admitted. He was fumbling around in the pack Morrigan had brought back from Breena's.

"What do you mean not this bad? How could a burn get worse with time?" she demanded.

Thomas looked over at her. He hesitated then decided he was going to have to tell her eventually, now was as good a time as any. "When Victor and I got to the cave, you were in pretty bad shape. Victor was sure he knew what those animals were, so he sent Morrigan off for help. In the meantime, he felt he needed to help you get through the night. You had a pretty serious fever and your wound looked awful. Anyway, he took you up to that pond above us and bathed you to bring down the fever." He paused when he saw the surprised look on Ariel's face. Then he continued. "While he was there, he cleaned your wound and noticed liquid seeping from the hole. He cut it open and forced the liquid out. There must have been a lot of venom in it because his hands were burned pretty severely. They were sore this morning, but he took that cream Breena sent with us and it seemed to help. Obviously throughout the day, the wound became more severe," Thomas finished. He stepped up to Victor, a bottle of salve in one hand and a thermos in the other.

Ariel grabbed the salve. "He's injured because he was caring for me. I'll take care of this. Nobody else needs to be exposed to these toxins." She carefully lifted one of his hands and started to slather salve across it.

"Breena also sent a powder, a different form of the medicine in that tea she made for you. Once I get it into this thermos of blood, I need to prop his head up so I can force it down him. If that venom has been working against his body all day, he's going to be extremely short on blood. That also explains why he's so weak." He set the container of powder down and began to shake the thermos.

After Dark

Once they had doctored Victor and forced the entire thermos into him, Ariel settled him into the sleeping bag. She only hesitated a moment before she removed his clothes, leaving him lying there in his underwear. If he stripped her naked to bathe her, he could deal with her getting him undressed for bed. This was all her fault. She should have seen that stupid animal coming. If she'd only reacted half a second quicker, neither one of them would be in this mess. She stood and started to pace the cave, but her leg hurt too bad to walk.

Thomas walked over and stepped in front of her. "Stop worrying. That medicine worked wonders for you. To be honest, neither one of us thought you were going to make it. Victor's not as bad as you were. He's going to be okay. He just needs a good night's rest and he'll be up and moving in the morning. I promise."

Ariel wanted to believe Thomas. Breena's tea had worked for her. The wound on her leg wasn't completely better, but at least she could walk on it a little. "I hope so," she finally said. "I'll take care of him tonight. It's the least I can do. It sounds like he's been taking pretty good care of me." Ariel paused at the look on Thomas' face. "With your help of course," she added with a smile.

"I'd like him to eat something, but at this point I think that's impossible. Why don't we all go to bed? It's been a long day and we're all beat." Thomas turned to go to his sleeping bag then stopped. "Breena sent that extra bag, is it going to be warm enough for you, or do you want to take mine?" he offered.

"No, it's warm enough. I also have that blanket. If I get cold, I can throw that on to keep warm. I want Victor to have the warmest bag tonight. I think he needs it more than I do. You're also going to keep the fire going, right?" Ariel questioned.

"Yeah. I'll throw a couple of the large logs on, that should keep it going most of the night. I know these caves get pretty chilly, but the fire kept us comfortable last night. Between the bag and the blanket you should be fine. If you get too cold just throw another log on or wake me up and I'll take care of it." He took Ariel's shoulders and turned her toward the sleeping bag. "Go to bed. We've done everything we can for him tonight. Trust me, he's going to be his usual annoying self in the morning."

Ariel gave him a smile she didn't feel and walked toward the sleeping bag. She pulled it closer to Victor's make shift bed then climbed in. Maybe between her and the fire he would stay warm and safe tonight. Hopefully Thomas was right and Victor would be better in the morning. She closed her eyes and eventually drifted off to sleep.

Chapter Four

Abby sat, huddled in the corner of the dark room. She was in a cave, she knew that much. They had walked almost all night. She was so tired by the time they finally arrived at their destination. As she stepped through the small opening, she entered a large cavern. She was then ushered through the room and forced to crawl through a small tunnel. It eventually opened into another internal cave. Off to one side was an opening that led to a small room. That is where they were housing her. The vampires had transformed the room into a prison. They fastened some kind of metal doorway to cover the entrance. The room was basically empty. Abby was secured to the rock walls with a chain and steel wrist manacles. There were two additional chaining stations inside the room.

Abby looked over at the new arrival. The vampires had carried her in last night. So far, she hadn't moved an inch. Abby wasn't sure if the girl was still alive. If she was, she must be unconscious. They probably drugged the new girl to control her, the same as they'd done with Abby that first night. She heard a door slide open and quickly looked up. Please don't let it be Hector, she silently pled. She was starting to get weak. If he kept feeding on her, there's no way she would have enough strength to escape.

Two vampires entered the room. They must be guards or something, Abby thought. A third vampire walked in behind them. She hadn't seen any of them before. The third one was wearing a long black robe, like he thought he was royalty or something. She glanced at his face. He looked evil and maybe a little crazy. His violet eyes were cold and empty. The way the first two vampires were acting, he must be someone important in their world. Abby sat motionless. She didn't know what was going on, but she didn't like it. She spotted Hector standing in the doorway watching. The robed vampire walked over and stood in front of Abby. "Stand up," he ordered.

Abby hesitated only a moment. She stood defiantly and looked directly at the vampire. He started to reach for her, then stopped abruptly. He grabbed the top of her head and pushed it to the side. Suddenly, he shoved her. She fell backwards onto the ground. The vampire swung around and roared, "Hector!"

Hector slowly stepped through the doorway and entered the room. "Yes sir," he answered.

"Explain yourself!" Radek glowered. "I gave specific orders that this one was not to be touched. Who disobeyed me?" he glared at Hector. "Was it you?"

Hector knew he had to do some quick talking to get out of this one. Radek was angry. He never tolerated anyone disobeying his orders. "I'm the one that fed on her, yes. I didn't have a choice," he added quickly. He could see Radek was about to throw one of his fits. "Do you still agree this was the best plan?"

"This is currently the best plan. I only put you in charge of this operation because it was your idea. I trusted you," Radek's face hardened. "But don't forget who is really in charge here, Hector. You work for me. I will not have my orders ignored by anyone. She is mine." Radek thrust a finger in Abby's direction. "Nobody will touch her again, not even you!" He finished on a yell.

Hector took a deep breath. "I was desperate," he said clenching his teeth. "I didn't callously disregard your orders. I can't hunt and keep her safe at the same time. You keep sending me young vampires. If I left her alone with any of them when I returned she'd be dead. Feeding on her was my only choice. We have that new one now." He shot a glance at the female lying in the corner. "I can feed off her if you will allow it. I have to eat," Hector argued trying to sound apologetic. He was growing tired of trying to appease Radek. He had to play along for a little longer. Then, if he was lucky, he'd be free forever.

Radek was livid. If he didn't still need Hector, he'd kill him right now. His vampires needed to know they could not disobey him for any reason. Hector was becoming a problem. Once this conflict was over and he had control of the vampire, fae and shifter communities; Hector would die. Radek knew Hector would continue to defy him. It was only a matter of time before he'd catch him again. He could make an example out of him then. "I will allow you to feed off the new female. But, you better not kill her. We need her to gain cooperation with her pack. You will not touch this one again, do you understand me?"

"Of course. I only need one to quench my thirst," Hector promised.

Radek turned back to Abby. "Leave me alone now!" Radek demanded. "I have plans for her tonight." The rest of the vampires left the room and shut the door behind them. Radek grinned.

Abby watched the vampire. His evil, sadistic smile gave her the creeps. What did he want with her? What did he plan to do to her?

Radek stepped forward and dropped his robe. He was completely naked. Abby inhaled with a gasp. Was he planning on raping her? What should she do? She considered her options for about half a second. When he reached for her, she shifted into a mouse. She ran the perimeter of the room, looking for a way out. She couldn't find one. There were no openings, not even a crack in the rock. She looked up in shock at the tremendous scream that erupted from the vampire.

"Hector!" Radek bellowed as he pulled his robe back on.

Hector threw the door open and ran inside. What could have happened? He looked around the room. The girl was gone. He stood there in surprise.

"Close that door!" Radek snarled. "She'll escape."

Hector quickly pulled the door shut. "Where is she?" He was still studying the room, but only saw one girl.

"Over there," Radek pointed to the corner in disgust.

Hector saw it now. A small field mouse huddled in the corner. He wanted to laugh but held it back. Radek was furious. He had big plans for this woman. He thought he could impregnate her and create an heir. Radek was excited at the prospect of having a shifting vampire for a son. He wouldn't even consider the possibility his heir could be a daughter. Vampires couldn't reproduce with other vampires. They needed another species. It was impossible for a female vampire to get pregnant. Their bodies couldn't change to accommodate a child. Some vampires created heirs with humans even though the process was lethal to the mother. Not Radek, he was appalled at the idea of mating with his food.

Radek was furious. This prisoner was not going to escape! He had captured a fae woman a few years back hoping to create an heir with her. It hadn't worked, she escaped before he impregnated her. That was just another example of how weak the fae were. It sometimes took years for a male vampire to create an offspring with the fae. His mother had been in captivity almost fifty years before she got pregnant with him. He would not give up on this shifter. He wanted a son and she was going to give him one.

Abby didn't need to shift back. She only used energy during the shift. She could stay a mouse as long as she needed to. She would not be attacked by a creepy vampire. She could wait until he left or just stay this way for days. They weren't feeding her much anyway. If she stayed a mouse, maybe the small amount of food they were providing would be enough to sustain her.

"Capture her!" Radek demanded looking at Hector.

Hector lunged for Abby. She scurried away. She was confident he'd never catch her. He continued chasing her around the room. Hector lunged again and fell onto the floor.

"Catch her, you idiot. Can't you move faster than that?" Radek insisted. "I came all the way out to this pitiful cave for her.

I will not tolerate this nonsense. She will turn back into a woman and provide me with an heir. Make her cooperate!" Radek stomped his foot. He was losing his temper.

"Exactly how do you suppose I do that?" Hector countered. "I captured her and held her here to give you a chance to negotiate with her pack. I can't make her cooperate with you if she doesn't want to. That is impossible and you know it," Hector grumbled. He was pushing it, which was dangerous, but he was getting so tired of Radek and his impossible demands.

Radek stood there watching as Hector tried to catch the small mouse. It was impossible. He had to admit that. He needed another plan. "I'm leaving. I need to get back to Lilith. She's still not herself since that human," he said with disdain as he paused, "covered her with holy water," he sighed. This was not working the way he had planned. Lilith wouldn't have sex with him. She claimed she was too self-conscious and weak since the woman had injured her. He was growing tired of this abstinence. Creating an heir with the shifter seemed like a perfect solution. Somehow she would have to pay for the inconvenience and frustration she caused him tonight. He had come all the way out here to this pathetic cave, just to be with her. How dare she not cooperate with his wishes? He was the king! He should have what he wanted anytime he wanted. This shifter would have to learn her place. If she continued to play games, it would be a fatal mistake. "I'll be back in a few days to try again. If she doesn't cooperate then, she will regret it. I won't tolerate such defiance in my subjects." Radek turned and angrily left the room.

Hector followed him out and shut the door behind him. He could feed later.

After Dark

Once the door shut, Abby remained where she was. This could be a trick. She wouldn't shift back until she knew she was safe. Maybe never. Not until she escaped anyway. She turned abruptly when she heard a moan from the corner. So, the girl was still alive. Was she injured or just disoriented? Abby considered shifting back to check on the other prisoner, but she was hesitant. She was safer as a mouse and shifting back and forth would use up too much energy. Energy she didn't have to waste. She decided to hold out for a while. If the girl seemed like she was in pain or needed help, Abby would shift back. In the meantime, she was staying a mouse.

* * * *

Lilith sat on the large branch, huddled near the trunk of the tree for cover. The vampire on watch still hadn't realized she was there. As she sat looking for movement, she tried to devise a plan. She needed to get back into the cave unseen. She was supposed to be incapacitated. Radek would be furious if he knew she'd been out hunting. She'd been so adamant tonight that she was still injured and too weak to have sex with him. She knew she was pushing it. Radek was getting frustrated and inpatient. She wasn't weak, she was just getting so bored with Radek. She wanted Hector, but that was impossible. He was off dealing with the shifters. He was surrounded by young vampires that would blab for sure if she went to visit on her own. If Radek found out about her and Hector, they'd both be dead.

Lilith's thoughts shifted back to the last time she saw Hector. She'd convinced Radek she needed to get out of the cave. She told him they needed to test her strength to see if she had recovered. The perfect test would be for her to deliver the new vamps to Hector. He was staying out in the woods, there wouldn't be any danger. Nobody knew he was there. Radek reluctantly agreed. Lilith cringed. So far nobody seemed to know about her little experiment. Hopefully, she could keep it that way. How was she supposed to know animals didn't turn completely like humans did? She just thought having a few vampiric animals would give them an edge. The idea had hit her on her way to see Hector that night. She'd gotten lucky. Hector didn't know how many vampires she was supposed to deliver. The fact she was five short had gone undetected.

That fox had been fast. She'd never seen anything like it. Those two new vampires didn't have a chance. Seeing the strength and agility in the fox is what made it impossible to resist when they'd come across the two coyotes. Okay, she had to admit the fox was a failure. She'd lost two men before they could kill the thing, but that's what made the idea so enticing. In her defense, there was no way to know if the young vampire had done things right with the fox. It was his first attempt at turning. She had to give it another shot with the coyotes. Those three vampires had fought well, but in the end the coyotes won. It had been a beautiful fight, she couldn't exactly say she regretted the attempt. If the coyotes wreaked havoc on Hector's vampires in the woods, she might be sorry later on. She'd been forced to choose between chasing down the coyotes and controlling the young vampires. She had to deliver the vampires to Hector. So she'd chosen the vampires thinking she could track down the coyotes later. She'd been wrong, they were long gone.

Her thoughts returned to Hector. What was she going to do about him? She was starting to worry. She'd gotten the impression he was growing tired of their secret affair, but that was impossible. No man grew tired of her, she was irresistible. Lilith always decided when things were over. No man dumped her, the thought was ludicrous. But Hector had refused her that night. He said it was because they were surrounded by vampires that were loyal to Radek. They were, but that's what made the idea more appealing. She'd gotten so worked up on her trip through the woods, imagining the thrill of cheating with Hector right under Radek's nose. Hector's refusal had infuriated her. Sure, she had yelled and screamed and maybe she was out of control but nobody rejected Lilith. She sighed, that had been the wrong tactic to take with Hector. Her tantrum had reminded both of them of Radek. Hector was even more put off with the idea after that. She'd made a lot of mistakes that night. She just hoped none of them would come back to bite her, literally and figuratively.

Well, there was nothing she could do about that now. She knew she had a temper and Hector's refusal had made her reckless. When she came across that black bear, she was itching for a fight. Trying to turn him had been impulsive. She was a better fighter than those young ones. She had been sure she could win a battle with a rabid bear. She'd been wrong about that, too. She glanced down at her thigh. All her wounds had healed except that one. Another reason she couldn't have sex with Radek. How could she explain that wound? She'd barely escaped with her life. The deep gouge from the bear's claw was nothing when she compared it to the agony those other vampires had experienced after being bitten over and over again by the coyotes and the fox. Once the vampires were down, the animals had ripped their throats out with their teeth, putting them out of their misery. Lilith hadn't had a choice; she had to plunge her knife through their hearts to eliminate the evidence. Dumb luck was the only thing that had saved her from that bear. She shuddered as she remembered the events of that night. The bear had swiped her with his paw, splitting open her thigh and throwing her several feet across the small clearing. Then, it had lunged for her. That's when his back leg got caught between two logs. That merely made the thing more angry. It only took an instant for the bear to get free, but that was all the time she needed to escape into the woods. That slight delay was the only reason she was still alive today. Lilith shifted her attention back to the cave. She smiled, the coast was finally clear. The rest would be easy. She jumped effortlessly from the tree and darted for the small opening.

* * * *

Ariel woke with a start. She sat up and started to panic. Where was she? She spotted the fire and then looked over to see Victor. Oh, she was in the cave. Just knowing that Victor was next to her calmed her down. That was strange. In the past, the only person that could calm her that fast was Dimitri. Maybe it was something about being a warrior. She started to lie back down, then took a closer look at Victor. He wasn't lying there in a peaceful sleep. He was curled up in the fetal position and his face looked tormented. Maybe his hands bothered him, or was he having a nightmare? She wasn't sure. If it was a nightmare, she knew enough to keep her distance. Her mother had awakened her one night while she was having one of her flashbacks. Ariel had almost thrown fire at her. She felt terribly guilty about that for months.

As she studied Victor, she realized he was shivering. She'd been planning on getting up anyway. She stood, unzipped the sleeping bag and carefully draped it over Victor's body. At least he wouldn't be so cold. She walked to her bag and realized her leg felt better this morning. Not completely healed, but better. She got dressed and went back to the fire. She'd start with tea for her, then she'd make coffee for the rest of the guys. Breena left specific instructions that Ariel would need at least one cup of tea each morning and one in the evening until the container was empty. The tea wasn't bad, but it did have a slightly bitter taste to it. She'd be glad when it was gone. Once the water was started, she settled back against the logs and watched Victor's restless sleep.

* * * *

The six-year-old boy laid shivering on the cellar floor. His mother had finally left, but the burns in his hands hurt so bad. He was trying to be brave like dad taught him. He was going to be a warrior someday. But he couldn't stop the tears from falling. Mother had been so angry. Earlier that day she had ordered him to pray. Pray for God to save him. Pray that the evil warrior inside of him would be released and he'd turn into a normal boy. He didn't want to be a normal boy. He wanted to be a warrior like his father. He prayed, but he prayed for a way to escape this nightmare. A way to get away from his mother. She had left him there for hours, kneeling on the cold packed dirt, his arms bound by those leather straps.

When she returned, he thought the bad part was over. He thought she'd loosen the straps then leave him locked in the cellar until just before his father came home like usual. He had been wrong. She walked to him and quickly sliced his leg with a knife. Then she stood back, watching to see if he would heal. He did of course, he was a warrior. That had infuriated her. She lit a candle and held a large metal crucifix over the flame. He was afraid of what she planned. He knew it was going to be painful.

His mother unbound one of his hands and pressed the red-hot metal to his palm. He didn't want to, but he screamed out in pain. He wanted to be strong. He wanted to be courageous like a warrior.

But it hurt so bad. He couldn't help it. She immediately unbound his other hand and went through the same ritual. She was chanting something. He wasn't really listening to her. He hated her. She yelled at him again and told him to pray harder. She said he wasn't being sincere. He needed to pray that God would save him. That God would forgive him for being such an abomination. Victor didn't know what an abomination was, but he didn't think he was one. She told him she'd be back later to see if her sacrifice had worked. Then she'd see if God had decided to have mercy on him and remove the evil warrior spirit from his body. She said if God forgave him, the evil inside would escape through the burning cross etched across his hands. Victor lay weeping on the cold floor for a long time waiting for the burning to stop.

Once his palms started to heal, he realized he wasn't tied up. In her rage, his mother had forgotten to fasten him to the leather straps hooked to the wall. Had God heard his prayer? Was this his chance to escape? He slowly rose, wiped the tears from his face with his sleeve and walked to the door. He peeked out and didn't see anyone. Victor slowly slipped outside then turned to softly close the door. As he was sliding it back into place two hands wrapped around his neck. It was her. She'd come back for him. She was even angrier now as she ushered him back into that cold, dark room. Victor suddenly realized he wasn't cold anymore. His hands still hurt, they felt like they were on fire, but he was actually getting too warm. He woke with a start. It took him a couple seconds to orient himself. Oh, he'd been having another one of those damn dreams. At least he woke before the beating. That beating had been one of the worst in his life. He looked around and saw Ariel studying him. Her face was sober and she was frowning.

He smiled over at her and tried to pretend everything was normal. He didn't want her to know he'd been having one of those flashes into his past. He didn't want to talk about that time in his life. Sleeping in these caves and the wounds on his hands must be getting to him. The instant he remembered his wounds he looked down to see if they had gotten any worse. They actually looked a little better. Whatever Thomas had done, it worked.

Ariel saw Victor studying his hands. "Breena sent some salve and a powder with Morrigan in case one of you warriors came in contact with the venom, too. She really is a miracle worker. Her tea and salve are working wonders on me." Ariel picked up a mug and poured a cup of coffee. She handed it to Victor and then poured herself another mug of tea. "How are you feeling?" she asked skeptically.

"A lot better, actually. What do I need to add that powder to? I should probably take another dose this morning," Victor asked.

"I'm not sure. Thomas added it to blood last night. Morrigan brought several more thermoses with him. Do you want another one this morning?" She started looking around, not sure where Thomas had put them.

Thomas climbed out of his sleeping bag and pulled on his pants. "Yes, he needs another thermos this morning." He picked up a black container and handed it to Victor.

"Wait," Victor started to protest.

"No," Thomas cut in. "Morrigan brought several of these back with him and you need it. You were in really bad shape last night, after dark I might add." He stopped and glared at Victor to make sure he got his point. "You are going to have one more thermos of blood this morning with that powder medication in it. You also need more of that salve smeared on your hands. If you're substantially better tonight, we'll discontinue the blood. You will have to continue with the salve until your hands are completely healed though. We need to drink that chocolate milk so you can have the powder in that tonight if you don't need more blood." He poured himself a cup of coffee and sat next to the fire. Thomas turned to Ariel. "Did you take the tea with your medication in it this morning?"

Victor took a deep breath. "Somehow I didn't get the memo," he said sarcastically. "You know, the one putting you in charge of this operation. I'm out for one night and you turn into General Patton," he smiled at Thomas.

"I'm the only one that's not injured, except for those two wolves over there that is. Since I don't speak wolf, I'm in charge. They can't argue," Thomas countered.

"Nice try, but no dice. I'll follow your directions this morning because I sort of agree with you. If things were reversed, I'd make you drink another thermos of blood just to be safe. Just so we're clear, you are not in charge. You're the rookie, remember?" Victor raised his eyebrows.

"Whatever," Thomas rolled his eyes. "Wanna fight for it?" He smiled a wicked grin.

"Some other time, hotshot. Today we have things to do," he shifted his gaze to Ariel. "Do you think you're up to traveling?"

"Maybe. How far do I have to walk?" She looked back down at her leg. It was feeling better, but she didn't think she was up to a long hike so soon.

After Dark

"It's a ways. What if I carried you? Then would you be up to traveling?" Victor asked.

Morrigan walked over to the fire and poured himself a cup of coffee. He snorted. "You think you're going to carry her on a hike all day long in your condition? You can barely carry yourself. How are you going to hold onto her with those hands?"

"You got a better idea?" Victor asked.

"Yeah, Austin and I can take turns with her. We can shift into a mule or something and she can ride wherever it is you want to take us." Morrigan looked over at Austin for approval. Austin nodded in agreement.

"That's not a bad idea. Do you think you could carry some of the supplies, too? We don't have a long way to go, but some of it is a pretty steep hike. It will probably take most of the day," Victor admitted. "We can't take the shortcut I used last night, it's too difficult especially with me and Ariel wounded. Plus, transporting the supplies would be impossible over that terrain."

"Mules can carry quite a bit without getting tired. They also do well on steep hills. I think if we switch off, we should be okay. I'm dying to know what you found yesterday on your tracking expedition." Morrigan sat down next to Thomas and leaned against a big log.

Victor filled him in. He told them about the cave where he thought they were keeping Abby and the smaller cave where he wanted to camp and conduct surveillance. At first Morrigan argued. He wanted to go in blazing, but eventually he saw the wisdom in Victor's plan. It would only be one more day and then Abby would be free.

They had a quick breakfast and then started to pack. They wanted to get an early start.

* * * *

Ariel was getting tired. They'd been traveling for hours. She was walking now and her leg was really bothering her. Riding Austin or Morrigan as a mule had made her butt sore. She couldn't bare another minute of riding, she'd rather walk even if it killed her. At least they hadn't seen any more vampiric animals. They were following a trail that led to the river. Victor said it wasn't too much further, maybe an hour or so. She couldn't wait to get to the cave. She needed to rest. As they came around a bend, they heard voices. The men slowed. Ariel didn't want to, but she followed their lead. Morrigan and Victor left the trail and eased forward. They were being careful, making sure they stayed behind the covering of the thick trees and brush. Ariel, Thomas and Austin followed a short distance behind.

Ariel knew the exact moment Victor and Morrigan spotted the men. They looked at each other then quickly retreated. Ariel was confused. She could see a portion of the men from a distance. There were four of them, but they looked like they were just drinking and partying. Why had Morrigan and Victor evaded them? They couldn't be much of a threat to two warriors, two shifters and a fae. Ariel followed as her group retreated back down the trail. She walked silently until they could no longer hear the men talking and laughing by the river.

"Okay, stop!" She demanded.

The men turned and looked at her in question.

"What gives? Why are we retreating because there are four men partying at the river?" She was exhausted and just wanted to continue on with the original plan. She didn't want to change routes now.

"Well," Morrigan said. "I'm retreating because they are not just men partying by the river. They are shifters. Well to be more specific, they are were-panthers."

"And?" Ariel prodded.

"And I don't think it's a good idea to get into a fight with panthers just before we try to rescue Abby. We may need to fight the vampires. You know, pick your battles, fight one war at a time and all that," Morrigan finished.

"I still don't get it. Why would we have to fight them?" Ariel asked.

"Panthers and shifters don't get along. Basically anytime we encounter each other, things turn ugly fast," Austin supplied. "Typically, it ends in a fight with several members of both sides injured. It's not worth it."

"Are you telling me you can't control yourself for ten minutes while we walk passed a few panthers on our way to the cave? What? Your animal instincts kick in and you become territorial or something?" Ariel said sarcastically.

"I can control myself just fine," Morrigan said impatiently. "Shifters don't normally have a problem with panthers. Panthers have a problem with shifters. Plus, I'm familiar with two of those men. They're worse than most. If they see Austin and me, they'll be itching for a fight. No matter what we do, they'll attack."

Ariel was silent for a moment. She was trying to figure out why panthers would have a problem with shifters. Finally she just asked.

"We can shift into anything we want. Anything that actually exists anyway. I can't shift into a mythical creature. Panthers can only shift into panthers. It's like we have the better toy I guess. They can't have the toy, so they want to fight to show they are better than we are. I can't explain it better than that because I don't really understand it myself," Morrigan explained.

"Men!" Ariel said exasperated. She turned to Victor. "So, what's your excuse? Why did you skedaddle so fast? I'm sure panthers aren't jealous of warriors."

Victor hesitated for a moment then shrugged. "Panthers in this area don't exactly care for me. I'd say compared to yours truly, they'd welcome a couple shifters with open arms. About five years ago we had a bit of a disagreement," Victor said wryly. "Let's just say, the panthers went home disgruntled and I got an extended vacation."

"Oh," Ariel said wide eyed. She remembered now. The girl Victor had been involved with when he got suspended for a year had been a panther. The panther pack was pretty upset at the results of the council meeting. Ariel didn't know the specifics, but she knew things hadn't gone well for anyone that day. Her father had come home extremely upset. She remembered him ranting in the library. He'd called Victor bullheaded and the panthers greedy and manipulative. As she recalled, he was also annoyed at the other council members.

"Okay. It looks like we don't have a choice, we have to take a different route. How long is that going to take?" Ariel said obviously frustrated.

"It will add about thirty minutes to the walk but once we get to the river, it's going to be a lot easier to cross. There's a bridge down this trail." They had come to an intersection where two trails crossed. "Taking that into consideration, we should only add about ten to fifteen minutes to the total trip time at most." Victor studied Ariel. "You okay?" he asked. "You look a little tired."

"Yeah," she sighed. "My leg's just getting sore, but I don't want to get back on that mule," she shot a glance at Morrigan. "My tailbone can't handle another minute on his back."

"How about a piggyback ride?" Victor asked.

"You're still recovering, I don't think that's a good idea. You only handed that pack off to Austin twenty minutes ago. You need a rest," Ariel objected.

"I feel fine. See?" He showed her his hands. "I'm almost completely healed. Better than you," he countered. He stopped and crouched down. "Come on, if I get tired you can walk again."

Ariel hesitated only a minute. She was so tired and if he was willing to carry her, she'd let him. She wrapped her arms around his neck. "Okay, I'm ready." Victor stood and she wrapped her legs around his waist. "Once we get to the river, we'll evaluate your condition and see if I need to walk again."

"Whatever you say," Victor laughed. It felt good to have her this close. He had definitely fallen for her. He didn't know what to do. He had tried to avoid her. That hadn't worked. Fate kept throwing them together. If he gave in and let things develop, he was sure to get hurt. He tried that once with Lakeisha. That relationship had definitely ended badly. He was never in love with Lakeisha but he had cared for her. It had been devastating to learn she'd been cheating on him. Then, she tried to blame him for her pregnancy. They both knew the baby wasn't his. He knew who the father was, but revealing that would have put Lakeisha in danger. He decided to refuse responsibility and take his lumps. He wouldn't provide for a child that wasn't his. But, he also wouldn't cause Lakeisha any trouble over her betrayal. His punishment had been hard. Leaving the warriors for a full year was the most difficult thing he'd ever done.

Victor had been thinking about his dilemma most of the day. The nightmare he had last night bothered him. It had been a long time since he'd thought about his mother. Was he subconsciously warning himself not to trust Ariel? Maybe his mind was trying to build those walls again. Unfortunately, his heart was telling him it was too late. His thoughts drifted to his father. He'd been so in love with his mother. Victor didn't think his father would ever get over that loss. He wondered if his dad ever regretted his decision that night. If he ever wished he'd chosen Victor's mother, Dannica, instead of Victor.

Dannica was like Dr. Jekyll and Mr. Hyde. She was loving, caring and sweet when his father was home. Once he left, she turned into a monster. How could you ever know if a woman was going to turn out that way? How could you really know her true character? Victor wasn't sure, that was the problem. He didn't think Ariel would ever harm anyone. Vampires didn't count. But he knew his father never would have married his mother if he thought she was capable of such atrocities. Victor knew ignoring his interest in Ariel was the safest course. Unfortunately, the more time he spent with her the more he was drawn to her. He wanted to act on the attraction. He wanted to be near her as much as possible.

Ariel relaxed a little. Her leg was still sore, but it didn't hurt as much now that she wasn't walking on it. She felt guilty about letting Victor carry her. Not enough to make him put her down though. She took a deep breath. He smelled so good. He had that muscular, woodsy smell. She didn't think it was just because he was in the forest. He always smelled good. She remembered smelling him in that dirty alley weeks ago. She'd caught a faint whiff just before his arms went around her. His smell was intoxicating but soothing somehow. She closed her eyes and enjoyed his closeness.

Ariel was still confused. They had shared that wonderful kiss at the cabin, but then she left with Morrigan. Since then, it was like Victor was avoiding her. He had taken care of her while she was sick, but she was unconscious at the time. Most of today he'd acted like he was avoiding her again. They really hadn't had a chance to explore their feelings. Once she recovered, he was sick. Maybe it wasn't the best time to get involved, but she wanted a chance to try. She wanted to get to know Victor better. She wanted another kiss.

They crossed the bridge and headed further into the forest. The trees were thicker here. Ariel insisted on walking the rest of the way to the cave. She spent the time thinking about Victor and the feelings she was developing for him. The more time she spent with him, the stronger her feelings. She already knew he was caring. He wasn't selfish and aloof, he just wanted people to think he was. On this trip, she'd gotten a better picture of just how good he really was. He'd risked his own life to care for her. Then, he risked himself again to scout for Abby. Ariel didn't think Victor had a selfish bone in his body. She'd never met anyone like him before. She knew if given the chance, she could fall in love with him. Knowing that scared her. She was worried she had already started to love this complicated man. One day he was kissing her, the next he was trying to avoid her. She had no idea how he felt. She had no idea if they had a chance. Only time would tell.

* * * *

They arrived at the cave and began to set up. Morrigan and Austin offered to gather wood. Everyone knew Morrigan just wanted a closer look at Abby's location while it was still daytime. Nobody said a word when they headed off into the forest. Thomas took care of the inside of the cave. Victor sat outside the door spying on the vampire's hideout with binoculars. Ariel stayed inside and helped Thomas for a while. She was a little tired, but surprisingly not as worn out as she thought she'd be. Breena's tea worked wonders. She looked around the cave and couldn't think of anything else to do inside.

"Hey, Thomas. Why don't you give me all the dirty clothes and I'll head down to the river and wash them? If we have a fire tonight and hang them across a rope or something they should be dry before morning." She started digging through her bag. She was sure there was a rope in there somewhere.

"Are you sure? Just because you're the only woman, it doesn't mean you have to do our laundry," Thomas said hesitantly.

Ariel laughed. "I don't mind. It'll give me something to do. You can cook dinner." She smiled at him as she handed him the rope. "And you can figure out how to hang this thing so I have somewhere to drape the clothes when I get back." She gathered up the dirty laundry and headed out the door.

Victor looked up as she exited the cave. "What are you doing?" he asked.

"Washing clothes," Ariel answered. She was trying to get her footing, but kept slipping on loose rocks as she slowly made her way down the incline.

Victor stood and placed a hand on her elbow to steady her. "Here, give me those." He reached for the clothes. "I'll do it. I don't think you should be out there alone. Not even in the daytime. There could be more of those animals close by."

"We'll both do it then." Ariel said as she handed him some of the clothes. "Nobody should wander around here alone. I've battled them. It's too dangerous for one person."

Victor hesitantly agreed. The river wasn't very far away, but it was secluded. If they ran into trouble, Thomas wouldn't be able to see or hear them. They would be on their own. It was safer to go together, but Victor wasn't sure he wanted to be alone with Ariel. Especially in such a secluded spot. It might be too tempting.

They reached the river and Ariel dropped the clothing on the ground. She immediately began pulling off her shoes. While she was here, she wanted to clean up. She glanced over and saw Victor leaning against the trunk of a tree, watching her. "You going to join me?" she asked casually as she pulled her shirt over her head.

"Right now I'm just enjoying the show," he said smiling. He didn't want to get too close to her. He wasn't sure he could stop himself from pulling her against him and kissing her, or worse. Especially now that she was stripped down to her underwear.

She gave him a coy smile. "I know you're not shy, you've stripped for bed every night without a second thought." She held up the bar of soap. "Come on, I have soap. I'll even wash your back," she tempted.

"That's okay. I'll wait," Victor insisted. "I like the view from here."

Ariel was confused and a little annoyed. Did she always have to make the first move? She walked over, grabbed his arm and pulled him toward the river. "Nope, that's not fair. Maybe I want a show this time," she teased with a smile. "You got enough of a visual the other day when you bathed me in that pond."

Victor couldn't stop himself. He grabbed her around the waist and pulled her in for a kiss. He'd been fighting this all day and he just couldn't fight it any longer. Her reference to the other day was too much. The quick memory of her lying on the ground, naked and beautiful was the final straw. Ariel wrapped her arms around his neck and deepened the kiss. She moved her sore leg in an attempt to get better footing and tripped over a rock. They both tumbled to the ground, laughing.

"My nick name is Grace," Ariel smiled over at Victor. He was just lying there, looking at her. He looked like he was debating whether to continue or not. Ariel decided to help him make up his mind. She slid closer, positioning her body against him and pressed her lips to his.

After Dark

Victor only hesitated a second, then he let go. To hell with safety, he wanted passion. He slid his hands down her body and enjoyed the moment.

Ariel couldn't move. She hadn't been intimate with anyone for years. Not since Tank. After three hundred years, she could be picky. She was now sated, exhausted and ecstatic all at once. She'd found a man who was not only hot and sexy, but he was good in bed. Well okay, this wasn't a bed but the concept was the same. All the warriors were large in stature, she wondered if they were equally large everywhere else. She smiled to herself, that probably wasn't a good question to ask right now. She wouldn't get an honest answer anyway.

Ariel wasn't ready to get up yet. She snuggled in closer to Victor. He draped his arm around her waist and they rested there, spoon style. She hoped he didn't regret their intimacy. She knew she didn't but Victor was a mystery. After a while, she turned around to face him and gently kissed him one more time. "We better get those clothes done. If we wait too long, we'll be washing in the dark," she reluctantly sat up. As she looked down at his bare chest she noticed for the first time Victor had a large tattoo of a dragon on the front of his torso. The dragon was breathing fire. The large flame spread from the front of his shoulder to the top of his chest. It was fascinating. How had she missed this? She remembered seeing something colorful, but she'd been too preoccupied to really pay attention.

Ariel reached out and traced the line of the dragon with her finger. She'd never seen a fae or a warrior with a tattoo before. She'd heard it was possible to get one, but very painful. For that reason, not many bothered. As she reached the fire, she felt a jagged edge. Was that a scar? But that was impossible. Warriors healed just like fae. They couldn't have scars, especially not one as large as this one was. She looked questioningly into Victors eyes and froze. He was staring at her with a cold, blank expression. Ariel felt like a barrier had just been erected between them. Was he angry with her? Once again, she was confused. The story of her life where Victor was concerned. She sat there motionless, waiting for him to make the first move.

Victor remembered why he avoided intimacy with fae. They knew he shouldn't have a scar. Humans didn't know any better. They just thought he'd had a bad accident. Fae always wanted an explanation. Well, anyone from the supernatural world wanted an explanation. Lakeisha had demanded one. How would Ariel react? He studied her, waiting for it to come. The questions, the demands, then the disappointment and anger when he wouldn't elaborate. It never came.

Ariel decided to let it drop. She wouldn't ask. Maybe someday he would trust her enough to share that secret on his own. She dropped her hand and smiled at him. "Ready to get wet?" she said lightly. "I never did get that sponge bath I started." She leaned in and sniffed then playfully wrinkled her nose. "Yeah, you need that soap worse than I do." She stood and held out her hand.

Victor stared into her eyes for an instant then grabbed her hand and stood. If she was going to let it drop, so would he. He swept her into his arms and headed for the river.

* * * *

Once they bathed and dressed, they stood on the bank and began washing clothes. Ariel was glad she hadn't said anything about his tattoo or the scar. The barriers she'd felt erecting were gone now. Victor seemed content again. He'd been gentle and caring as they'd bathed each other in the water. His kisses were so addictive. She didn't want to ruin the mood, but she was curious about the panther and was debating whether she should bring it up or not.

Victor was watching Ariel. He could tell she wanted to ask him something, but she was holding back. So, he wasn't going to escape a conversation about the scar after all. He wasn't surprised. The surprise had been her lack of questions before. They might as well get it over with. "Go ahead ask," he said flatly.

Ariel looked at him in surprise. How did he know she wanted to ask him something? She had been so deep in thought, she must have let her face show her curiosity. Well, it was too late now. She had to ask. She just hoped it wouldn't make him push her away or close himself off again. "I was just wondering about what you said earlier today," she paused.

Victor was confused. Earlier today? What was she talking about?

"You know, when we changed our route to avoid the panthers?" she said hesitantly.

"Oh," Victor said quietly. This wasn't about the scar, it was about Lakeisha. He was still shocked. Why wasn't Ariel curious about something so unusual?

Ariel watched Victor for a reaction. So far, he wasn't getting angry. She'd just ask and deal with what came next. "Well, obviously I know a little about what happened five years ago." She looked at him. His face was sober and didn't reveal anything. "Not details. Dad would never break confidentiality that way. I don't know any more than anyone else does." She hurried on, not sure how to continue.

Victor didn't really want to talk about Lakeisha, but he'd rather talk about that than his mother. He walked over and took her hand. "What do you want to know about Lakeisha?" he asked.

"Lakeisha? Was that her name? The were-panther?" she asked.

"Yes," Victor answered. "Go ahead and ask whatever it is you want to know," he prodded.

Ariel took a deep breath. "Well, I know you probably don't like to talk about that time in your life. I'm also sure it must have been awful. I know you hated being suspended for a year. I just wondered what you would be willing to tell me about it," she confessed.

Victor almost laughed. When Ariel looked up at him, she looked guilty. Like she'd just been caught with her hand in the cookie jar. He'd make this easy for her. Maybe she deserved an explanation. He wasn't sure what he was going to do about Ariel and his feelings, but he did know he wanted her to understand him. He needed her to understand him. He had never cared what people thought before, but he cared about Ariel's opinion for some reason. He didn't really understand why, but it was important to him that she knew he didn't reject his own child. He was still holding her hand. He guided her toward a fallen tree, sat down, then pulled her down next to him. He hesitated.

"Look. I don't need all the gruesome details," Ariel began. "That's not what I'm asking. I was at my parents' house that night the council met. Dad was pissed when he got home. He stalked straight into the library and started mumbling. He does that sometimes, but he's usually more aware of his surroundings. That night, he didn't notice me at first. I was sitting in his big chair reading. I heard him say something about you being a stubborn, bullheaded warrior with no sense and the panthers being greedy opportunists. I can't remember exactly what he called his fellow councilmen, but it wasn't flattering. He was also upset with them. Then he realized I was in the room. He told me to tell mom he had to go back out and he left. I was a little worried about him. He stayed out pretty late but I have no idea where he went," Ariel paused. "Anyway, I guess I'm curious to know why an innocent man would accept a punishment he didn't deserve."

"Why do you think I was innocent?" Victor asked, truly curious.

"Dad knew you were innocent. That's why he thought you were stubborn and bullheaded. If dad knew you were innocent, you were," Ariel said simply.

"You have a lot of confidence in your father's opinion," Victor answered.

Ariel paused while she considered that. "I guess I do. I'm not young and naive." Ariel looked at him intently. "I know my father. There have been times he's questioned someone's guilt. A few people he felt were guilty, but maybe not as guilty as they appeared. Does that make sense?" she asked.

"Yes. I think so," Victor admitted.

"Not with you. He knew you were innocent. He was sure of it. If my father was that sure you didn't do it, then you were innocent. It's that simple. Dad is big on justice and accepting the consequences of your actions. He couldn't have been that sure of your innocence if you were even a little guilty," Ariel answered.

Victor was surprised and touched. He studied Ariel for a long moment. "I knew your father was frustrated with me, but I didn't know he felt that strongly about it," Victor admitted. He assumed his lack of defense had made him look guilty to everyone on the council. "By the way, he went to see my father that night. After the council meeting I headed out to talk to dad. He needed to know I was going away for a while and why. After I explained the situation to him, he understood my decision and stood by me when your father showed up. Oberon tried to convince dad to talk to me. He wanted dad to convince me to trust him. When your dad left, he was just as frustrated with my father as he was with me. Obviously he didn't get anywhere with either one of us. We're both bullheaded," Victor said smiling.

"I'll try to remember that," Ariel said. "Anyway, I guess I just wondered what happened. How did you end up in front of the council that night?"

Victor took a deep breath. He studied her for a long moment. Should he trust her? Probably not, but he was going to with this. Most of it anyway. "I've never really been serious about any woman. I'm sure you know the womanizer rep I have. I guess on one level I've earned that reputation. Not completely, most of the things that are said about me are over exaggerations. But I have been with a lot of women." He was watching Ariel to see how she reacted to his confession.

"Victor, you've lived several centuries just like me. I'm not some innocent maiden. I've been with a lot of men myself. What does that have to do with what happened five years ago?" Ariel asked.

Victor looked down at their joined hands. "I'm not sure," he paused. "I met Lakeisha at the club. I noticed her as soon as she walked in. She was beautiful and seemed so alive. It was hard not to feel something for her. We talked for quite a while that night. When she left I didn't think I would see her again, but she started to come to the club on a regular basis. We slowly got to know each other and began to date. Eventually we were spending all our free time together," he paused again. "Even though I'd been with a lot of women, Lakeisha was the first one I truly cared about. We gradually got to the point where we were basically living together. Either she'd stay at my place or I'd stay at hers. Sometimes I considered spending the rest of our lives together, but we had a lot of problems. She was frustrated with my schedule. Even back then, the warriors spent a lot of time at night protecting the human population. Plus, she didn't like the time I spent at the club."

"Wait," Ariel interrupted. "You were serious about this girl, you considered spending the rest of your life with her, but you were still hanging out in clubs? I realize your rep is exaggerated, but don't you think that was a little out of line? You know you have a rep, but you thought she would trust you while you went clubbing?"

"Not clubs. The club," Victor corrected.

"I don't know what club 'The Club' is. But what difference does it make which club you were hanging out in? The point is, why would you continue to spend time in a place like that if you were in a serious relationship? It's kind of an unspoken rule that if you're sitting around in a club, you're probably trolling for a date.

Other women are going to approach you, hit on you. Especially someone as attractive as you are," Ariel said surprised.

Victor smiled. She didn't know he owned the club? He thought everyone knew that. "I had to spend time at my club. It doesn't run itself and my employees expect to get paid. I know that's narrow of them, but I have payroll, supplies to order, personnel issues to deal with. You know, basic business operations," he was still smiling.

"You own a club? Which one?" Ariel asked.

"Bojan Taverns," Victor admitted. "It's a lot of work, but I still love it. So yes, I cared about Lakeisha but I still had to spend time at my club."

Ariel looked at him wide eyed. "You own Bojan Taverns? I love that place," Ariel confessed with excitement. "Well, I admit, I've only been there twice. It's hard to get in. If I'm in the mood to have a drink with a friend, I'm not patient enough to stand in the parking lot for a couple hours before I get my beer," she smiled.

"Well there is that," Victor laughed. "I can't really help the crowds. Well, honestly maybe I could, but I won't. It's good for business."

"You do know you own the coolest, hottest club in the city don't you? I'm curious, how did you come up with that name?" Ariel asked, amazed.

Victor looked at Ariel for a few seconds. She was really excited about his club. That was unexpected. Most women hated the fact that he owned a business centered around alcohol and women. They didn't trust him. That was twice in one day Ariel had surprised him. "It's not very original," Victor confessed. "Bojan is Slavic for Warrior. So basically it means Warrior Taverns," he admitted.

"I love it!" She laughed. "I never would have guessed. So, do you think you could get me in sometime? You know, without the two to three hour wait in the parking lot?"

"I'll see what I can do. I have pull with the owner," he laughed. "You're pretty easy to impress."

"No. I'm not," she disagreed. "But you own Bojan Taverns. Wow! That's all I can say." She leaned over and gave him a long hard kiss. He kissed her back, but gave her a strange look. Ariel shrugged. "With this new information, I just needed to check. You know, see if it felt any different now that I know how important you are."

"And?" Victor asked raising his eyebrows.

"Nope. I've liked your kisses since the very first one. I guess you can't improve on perfection. Not even if you are the big shot owner of Bojan Taverns," she grinned. "But you've distracted me. Tell me the rest of the story," she inquired.

Victor sobered. "Where was I?" he asked.

"You and Lakeisha were pretty much living together, but she didn't like your schedule," Ariel supplied.

"Right. So we started to fight a lot. She'd try to talk me into blowing off the warriors, or leaving the club to the manager. I wouldn't shirk my responsibilities for her and she didn't like it. I knew she started to go out again. I think she went out anytime I worked late or had to patrol all night. Eventually she met someone else I guess. I don't know how long she'd been seeing him, but it was at least a couple of months. I came home early one night and caught her taking a pregnancy test. She tried to convince me it was mine. It wasn't. I told her I knew she'd been cheating. She was surprised at that. She thought she'd covered her deception so well I'd never know. She was upset and started crying. She said she wasn't sure whose baby it was. Apparently she'd been intimate with both of us during the same time period and got pregnant. I made it clear it was over between us. I told her she should try to make things work with the other guy because he was the father of her baby."

"What made you so sure?" Ariel asked.

He studied her. Should he tell her he'd had a vasectomy? They had just had sex without protection as far as Ariel knew. Maybe she had a right to know. "We were intimate earlier today. I didn't use protection. Did that worry you?" Victor asked.

"No," Ariel admitted. She was confused at the change in conversation but thought it must have relevance so she'd go along with it. "Not at all," she took a deep breath. "I don't know how familiar you are with the fae and their ability to reproduce," she began.

"I guess I don't know much. I just assumed they were like everyone else," Victor admitted.

"Well everything works the same," she laughed. "But it's difficult for fae to get pregnant. Then, most fae have dicey pregnancies. A lot of us lose the baby. We have an abnormally high rate of miscarriages. That's why you don't see large families in the fae community. Most couples are thrilled if they have one child. I guess its nature's way of controlling our population. We live so long, if we had tons of kids, we would probably over populate."

"Oh," Victor said thoughtfully. "I guess that's true. I honestly never thought about your family sizes or why they were so small," Victor admitted.

"Well anyway," Ariel continued. "We could have sex a hundred times and the chances of me getting pregnant would be pretty low simply because I'm fae," Ariel hesitated. How much should she explain? She was about to trust him with part of her secret, he was trusting her with his. But, how much should she tell him? She decided to keep it simple.

"So, that's why you're not worried? Because there's only a small chance you could get pregnant? That sounds pretty reckless to me," Victor stated.

"No, that's only part of it." Ariel took a deep breath. "When I was very young, a teenager actually, there was an incident. My body was traumatized. I healed, but we don't know if the trauma caused permanent damage. You know, because it's already so difficult to get pregnant and carry full term. Obviously a fae's reproductive organs are already vulnerable. The trauma could have made my situation worse. I won't know if I can have a child until I actually try to have one. Since I've never met anyone I was that serious about, I have no idea what my future holds," she paused. "In the meantime, Breena has concocted some great birth control. I guess it's kind of like the pill humans take, but I only have to take the herbs once a month and I'm covered. You don't have to worry, Victor. I'm not going to get pregnant and I'm not going to try to blame you for anything like Lakeisha did," Ariel said sincerely.

Victor watched Ariel intently. "I'm sorry you're faced with that," he said genuinely concerned for her. "I imagine it's hard, wondering if you can ever have a child if you decide you want one. I think it would be easier knowing, one way or the other. At least you would know what you were up against and could deal with it." He ran his hand over the top of her head and through her hair. "I'm sorry," he said again as he leaned down and kissed her gently.

Ariel blinked back tears. She hadn't expected Victor to be so understanding and sympathetic about her situation. His gentleness touched the deepest part of her soul. She cleared her throat. "Anyway, that's why I'm not worried. Can I ask why you brought that up?"

"I was trying to answer your question about how I could be so sure the child wasn't mine," he paused. "I didn't know your situation earlier, but I didn't use protection either." He stopped to let that sink in.

Ariel hadn't thought about that until now. He hadn't used protection. Why not? After what happened five years ago, you would think Victor would be extra cautious. "Why didn't you?" She asked.

"About fourteen years ago I had a vasectomy," Victor said bluntly. "So, now you understand why I couldn't have been the father of Lakeisha's child five years ago. I shoot blanks so to speak."

Ariel looked at him in shock. "Did you explain that to the council?" She stood up, no wonder her father had been adamant Victor was innocent. How could the council justify their punishment in the face of such undeniable proof? She was pacing the small area, obviously agitated.

"Sit back down Ariel. I didn't tell them," Victor admitted.

Ariel looked down at Victor in shock. "Why not!" She demanded. "You had the perfect defense. One nobody could have argued with but you didn't tell them? That doesn't make any sense," she said angrily.

"If you will sit back down I'll try to explain," he coaxed.

Ariel stood, glaring at Victor for a moment. Then, she walked over and sat back down next to him. "Okay, spill it. And this better be good. If not, I'm going to have to rethink my previous admiration. You might own the hottest night club in the universe, but I'm afraid this new information makes me question your sanity." She finally smiled at him. "I can't be seen in public with a moron you know. I have a reputation of my own to protect."

Victor didn't smile. He was still very sober. He knew Ariel was joking, but he wasn't sure what to tell her or how much to explain. She was the daughter of the council leader. If he found out, Oberon wouldn't let it drop. Lakeisha's life could be in danger all over again.

"What is it that you are struggling with, Victor?" Ariel asked pointedly.

Victor took a deep breath. "I think you have a right to know a little background and I want you to understand the situation. I just don't know how much I should tell you. How much I have a right to tell you. More importantly, I don't know who you will tell once we get back to civilization."

Ariel's eyes never left Victor's. "You're worried I'll share this information with my father?"

"Yes," Victor admitted.

"And you don't want him to know," she concluded.

"No. I don't," Victor stated.

"Then I won't tell him," Ariel said simply.

"Just like that?" Victor asked in disbelief.

"Yeah. Just like that," Ariel stated. "I don't know if you are aware, but you're not the only one that's been brought before the council. I think you were still gone at the time, but the council wanted information from me. I wouldn't give it, so they brought charges up against me. I was ordered to appear before the council and tell them what they wanted to know. I still wouldn't talk."

"I heard you were taken before the council, but I didn't know the details. What did they want to know?" Victor asked curiously.

"Do you know Mr. and Mrs. Jackson?" Ariel asked.

"I've seen them when I've gone into the store. Basically exchanged a cordial hello, but that's it. I don't really know them," Victor admitted.

"Well, Mrs. Jackson has an addiction. She gambles," Ariel admitted.

"Really?" Victor asked, surprised. "That stuffy old lady is a closet gambler. Who would have guessed?"

"Just like you are trusting me with your secret, I am going to trust you with mine. What I'm going to tell you, nobody else knows.

Not even my parents. I'd like to keep it that way." Ariel wanted reassurance Victor wouldn't tell anybody her secret either.

"Your secret is safe with me. Do many people know about Mrs. Jackson?" he asked.

"A few, not many. She even tries to hide it from her husband, but I think deep down he knows," Ariel stated. "Anyway, Mrs. Jackson sometimes jacks money from the store till to cover a lost bet." She laughed as Victor looked astonished. "It's their money. There's really no harm in it as long as she only takes small amounts," Ariel paused. "The problem comes in when her bets are more substantial. There's been about a half a dozen times when she's taken a few hundred from the till."

Victor's eyes narrowed. "How does she explain that to her husband?" He was sure he didn't like the direction this story was going.

"When the take is bigger, she has always blamed someone in the store at the time. Honey, someone must have taken it while I wasn't looking. I was over in that corner helping Tianna and couldn't see the register. Frankie was standing right there, looking at key chains. Maybe he took it while I was busy. You know his family has been struggling the last couple months," Ariel mimicked.

"You're not serious!" He said incredulously. "She really blames an innocent customer for her deception?" Victor asked.

"Yes, but it doesn't usually go anywhere. Typically Mr. Jackson shows up on dad's doorstep demanding action and compensation. Dad takes him into the library, talks to him for a while and calms him down. He reminds Mr. Jackson he can't accuse a good standing member of the community of such a crime without proof. Mr. Jackson admits he doesn't have proof and concedes theft would be out of character for the accused. He goes on his way without another word. That's why I think he knows. I think it's all for show," Ariel accused.

"Then they're both dishonest," Victor said, appalled.

"Yes. They are," Ariel said with disdain.

Victor looked at her. He noticed for the first time she was angry with the Jackson's. "So, what does this have to do with you and the council?" Victor asked.

"Like I said," Ariel continued. "Usually Mr. Jackson is satisfied with complaining to dad. However, they found an easy target. Someone that was new to the community. Someone most people didn't trust." Ariel hesitated, looking at Victor. He made a movement with his head, urging her to continue.

"A few years back a stranger came into town. He was a drifter. He was fae, but nobody knew him or his ancestry. Several members of the community didn't trust him. You know how they are, especially the older generation. They think of themselves as above the rest. Maryann and Frank Saunders are the worst. They consider themselves ancient aristocrats and act accordingly. Maryann made a project out of getting Tank to leave town. It became a personal vendetta for her. She believed the ends justified the means, no matter how bad her behavior became. She was really quite ruthless about it."

"This guy's name was really Tank?" Victor questioned. "No wonder he clashed with the Saunders and others. He didn't have a chance."

After Dark

"Actually, that was a nickname. Tank refused to reveal his true identity and lineage, which of course made matters worse. If he won't tell us his name, he has something to hide. They accused. He must be a criminal on the run and so on," Ariel sighed. "Almost no one accepted him for what he was. A simple drifter trying to find himself. He wasn't a bad guy. He was just a wanderer with a better pedigree than anyone in our community."

"It sounds like you accepted him." Victor could tell there was more to the story. He decided to wait patiently. He looked at the sun, they still had time.

"I did. Tank was a good guy. We dated for a while and had some fun. I wasn't looking for anything more, just a good time. I thought that's all he wanted too," Ariel reflected.

"But that wasn't the case? He wanted more?" Victor surmised.

"Yes. He told me he was in love with me and wanted us to move in together. I was shocked. It blindsided me. I guess I should have realized, but I wasn't looking for anything serious so I was oblivious. He realized right away from the shocked look on my face I didn't want the same thing. He was really cool about it. He told me he knew it was a long shot, but he had to try. He needed to let me know how he felt before he moved on. I guess he didn't want to leave and always wonder if things might have been different. Like I said, he was a good guy. I broke his heart and he tried to sooth me. He didn't want me to feel bad or guilty about not loving him back. He told me he was headed for Denver. He had a distant cousin there he planned to stay with for a while."

Victor thought he knew where this was leading, but he remained silent. He'd let Ariel tell the story in her own way.

"He got an early start the next morning. He left before I got up," she smiled. "He didn't want an emotional goodbye. That was just like Tank. Anyway, he left a note on my pillow. It told me the route he was taking and how to find him once he reached Denver. He planned to take the scenic route, so it was going to take awhile to get there. If I ever wanted to blow this stuffy town and have some fun, I should look him up." Ariel smiled at the memory.

"You cared for him," Victor observed.

"Yeah. I'd been alone for a long time and Tank made me laugh. We had a lot of fun together, but it just wasn't there for me. Do you know what I mean? I think we could have been happy for a while, but I knew he wasn't the one. He wasn't a man I could devote the rest of my life to. I wouldn't be happy or content with him forever. Maybe if I was human, but fae live a long time. I can't settle. It has to be real for both of us before I'll consider spending my life with someone."

"So let me guess, Tank left town and the Jackson's accused him of theft," Victor said flatly.

"That's basically the short of it. Tank left that morning. I needed a few things so I stopped by the Jackson's store. Mr. Jackson was in a huff. He barreled over to me as soon as I stepped in the door. He demanded to know where Tank was. He accused him of stealing two thousand dollars right before closing the night before. I told him Tank couldn't have stolen the money, he was with me all night and then he left town this morning before the store opened. That made it worse. Mrs. Jackson shrieked that Tank had robbed them blind and then skipped town. They'd never see their money again. It got pretty out of control. Avery from the council walked in and of course took the Jackson's side. He and my father have never really gotten along and he's never approved of me. Avery called an emergency council meeting to formally charge Tank with theft.

He verbally accosted my father over my loose and inappropriate behavior. He demanded I tell them everything I knew about Tank's whereabouts. You would have thought it was the 1800's, and I was wearing a scarlet letter on my shirt. The community was afraid to come near me. It was just too much. I was pissed. I couldn't believe such condescending behavior was coming from Avery of all people. Do you know his son? He is the most disgusting, perverted, dishonorable man I've ever met." Ariel was furious, she took a deep breath to calm herself. Just thinking about that time still made her so angry.

Victor was angry, too. He couldn't believe the community would support the dishonest merchant over the council leader's daughter. He knew he hadn't gotten a fair break, but that was his own fault. If he had told the council about the vasectomy, he wouldn't have been punished. Ariel on the other hand was innocent, so was this Tank guy. He'd just been an easy target for a few dishonest people.

"The whole thing made me so angry, I rebelled I guess. I refused to tell my father anything. I refused to talk to the council. I got into a few less than lady like arguments with some of the elite members of society," Ariel said in her most snooty accent. "Eventually I was called before the council myself. Avery wanted to charge me with obstruction, aiding and abetting and contempt. The list went on and on. The contempt part was certainly accurate. I'm not sure it's possible to have more contempt than I did for a few people in this community," Ariel admitted.

"Your dad couldn't help you?" Victor asked.

"He probably could have, but I wouldn't let him. He was pretty upset with me. My parent's never met Tank, they were in France visiting my aunt while he was in town. Dad got back the night Tank left for Denver. But he believed me and he knew Mrs. Jackson's history. He was confident he could help Tank and keep me out of it. I refused. I couldn't let Tank suffer because of the Jackson's dishonesty. With Mrs. Jackson's history, dad probably would have gotten Tank off the hook. I don't know, but I wasn't willing to chance it. I didn't want Tank anywhere near the council. I didn't even want him to know what happened, but I had to tell him. I was worried he might change his mind and come back to town. I called his cousin and explained what happened. I warned him to keep Tank away. He promised me he would. I have never seen or heard from Tank again," Ariel answered.

"Did Tank or his cousin know you were in trouble with the council?" Victor wanted to know.

"No. I kept that part from them. If they knew, Tank would have been on the first plane back here. He wouldn't have let me protect him that way. Tank was an honorable man and I think he really loved me. He would have protected me at all cost. I couldn't let him do that. Especially after I had broken his heart," Ariel admitted.

"So, what happened with the council?" Victor asked.

"They brought me in, tried to question me. Of course I was uncooperative. They tried to put pressure on my father, which upset me. I'm sure it was supposed to. They thought I'd break and tell them what they wanted to know if they harassed dad enough. I couldn't do it, not even for dad. I figured he was a grownup and he could handle himself. I had to protect Tank. Their tactics only made me angry and more uncooperative. They kept me there for hours, but I wouldn't give them anything. Finally, they had to let me go. They didn't have any proof I knew anything. They didn't even have proof that Tank was guilty, which he wasn't. It would have been difficult to charge me or punish me in any way, especially with dad and Orin there. I was given a long lecture on community responsibility and set free. Apparently, they thought they could make me feel guilty about not cooperating. I didn't," she finished with a smile. "And one day I will pay Mr. and Mrs. Jackson back as well as Maryann and Frank Saunders. Avery's on my list too. I don't care if he's a council member. In my opinion, they are all out of control. Someone needs to put them in their place." She stopped and watched Victor. He was just sitting there silently. Maybe she shouldn't have shared her story with him. What was he thinking?

Victor finally spoke. "Your secret is safe with me. You don't need to worry about that. Do any of those guys or the rest of the community still give you a hard time?"

"Not really. I obviously don't get along with any of them. There are a few others in the community I had words with that don't particularly like me, but they're civil for the most part because of dad," Ariel admitted. "After about a year I went to visit my aunt for a while. When I came back, most people wanted to pretend like nothing ever happened."

"I'm sorry you had to go through that," Victor said sincerely. "I won't be shopping at the Jackson's anymore. I'm not sure I could get out of their store without having an incident with those two myself," Victor smiled. "I'm afraid it won't hurt their business much. I really don't go there very often."

"You don't have to stop shopping there because of me. You shouldn't inconvenience yourself just because I can't stand that couple," Ariel said soberly.

"It's not just for you. I refuse to give those type of people one cent," Victor told her. "They don't deserve my money."

"Thanks," Ariel told him. "It's nice to have your support. It was a difficult time for me. I guess it was a difficult time for you too," she sobered. "I'm sorry about Lakeisha. I wish you hadn't been hurt that way. I still don't get why you protected her though. Why you accepted punishment rather than reveal the truth."

"I guess the easy answer is I felt like she needed to be protected. I know that's hard to understand," he glanced at Ariel. She was watching him intently. "Lakeisha had an affair with someone that was an enemy to her pack. She was terrified of the consequences if anyone found out. If they knew who the father really was, they may have killed her for consorting with the enemy. It was also possible they would have caused a miscarriage to eliminate the child. At the very least she would be banished from the pack. Lakeisha isn't strong like you. She would have been lost without her pack. I know she betrayed me, but I couldn't let her face something like that alone. I don't think she could have raised a child on her own. I didn't want to be with her anymore, but I still cared. It was easier to keep quiet and deal with whatever punishment the council gave me. I could get through a year without the warriors, but I drew the line at providing for another man's child," Victor stated simply.

Ariel blinked. She wanted to say something, but she was astonished. Victor had cared for this woman. He had actually considered spending the rest of his life with her. A woman who never accepted him for who he was. Lakeisha had expected him to stop working with the warriors and leave the club to his subordinates. That would have been out of character and basically impossible for Victor. When he refused, she cheated on him, got pregnant by a pack enemy and then accused him of being the father. If that wasn't enough, she lied to the council and demanded excessive amounts of money to support a child she knew all along wasn't Victors. But did Victor get angry? No, he protected her. He sheltered her and accepted a punishment that was extremely hard on him so Lakeisha could keep her pack and evade any consequences for her actions.

Victor was uncomfortable. Ariel was just staring at him. What was she thinking? Would she really keep the secret? He wished she would say something.

"I don't know what to say," Ariel admitted. "I'm dumbfounded. I hope Lakeisha appreciates what she gave up. You gave so much for her and didn't receive anything in return. Well, you did get heartache and punishment. I just hope she knows what she had," Ariel paused. "I guess you should know, you are a much better person than I am. I couldn't do that. I don't think I could protect someone who betrayed me so completely, so callously. You are proof that no good turn goes unpunished. I'm so sorry Victor," she said soberly. "I'm sorry you got involved with such a selfish woman. You are the most unselfish man I've ever known. I think Lakeisha took advantage of your goodness. All I can say is I'm sorry for that," Ariel finished soberly.

"You make me sound like I'm a saint. I'm not. I just did what had to be done. I did what was best for everyone involved," Victor answered.

"How was it best for you?" Ariel asked.

Victor shrugged. "All I can say is I don't regret my decision. I did what I had to do. Now it's over. It's in the past. Maybe you can't understand. But I hope you will still keep your promise. That you will keep my secret to yourself." He was worried he'd said too much. For the first time in his life he was putting his trust in a woman. Trusting her to keep her word. It made him very nervous. "I know this all happened a long time ago, but it's possible that Lakeisha could still be in danger if anyone knew the truth. Her child would be about five now. He or she could also be in danger if the real father's identity was revealed. I need to be sure you won't tell anyone about this," Victor pled.

"I won't tell anyone. I don't agree with you. I don't think Lakeisha should have gotten off without consequences, but I promised I wouldn't tell anyone and I won't. You can trust me, Victor. I'm not Lakeisha. All women don't betray the people who care about them. If nothing else, I would think my story about Tank demonstrates that," Ariel looked around. "It's going to be dark soon. We should probably get back to the cave," she stood. She was a little hurt that Victor doubted her. Okay, she was hurt a lot. She'd trusted him as much as he trusted her. Yet, he stood there looking at her like she'd break her promise and blab the first chance she got.

Victor stood, too. He almost left things the way they were, but he couldn't. They had both shared a lot this afternoon. Ariel was also trusting him to keep quiet about Tank. Was he being unfair to doubt her? He wanted to go back to the cave feeling confident things were okay between them. He wanted to feel close to her again. He didn't like the distance his doubt had created between them. He took her hand and pulled her to a stop.

After Dark

Ariel looked back at Victor. She wanted to get away from him. Victor had hurt her. She needed to escape and surround herself with other people. She was surprised when he pulled her against him and kissed her. It wasn't a gentle kiss either. It was full of passion and intimacy. Ariel forgot her disappointment and accepted this as his apology. All she could think about was Victor and the feelings he erupted deep inside her. It felt so good to be held by him, kissed by him. She wished they never had to stop.

Victor slowly pulled back and grinned. "Now I'm ready to go back to the cave." Once they gathered up the clothes, Victor took her hand and headed down the trail to join the rest of the group.

Chapter Five

Thomas had dinner ready when they returned. They'd made good time. The sun was just setting as they entered the cave. Victor and Ariel hung the clothes across the rope then sat down to eat. Morrigan seemed to be in pretty good spirits. Ariel was happy and content for the first time during this trip. Well if she was honest, the first time in her life. "So, Morrigan. What did the two of you find today?" she asked.

Morrigan looked up. "We got a pretty good look at that cave. The bad news is, I think there's only one way in. We are going to have to go in through the front. The good news is the cave can't be that deep but it could be long. Unfortunately, that means there could be off-shoots winding throughout the entire hillside. Austin and I scouted the whole area. There's only one way in for us. That also means there's only one way in or out for them. They can't sneak up on us," he looked over at Austin.

After Dark

"We think it might be a good idea to go in later tonight." Austin looked over at Victor. "We know you wanted to wait until tomorrow, but just hear us out. Once it gets completely dark, the vampires will leave. If we go in after dark, the cave should be fairly empty."

"I agree we should go in after dark. But you agreed to wait until tomorrow," Victor countered. "I'd like to stick to our original plan. Tonight, I want to scout their activity. We need to see if they all leave together or if they leave in shifts. I think the more information we have, the better off we're going to be. We need to be prepared. Not only for us but also for Abby's safety," Victor argued.

"But she's right inside. I know she has to be scared," Morrigan insisted. "We need to get to her as soon as we can."

"I disagree," Thomas put in. "I agree with Victor. I think we should take tonight to watch their behavior. Then, I think we should take tomorrow to prepare for an attack."

They all looked at Thomas. "What did you have in mind?" Ariel asked.

"Well that kind of hinges on you," he confessed.

"Me?" Ariel asked. "How?"

"I spent a lot of time here by myself today. I used that time to scout the cave and its surrounding area with Victor's binoculars," he smiled at Ariel. "I have an idea."

"We're listening," Victor pushed.

"I think we should spend the day tomorrow booby trapping the immediate area. None of us have really scouted inside that cave. Once we get in, we might have to fight for our lives. If we can rescue Abby and get back out, it would be nice to have a little buffer. A cushion to help us sneak back to this cave unseen," Thomas supplied. "Especially if we are going to go in at night. It's not going to do us any good to get back to the cave if all the vampires follow us here."

Ariel smiled. "I get it. We set up some traps that I can catch on fire as we leave. The smoke and fire will shield us. The vampires won't be able to follow. They won't know which direction we went," she was excited. This was a good idea.

"Why can't we go in tonight and you can set whatever is in our path on fire as we leave?" Morrigan pressed.

"Because," Ariel answered. "I need to set it up so only the things I want to catch on fire will burn. The last thing we need is to cause a forest fire. We could all get trapped and die if the fire gets out of control. I need to create buffers around whatever I catch on fire." She put her hand on Morrigan's arm. "I know you're anxious to get to Abby. I know you're afraid for her. But if we watch the cave tonight, one more day isn't going to hurt. We'll know if Hector, Radek or Lilith show up. If they do, we can rush in and help. If not, we set things up tomorrow and go in prepared like Victor suggested. Trust me. Vampires are up all night so they sleep most of the day. If nothing happens while we watch tonight, Victor's plan is the safest for everyone. Abby will be safe during the day," she paused. "Victor?"

"Yeah," he answered.

After Dark

"If we shave some branches into arrows, can we rig up a system that you could set off by throwing those nifty ninja stars?" She smiled at him. She thought those were so cool. She'd seen him use them that night in the alley.

Victor smiled. "Good idea. If you guys help me make the arrows, I can handle the rigging and the throwing."

"I don't like it but I guess I see the wisdom in your plan," Morrigan confessed. "Prepared is always better. Do you promise we will go in tomorrow night, no matter what?" he asked.

"Yes," Victor promised. "I know you're anxious, Morrigan. I am too. Based on everything we talked about the other day we have to act quickly. Abby could be getting weak. We need to get her out of there soon. I just want to make sure we get back out once we're in."

"I agree," Morrigan answered defeated. "Who's going to scout the activity tonight?"

"I'll take the first shift," Victor offered. "We should only need one more volunteer to get us through the night. Thomas, are you up to it?"

"No," Morrigan answered. "She's my sister. I'll take the first shift. When I get tired, I'll wake you up, Victor. I can sleep in if I need to and once Thomas and Austin wake up in the morning, you can go back to sleep. We all need to be well rested for tomorrow night."

"That works for me," Victor agreed. "If I'm going to be up half the night, I want to go to bed early." Victor rinsed his plate and set it off to the side. "Anyone mind if I turn in?" he asked.

Thomas got up and walked to his backpack. "We still need to put some more salve on your hands and I added some of that powder to this chocolate milk. Gag it down quickly. I think it's going to taste worse than the blood." Thomas handed Victor the chocolate milk and the salve.

"Thanks, but I don't think anything could be worse than drinking blood with or without that powder mixed in." Victor smiled at Thomas. "I think I should be healed by tomorrow morning. Breena's a miracle worker." He guzzled the chocolate milk and headed off to set up his sleeping bag.

Ariel was already there. She took the salve from him. "I'll take care of that," she said as she put the salve aside. "Can you help me with these?" she asked as she unrolled the lighter bag. She unzipped it and spread it out on the ground. She looked at Victor hesitantly with a question in her eyes.

Victor understood. He unrolled and unzipped the second bag then spread it out on top of the first one. He smiled over at her then whispered in her ear. "I don't mind if you don't." He glanced over his shoulder at the others.

"I don't mind at all," she answered. "Let me take care of your hands. I'll join you after I clean up the dishes."

"I've got the dishes tonight," Austin chimed in. "Ariel did them last night and again after breakfast." He glanced over at her. "It's been a long day for you, too. I think you should get as much rest as possible. You're not healed yet, either."

Thomas walked over and handed Ariel her container of salve. She'd had the medical tea with dinner. "Do you need help with this?"

After Dark

Victor reached out and took the salve from Thomas. "I'll take care of it. I want to check the wound anyway. I need to make sure it's still healing," he turned to Ariel. "Sit on the sleeping bag so I can examine your leg," he grinned. That wasn't all he wanted to examine.

Once Victor was finished with Ariel, she opened his salve and took one of his hands. She gently rubbed the oily liquid into both palms. He was right. His hands were nearly healed. They absorbed the salve almost like lotion. She changed into a t-shirt and snuggled in next to him. Victor propped himself up on one elbow, leaned down and kissed her gently. "Thanks," he said sincerely. "You sure you don't mind sharing? It might be awkward once we get back home." Victor had zipped the two bags together to create one double bag.

"What do you mean?" she asked.

"You know my rep and my lack of standing in the community. You on the other hand are the council leader's daughter. People will talk. Some won't approve. It might be uncomfortable for you if those guys talk about the sleeping arrangements while we were out here." Victor signaled toward the other men. "I just want to make sure you've thought this through."

"There's nothing to think about." She grabbed his neck and pulled him down to her then kissed him passionately. "Goodnight, Victor." She settled back into the bag.

"Goodnight Ariel," Victor said laughing. He pulled her close and settled in for the night.

* * * *

Victor sat in the darkness, watching the cave. There was very little movement. Morrigan had reported the same. Apparently most of the vampires left once it got dark and were out for the entire evening. If that was their normal routine, fate was on their side. Neither one of them had spotted Hector, Radek or Lilith. Victor knew Hector had to be around somewhere. He might be holed up in another cave close by, or he might be guarding Abby himself and feeding on her like Dimitri had suggested. Either way, Victor knew they must be prepared. Hector wasn't stupid. He'd orchestrated the ambush that killed Thomas' father, Luke. He'd also assassinated Marlena, Alex's mother and their former queen. They would have to be on their toes tomorrow night.

Victor heard movement behind him. He pivoted and saw Austin quietly moving in his direction. "Morning," Victor whispered.

"Morning," Austin answered. "I'm awake, so I thought I'd relieve you and let you get a little more rest before daylight. I won't be able to go back to sleep anyway."

"You sure? I'm okay for a couple more hours," Victor offered.

"No, I'm sure. If I try to go back to sleep, I'll just lay there restless until morning. I might as well make myself useful. Have you seen anything unusual out here?" Austin asked.

"Nope. There's been very little activity down there and nothing alarming. There's no sign of Hector. Keep an eye out for him. I think he's going to be our biggest obstacle tomorrow night.

I'm worried he's guarding Abby himself. Maybe feeding off her so he doesn't have to hunt," Victor said soberly.

"I was thinking the same thing, I just didn't want to mention that to Morrigan. Abby might be really weak when we reach her. I'll make sure I take a couple of those protein shakes and some jerky and nuts in with us. If we can get her a little protein, she should be able to make it back to the cave. We're going to have to stay here the rest of the night anyway. That should give us plenty of time to gorge her before we set out in the morning," Austin offered.

"Sounds like a good plan. I'll leave the doctoring to you and Morrigan. You'll know how to get her strength back up if we need to. Let's just hope we're wrong and she's doing fine. Make sure you don't forget the shakes though. If she's so weak she's passed out or something, we'll have to force feed her and liquid is the easiest," Victor stood. "Thanks for the respite. I'm still a little tired." He walked back to Ariel and climbed into bed.

* * * *

Victor slowly opened his eyes and saw Ariel crouched next to him. He looked around and realized they were alone. When he looked back at Ariel, she was smiling.

"Morning," she said quietly.

"Morning," he sat up. "Where is everyone?" he asked as he rubbed the sleep from his eyes.

"Outside. We've all been up for a while, but you were sleeping so soundly we thought we'd let you rest and recover," she answered. "Are you hungry?"

Victor smiled. "Yeah," he answered as he grabbed her around the waist and pulled her on top of him. "I am," he crushed his mouth to hers in a long intense kiss.

"That wasn't exactly what I meant," Ariel said, breathlessly.

"You have too many clothes on." Victor protested as he pulled her shirt over her head. He opened the sleeping bag and pulled her inside, pressing his mouth back to hers.

"Maybe we should let you sleep in more often," Ariel said, laughing as Victor slipped her pants down the length of her legs.

"Umm, maybe." Victor said absently as he ran his hands up her body. His mouth returned to hers and they were lost in each other and the heat of the moment.

Victor was watching Ariel. She was lying next to him, eyes closed, looking relaxed and content. He was definitely in trouble. He hated to admit it, but he had fallen for her. He had fallen hard. How had he let himself fall in love? He knew yesterday should have been a onetime deal. He hadn't planned a repeat of that intimacy, but he couldn't help himself. When he woke up and saw her hovering over him his heart did a little flip. She looked so beautiful and angelic. When he realized they were alone, he had to have her. She was irresistible. He just hoped he could survive the consequences. How had he lost complete control in such a short amount of time?

After Dark

Ariel could feel Victor watching her. She slowly opened her eyes and grinned. "Well, that was certainly unexpected," she said, still smiling. She sat up and studied him. Ariel never knew what to expect from Victor. He was so unpredictable. His reactions were never simple or what she expected.

"What?" he asked narrowing his eyes at her.

"Nothing," she said innocently. "I just never know which Victor I'm going to encounter when I open my eyes," she said honestly.

"What do you mean by that?" he asked, furrowing his brow.

"Well," she said hesitantly. How was she going to explain this? "Sometimes it seems like you are fighting the attraction we feel for each other. I never know if you are going to regret something we do. I don't know where I stand with you. Like our first kiss. I kissed you and you acted like it was completely unwanted, but the next thing I know you're kissing me. I just never know which guy I'm going to find when I look into your eyes. Does that make sense?"

"Oh," Victor wasn't going to try to explain that one. He hadn't considered how his actions were impacting Ariel. His indecision really wasn't fair to her. He smiled his most charming smile. "So, which Victor am I right now?"

"The charming, sexy one I think," Ariel answered as she moved in and gave him another kiss. "We should probably get up before someone decides to come check on us. I'm sure they're wondering what's taking so long. I told them I'd be back in a couple minutes." Ariel realized she wasn't going to get an explanation, so why press. It would only ruin the moment and she wanted to enjoy this as long as she could. It was too perfect to mess up.

They both got up and got dressed. Victor grabbed a quick snack before they headed outside. "Oh," Ariel turned to Victor. "I forgot to ask about your hands. Are they completely healed now or did you need more salve?"

"How did they feel?" Victor asked with a big grin.

Ariel smiled. "Pretty good a few minutes ago. But really, are they still sore or are they healed? My leg feels good today. I think given a couple more days, I'll be back to 100%."

"Yeah, they're healed. I don't think I even need that cream anymore. I might take one more dose of the powder tonight, just to be sure. Breena said you should continue the tea until it's gone. How many doses do you have left?" he asked.

"Probably two or three days' worth," Ariel admitted. "It's not bad, so I'll follow Breena's orders. The last thing I want is a relapse. You should do the same. I realize it doesn't taste great, but an extra dose won't hurt you. If you short yourself, it might."

"Agreed," Victor paused to look around. "You guys have been busy," he was surprised. Ariel and the guys had set up several pockets of dried brush and sticks. It would be easy for Ariel to set them on fire. They had cleared the foliage away from each one to make sure once the fire started, it couldn't spread to anything else. They had strategically placed the pockets so it created a path, but the trail wasn't obvious unless you were looking for it. The green brush would create tons of smoke.

After Dark

Thomas approached the two enthusiastically. "So sleeping beauty, you finally decided to get up?" he asked. He didn't notice Ariel trying to hide a grin. Victor caught it though and had to fight to keep his face serious. He understood the private joke.

"Those are perfect Thomas," Ariel cut in. She was biting her tongue and wanted to change the subject. "With my design and your expertly created path, I think this is going to work great!"

"We still need to work on the arrows you talked about. I wanted to wait for Victor to start on those," he turned to Victor. "You need to help us figure out where to place the traps and the size of the arrows. We don't want you to throw the ninja star and have the arrow fall to the ground. The vampires could use them as weapons against us."

"Right," Victor became all business. The group worked the entire day setting up their battlefield. If they were attacked by vampires, they were as prepared as they could be under the circumstances. Victor felt pretty good about their odds. He just hoped the vampires held to the same pattern as last night. If the vamps left at dusk again, the group could wait an hour, sneak in and be out before the majority of the vampires returned.

The small group sat in front of the fire hashing out their final plan. All of them would go in together. It was impossible to know what they would encounter once they entered the cave. They wanted all the help they could get. Victor had plenty of stars but he wouldn't use them inside unless he had to. He'd stick to his dagger and save the stars for outside. Ariel had a couple mugs of tea with dinner. One with medication and one without. She wanted to make sure her energy level was up. She'd need fire inside and outside. Thomas had prepared another pot of tea in the event they needed more, all they had to do was heat it back up. He also made sure the blood was handy and everyone knew what to do if both he and Victor were severely wounded. Morrigan and Austin were the most vulnerable. They didn't heal as quickly as the others. If they were injured, they had a medical kit and some protein shakes to help them get through it. They all felt prepared. Well, as prepared as they could be anyway.

Victor was explaining the layout of the cave. He'd been in the main section a few decades ago. Nobody thought the general layout could have changed much. "As soon as we walk in, there's a large open area. We're not going to have any cover. I suggest we go in as quietly as possible. There were a couple tunnels leading off that main section. I only recall two and one of them is really small. I'm not sure the vampires could even get through it. I can't. The only one here that might be able to traverse that area is Ariel. What is Abby's size compared to Ariel's?" He looked to Morrigan in question.

"Abby is pretty small," Morrigan admitted. "She's maybe four inches shorter and she's petite. She'd be able to fit through a tunnel none of us could get through," Morrigan finished, obviously beginning to worry.

"Don't stress too much over that," Victor assured him. "Just because Abby can get there, it doesn't mean they'd let her. Hector wouldn't want to give Abby access to any area he hadn't scouted out himself. He's about your size, so I'm fairly sure he's not hiding Abby anywhere you can't go."

Morrigan relaxed a little. "You're probably right. Her size might help though if we get into trouble. She could hide while we fight if she's too weak to join in. Don't let her size fool you, she's strong and feisty. She won't sit out if she thinks she can help," Morrigan finished proudly.

"All right then," Victor said as he sat back against a log. "I think we're ready. I'll go watch and let the rest of you know when it's safe to head out." Victor stood and walked to the cave opening.

Morrigan followed. "Do you mind if I watch with you?" he asked. "I don't want to crowd you, but I'm anxious. At least watching will be doing something!" He added.

"It's all yours," Victor handed Morrigan the binoculars. "I can see pretty well without them. We'll both decide when the time is right to go in."

* * * *

The group silently slid into the cave. It was dark, but the moonlight illuminated the area enough to see the main section was empty. Victor led them to the small tunnel. He was going to go first when he was stopped by Morrigan. "I think I should shift into a bat or something and take a look," Morrigan whispered. "The vampires won't expect it and I can come back and report what I find."

"Okay, if you hurry. I feel like a sitting duck out here in the open," Victor agreed.

Morrigan shifted into a bat and flew through the passageway. He returned almost instantly. He shifted back and turned to Victor. "Once you get through the tunnel there's another open area. It's smaller, but still pretty large. There are four vampires. They appear to be guarding a door. I assume that's where they are keeping Abby.

It looks like it was another smaller cave, but they have erected a metal door to close it in."

"How do you want to handle this?" Thomas asked. "We can only go in one at a time and that's going to put the first man at a disadvantage with four vampires."

"That's not exactly true," Austin put in. "Morrigan and I could shift into bats again. We could fly to the cave and wait for the third man. Once you enter, we could shift back. That would make three of us against four. It shouldn't take very long for the two remaining members to join us."

"What about your energy levels?" Victor asked. "Will that take too much out of you, especially you?" He turned to Morrigan. "You've already shifted twice."

Morrigan pulled out two small bags of peanuts and handed one to Austin. He tore it open and dumped the entire package in his mouth. After a couple seconds he swallowed. It wasn't necessary, but he didn't want these guys to worry. "Not anymore. Problem solved," he smiled.

Victor had to laugh. "Okay, you and Austin turn back into bats. I don't think they'll be suspicious if you stay the same animal. Plus, it's not unusual to have bats in these caves. I'll go next."

"Why you?" Ariel interrupted. "I think I'm the better choice. I can throw fire across the room and get the closest vampire before he even reaches the tunnel," she argued.

"No way!" Thomas and Victor said at once.

"Why?" Ariel pressed.

"No," Victor said with finality. "Thomas, I'll go next. I want Ariel to come after me. You take up the rear. That way, if any vampires approach from this side, you'll have her back."

"And who has Thomas' back?" Ariel asked.

"Thomas is capable of getting his own back," Victor said impatiently. "You're not going in first, so just deal with it. We need to hurry." He turned back to Austin and Morrigan. "You two ready? Once you enter, I'll follow. Obviously it's going to take me a little longer to crawl through that small space than it's going to take the two of you to fly it. Be ready to switch as soon as I come out."

"Got it," Morrigan answered then immediately shifted and hovered above them. Austin followed and the two of them flew through the tunnel. Victor followed.

"Your turn," Thomas said as he gently pushed Ariel toward the opening.

"Men!" Ariel mumbled as she entered the small space. It made more sense for her to go first but because she was a woman, she had to be protected. She finally understood why Alex and Breena were so mad that morning at the cabin. Their men had been condescending morons, too. It must be the testosterone. As she exited the tunnel, she heard a loud scream. She looked up to see Victor stab the final vampire. He vanished into dust.

"What was that about?" Thomas demanded as he stood.

"Austin missed his target and one of the vamps let out a yell," Victor supplied. "Someone help me with this." He was trying to pry a lock open with his dagger.

Austin pulled a key off a hook near the door. "Try this," he said as he handed the key to Victor. Victor unlocked the door and pushed it open. Victor, Morrigan and Austin rushed into the room. Thomas was behind them, but stopped in the doorway. As he turned and pulled Ariel into the room, he noticed she was a little off. "I'll guard the door while you figure out how to get them unchained. Hurry, there's another tunnel leading out of this cave. If anyone's down there, we'll have company soon."

Ariel was barely listening, somewhere in the back of her mind she was confused by Thomas' reference to 'them.' She couldn't focus on that, she was trying to gain her composure. These small dark rooms were bringing back too many memories. Her annoyance had gotten her through the tunnel but once inside this room, she froze. It was like she was shoved through a time warp. Abby was huddled on the floor, wrists chained to the wall. She looked frightened and weak. It was obvious she'd been crying. Ariel slammed her eyelids shut to block out the image of herself huddled in the exact same position. She had to get through this. They didn't have time to deal with one of her panic attacks. She reached her hand out for Victor, but he wasn't there. Her hand just sliced through the air. She opened her eyes and looked toward Abby. Morrigan was sitting by her side. Austin was right behind him opening one of the protein shakes. Abby was sobbing, she must have realized her brother had arrived to save her. The tears were flowing down her cheeks nonstop. Morrigan pulled her into his arms and tried to sooth her. Ariel closed her eyes again. She had to settle down. She remembered how it felt when Dimitri rushed in that morning so long ago. She was a mess just like Abby was now. Ariel was breathing too quickly. If this continued, she'd hyperventilate and pass out. "Breathe slow," she told herself. Being close to Victor would help her. Just like in the cave. Where was Victor? She just needed to know he was near. If she could feel his touch, she'd be okay. She looked around and saw him on the other side of the room.

He was kneeling beside a woman. Oh, that's what Thomas meant. There were two prisoners. Ariel watched as Victor tried to brush the hair back from the woman's face. She lashed out and knocked his hand away.

"Lakeisha," he said softly.

Ariel inhaled in shock, she almost let out a gasp but stopped herself just in time. She'd been trying to stop the panic but now watching Victor and realizing who that woman was, sent an arrow straight through her heart. She stumbled back against the wall. It was like she'd been sucker punched. "Get a grip Ariel," she told herself. You can't do this right now. At least she didn't feel like panicking anymore. She was too hurt and angry now. The woman had to be Victor's old girlfriend.

Lakeisha was huddled in the corner. She wouldn't look up at Victor. She was sobbing and holding her arms over her head. Every time Victor tried to pull at her arms, Lakeisha lashed out and knocked his hand away. He was trying to be gentle, but Lakeisha started flailing her arms striking out at him. He softly called her name again with no response.

"Kei," Victor said quietly. "You have to stop this." That seemed to pull the woman out of her trance. Her head popped up and she gazed at Victor.

Ariel's attention was transfixed on Lakeisha. She was so beautiful. She had long ebony hair that looked like silk. As Victor brushed the woman's elegant hair aside, Ariel saw how stunning she was. Her silky hair framed a delicate face with an olive complexion.

146

Her features flowed together to create a flawless and angelic picture of perfection. Ariel thought she could be a super model. No wonder Victor had fallen for her.

"Victor?" Lakeisha questioned. Then she flung herself into his arms. "Oh Victor," she sobbed. "You have to help me. Please don't leave me here. I know you're angry with me but please, you have to take me with you. You can't leave me in this awful place. I need you to help me, Victor." Lakeisha began to sob.

"Shh," Victor whispered. "I'm going to help you," he soothed.

Ariel blinked back tears. Victor was still in love with this woman. That was the only explanation. He was caressing her and soothing her in such a loving way. The woman was sitting in his lap. Ariel couldn't stand it. She turned away and walked toward Abby. "Are you okay?" she asked.

Abby finished off her first shake and looked up at Ariel. "I will be now," she sniffed. "We have to get out of here before Count Creeptacula comes back though."

Thomas was alert now. "Who is that? Are you talking about Hector?" he asked.

"No," Abby answered. "Hector was bad. At first he fed on me every night, that was bad enough," Abby shuddered. "As he fed, he rubbed himself against me almost like he was getting off on it. It was disgusting. But then the king came by. He was just creepy and a little terrifying."

"When?" Thomas pressed. "When did Radek come here?"

"It's hard to know. There's no light or windows. I think it was probably two or three nights ago," Abby answered.

"What happened?" Thomas asked.

Abby took a deep breath. "He was angry Hector had been feeding on me. He ordered him to stop. Radek said I was his. After that he yelled at Hector awhile, then he ordered everyone out of the room. He came over by me and dropped the long robe he was wearing. He was completely naked underneath," Abby shuddered again.

"What!" Morrigan exclaimed.

Abby looked at him, she had to pretend like it was no big deal. "He dropped his robe and started to come at me. I hesitated for about half a second and then I turned into a field mouse," she admitted with a smile. "That really pissed him off." She gave Morrigan a huge grin.

Morrigan was horrified and proud of Abby at the same time. He decided he'd shelf the horror. Freaking out in here wouldn't do any good. "Good thinking, sis." He gave her the best smile he could muster. "Then what happened?"

"He was really angry and ordered Hector to catch me and force me to shift back. He couldn't of course. The king said he'd be back in a few days. That's why I'm worried he could return any time. He rambled on about wanting an heir. He thought it would be cool to have a shifting vampire to leave his empire to. He said I was going to pay for being uncooperative. He told me his subjects didn't disobey him," she finished. "Since then, Hector's been feeding off her." She motioned to Lakeisha in the corner.

Austin looked over at Thomas. "I can't get these manacles off. How are we going to get them out of here?" he asked as he handed Abby another shake. "Drink this, you're still pretty weak."

Abby grabbed the shake and took a big gulp. "Once I finish this second shake, I think I can shift. Don't worry about getting me out of these, I can shift into something small and then shift back. The chains will be off me in no time. You need to figure out something for her." She pointed to Lakeisha. "She can only shift into a panther and that's not small enough to remove the metal wrist bands. She's stuck unless you can figure out a way to get them open."

Lakeisha began to sob loudly. Victor ran a hand down her hair and tried to sooth her. "Lakeisha you have to be quiet. We're not going to leave you here, we'll figure something out. In the meantime, you have to stop this. You're making too much noise. The vampires are going to hear you. We can't get you free if we have to fight the vampires."

Lakeisha took a big shuddering breath and snuggled in tighter to Victor. Ariel couldn't take anymore.

She walked over to the cozy couple. "Get out of my way," she demanded looking directly at Victor.

Victor looked at her skeptically.

"Move," she demanded. "We need to hurry."

Victor shifted slightly and set Lakeisha on the ground. He remained close, letting Lakeisha retain her vice grip on his arm. He was skeptical, but wanted to see what Ariel was up to.

After Dark

Ariel moved in and crouched next to Lakeisha. "Don't move a muscle," she warned. But deep down she hoped Lakeisha would move, she deserved a little pain. A good deep burn would be poetic justice as far as Ariel was concerned.

Lakeisha was terrified. She quickly looked at Victor and then back at Ariel. "Okay," she finally said. Then she grabbed Victor's hand and held on tight.

Ariel rolled her eyes. What a drama queen. Yeah, this woman was beautiful but she must have been pretty high maintenance. Apparently that's what Victor liked, beautiful and delicate. She felt another stab in her heart. She was feisty and aggressive. She'd never be delicate, she was too independent. She'd better clear her head and get to work. Ariel picked up one of Lakeisha's hands and studied it. She took a deep breath and concentrated on the fire. She shot a laser beam directly onto the chain loop closest to the band. It quickly heated then the beam sliced through the metal. She looked at Lakeisha. "If you want the other one off, you're going to have to let go of him."

Lakeisha immediately pulled her hand away from Victor's and held it out to Ariel.

Victor looked at Ariel in astonishment. He knew she could create fire, but he had no idea she could channel it into a laser beam. She truly was amazing. Victor stood and held out a hand to Lakeisha.

Once Lakeisha was on her feet, she turned to Ariel. "Thank you so much..."

Ariel couldn't help herself. She lashed out and punched Lakeisha in the face. Her aim was perfect. Lakeisha dropped like a sack of potatoes.

Victor was horrified. "What in the hell do you think you're doing?" he said, glaring angrily at Ariel. "You knocked her out cold."

"Yeah I did," Ariel said as she turned toward Thomas. "Let's get out of here while we still can."

Victor didn't know what was going on, but he wasn't finished. He reached out and grabbed Ariel's arm. "Wait a minute."

Ariel froze. She couldn't handle Victor's touch. If he didn't let go, she'd break down right here. She slowly turned to face him. Her eyes hard and cold. "Let go," she said flatly. They stared at each other for the briefest second. "You'll need to carry your girlfriend if you want to save her." She pulled her arm free and walked out the door.

Thomas enjoyed seeing Ariel punch Lakeisha. It was about time someone did something to that woman. But now he was worried. He caught a glimpse of the tears and agony in Ariel's eyes as she walked by. She had obviously misinterpreted Victor's actions. She didn't realize he was too kind hearted to let anyone suffer, not even Lakeisha. Thomas hurried after her.

Victor was flabbergasted. What had gotten into Ariel? He couldn't understand it. She just hauled off and slugged someone who was obviously scared, weak and helpless. She used enough force to knock her out. Apparently she wasn't the woman he thought she was. Maybe it was better he found out now. Was that what happened to dad? Had he fallen in love with the woman he thought Dannica was only to find out later she was someone completely different? From what he heard their courtship had been short. Maybe dad never saw the real woman until after they were already married. Back then, people didn't get divorced. There was still a problem with that theory though. Victor knew his father never would have left him home alone if he knew his mother was that vicious and evil. He shook his head in confusion. He wasn't going to figure things out tonight. He gently picked Lakeisha up and headed for the door.

* * * *

Thomas was half way across the cave. He was keeping an eye on Ariel as she approached the tunnel. Suddenly, Hector jumped out from the shadows and grabbed Ariel around the neck.

"NO!" Victor yelled. He had just passed through the metal door when he saw Hector. Ariel was in trouble. He needed to help her. He almost dropped Lakeisha right there. At the last moment, he realized what he was doing and shoved Lakeisha into Austin's arms. He began to dash across the opening and stopped. Thomas had already taken care of her. Ariel was standing nearby, but she was no longer in danger. Thomas had lunged at Hector so fast, he hadn't seen it coming. Hector was thrown to the ground. He relaxed his hold on Ariel enough that she darted away. Victor was grateful to Thomas, but he was upset he hadn't been there for her himself. He would have been if Ariel hadn't knocked Lakeisha out and left him to deal with the problem.

Thomas was now attacking Hector with all his might. Victor realized he wasn't applying a death blow on purpose. He kept attacking, causing Hector as much pain as he could without killing him. Thomas was getting vengeance. He obviously wanted Hector to be punished for the pain he had caused Thomas' family. Victor couldn't blame him, but they needed to get out of this cave. Thomas was putting the rest of them in danger. Thomas' father, Luke, had done the same thing after his wife's assassination. Luke had put all the warriors in danger in an attempt to stop and punish Hector. Victor approached Thomas, but was stopped by Ariel.

"Stay out of his way. He needs this," she said angrily. "If you're worried about those women..." she jerked her head toward Abby and Lakeisha. "You, Morrigan and Austin can escort them back to the cave. I'll stay here with Thomas. We're not leaving until he's satisfied." She had shifted slightly to block Victor's path.

"We're all staying together so you better hope he gets satisfied soon," Victor glowered.

Abby was mesmerized by Thomas. She'd never seen a warrior fight before. Now she knew why they were referred to as warriors. She certainly wouldn't want to be up against him. He was using every fighting technique Abby had ever heard of to attack Hector. It was clear he wasn't just trying to kill him. He wanted Hector to suffer. Abby was glad. She didn't know what that said about herself, but she was. If that made her a bad person, she could live with that. Hector had snuck into her home, abducted her and then fed off her for days. He was disgusting and sadistic. She wanted him to pay. He certainly hadn't cared what impact his actions had on anyone in her family. Why should she care about him?

Abby continued to watch as Thomas punished Hector. She found her thoughts shifting to Thomas. He was definitely sexy. He had such broad shoulders and his waist was slim. His build was muscular and taught. She suspected he had great abs under that t-shirt. Her imagination was getting out of control. She needed to focus on something else, but she couldn't pull her eyes away from Thomas. Watching him was too fascinating and enjoyable.

Ariel saw movement just in time. Several vampires stormed the cave. They came from the second tunnel. How many vampires were in there? How big was that cave? She started throwing fire. She had to protect Thomas. The vampires were coming at her fast and hard. She couldn't keep up. One slipped through, she kicked out then spun around and got him with fire. Ariel didn't really care how long Thomas kept this up. She understood the need for vengeance. She didn't look at what Thomas was doing as wrong or excessive. She thought it was therapeutic. She always suspected Dimitri had done something similar to the men that had kidnaped her. She hoped the one that tried to rape her had received plenty of pain before his death. She had no doubt Dimitri had killed them. She knew him well enough to know he wouldn't let their atrocities go unpunished.

The vampires were coming too fast for Ariel to handle them all. She realized Victor had joined the fight. He was only using his dagger. She knew he was saving the ninja stars for outside. She hoped they made it out before the whole coven returned from hunting. She would not interfere with Thomas but if he didn't hurry up, there might be too many vampires for her and Victor to handle on their own.

Four vampires got past her and were heading directly for Thomas. She had to stop them. He wouldn't see them coming. She kicked out and knocked another vampire down then killed it. The vampires were getting closer to Thomas. She only hesitated a moment then she threw a long stream of fire that struck all four vampires. They weren't killed, but they were injured enough to stop their attack on Thomas. Victor quickly stepped in and killed all four of them almost instantly. He was good. Ariel took a deep breath trying to relax. She didn't like to do that. Funneling so much fire took a lot out of her. She continued to fight off vampires, but her reflexes were slower now. She hoped Thomas would finish soon, she was getting so tired. She needed a short break to regain her strength, or she was going to get hurt.

Hector pulled a knife from his boot. He swung out and stabbed Thomas through the leg. Thomas went down. His leg was bleeding pretty badly, the wound looked deep. Ariel almost finished Hector off, but she couldn't deprive Thomas of that pleasure. Instead, she threw a ball of fire and struck Hector in the leg. "Now they were even," she thought as Hector let out a scream and looked her way.

Abby gasped as Thomas was stabbed and fell to the floor. "We need to help them," she said anxiously as she looked toward her brother.

Thomas regained his composure and lunged at Hector. The punishment resumed.

"He's fine," Morrigan assured Abby. "We can't leave Austin and the panther. We have to stay here in case additional vampires arrive and try to attack. Trust me, he'll be fine." Morrigan hoped he was right. He needed to protect Abby, too. But he knew if he told her that, she'd be angry and defiant. If she thought they were protecting Austin and Lakeisha she wouldn't argue.

Hector had to be in pain. Thomas would slice him, then kick or throw him into the wall. Currently, Hector was on the ground struggling to get up. Ariel periodically watched the match between the warrior and the vampire. She couldn't focus on them, she was in a battle of her own. But it was painfully obvious Hector wasn't a very good fighter. He was smart and seemed to be good at planning tactical attacks but when it came to hand to hand combat, he was no match for Thomas. He didn't have a chance.

Victor saw several more vampires slip through the tunnel. How much longer was Thomas going to play with Hector? He understood, he really did. But he wasn't willing to sacrifice any of their group to appease Thomas' need for punishment. If the vampires kept coming, someone was going to get hurt. He glanced over at Ariel and saw her throwing fire at five additional vampires one after the other. She looked tired, Victor observed as he plunged his dagger through the heart of another vampire. He was so confused about her. He kicked out and another vampire flew across the room. She seemed amazing, good and kind at first. After what happened in that room with Lakeisha, he didn't know what to think anymore. He knew he was in love with her, but he wasn't sure he could trust her. He ducked then pivoted and killed another vampire.

Thomas was relentlessly attacking Hector. This vampire was responsible for the death of both his parents. He wanted him to pay. He needed to pay for assassinating Marlena and ambushing the warriors. As far as Thomas was concerned, Hector was responsible for his father's death too. Hector hadn't killed Luke himself, but he had planned the attack that led to his death. He also needed to pay for kidnaping these two women and terrorizing them for days. Out of the corner of his eye, he saw a ball of light. Ariel was throwing fire. He immediately snapped out of his anger driven trance. While he was torturing Hector, he was also endangering the rest of the group. If anyone got hurt, it would be his fault. The other vampires had realized they were here and had started to attack. Thomas stabbed Hector one more time in the ribs and then plunged his knife directly through Hector's heart. Hector vanished in a puff of dust.

It felt good to know he was gone forever. Hector couldn't hurt anyone ever again.

Ariel turned to Thomas. "Feel better?" she asked with a smile as she killed another vampire.

Thomas realized Ariel understood. She supported his need for justice. He wouldn't forget the backup she gave him. She kept him safe while he took care of Hector. Once they got back, he would try to return the favor. To start, he was going to have a chat with Victor.

Victor stood by Thomas' side. "Now that you're finished with that, can we get the hell out of here?" he asked.

Thomas turned to Victor. He thought they were going to have an argument but Victor was smiling. Thomas immediately relaxed. So, Victor understood why Thomas had to make Hector suffer too. "I think that would be a good idea," Thomas answered. "Any thoughts on the safest way to escape?" He turned and plunged his knife into the chest of a vampire. Victor turned in the opposite direction and did the same.

The three of them looked around the cave then at the tunnels. The vampires had stopped invading. Their small group was the only occupants inside the cave opening now. Hopefully, all the monsters inside were dead. But they still had to worry about the ones outside hunting for food.

"I don't like it, but I think we need to send you and Ariel through the tunnel first. It would be nice if you could go together. I don't want anyone walking into a mass of vampires alone. I have to carry Lakeisha and Abby's still a little weak. She needs to be buffered between Morrigan and Austin. I'm thinking we should have Austin shift and fly all the way outside to see what we're up against. The vampires can only come at us from the tunnels. That gives us the advantage. Ariel can get most of them with fire as they exit. What do you think? I'm open for suggestions."

Austin was by his side. "Here take her," he pushed Lakeisha toward Victor. "I'll be right back." He was instantly a bat and disappeared through the tunnel.

"Well," Victor sighed. "I guess that answers that. Now we wait."

In no time at all, Austin returned. He flew to Morrigan and shifted back. "Hurry, right now there's nobody out there. I think we can get out of the cave before the vampires arrive."

Thomas grabbed Ariel's arm and pulled her toward the tunnel. "We're first," he said as he continued through the hole. Victor went next, carrying Lakeisha on his back as he crawled through the small space. Morrigan, Abby and Austin took up the rear. The group was just exiting the cave and entering the woods when a group of about twenty vampires appeared on the small path.

"Keep going," Ariel called. "I've got this. I'll start lighting the fires and we'll be fine. Thomas, you get my back. Everyone else head for the cave."

Victor paused. He wasn't going to leave Ariel and Thomas alone to fight off that many vampires. He knew they could probably handle it, but there was no way he was going to leave them alone out here. They were all tired, especially Ariel. "Morrigan, you and Austin get Abby to the cave." He shifted Lakeisha over his shoulder, fireman style. "I'm hanging back to help these guys," Morrigan didn't hesitate. The three of them hurried off toward shelter.

Ariel turned on him and was about to argue.

"Don't waste your breath," he barked. "I'm not leaving without you."

Ariel flung a ball of fire at the first wood pile. It ignited immediately. The vampires hesitated then three of them lunged forward. Victor threw a star and set off the first trap as they ran passed. It worked perfectly. The arrows flew toward the vampires, striking two of them and killing them instantly. He threw another star and struck the third one in the chest. The dust mixed with plumes of smoke and disappeared in the breeze. The three of them continued running through the forest, Ariel igniting the wood, Victor setting off arrows and Thomas watching their backs as vampires disintegrated behind them. They all stopped to survey the immediate area for vampires before they made their final trek to the cave. Once they were sure the coast was clear, they scurried up the incline and ducked inside.

Abby and Austin were eating large chunks of jerky. Morrigan was munching on peanuts. Lakeisha had finally come around. Victor placed her on the ground next to the fire pit. "Just sit there, I'll build a fire. You'll be warm in a minute." Victor started gathering small pieces of wood.

Ariel couldn't watch Victor care for Lakeisha all night. She felt like she was dying inside and she was so tired and weak. She grabbed her sleeping bag and moved to the corner of the cave. She'd be warm enough for one night and she needed to be as far away from Victor and Lakeisha as she could get. She didn't even say goodnight to anyone. She just laid out the bag and climbed inside. She was facing the wall of the cave for privacy. Her eyes had started to water and she didn't want to invite conversation with anyone. She certainly didn't want them to see her cry.

Victor scowled as he finished building the fire and stood. He spotted Ariel in the corner. He really didn't understand what was going on with her. She was acting so strange tonight. It was like she didn't want anything to do with him. The idea he had lost her so soon after he found her tore at his heart. He didn't know what to do. He'd never been in this situation before. Could he live without her? He might have to. He ran his hand through his hair. Sometimes life seemed so unfair.

Lakeisha was studying Victor. For the first time, she realized he was in love with Ariel. The idea stung a little. She had convinced herself that Victor was incapable of love. It was her way of dealing with the rejection. Sure, she was the one that cheated but Victor had rejected her over and over again. That's why she eventually started going out with friends. She regretted the hurt and pain Victor had suffered because of her actions. But, she didn't regret taking control of her life again. Before the abduction, she had been happier than she'd ever been in her entire life.

She glanced over at Ariel. Is that what her anger was all about? Was Ariel in love with Victor too? Well who could blame her, for the love or the anger? Lakeisha had been a basket case back at the cave. She wasn't sure what happened. She was so scared and disgusted by Hector. When the door opened, she just couldn't face another feeding. Then, Victor called her by the nickname he'd given her. Nobody used that name but Victor. For just an instant it was like she'd gone back in time. He was being so gentle with her. She'd just lunged at him. She was falling apart and needed Victor to steady her. Ariel must hate her. If they were a couple, Ariel had a right to be upset just for the events of tonight. Then if she knew about five years ago... Lakeisha's thoughts trailed off.

She glanced back at Victor. He looked so miserable. She would have given anything for him to feel that way about her. She had longed for him to look at her the way he looked at Ariel, with so much love and desire. She always thought she'd be devastated if Victor ever fell in love. She wasn't though. Underneath the pain and jealousy, she was actually happy for him. He was such a complex individual. Lakeisha hoped she hadn't caused problems for him again. The last thing she wanted to do was cause Victor more pain. She stood and walked to him. "Thanks again for helping me tonight. I know you didn't have to. Most people would have left me there after what I did to you five years ago." Victor was looking at her, but Lakeisha knew his mind was elsewhere. His mind was on Ariel. She stood up on her tip toes and kissed him on the cheek. "Goodnight, Victor. I'm tired and I'd like to get some sleep. I haven't really slept for days."

"Oh," he seemed to snap back. "Do you want the sleeping bag?" he asked.

"No. I'm going to shift for the night. I'll be more comfortable and I'll stay warmer that way. Thanks again for everything." She walked to the other side of the room and turned into a panther. She curled up and was out almost instantly.

Chapter Six

Victor couldn't sleep. He hadn't slept all night. He'd been watching Ariel. There were a couple times he thought he heard her crying. But that was ridiculous, what would she be crying about? He was angry and confused. Things had been so good yesterday morning. He was actually happy for the first time in his life. Then, fate slipped in and yanked the rug out from under his feet. Now he was sprawled on the floor, battered and bruised. What was he supposed to do? He didn't know anything about relationships or women. He was out of his element. If Ariel was violent like his mother, he should just forget her. He looked around the small cave, the sun should be up now. It was still early, but he could tell it was morning. He'd need to get up soon and strike camp. It was going to take a couple days to get home and he was anxious to get out of this forest. He looked back to Ariel. All he really wanted to do right now was climb into that sleeping bag and hold her close. He wouldn't. He couldn't. If she didn't want him, he wouldn't put her through the discomfort of rejecting him.

Victor watched as Ariel quietly slipped out of her sleeping bag and snuck out the door. She had slept in her clothes. That was odd. Should he follow her? She knew better than to go out on her own. So far they hadn't run into any more vampiric animals, but that didn't mean they weren't out there. He didn't like her outside by herself, but he wouldn't follow. She obviously wanted to be alone.

Ariel stumbled down the trail. She wasn't really paying attention to where she was going. She just had to get away. She was a little surprised when she entered the clearing where she and Victor had washed clothes. It was also where they had first made love. She sat on the ground and laid her head on a fallen tree. They had sat on this tree for hours talking and getting to know each other. Had that only been two days ago? So much had happened since then. The tears were flowing now. She couldn't stop them, she didn't even try. Victor was gone. He was in love with Lakeisha. It didn't matter what happened between those two. Ariel couldn't settle. Just like she wouldn't settle for Tank because she didn't love him. If things didn't work out this time with Lakeisha and Victor, she still couldn't have him. She couldn't be in a relationship with Victor knowing he was in love with someone else.

She curled into a ball and wept. Her heart ached and she felt so hollow and alone. She suddenly realized she was in love with Victor. She hadn't wanted to admit that to herself. She'd refused to evaluate her feelings before, when things were going so well between them. Now that she knew there wasn't a chance for them, why continue to deny it. She had fallen totally and completely in love with Victor. So, this is how it felt to lose someone you loved. She hoped she hadn't put Tank through this kind of pain. He was such a good guy. Maybe karma was catching up to her. She'd broken Tank's heart, now it was her turn to have her heart broken.

After Dark

She was crying uncontrollably now. She couldn't stop herself. She wrapped her arms around her waist and let the pain overcome her.

Lakeisha woke just in time to see Ariel slip out the door. She wanted to talk to her, maybe this was a good opportunity. She decided to stay in the form of a panther and slipped out of the cave. It was a nice day, a little cool but not too bad. They should have an easy trip home. She assumed they would be traveling today. It didn't make sense to stay this close to the vampire's lair. She wanted to get home. She missed her husband and her son. She looked around but couldn't see Ariel. Maybe she'd gone for a walk. She set off down the trail.

Lakeisha stopped when she heard a noise. Was that someone crying? She silently slipped through the trees until she saw Ariel lying on the ground in a fetal position. She was weeping uncontrollably. Lakeisha could almost feel the agony as Ariel laid there crumpled and broken. It tore at her heart. What could she do? The last person Ariel would want to see right now was Lakeisha. Victor was such an idiot. If somebody didn't step in, they might lose each other over stupidity. As much as she hated to admit it, there was nothing she could do for Ariel right now. If she interrupted, Ariel would be embarrassed and completely shut her out or punch her again. There's no way she would listen to anything Lakeisha had to say. Interrupting her now would just make things worse.

Lakeisha slowly backed away from the clearing. She'd head up river and go for a swim. Ariel needed time to herself right now. Maybe after Lakeisha dried off, she'd go back and see if Ariel was okay. She didn't know how to help. Most of all, she was worried this was somehow her fault. She believed her actions in the cave were the reason Ariel and Victor were suffering and avoiding each other. She needed to find a way to fix it. She continued to ponder the situation as she slowly headed for the river.

Ariel had cried herself out. She didn't have any more tears to give. She rested on the ground awhile, too weak to get up. She was emotionally drained and didn't care about anything. The sun was shining brightly now. The rest of the group would be awake. If anyone came looking for her, she'd be embarrassed if they found her this way. She had to clean herself up. Ariel slowly rose and walked to the river bank. She sat down and washed her face with the cool liquid. Hopefully that would erase the evidence of her breakdown. She slipped off her shoes and rested her feet in the water. She was staring vacantly across the river when she heard Lakeisha.

"Ariel?" Lakeisha said softly. "I know you dislike me but could I have just a few minutes of your time?" she asked hesitantly.

"If you're here for an apology, I'm not sorry," Ariel answered.

Lakeisha smiled. This woman had grit. Even in her present condition, she was feisty. "I'm not," Lakeisha said honestly. "I'm not asking for an apology and frankly if you gave one I'd be disappointed in you. You wouldn't mean it and I think maybe I deserved the knock out yesterday." She was standing next to Ariel now. The woman looked awful.

Ariel was surprised. That certainly wasn't what she'd expected. She looked up at Lakeisha. "Then what do you want?" she asked.

"Just to talk to you for a minute. Can I sit down?" she asked motioning to a nearby rock.

"Go ahead," Ariel shrugged. "I was just about to leave anyway. I need to get my stuff cleaned up so we can leave. I'd like to get home."

"This won't take long," Lakeisha pressed. "Please, just give me a few minutes."

"Does Victor know where you are, or will he start looking for you?" Ariel asked. She couldn't face Victor yet. "I had to witness your happy reunion yesterday. I'd rather not be here for the joyous day after," Ariel said bitterly.

So, she'd been right. Ariel thought there was something going on between Lakeisha and Victor. How could she possibly be that dense? Victor was obviously in love with Ariel. Plus, Lakeisha had caused him so much pain. They hadn't seen each other in over five years. Surely Victor had gone on with his life the same as Lakeisha had. Even if she wasn't married, Victor would never give her another chance. She had cheated on him, betrayed him and caused him a year's suspension from the warriors. She'd have to tread lightly, but somehow she had to convince Ariel there was nothing between her and Victor.

"No, I didn't tell Victor where I was going. But he won't come looking for me either. If he went looking for anyone it would be you," Lakeisha said softly.

"Lakeisha, I don't know how you feel about Victor, but I saw him with you yesterday. He's still in love with you. If you don't feel the same, please just make sure he knows that right away. Don't hurt him again. He's been through enough because of you," Ariel moved to stand up.

"Ariel, please just give me five minutes before you leave," Lakeisha practically begged. "I promise it will be worth your time." Ariel was definitely in love with Victor. She thought he was in love with someone else, but she was still trying to protect him.

Ariel looked at Lakeisha and sighed. She didn't want to hear anything the woman had to say. She didn't want to look into that gorgeous face for one more second. But, she knew Lakeisha wouldn't give up. If Ariel walked away now, she'd be trying to avoid Lakeisha all day. "Fine, but make it fast," Ariel said settling back against a rock.

"You said Victor is still in love with me," she began. "That's impossible because Victor was never in love with me." Ariel started to object but Lakeisha cut her off. "No," Lakeisha said forcefully. "Just hear me out. Victor cared for me. I know he did. He may have had some kind of love for me. I don't know, Victor is complicated. I do know, without a doubt, Victor was never in love with me. That was our problem," Lakeisha confessed.

"If you were too blind to see Victor's real feelings for you, that's your problem. I watched him yesterday. He's still in love with you," Ariel countered.

"From where I'm sitting Ariel, you're the blind one here," Lakeisha said flatly. "You obviously can't see how strong Victor's feelings are for you. You have what I always wanted and you just can't see it," Lakeisha said vehemently. "But that's not what I'm here to talk to you about. Before you get mad I want to tell you about me and Victor. Maybe then you'll understand."

"Victor already told me about you. I think I'm up to speed there," Ariel retorted.

After Dark

"I don't think so," Lakeisha replied. "I'd like to tell you my story," she continued before Ariel could interrupt or leave. "The females in our pack are sheltered. The men haven't learned about women's lib and all that. We are expected to keep the camp, cook the food and prepare for marriage. The men go out to clubs and parties, but typically the women don't. We're not even supposed to go into the city. My best friend Andrea and I didn't agree. We were twenty eight years old, but we had to sneak out just to go to the mall. One day, we hooked up with two other girls, Chelsea and Leslie. They were shifters.

Panthers are supposed to hate shifters, but we didn't. I thought that was another stupid rule. Why should I hate a group of people just because they can do something I can't? Anyway, the four of us became very good friends. We are still best friends," Lakeisha paused. "Chelsea and Leslie wanted to go out for Andrea's birthday. They talked us into going to a club to celebrate. They said they knew the perfect spot. There was this hot club in town, but we'd have to go early and wait in line to get in.

I'm sure by now you've guessed it was Bojan Taverns, Victor's club. The four of us stood in line for two and a half hours, but it paid off. We were part of the first group in when the doors opened. We got this great booth in the corner. The four of us were laughing and having a great time. That's when I first saw Victor. He walked out of his office and went straight to the bar. He visited with Rocky for just a minute then left through the back door. That was enough for me. I was hooked. I don't know what happened, it was like I became instantly obsessed. My friends discussed how hot and sexy Victor was like girls do, but then they forgot him and went back to partying. I didn't. I couldn't stop thinking about that sexy stranger.

The following week, I snuck away and headed back to Bojan Taverns. I had to see Victor again. I never thought for one minute I would actually speak to him. I believed he was completely out of my league," Lakeisha paused.

Ariel kept telling herself to leave. She didn't want to hear this story, but she couldn't. She had to admit she was curious. She wanted to hear Lakeisha's side of things. She already knew Victor's. Regardless of his feelings for her, Ariel was still in love with Victor. She needed to know what had happened with Lakeisha.

Lakeisha leaned down and cupped her hands, filling them with river water. She took a drink and then continued. "So, I waited in line again. This time I was out there for about three hours. I'd arrived late, so I missed the first wave of admissions. I kept telling myself I was being stupid. I should just go home and forget the sexy stranger. I couldn't. I had to see Victor again. It's hard to explain. I guess what I'm trying to tell you is that my feelings for Victor were unhealthy from the start. Once I finally got into the club, I sat at the bar. I figured I'd be more likely to see Victor that way. I had no idea who he was at the time, but I figured he must work there because he had come from the backroom that first night.

I was completely shocked when he came over and sat next to me. He introduced himself and talked to me all night. This beautiful, sexy man spent the entire evening with me. I left that night knowing I'd be back. My obsession was a hundred times worse now. I kept going back to the club to see Victor any time I could. Eventually we started dating. I was twenty-eight, but I remind you I was so naive and sheltered. I fell in love with Victor right from the start. I was like a drug addict, I had to have my Victor fix. I know that sounds bazaar, but it's the only way I can explain it." She looked over at Ariel for a response, but didn't get one so she continued.

"Eventually Victor and I were spending every night together. I moved to the city to be closer to him. I kept telling myself I was happy. This was what love was all about. For a while it worked. I convinced myself everything was normal. Everything was the way it should be. I finally had to admit the relationship was one sided. I was living with this twisted obsession that I believed was true love. Victor was my world. He was everything to me. I wanted it to be the same for Victor but it wasn't. We started to fight. The fights were always about him going to the club or hunting with the warriors, but that wasn't really what upset me. I just wanted Victor to love me. If he had just loved me, I wouldn't have cared how often he left or how many other responsibilities he had. I just wanted to be loved by him. I knew Victor cared, but he wasn't in love. What we had wasn't enough," Lakeisha confessed.

"The longer we stayed together, the more I lost my identity. My whole life became Victor. I gave up my friends because I didn't want to be gone if Victor happened to be free. Everything I did was aimed at gaining Victor's love. I finally told myself he was incapable of love. I decided I would just have to love him enough for both of us. Of course, that didn't work either. You have to know how complicated Victor is. He's been through a lot. I know the situation with me only made things worse. I am truly sorry for that. I'd like to say if I had it all to do over again I'd do things differently, but I honestly don't know that I could have." Lakeisha looked out across the river, deep in thought.

"I guess you could say my friends staged an intervention," Lakeisha continued. "They saw what was happening to me and they stepped in. One night they came to my place determined to help.

By this time I wasn't visiting my pack or even my parents anymore. Like I said, my whole life was Victor. They forced me to go out with them. We went to a club on the other side of town and just hung out. I was anxious and stressed all night long. What if Victor called and I wasn't home. What if he stopped by for the night and went home alone because I wasn't there for him. It took almost the entire evening but I finally relaxed a little. By the time I got home I had to admit I'd enjoyed spending time with my friends again.

They came by every Friday night and we went out. One night I met Ryker and he changed my life. I know it wasn't fair to Victor. It wasn't fair to Ryker either. The problem was, I'm going to use the addict scenario again, I couldn't give up my Victor fix. I gradually fell in love with Ryker. This time it was a healthy love. It took me a long time though. I thought I was still in love with Victor. I couldn't leave him. The love I share with Ryker is pure. It's a lot healthier and most important, it's mutual. That's something Victor and I never had and we never would have. I know, I was there. Victor was never in love with me, Ariel. He cared for me. He tried to make me happy, but he was never in love with me. Do you understand?" she asked Ariel.

"I guess I understand. I'm just not sure I believe you," Ariel admitted.

"Until you have someone that truly loves you, it's hard to know how wonderful it is. You think Victor loved me. But I know he didn't. I also know I wasn't really in love with Victor. I'm not sure what it was, but it was obsessive and unhealthy and destructive. Ryker and I have been together for five years now. We are still madly in love. In fact, I love him more now than I did back then. We have a wonderful life together with our son. You and Victor have that possibility if you don't mess it up."

After Dark

"What!" Ariel said angrily. "Are you telling me you are still with the father of your child?"

"Yes," Lakeisha said almost guiltily. "We got married mid-way through Victor's suspension."

Ariel shot to her feet. She was pissed now. She swung back around and faced Lakeisha. "So, let me get this straight. You cheated on Victor, got pregnant, unjustly accused him of abandoning you and his child, then you went back to camp and hooked up with the real father. The two of you wait a few months, then you get married and live happily ever after. Victor, on the other hand has suffered intensely for the past five years for a crime he didn't even commit. Do you realize he's still afraid to tell anyone your secret because he fears it will put you in danger? He wouldn't even tell me the specifics. He just said the father was an enemy to your pack and you would suffer for hooking up with him. No matter what Victor does, he will always suffer for your actions. He will be punished for the rest of his life. But hey, I'm so glad you're happy. I should knock you out again just for that," Ariel growled.

Lakeisha didn't understand. What was Ariel saying? Why was she so angry? "What do you mean Victor is still being punished? He served his time and when he returned he was reinstated as a warrior. I checked. I had to make sure he had his life back. Please explain what you mean."

Ariel glared at Lakeisha. "You really are naive. Your actions have damaged Victor's reputation for the rest of his life. He will never truly have respect in our community." Ariel sat back down and sighed. "It is very difficult for fae to get pregnant. Once a pregnancy occurs, it's no guarantee there will be a child. We have a high rate of miscarriages. Because of this, having a child is sacred.

Turning your back on that child is unforgivable. Victor has been labeled. Many members of the community believe that child was his. Why wouldn't they, he was punished for his transgressions. Because of that, they don't trust him. They believe he lacks integrity. Most keep their opinions to themselves, they just snub him or avoid him. There are a few that are very vocal about it though. Some of them even tried to prevent him from rejoining the warriors when he returned. The past five years have been very difficult for Victor. And thanks to you, it's not going to get better any time soon."

Now Lakeisha stood and began to pace. "I am so stupid!" She exclaimed. "How can I fix this?" She turned to Ariel, tears in her eyes. "I have to fix this. What can I do? My uncle and my father forced me to go before the council. If I go to the council, will that fix it? Will the community find out Victor was innocent if I go to the council?" She was starting to get hysterical. "I really have ruined Victor's life. Ariel, I am so sorry! I have made things so difficult for you. After what his mother did to him, what his father has gone through, how could I have been so stupid? You have to help me fix this."

"Wait," Ariel said firmly. "What do you mean after what his mother did to him?"

Lakeisha stopped abruptly. "You don't know about his mother? Oh, Victor!" She said exasperated as she closed her eyes. She was still pacing, trying to decide if she should tell Ariel what she knew. She took a deep breath. "Victor's mother tried to kill him," she paused.

"His scar," Ariel said quietly.

After Dark

"Yes," Lakeisha answered. "I think that's why he opened the..."

"Lakeisha!" Victor roared. "After everything I sacrificed for you, everything I did to keep your secret, I would think you'd have enough respect for me to keep mine. I told you those things in confidence. You don't have the right to share them with anyone."

Ariel and Lakeisha stared at Victor. He was so angry. He was just standing there, hands clenched, his breathing ragged. How long had he been there? They were both wondering how much Victor had heard.

"I'm sorry," Lakeisha finally said. She looked back at Ariel then turned to Victor. "Well, actually, no I'm not. Ariel has a right to know what she's gotten herself into. She has a right to know your history."

"I'll be the judge of what Ariel has a right to know about my family and my life," Victor shot back. "Not you."

"Victor, your history is the only thing that explains your complicated personality. You can't care about a woman and keep that part of you locked away. You know that. Stop being an idiot and explain things to her." Lakeisha was watching him closely. He was still angry, but was he also angry at Ariel? "Don't tell me you're still upset with her for punching me yesterday."

"Of course I'm angry at her for that. You were weak and defenseless. Ariel was out of line." He shifted his gaze to Ariel and saw her narrow her eyes at him.

"Well you can stop it right now," Lakeisha shot back. "I'm not angry at her. In fact, I happen to understand why she did it. I probably deserved it. If you weren't so busy being a moron, you'd understand why she did it too. Until you figure it out, mind your own business. This is between Ariel and me. It has nothing to do with you." She turned to leave, then stopped and looked at Ariel. "Can I talk to you later about how to fix that other problem? It's important to me."

Ariel nodded then watched Lakeisha disappear. She had to admit, Lakeisha wasn't the woman she initially thought she was. Yes she was naive, but she wasn't as callous and manipulative as Ariel had believed. She looked at Victor then turned and headed back to the cave.

Victor was left alone by the river. Had all the women on the planet gone mad? He wasn't happy with Lakeisha. She had no right to tell Ariel his mother had tried to kill him. Then, she'd almost spilled his other secret. Lakeisha knew how important it was for him to be anonymous. She knew he didn't want anyone to know he owned that business. Why had she betrayed him? Especially after he'd sacrificed so much for her? And what was that nonsense about her deserving the sucker punch Ariel gave her yesterday. He would never understand women. He slowly made his way back to the cave. They needed to head out. As it was, they would already be pushing it. If they left right away, they might still make it to the cave before night fall.

Lakeisha was furious with Victor. He'd finally fallen in love and he was going to ruin everything. Ariel was just as stubborn. Realizing she had ruined Victor's reputation had been a blow. She was going to find a way to fix that. If Ariel wouldn't help her, Ryker would. They would fix everything. She stopped abruptly when she heard the growling. She looked up and saw a bear. Or was it a bear? She knew there were black bears in this forest, but this bear was huge. It was so muscular and its teeth looked sharp and jagged. Whatever it was, she had to get out of here. Even as a panther, she'd be overpowered. She started to back away as the animal charged.

Ariel came around the corner to see Lakeisha and the vampiric bear. She knew what it was instantly. She didn't think, she just rushed forward. Lakeisha was fast, she had turned into a panther but she wasn't trying to fight the bear. She was just trying to avoid it. "Keep that up," Ariel yelled. "This thing is dangerous. Its blood, its venom is toxic. Whatever you do, make sure you don't get bit!" She called.

Lakeisha seemed to understand. She'd let the bear charge her then she'd dart away. At one point the bear seemed to realize Ariel was there and might be an easier target. It turned and charged her. Ariel didn't hesitate. She started to throw fire. She hit it in the chest, time after time but it kept coming. Lakeisha jumped in front of the bear again. She was drawing its attention away from Ariel. They couldn't keep this up forever. Ariel was trying to think. What could they do? She didn't have a dagger. She'd never needed one. The bear came too close to Lakeisha and Ariel threw fire at it again. The bear let out a loud growl as the flames burned its face. It turned back to Ariel and charged again. The fire seemed to singe the bear, but it wasn't doing enough damage. Lakeisha jumped forward and drew the bear back to her again.

Victor was still deep in thought when he heard it. It sounded like a bear, but what if it was one of those animals bitten by a vampire. He started to run. As he came around a bend in the trail he saw it. The bear was huge and it was charging towards Ariel. She was still recovering, he would not let that thing get to her. She might not survive another attack. Lakeisha jumped between them and the bear charged her. As a panther, Lakeisha was quick. The two women were doing a good job of keeping the bear at bay, but they couldn't keep this up forever. Ariel was throwing fire, but it didn't seem to faze the bear. Victor pulled a star from his pocket. His aim would have to be perfect. If he could injure the bear enough, maybe he could slip in and stab it through the heart.

The star hit the bear between the eyes. It turned on him and growled. So, that hadn't worked, all he'd done was make it angry. He pulled several more stars from his pocket. He threw them one after the other, hitting the bear in the same spot. Right between his eyes. Ariel joined in and started throwing fire one after another into his face. Finally, the bear went down. Victor didn't hesitate. He was on the bear instantly and plunged his dagger into its heart. Then, he jumped back and watched. He couldn't tell for sure if the bear was dead, but he didn't want to come into contact with that venom again. Lakeisha shifted back. The three of them stood there in silence.

Finally Lakeisha asked. "Is it dead?" she looked to Victor.

"Yeah. I think so," he confirmed.

"What is it?" she asked.

"A black bear that one of the vampires tried to turn. It doesn't work, but they become strong and fast like this bear. See the teeth? They're like vampires' teeth. Don't touch it. Any liquid on that thing is toxic. Both Ariel and I can attest to the lethal qualities of that liquid."

"What do we do with it? We can't just leave it out here in the open. A child could touch it and who knows what that toxin will do to a human," Ariel said.

After Dark

"No. We have to bury it," Victor stated. "One of you will need to go back to the cave and get me a shovel."

Ariel spoke up. "I'll go. I'll send the other men back to help you too. You can't get that thing into a hole by yourself without coming in contact with it. I realize you're healed now, but be careful. I don't think either one of us should come in contact with that venom again. Our bodies might not be able to fight it off so soon after the last time." She turned and jogged up the trail.

"You and Ariel have come into contact with one of these before? How come she didn't know her fire wouldn't kill it then?" Lakeisha asked.

Victor watched Ariel as she ran up the trail. "Ariel and Morrigan were attacked by a couple coyotes in this same condition. One of them bit Ariel. I came in contact with the venom while I was cleaning her bite. She's right. It's very toxic and neither one of us should risk coming in contact this soon. You shouldn't either. Check yourself and make sure you're not bit. You also need to make sure you don't have any of its blood or saliva on you. It could be fatal."

Lakeisha did a thorough check and was satisfied she wasn't in danger. Once Thomas, Morrigan and Austin arrived she excused herself to go back to the cave. "I'll clean things up so when you guys are finished we can head out," she called as she started up the trail.

Lakeisha and Ariel had everything packed and ready to go when the men got back to the cave. Victor took the lead and headed down the trail. The rest of the group followed. Ariel held back. She wanted to be alone. She had a lot to think about. She'd seen Victor with Lakeisha. It had been obvious to her he was still in love. He was so gentle and caring with her. But all the things Lakeisha told her kept coming back. Plus, while they battled that bear he didn't act protective of Lakeisha. He actually seemed more protective of her. That was confusing.

She couldn't stop thinking about Victor's mother. Had she really tried to kill her own son? Obviously, she had. That's why he had such a big scar. No wonder he didn't want to talk about it. What would it be like to grow up with a mother who didn't love you? A mother who at some point tried to kill you. She couldn't even imagine it. Her parents were so caring and protective. That explained Victor's hesitance to get involved with her. Well that and the fact he was still in love with Lakeisha. But, was that why he was so complicated and confusing. Why he wanted people to think he was careless and aloof? Was that why she felt like he was fighting his attraction to her? Maybe he struggled with relationships with all women. Probably. How could he possibly overcome something like that? She thought of the incident she'd had as a teen. The emotional baggage had followed her for centuries. She still had nightmares and panic attacks, but they had been strangers. What if it had been someone she knew? Someone that was supposed to love and protect her. Could she ever get over that? Probably not.

There were so many things going through her mind. She'd been deep in thought the entire trip. She looked up and was shocked to see they were at the cave. She also realized it was getting dark. They all went to work setting things up for the night. Luckily there was wood left over from a few nights ago. Thomas was preparing to start the fire. Ariel stepped up and with the flip of her hand the fire was blazing.

Thomas looked over at her. "Thanks," he said smiling. "That kind of comes in handy." He put a pot on the coals and began to heat some stew and water for tea and coffee. "Hey, you've missed two doses of your tea. You went to bed last night before we could make it and then you were gone this morning when everyone else woke up. I think you should have two cups tonight to make up for it."

Ariel smiled at him. "That's fine with me. I feel a little weak and dehydrated, I think I could use a couple of cups. I'll make sure I get another dose in the morning." She crossed her heart with her hand. "I promise."

They were all tired from the long day. Once dinner was over, everyone retired to bed. Ariel was so exhausted. She hadn't slept at all last night and then that bout of hysterical crying wiped her out. On top of everything, they had that fight with the bear and their long hike all day. She closed her eyes and immediately fell asleep.

Victor was beat. Ariel hadn't talked to him at all today. If he had any doubt before about her feelings, he was positive now. Ariel had changed her mind. She didn't want a relationship with him. Realizing that hurt more than he could have imagined. He had finally fallen in love and immediately lost her. For the first time in his life he felt like he understood his father. He understood the betrayal and the pain that kept dad imprisoned on the farm. Victor slowly climbed into his sleeping bag. All his energy was gone. He felt numb and alone. He closed his eyes and eventually drifted off to sleep.

* * * *

Ariel closed the door to her room with a sigh. She was spending the night at her parent's house. She didn't want to, but they had been so happy to see her. She could tell they'd been worried while she'd been gone. They needed her close to assure themselves she was safe. She'd spend one night with them and tomorrow she could escape to the solitude of her own home. She could act like everything was okay for a few more hours before she shut herself off from the world for a while.

Her thoughts drifted back to the long hike through the woods that morning. They'd gotten a late start because both she and Victor slept late. Nobody mentioned it. Abby, Morrigan and Austin had held back a little so they could visit and avoid the tension between her and Victor. Thomas and Lakeisha stuck it out. It was clear they were both uncomfortable and anxious to get home. At one point, Lakeisha maneuvered Ariel to the side. They'd spent over an hour trying to come up with a plan for Lakeisha to improve Victor's standing in the community. Ariel didn't know how to fix things but she agreed to talk to her father once they got back.

When they reached the cabin things got a little better. Dad kept his promise and had an army waiting in case there was trouble. Morrigan's parents, Mason and Jackie, were there with about a dozen pack members. They mostly stayed outside, guarding the yard. Ariel's parents, Oberon and Mara, had spent the last three nights at the cabin with Orin and Breena. All the warriors were there as well. Dimitri and Alex had also been staying at the cabin the past four nights. Alex wouldn't leave until she knew Thomas was safe. Ariel didn't know how they all managed in such a small space with so many people.

One good thing had come out of this. The fae and Morrigan's shifters were now close allies. The stress of the past several days had brought them together. Oberon, Dimitri and Mason seemed to work great together. The three of them had organized a large group under difficult conditions. Everyone there had been prepared for battle. Ariel was glad they hadn't needed the backup, but it was nice to know it was there. All the shifters had left soon after the group had arrived. Ariel suspected they were off to have a private celebration. Mason stayed to participate in a brief discussion with the panther leaders. The panthers were now hesitant allies with the fae, but they were still apprehensive about a long term commitment that aligned them with the shifters. Ariel's thoughts drifted to Radek. She wondered if he knew Hector was dead yet. Part of her hoped so. She knew learning Hector was dead and his prisoners were gone was going to infuriate him. On the other hand, she wanted time before his next attack. She knew they could all use a break.

Ariel stripped off her clothes and climbed into bed. The events of the last few days replayed over and over in her head as she slowly drifted off to sleep.

* * * *

Lakeisha was finally home. Once they reached the bridge, Victor gave her his cell phone so she could call her parents. They were so relieved to hear she was safe. Her father, Cayden, and Ryker's father, Numair, had traveled to the cabin to bring her home. As pack leaders, they thought it would be a good idea to have support when they encountered the shifters. Surprisingly having so many leaders in one place had presented an opportunity to form a semi-alliance with the rest of the group. Both men were grateful for Lakeisha's safe return. They promised to work with the fae and the shifters if Radek attacked again.

Numair had signaled for Ryker to come home as soon as he heard she was safe. That was one advantage to being a panther. The leader could communicate with any member of his pack instantly. It was hard to explain that ability to outsiders. The leader couldn't read his pack's mind, but he could send a message that was always heard by the members of his pack instantly. Lakeisha hoped Ryker would be home when she arrived. As they pulled in the drive, she realized he hadn't made it back yet. She had so much to talk to him about, but that could wait until tomorrow. Tonight, she just wanted time with her husband. She hoped he'd be here soon. She couldn't understand the way Ariel and Victor were behaving. It made her even more grateful for Ryker. Trae was staying with Ryker's parents tonight. Lakeisha had checked in on him on their way home, but he was sleeping so soundly she decided to leave him there until morning. First thing tomorrow she'd talk to Ryker about Victor then they'd go collect their son. Ryker would know how to make things right again. Lakeisha climbed into bed and patiently waited for her husband to arrive.

* * * *

Radek was explosive. He'd already broken every lamp in the room. He was now throwing chairs and knocking things off shelves. Lilith wasn't in the mood to console him. Hector was dead. How was that possible? Now she was stuck with Radek. She'd been playing both men for months, but she honestly thought Radek would be the one to get himself killed. She'd hoped to be Hector's queen forever, not Radek's. He was such a bore and she was so tired of dealing with his tantrums. At least with Hector, the sex had been good. Well, great actually. Radek would kill her if he ever found out she'd been sleeping with Hector, but really Radek was boring.

After Dark

Anyway, vampires weren't supposed to be monogamous. It wasn't the way they were made. Lilith was going to have to find another partner eventually. She'd have to be very careful. Radek was too explosive to make mistakes. She'd wait awhile before taking another man to her bed.

Right now her attention was focused on the fae queen, Alex, and that annoying human. That woman in black was going to pay for throwing that holy water on her. She'd been down in bed for almost a month. She still wasn't back to normal and the deepest scars were going to last the rest of her life. She owed that human. Nobody messed with Lilith and got away with it. She jerked back to attention when Radek flung another chair and almost hit her. He was going to be in a rage for hours. Lilith slipped out the door and headed back to her room. If he questioned her about it, she'd blame it on her wounds. He seemed to be buying that for now. As she walked down the corridor, she thought about Hector. It was inconvenient that he'd gotten himself killed. Now she had to change her plans. Whoever killed him would have to be punished of course. The shifter community was in for a shock. They had no idea what was coming their way. Sure, they rescued their pathetic daughters but they had killed her lover in the process. Lilith's revenge was going to be sweet. She smiled as she entered her room.

* * * *

Victor stopped at the club on his way home. He was sure everything was fine. Jack knew what had to be done and was good at troubleshooting. He was only stopping by for his own peace of mind. It had been a terrible day. He and Ariel still weren't talking. Any doubts he had about their status were eliminated on the long trek home today. She'd verified his worst fears. There was no hope. Ariel didn't want him anymore. He noticed her talking to Lakeisha during part of the day. That made him nervous. They were being secretive and their topic was clearly something serious. He had to trust Lakeisha to keep her word. With their history, it was hard to trust her with anything. But, she'd promised him she wouldn't tell Ariel anything else about his life. Not his family, or his businesses. He hoped she'd keep her word. If Ariel didn't want him in her life, she didn't need to know anything about him.

He walked through the back door and into his office at Bojan Taverns. This was home. He was grateful Dimitri agreed to give him some time off. Hector was dead and Victor needed to focus some energy on his businesses. The club should be covered, but he would need to do paperwork at Tèarmann. He'd go there tomorrow and check in. He had a good staff. He was lucky that way. Both places practically ran themselves in his absence. He looked around the room, but didn't see anything pressing. He walked into the club and checked in with Rocky. Apparently things had been going smooth in his absence. No surprises. He left a message for Jack to call him and headed to his apartment.

* * * *

Ariel picked up the phone and groggily said hello.

It was Alex. "Hey, are you still in bed?" she asked. It was past noon.

"Yes," Ariel barked. "I got a little drunk last night. What do you need?"

"I'm coming to get you," Alex told her. "I'll be there in two hours. That should give you plenty of time to shower and get dressed. Drink plenty of coffee. You're grumpy enough without the hang-over."

"I don't want to go anywhere," Ariel argued. "So, don't bother coming by."

"You've been locked up in your house alone for over a week now. I'll be there in two hours, Ariel. I suggest you shower because we are going out. I'm taking you to lunch and then we're going shopping. I've been patient with you long enough. Get up, get showered and get dressed." Alex hung up the phone and turned to Dimitri. "She drank herself silly last night. I can tell she's got a hangover. It's certainly going to be a pleasant day," Alex moaned.

Dimitri laughed. "I'm sure you'll survive," he pulled her onto his lap. "You handled her very well. She'll be ready when you get there. So, did I hear you say you have two hours?" He gave her a sly grin. "I'm free right now. How about a swim?"

"Sure, I always love your creative water games." She laughed as Dimitri stood up and carried her to the pool.

* * * *

Alex and Ariel were sitting in the corner of the small deli. Ariel still looked awful. She'd showered and dressed, but Alex could tell she'd lost weight and she was miserable. "Why don't you just go by and see him?" Alex asked. "Unless you talk to him, you're not going to know if Lakeisha was right." Ariel had filled Alex in on most of the trip.

"I can't," Ariel confessed. "If he wanted to see me, he would have called by now. I haven't heard a word from him. He must have realized he's still in love with Lakeisha but he can't have her because she's married to the father of her child. Why would he want to see me? You saw her, she's beautiful. Victor doesn't need to settle when he can have someone as gorgeous as Lakeisha."

"First of all, Lakeisha is beautiful but so are you. Did I tell you the first time I saw you, I thought the same thing? I figured I didn't have a chance with Dimitri with you around. You can imagine my relief when I found out your relationship was strictly platonic," she paused and smiled. "You reminded me of a super model," Alex confessed.

Ariel laughed. "That's funny. It's the exact same thing I thought about Lakeisha. She doesn't have a flaw. Her complexion, her figure, everything is perfect."

"So are you," Alex paused. "Well, you were until you stopped eating. Finish that sandwich," she pointed to Ariel's plate. "I still can't believe Lakeisha married her lover after the problems she caused with the council. How could she let Victor suffer all this time? Maybe it makes me a bad person, but I'm glad you knocked her out. She deserved it," Alex smiled. "I just wish I'd been there to see it," she paused. "Oh, that's the human talking, not the queen of course."

"I'm pretty sure that didn't win me any points with Victor. He still seemed angry about it when I left the cabin." She took a bite of her sandwich. She wasn't hungry, but she knew Alex wasn't going to let her get out of this deli until her food was gone. "It's hopeless, Alex. I finally fell in love and I lost him after just a few days."

After Dark

They sat in silence while they finished their lunch. "Well," Alex finally said. "I'm stuffed. Are you ready to shop? That little boutique down the road has a sale today. I want to see if I can find some new shoes to go with that awesome red dress I just bought. If I'm lucky, I'll find a matching bag."

Ariel laughed. "You and your shoes. Do you even know how many pairs you own?"

"Nope. But you can't have too many shoes," Alex said enthusiastically. "Once we're finished there, I thought we could cut across the park and hit the shops on Broadway. Ready?" She dropped some cash on the table. "It's my treat, I forced you today."

"I'm ready. Let's go," Ariel stood and headed for the door.

They were in and out of the boutique pretty quickly. Alex found her shoes and was out the door. They were strolling through Central Park when Ariel heard Victor's voice. She grabbed Alex's arm and pulled her onto a nearby bench. They couldn't see Victor, but his voice was coming through loud and clear. It sounded like he was lecturing a child. It soon became obvious the boy had stolen a wallet from a tourist. Victor demanded the kid take him to his parents. The boy was making excuses. Victor gave the kid a choice between his parents or the police. The child finally relented and chose his parents. Ariel still didn't know where Victor was. She and Alex scanned the park. He finally appeared out of a stand of trees with a young boy in tow. The child hesitantly approached a woman sitting by the lake. She was wearing large glasses and a hat that was lowered to cover most of her face.

Ariel and Alex could no longer hear what Victor was saying. He unexpectedly sat down next to the woman. She hesitantly removed the hat and glasses to reveal a huge black eye. The whole side of her face was swollen and looked sore. Victor brushed her hair away from her face and then ran a finger across the bruising. He was still talking to her. Ariel thought he was either asking her questions or comforting her. The woman began to cry. He wrapped his arm around her and held her while she wept. He was still speaking quietly as she sobbed into his chest. Eventually she regained her composure. After a short time he stood and held out a hand. The boy took his mother's hand and the three of them began to walk out of the park.

Ariel was shocked, but Alex was curious. Where was Victor taking these two? Surely they weren't going to the police. Victor wasn't angry anymore. He was gentle and caring with this woman. She was a stranger to him, but somehow Ariel knew Victor was going to help her. She was struggling with what she just witnessed. She turned to Alex. "This might sound strange, but he's acting the same way with this woman as he acted with Lakeisha in the cave. It's obvious she's been abused. She was probably beat up by her husband or a boyfriend. Victor couldn't know her, but his actions and demeanor were so loving and gentle." She glanced at Alex. Ariel was confused. Had she been wrong about Victor's feelings for Lakeisha?

Alex hesitated. "Have you ever stopped to consider the possibility that Victor is just a kind hearted soul?" She glanced at Ariel. "Maybe he just has compassion for those in need. I know he tries to act tough and thick skinned, but deep down I think he's extremely soft hearted and vulnerable. Maybe you misinterpreted what was going on in that cave." Alex knew she was right, but she had to be subtle. Ariel had to think she'd figured this out on her own. "Maybe you should take some time to re-evaluate what you thought you saw."

After Dark

They left the park as they followed Victor and his two new friends. After a few turns they finally ended up in front of Lavena Tèarmann. It was a shelter for women and children. Victor escorted the small family to the side of the building. He pulled out a key, opened the door then slid inside. Alex and Ariel looked at each other, confused. How was Victor associated with this shelter? Alex was going to find out. She'd been trying to talk Thomas into holding a charity event for the women's shelter for the last several months. So far, Thomas was resisting. He kept putting her off but his excuses were getting weak. Maybe Victor had an in and could help introduce her to the right person to make her event a reality.

They spotted a coffee shop across the street. "Let's sit out there and see what happens when he comes out," Ariel suggested.

Alex and Ariel were discussing this new development over coffee when Victor left from the same side door, minus the woman and child. They were both throwing out ideas, trying to figure out what his connection was to the place. "I've been wanting to host a charity event for this shelter anyway. Let's just walk over there and do some subtle investigating," Alex suggested.

"I'm game," Ariel agreed. "You'll have to do most of the talking though. I don't know much about hosting a charity event."

They finished their coffee and casually strolled across the street.

Hours later the two friends sat in the library at Alex's house waiting for Dimitri to arrive. Ariel had a few questions for him. He had to know Victor's secret. The door opened and Dimitri strolled in. "Hey," Dimitri greeted Ariel as he pulled Alex in for a quick kiss. "It's good to see you out and among the living."

"Very funny," Ariel snorted. "I have some questions for you. Do you have a minute?"

Dimitri looked to Alex in question. She wasn't giving him any clues. "Sure," he walked to the bar and poured himself a glass of wine. "You want anything?" he asked.

"No thanks," Ariel scrunched up her nose. She'd had more than enough the night before.

"So, what did you want to talk about?" Dimitri sat in the big chair.

"Victor and Lavena Tèarmann." She thought the direct approach would be best.

Dimitri looked surprised, then resigned. "How did you find out about Lavena Tèarmann?" He asked.

Alex broke in and explained what happened in the park.

"So, let me get this straight. The two of you saw Victor helping an abused, helpless woman and her young son and decided to spy on him? Then, you see him take this woman, who obviously needs help, into a woman's shelter and you get suspicious? Then you actually go inside to investigate? Don't you think that was a little rude and inappropriate?" he asked.

"No," Alex answered. "Not at all. At first we were curious. Then, I wanted to know if Victor was associated with the shelter or had a friend there. You know I've been trying to set up a charity event for the shelter. As I recall, you've been just as standoffish and evasive about it as Thomas. Why is it such a big secret?"

"Victor wants it that way," Dimitri stated simply.

After Dark

"Why?" Alex asked. "It's such a good thing he's doing. Why would he want it to be a big secret?"

"I'm not sure. It doesn't really matter though. That's the way Victor wants it so we respect his privacy," he paused. "Something the two of you should try for a change."

Ariel stood and walked to the window. Is that what Lakeisha had almost told her? What Victor was so angry about? What was it Lakeisha said? Victor's mother tried to kill him. Maybe that's why he opened...was she going to say Lavena Tèarmann? She stood quietly contemplating this new information. Chances were pretty good that his mother hadn't just decided to kill him one day. How long had she abused him prior to that horrible incident? It would make sense for Victor to open a shelter for women and children if he had come from an abusive background. Maybe he was providing these victims a sanctuary because he didn't have one himself. She turned back around and realized Alex and Dimitri were watching her.

"You okay?" Dimitri asked.

"Yeah. I'm fine," she said trying to sound casual. She walked back over to her chair and sat down. "You two finished arguing?" she countered.

"We weren't exactly arguing," Dimitri smiled. "That's just what happens when I don't agree with everything Alex says. She gets a little testy that way." Alex was perched on the arm of his chair. Dimitri gave her a subtle yank and pulled her onto his lap. Then, he leaned over and gave her a quick but loving kiss.

Ariel wondered if they knew how lucky they were to have each other, to love each other so completely. They were blessed to know

192

the person they loved, loved them back unconditionally. "Alex, what are you going to do with this knowledge about Victor and his shelter?" She was beginning to think they should just leave it alone. Pretend they didn't know.

"Nothing for now," Alex admitted. "I still want to have a charity ball and donate the proceeds to Lavena Tèarmann. I think it's a really good cause. I thought so before I knew it belonged to Victor. Now I'm even more passionate about it. I may just have my event and send them a check. You know, leave Victor and the shelter out of the loop completely?" She smiled at Dimitri. "That way, everyone gets what they want."

Ariel grinned. Alex never did back down when she thought she was right. It was a good quality in a queen. They were lucky to have her.

Dimitri cleared his throat. "So Ariel," he paused. "What are you going to do about Victor?" he asked.

"What do you mean?" she said defensively. "There's nothing to do."

Alex broke in. "I don't think you should let him get away with avoiding you. The two of you need to talk things out. In light of everything we discovered today I'm not sure you interpreted the situation correctly. Chances are, he also misjudged what has been going on."

"Look," Ariel began, "I understand the two of you are madly in love and you want the whole world to be as happy as you are. It's different with me and Victor. I have baggage, so does he. Things could never be as simple as it is for the two of you."

After Dark

"First of all, it wasn't exactly simple for me and Alex. We had some things to overcome before we got to where we are today. Relationships take work and courage." He smiled at Alex, grateful they had talked things out instead of splitting apart like Victor and Ariel were doing.

"Are you saying I'm a coward?" Ariel asked. "Because I recall telling you that a short time ago and you disagreed."

"Is that what this is about? Does your past have anything to do with your behavior toward Victor?" Dimitri was serious now.

Alex noticed the shift. She had no idea what Dimitri was talking about, but she thought it would be best to give him some space and let him pursue this topic. She stood and moved to the chair adjacent to his.

Ariel glared at him. Was he actually going to bring that up in front of Alex? Had Dimitri already told Alex about her past? Ariel had recently decided to tell Alex the story, but Dimitri didn't have the right to share something so personal without talking to her first. She looked over at Alex, wondering if her face would reveal anything.

"No," Dimitri stated flatly. "I haven't told her anything. It's not my secret to share."

Ariel was relieved. But how could they have this conversation with Alex in the room? She didn't know what they were talking about. She looked back at Alex. There was no indication this was a problem for her.

"Please tell me you're not angry with Victor over what happened to you in that cave. You didn't panic. You pulled yourself out of it," Dimitri continued.

"How do you know that?" Ariel asked truly perplexed.

"Thomas," Dimitri said simply.

"What does Thomas know?" Ariel asked.

"As far as I know, nothing. Not specifics anyway. However, he was the one that came to your aid that night in the safe room. He also saw your reaction once you stepped into that room. He said you went ghostly white when you saw Abby chained to the wall. He was starting to get concerned when you snapped out of it. So, answer my question. Please tell me you're not being that unfair to Victor. That you aren't angry with him for leaving your side to give aid to Lakeisha."

"Of course not," Ariel answered.

But Dimitri saw the hesitation, so he pressed on. "Good. I'd be disappointed in you if you were angry with him for something that was completely out of his control. It would be extremely unfair to hold something like that against Victor. I was afraid when you reached for him and he wasn't there, you jumped to the wrong conclusion. In your panicked state, you needed comfort and he was across the room comforting Lakeisha. It would be like you to assume he had abandoned you for her. I know you pretty well, I can't tell you what a relief it is to hear I was wrong. I assume you haven't told him anything about your past," he questioned.

Ariel glanced at Alex again. She still hadn't said anything. She was just sitting there quietly allowing her and Dimitri to continue this cryptic conversation. "No. Why would I tell him about that?" Ariel countered.

"Oh I don't know, because you care about each other. Because if you're going to try to have a relationship, it's something he should be aware of. Because if he had known about your past, if he was aware of how small dark spaces remind you of that terrible incident, he would have been standing by your side giving you strength and helping you deal with the trauma of seeing Abby chained to that wall. Instead, he went in blind. Victor has only seen you strong and courageous. When he walked into that room, the thought never would have crossed his mind to check on you to make sure you were okay. He didn't know there was any possibility you wouldn't be. All he saw was someone he once cared about chained to a wall, cold and weak and scared. Being Victor, he didn't have a choice. It's not in him to do anything other than what he did. If you don't understand that, you don't know Victor very well," Dimitri paused. He glanced at Alex. He'd figure out what to tell her later. This was too important. He couldn't let the opportunity pass him by.

Ariel was shocked. Did Dimitri think this was all her fault? That she was being unfair to Victor. Had she been? She had to admit she was hurt when she saw him tending to Lakeisha. She'd done exactly what Dimitri had suggested. She had needed Victor and he wasn't there for her. She'd expected the impossible. Dimitri was right, Victor couldn't have known she'd be upset by the scene in that room. Yet, she'd felt betrayed when he comforted Lakeisha instead of her.

"So," Dimitri continued. "This is all because Victor didn't respond to Lakeisha the way you would have? The way you think he should have?"

"What do you mean by that?" Ariel asked.

"Well, you can correct me if I'm wrong but here's what I think happened in that room. The group of you walked in. You have flashes back to your past. Somehow you overcome them and realize Victor is helping Lakeisha. He's comforting her. Trying to calm her down and assure her that you guys won't leave without her. Being you, this makes you angry. You think Victor should be upset with Lakeisha. He shouldn't be comforting her, he should be arguing with her. Demanding an apology or an explanation. How could she have done those terrible things to him? After all, she cheated on him, got pregnant and then blamed him for her indiscretion. Victor was punished for something he was completely innocent of. He should be irate. You would have been furious. So, because Victor didn't respond the way you would have, you can't forgive him. You got angry. Angry at Lakeisha for causing Victor pain. So angry you knocked her out the first time you had the chance. But also angry at Victor. When he didn't respond the way you expected him to, you concocted some ridiculous fantasy that he's still in love with the girl that ruined his life.

Ariel, if you can't love Victor for who he is, you don't deserve him. If you're angry at him for caring about the wellbeing of another person, regardless of who that person is, the two of you don't belong together. Victor's compassion is what makes him the man that he is. I doubt I have as much goodness in my entire body as he has in his little finger. If he has to change for you, if he has to lose his compassion for you to love him, you don't deserve him."

Why was Dimitri being so hard on her? She hadn't expected this reaction from him. She thought he would be supportive. She expected him to comfort her. Instead, he was taking Victor's side. Twisting this around and making it sound like she was the one being unreasonable. Was she? If she was honest with herself, everything Dimitri had said was the truth. She was angry with Victor. How could he forgive Lakeisha so easily? How could he care about her so much when she had caused him so much pain? Was she trying to change who Victor was? Was she giving up on him because he hadn't reacted the way she thought he should have? She didn't know. She thought again about the things Lakeisha had told her. Was it possible this was all a misunderstanding and she was wrong about everything? But Victor was angry with her. She knew he was upset that she'd punched Lakeisha in the face. But there was something else, too. Did it have to do with his mother?

"What are you thinking so hard about, Ariel?" Alex asked. "What's troubling you?"

She turned to Alex. She sounded so concerned. After everything that had just been said between her and Dimitri, Alex wasn't even going to ask for an explanation. She was fine with being left in the dark. "I was thinking about something Lakeisha said to me. I was also thinking at least part of what Dimitri said was true. I have been angry with Victor for how he handled things in the cave." She glanced over at Dimitri. "I'm going to have to think about that and decide how much of what you said was true, but at least part of it is right on," she paused. "But Victor is also angry with me. I know he's upset because I hit Lakeisha, but I think there's something else. He walked in on a conversation Lakeisha and I was having. She told me something that was supposed to be a secret. I think she was also about to tell me about Lavena Tèarmann. He was furious with her. I don't know if it was for what she was about to tell me, that he opened the shelter, or if it was because of what she did tell me." She looked over at Dimitri. "Is he that sensitive about the shelter?"

"He's pretty sensitive about the shelter. But I don't know what else Lakeisha told you. It's hard for me to have an opinion with the information you've provided. However, I don't think Victor would be angry with you because Lakeisha told you his secrets. How could he blame you for that?"

"I don't know," Ariel confessed. "I just know he is angry with me. I thought it was for punching the woman he loved, but if I'm wrong about that, why is he so mad at me?" She stood again and walked to the window. Should she tell them about Victor's mother? She knew she could trust them. Dimitri had kept her secret for hundreds of years. She hadn't known Alex very long, but she trusted her. Maybe they should know. Maybe Dimitri already knew. She turned back and took a deep breath. "I'm going to tell you something that can't leave this room," she paused to look at each of them. "Dimitri, you may already know. I don't know. You are good at keeping secrets and I'm sure you would keep this one if Victor confided in you."

Dimitri nodded. He would. He would keep anything Victor told him in confidence to himself.

"Lakeisha and I were talking. She didn't understand our community. She thought that once Victor finished his year suspension, everything would go back to the way it was before. She thought the community would embrace him. They would feel he served his time and accept him back into the fold so to speak."

"That's a little naive," Dimitri muttered.

Ariel smiled. "Yeah, I told her that. I explained what Victor has been going through the past five years. I also told her he'll probably be ostracized for a long time, forever by some members of the community. She was horrified. She started to go on about how she'd ruined his life. How she had to fix things. By the way, I think her and her husband might want to have a meeting with the two of you and my father. Are you willing to talk to them? I need to know what to tell her if she calls. She was pretty adamant that she and Ryker, that's her husband, had to do something to help Victor."

"Of course," Alex answered for both of them. Dimitri nodded in approval.

"Anyway, during this rant she said something about Victor's mother. I didn't understand, so I asked her to explain," Ariel continued.

Dimitri stiffened. If Lakeisha had told a secret about Victor's mother, no wonder he was angry. For Victor, that would be a worse betrayal on Lakeisha's part than cheating on him with another man. Alex would keep the secret, he was sure of it. But once Ariel left, he'd have to fill her in on a couple things and make sure she knew how big of a secret this really was.

"Lakeisha was surprised I didn't know. She was also frustrated with Victor for keeping it from me. She said Victor's mother tried to kill him. Then she said something like I always wondered if that's why he opened the... but she didn't get a chance to finish. Victor interrupted. He told her she didn't have a right to share that information with anyone. Victor hasn't spoken to me since. Actually, he didn't speak to me that day. His whole conversation was directed at Lakeisha. To be honest, he hasn't spoken to me since we were in that cave, rescuing Lakeisha and Abby," she looked to Dimitri. She was going to ask him what he thought, but she was surprised at the look on his face. "You know something else, don't you?" she asked.

"Yes," Dimitri answered. "But it's not anything I can share. Someone took me into their confidence and shared some information with me. I can't betray that confidence. I hope you understand that."

"Of course." She did, but she really wanted to know what Dimitri was so upset about. She wanted to know anything that had to do with Victor. "You've kept my secret all this time. I don't expect you to share someone else's secret with me," she turned to Alex. "Speaking of my secret, I already decided to tell you about that incident someday. I trust you and I have no problem with you knowing what happened to me. I know you won't tell anybody once you know. I just haven't felt up to reliving that awful time again. I've had plenty of flashbacks the past few weeks," she turned to Dimitri. "I'd like it if you would fill Alex in. Tell her the story. Then if you have questions," she turned back to Alex, "you can ask me personally." She looked at Dimitri again. "If you're willing that is. It would really help me. It would save me from living the nightmare again. I have enough to deal with right now. Alex has been very patient with both of us today. She deserves to know what all the cryptic conversation was about," she smiled at Alex.

"No. I don't deserve to know," Alex protested. "If you want me to know, that's one thing but don't have Dimitri tell me anything just because you think I'm curious or because I overheard the two of you. I don't need to know anything until you are comfortable with me having that knowledge," she insisted.

"I know," Ariel said, touched by Alex's understanding. "But like I said, I already decided to tell you. I was just waiting for things to settle. I was waiting until I felt better about everything that's going on. If Dimitri is willing to do the hard part for me, I can talk to you about it all later." She looked to Dimitri in question.

"I'll talk to her." He walked over and pulled Ariel into his arms. "Don't get too mad at me for what I said about you and Victor. I strongly felt you needed to hear it. I hope you'll think about what I said. Think about your actions, not just Victor's. Very rarely is one person to blame for the entire situation. From where I'm sitting both of you are at fault. Both of you reacted based on your individual experiences, bad experiences, and jumped to conclusions. I believe they were wrong conclusions. I also think the two of you could work this out, but it has to be important enough," Dimitri paused. "You have to decide if you love Victor enough to overcome his ghosts. You have some ghosts of your own, but I think Victors are bigger and darker. He needs someone strong enough to stand by his side, even when he pushes them away." He kissed her forehead and released her. "If that's not you, if you can't be that person, please back out now. He doesn't need any more heartbreak in his life."

Ariel nodded. "I understand," she gave Alex a hug. "Thanks for everything. I'm beat and I have a lot to think about. I'm going to head home," she turned to leave. "I'll talk to both of you later. Thanks for being there for me, even when I tried to push you away." She smiled at them and walked out of the room.

Dimitri sat in silence for a long moment. Then he turned to Alex, took her hand and began to fill her in on Ariel's past.

Chapter Seven

Two days later, Ariel was still confused about the situation with Victor. She'd gone over everything in her mind a million times. She could admit Dimitri had been right. He was actually right about everything. She had been angry with Victor for abandoning her to comfort Lakeisha. The thought hadn't even crossed her mind that he was oblivious to her distress. She expected the impossible and was disappointed. Big surprise. He was also right about the rest. She was upset because Victor hadn't been angry with Lakeisha. She realized she was angry with him for the very thing that had made her fall in love with him in the first place. She admired his kindness and his selflessness. If you added the whole community together, Ariel didn't think the kindness or goodness found in their whole society would balance even a fraction of Victor's character. He was a better person than she was, she knew that for sure.

After Dark

She had also come to realize that if Victor had behaved the way she thought he should have, she would have been disappointed in him. If he had gone into that cave, saw Lakeisha chained to that wall and railed on her about their past, or worse left her there for Ariel or Thomas to deal with, a piece of the love and respect she had for him would have died. She wasn't angry with Victor anymore. She just wanted him back. But Dimitri's request kept haunting her. Victor had suffered enough. It was going to have to be all or nothing. She was still trying to figure out if she could give him her all. Did she love him enough to battle his demons? She thought about Alex and Dimitri. If Victor loved her too, she thought she was up for the challenge. That was the problem, she didn't know how Victor felt. She'd never been insecure, but she felt that way when it came to Victor. She didn't know if she was good enough for him.

The phone rang and interrupted her thoughts. "Hello," she said without even looking at the caller ID. She glanced at the clock, it was only ten.

"Hi," a voice answered on the other end. "It's Lakeisha. I hope you're still okay with me calling," she said hesitantly. It had been longer than she planned, but she still wanted to make things right.

"Sure. I'd basically given up on you though. I thought you changed your mind," Ariel confessed. "Have you?" she asked.

"No," Lakeisha answered quickly. "Ryker and I have discussed this thoroughly. We want to do the right thing. The problem is with our packs. They're worried if we come clean, it's going to cause complications with our communities. They don't think right now is the best time to confess. The leaders are worried about Radek and how he's going to react to Hector's death and our escape. His plan was foiled. He has to be furious."

"So, they think if you talk to my father, Dimitri and Alex the fae community is going to turn against them?" Ariel asked, slightly offended.

"They do. We don't," Lakeisha admitted. "Ryker and I have decided to ignore the guidance of the leaders and set up a meeting if you're still willing to help. We will accept any punishment they want to give us. We just ask that they don't punish our people because we made a mistake. Do you think they will promise us that? Will they keep the alliance they formed at the cabin if Ryker and I admit to our crimes?"

Well, this was a strange twist. She couldn't make promises for her father or the others, but she was pretty sure they wouldn't take anything out on the were-panthers. To begin with, this was about clearing Victor's name, not punishing Lakeisha and Ryker. "I can't make any promises for the queen or the others, but I really don't think you have anything to worry about. My father wouldn't punish your people for something that happened a long time ago. Something that you and Ryker did to one of ours. For that matter, neither would Alex nor Dimitri. When do you want me to set up the meeting?"

"Our schedule is free. The sooner the better. This has gone on long enough. We want to get the ball rolling. How is Victor?" she asked hesitantly.

Ariel took a deep breath. "I really don't know," she admitted. "I haven't seen him since we left the woods."

After Dark

Lakeisha was quiet for a long time. Ariel wondered what she was thinking. She was just about to tell her goodbye when Lakeisha spoke. "I know I don't have the right to ask you this and I think I already know the answer, but do you love him Ariel?"

Ariel hesitated. No, Lakeisha didn't have the right to ask but she wasn't ashamed of her feelings, so she would answer anyway. "Yes I love him," Ariel confessed.

"Have you told him?" Lakeisha questioned.

"No," Ariel answered. "I don't think I'm ready for him to know that yet."

"I don't understand. Why not? What possible reason could you have for keeping something that important from Victor?" Lakeisha asked.

"I don't know if I love him enough," she admitted.

Lakeisha was confused. "What do you mean by that?"

"I have to love him enough to help him fight his demons. Before I let him know how I feel, I need to have enough confidence in myself and my strength to know I won't let him down. I won't abandon him for any reason, not even if he tries to push me away. I have to love him enough to know I won't hurt him even if he hurts me. I'm just not sure I'm good enough or strong enough to stand by his side. If I'm not, it's better for him if he doesn't know how I feel," Ariel confessed. Why was she telling all this to Lakeisha? She hadn't even talked to Dimitri or Alex yet. It was too personal.

Lakeisha took a deep breath. Ariel really was perfect for Victor. She just hadn't figured it out yet. "Well I think that's your answer," she finally acknowledged.

"What's my answer?" Ariel asked.

"If you weren't good enough, strong enough and didn't love him enough. None of those things would matter to you. The fact you are struggling with those very things tells me you are the perfect woman for Victor. You are probably the only woman strong enough to break through his defenses. Victor is complicated and you are right, once things get too serious or too scary for him, he'll probably try to push you away. You won't tolerate that though and you shouldn't. He'll need you to stand up to him. You know you love him. Now you just have to love yourself enough to believe he could love you too. For what it's worth, I know he loves you. Have a little faith Ariel and believe in yourself. If you do, the two of you could have a great life together. I know it."

Tears were swimming in Ariel's eyes. How did this woman, a woman she had just met, know exactly what Ariel was struggling with? She was insecure. Her baggage made Ariel feel undesirable. She wondered if Victor would really love her if he found out she was weak. If he knew she had a hard time dealing with her past. If he did love her, he loved her for the woman he thought she was not the woman she really was. Could he love her enough to help her deal with her baggage, too? Was she worth the trouble? How had Lakeisha known Ariel didn't believe in herself?

"Ariel, are you still there?" Lakeisha asked.

"Yeah," Ariel wiped away a tear. "You just struck a nerve," she admitted.

After Dark

Lakeisha paused. "I'm sorry. We don't know each other well enough for me to give you a lecture. I only wanted to help. I hope I haven't offended you again."

"Oh," Ariel said in surprise, "that's not what I meant. Of course you didn't offend me. I think you know me better than you think though. You also know Victor very well. Thank you for your encouragement. I was just surprised by how insightful you are. I have been feeling a little inadequate and vulnerable. Maybe I'm supposed to. Maybe two people should be vulnerable if they want to try to have a life together. Anyway, I'll call my father and Dimitri and get back to you. I'm sure they can schedule something in the next couple days."

"Thank you," Lakeisha said sincerely. "And Ariel, I know the two of us didn't get off to a very good start but if you ever need someone to talk to, you know where to find me."

"Thanks, I'll think about it. Will you be home for a while? I'll call you back as soon as I have a date and time."

"I'll be here. Talk to you soon," Lakeisha hung up.

Later that afternoon, Ariel was sitting in the back seat of Ryker and Lakeisha's car. They were nervous about the meeting, so Ariel agreed to go with them and make introductions. Lakeisha had met everyone at the cabin, but she was still terrified. Ariel saw Lakeisha grip Ryker's hand. She was shaking. Why were they so nervous about this? She decided to ask. "You two are as jumpy as a cat on a tin roof. What gives?"

Ryker answered first. "We are worried about our punishment. We have a son. I know it's asking a lot, but we just hope your people will take that into consideration. It would be extremely hard on him if our punishment took both his parents away from him."

Lakeisha jumped in. "We will accept anything your leaders see fit to impose. We committed the crimes against Victor, we will accept the consequences. It will just be a lot more difficult if Trae also has to suffer for our actions."

Ariel was shocked. These two thought they were going to be punished? Ariel didn't think that was even possible. They weren't part of the community. They didn't fall under fae law. If there was going to be a punishment, it would have to come from their pack leaders. Ariel was pretty sure of that. She'd never heard of anyone outside their community being punished by the council. "Um, I can't say for sure but I don't think our community can punish you for your actions. We'll ask my father when we get there, but that's not what this meeting is about. It's about getting the truth to the right people so they can help clear Victor's name. I don't think this is about you guys," Ariel winced. That sounded kind of rude.

Lakeisha turned to her. "I hope you're right. But whatever they decide, we will honor their decision. I am the one that caused this. I will accept the consequences for my actions no matter how hard it might be." Ryker gave her hand a gentle squeeze.

"We will accept the consequences," he glanced at his wife. "We're both at fault. I never should have let Victor get punished for my indiscretion."

Ariel glanced up. "We're here. Just pull into that gate right there. It looks like my father's already arrived. Take a couple deep breaths and calm down. They are all good, fair people. They're not going to make this harder on you than it needs to be." The car had come to a stop, so she stepped out of the back seat.

After Dark

Ariel walked to the door and waited for Lakeisha and Ryker. She rang the bell then walked in, they were expected after all. Ariel didn't want to make the two panthers wait longer than necessary. They were a nervous wreck as it was. She assumed everyone was in the library, so she headed that way. Alex stepped through the doorway. "Ariel," she said taking her hands and kissing her gently on the cheek. "Hello again, Lakeisha." She walked toward them. "And this must be Ryker. Welcome to our home," she said as she held out her hand.

"Thank you," Ryker and Lakeisha answered at once.

"We're going to do this in the library. It's the most comfortable room we have, and it has enough seating for everyone." Alex turned and headed for the library expecting the rest to follow.

Ariel took time to reacquaint Lakeisha and introduce Ryker to her father and Dimitri. Then she suggested the two would be most comfortable on the couch. That way they could sit together and lean on each other for comfort. Lakeisha smiled at her in gratitude. "Thank you," she whispered as Ariel walked toward her father.

"Dad," Ariel leaned in and whispered softly. "They are extremely nervous and they think you are going to punish them. They're worried about their son. Be gentle." She smiled and started to leave the room.

"Oh," Lakeisha called out. "Ariel, we were hoping you wouldn't mind staying. You already know most of this, but we would like you to hear it all."

Ariel looked to her father in question. This was unusual. Typically a civilian wasn't allowed in this type of proceeding.

Oberon nodded his approval and turned to Alex. "I'm comfortable with the arrangements if you are my Queen."

Alex rolled her eyes. "I'm comfortable with Ariel staying." She narrowed her eyes at Oberon. "I'm not comfortable with your formality. I've told you a million times, just call me Alex. The 'my queen' stuff makes me feel ridiculous. Please sit, both of you." She motioned to Ariel and Oberon and then to two of the chairs. Alex saw Dimitri grinning out of the corner of her eye. He would pay for that later.

Lakeisha did most of the talking at first. She basically told them the same story she had shared with Ariel in the forest. She confessed to having an affair with Ryker while she was still seeing Victor. She had slept with both Victor and Ryker within days of each other, lending credibility to her claim she wasn't positive at first who the father was. She also admitted to lying to the council. She had told them she was certain Victor was the father even though she really didn't know which man was the father of her child.

Dimitri stopped her at that point. "Just so I'm clear, did Victor or Ryker ever use any kind of protection when you were intimate?"

"No," Lakeisha admitted.

"Never?" Dimitri pressed.

"No," Lakeisha said again. Wondering about the question.

Oberon stepped in. "You were seeing Victor for several months. I would assume you were intimate during most of that time. Didn't you ever talk about protection or how you were going to make sure you didn't get pregnant?" he asked.

Lakeisha thought about it. They never had talked about protection. Why hadn't she got pregnant with Victor? She was sheltered and hadn't even considered birth control until she realized she was pregnant. Then she scolded herself for being so stupid. She took a deep breath. "No, we never talked about it. I know I was old enough to know better, but I really was naive. Victor never brought up the subject of birth control and to be honest, I never thought about it. I never considered the possibility I could get pregnant until I started having symptoms. Believe me, that afternoon standing in my bathroom looking at a positive pregnancy test, I scolded myself over and over for being so stupid. I don't know why I never got pregnant with Victor. Now that I think about it, that's strange. As many times as we...well, uh...I should have." She looked at Ariel in question. "Why didn't I?"

Ariel wasn't going to answer that. If Victor never told Lakeisha he had a vasectomy, it wasn't Ariel's place to fill her in. Plus, she'd promised Victor she wouldn't tell her father about the things they talked about that day in the forest. She wasn't going to break that promise for anything or anyone. She shrugged and hoped Lakeisha didn't press her further.

Oberon and Dimitri looked at each other for a few moments. "I think you will have to ask Victor to explain if you really want an answer to that question," Oberon finally answered. "Nobody in this room is in a position to speculate."

Ryker put an arm around Lakeisha in support. "I'll take up where Lakeisha left off if that's all right," he requested.

"Okay," Oberon agreed.

"After the council meeting Lakeisha went back to her pack. Her father didn't let on, but he didn't believe her. Cayden and

Lakeisha's mother, Tilly, had met Victor several times. They believed him to be an honorable man. Cayden couldn't believe Victor would father a child and then abandon Lakeisha and her baby; his baby. We didn't know it at the time, but he ordered her brother, Corbin, to follow Lakeisha whenever she left camp." He paused and looked at Lakeisha. "I guess we were both naive. Anyway, Lakeisha and I were in love. We couldn't stay away from each other. One day, about four months after the council meeting, Corbin caught the two of us together. We had gone into the forest and were having a picnic in a meadow."

Lakeisha took up the story. "Corbin ran home and got my father. My uncle Scott, the pack leader at the time, followed them back into the forest. The three of them marched into the meadow and basically caught us red handed. We were right in the middle of a very passionate kiss," Lakeisha blushed.

Oberon smiled inwardly. This woman was so innocent and naive. No wonder she'd gotten herself into this mess.

"They demanded an explanation," Ryker added. "I think Cayden had already figured it out. He didn't seem angry, just disappointed. His brother, Scott, on the other hand was furious. He grabbed me by the shirt and marched me back to camp. I was sure he was going to kill me. Our packs had been feuding for centuries. Instead he called my father, who was our pack leader and basically arranged a trial for us both.

The leaders from my pack and the leaders from Lakeisha's pack ordered us to tell our story. We confessed to everything. They decided to hold off on deciding a punishment until the baby was born. My pack was taking the position that if the child was Victor's, I hadn't committed a crime. If it was mine, a punishment would be decided. Two months later Trae was born. It was evident from the beginning he was a pure blooded panther. He was mine. There was no doubt, a pure blood can shift basically from birth. If he had been half warrior, he wouldn't have been able to shift until his teen years. Plus, he would have had some of the warrior traits. He didn't. He was mine."

Lakeisha took over the story. "The leaders reconvened to determine our fate. I was so terrified they were going to harm my baby. He was innocent, but the feud had been going on so long. I could handle any punishment except the death of my child. Ryker's pack and my pack discussed the situation for a long time. Ultimately, they decided Ryker and I would have to suffer the same punishment we inflicted on Victor. We would each have to be banished from the pack for an entire year. We had a choice, we could be banished separately, one at a time or we could leave together and be isolated for two years. We chose two years," Lakeisha paused. She had tears in her eyes. "I was so grateful. The punishment was going to be difficult, but I could handle it. They weren't going to take my baby."

Ryker held Lakeisha a little tighter. "Once we made our choice, the pack leaders wanted to know my intentions. Did I plan to marry Lakeisha and accept responsibility for our child? Of course I did. We were married immediately. They allowed us to stay in the camp overnight, but ordered us to prepare to leave in the morning. Lakeisha and I spent the night in the loft of her parent's barn. We thought we were alone. We were discussing our future and what we were going to do, where we were going to live, how we would provide for Trae. Then, we started to talk about Victor. We both felt something had to be done to clear his name. We thought if we came before the council and confessed, maybe you would cancel his punishment. Maybe he wouldn't have to serve his last six months suspension. We both agreed that was the first thing we would do. In the morning, we would leave and seek you out Oberon."

"Obviously that didn't occur," Oberon prodded. "What happened?"

"My Uncle Scott overheard our conversation," Lakeisha confessed. "In the morning, he stopped us. He said there had been a change in plans. Ryker and I were not allowed to leave camp for any reason. We would be sequestered there for three months. Once that time was over, we were going to be escorted to Ryker's camp where we would have to remain for three months. When the six months were over, we would begin our banishment.

I tried to argue. I didn't understand what had changed. Uncle Scott wouldn't discuss it. A couple weeks later my mother finally told me the rest of the story. Uncle Scott heard our plans. He'd been listening to find out where we were going to go and panicked. He called another emergency meeting with Ryker's leaders. They decided it was too dangerous to let the fae know of our deception. They believed if you knew, you would start a war or silently attack our packs for revenge. After all, one of your warriors had been punished unjustly. My uncle had made such a big deal over Victor's refusal to provide for his child and all along it wasn't really his. My uncle was a proud man, he couldn't face the humiliation and he was afraid of the consequences. He believed until the day he died, he had made the right decision for our pack."

They all sat in silence for a moment. Finally Lakeisha said softly, "I am so sorry for all the pain I have caused Victor. It was stupid for me to think once his suspension was over, everything would be okay. I have regretted that suspension every day for the past five years. It took Ariel to open my eyes and see Victor was still being punished unjustly. Ryker and my pack contributed to Victor's pain, but I strongly believe the majority of the responsibility rests with me. I am prepared to do whatever I can, whatever you wish, to make things right. My only hope is that you will consider my child in this. If you want to throw me in prison I will go. Please don't take both of Trae's parents away from him though. Don't make him suffer for my mistakes," she pled.

Alex stood and walked over to stand in front of Lakeisha. "This is not about punishment." She took a deep breath. "I think everyone involved in this thing has been punished quite enough," she turned to Dimitri and Oberon. "Do you agree?" she asked.

They both nodded. "This is about making things right for Victor. The two of you have more than served your time for the mistakes you made. Now, let's fix this for Victor. Let's truly give him back his life," Alex said softly.

"How can we do that?" Lakeisha asked. "The community needs to know he was innocent. Somehow we need to clear his name."

"I agree," Alex said. "And I think I know just how to do that. Why don't you leave the details to us? I think all I need from you is a signed statement admitting your parentage. Both of you will have to sign it of course with an explanation of how you know, without a doubt, the child is Ryker's and not Victor's. Are you willing to do that?" Alex asked.

"Of course," Ryker answered. "If you want, we will also have a paternity test and provide you the results. We will do anything we can to make things right."

Oberon interrupted. "We cannot force you to take a paternity test. However, I will tell you having those results would prove without a doubt Victor is not your child's father. If anyone questions our actions, it would be undeniable evidence in Victor's favor. If you don't have someone your pack uses, I'm sure Bastian would take care of it."

"I'm familiar with Bastian," Ryker answered. "We'll schedule the tests immediately. Once we get the results we will hand deliver them to the queen," he looked at her shyly.

Alex smiled at him. "That would be very helpful. Thank you. Now, I think we have everything we need from you two for now. I'll have your statement typed up and when you bring me those test results, you can sign the statement before witnesses. Trust us to do what is needed to finish the process. Victor will be cleared of any wrongdoing, I promise you that. I would also like to thank you for your willingness to come forward. It would have been much easier to leave things as they were. It's nice to see you both have too much integrity for that. It is an honor to continue our alliance with your packs during this difficult time. I realize our alliance with the shifters complicates our association with the panthers. If it's not possible now I hope, if you become pack leader someday, we'll be able to make that alliance more permanent." She looked back at Dimitri. "You are both welcome to stay for coffee. But afterwards we have some private matters to discuss," she motioned to the tray.

"Thank you," Ryker said sincerely. "But I think we would like to get back to our son. He's young and he still gets a little nervous when Lakeisha's not around. Her abduction was pretty hard on him."

After Dark

"Of course. I'm sorry you had to go through that terrible ordeal," she said to Lakeisha. "We hope that's something we'll be able to avoid in the future. Unfortunately, Radek seems to delight in abducting people as much as his father did."

Ryker turned to Ariel, "do you need a ride home?"

She looked to her father in question. Oberon answered. "No, thank you. I'll drive my daughter home once we're finished here. Thank you again for your cooperation in this. I too look forward to working with you in the future."

The four of them listened as Ryker and Lakeisha left the house. They watched their taillights as they pulled onto the highway. Then they sat in silence, each of them lost in their own thoughts. Finally, Ariel spoke. "Well maybe I shouldn't have knocked her out after all," they all laughed.

Dimitri pulled Alex into his arms. "I think we all have a lot to be grateful for," he looked over at Oberon. "Apparently the council isn't the only group of leaders that make bad judgments sometimes. Can you believe those two packs, holding their own children hostage like that? And for what? To protect their pride and their egos. It's amazing."

Oberon agreed. "Those two received a sentence of two years, but in reality they served two and a half. Basically, they served the first six months in prison. They didn't have walls, but they couldn't leave either."

"I want to get this resolved as soon as possible. Once I have the documentation from Ryker and Lakeisha, what do we have to do to clear Victor's name? I assume as queen I have some authority. Can I expunge his record or something?" Alex asked.

The group spent over an hour discussing policy and formulating a plan. They were all determined to clear Victor's name at all costs. There were some members of the community that would never accept Victor, part of that had to do with his father. But most of them would welcome him with open arms if they knew he was innocent. Especially since he had already served his sentence without complaint.

Oberon stood. "It's getting late. I need to get home. Ariel, are you ready?"

"Sure," she stood and turned to give Alex a hug.

"Thomas should be here at seven. We're going to dinner and then we're going to stop by Victor's club for a drink." Alex paused, waiting for a reaction. "We'd like you to join us if you're up to it."

Oberon froze. He wasn't sure what had happened to his daughter in that forest, but he knew it had something to do with Victor. He suspected Ariel had fallen in love with the man, but somehow everything had gone terribly wrong. Personally, he hoped they would work things out. He'd be proud to have Victor as a son-in-law and he thought Victor and Ariel might be good for each other. They both had terrors in their past. Maybe they could heal each other's souls. If it was meant to be, Oberon believed fate would work it out.

Ariel was debating with herself. She wanted to see Victor, but she was afraid to. She loved him, but did he love her? Should she fight for him like Alex had suggested or just let things be? She wasn't sure what the best course of action was.

"Stop over thinking it," Dimitri finally grumbled. "Do you want to have dinner and a drink with us? Put everything else aside and just think about that."

"Okay," she exhaled. "Fine, I'll go to dinner and have a drink with you. If it all goes terribly wrong, you have nobody but yourself to blame." She glared at Dimitri. "Should I be here at seven then?"

"Yeah," Alex said enthusiastically. "I'm so glad you're going to join us. It's been a rough day. It will be nice to go out with friends and relax," she turned to Oberon. "Thank you for helping with this. I know it's just as important to you, but still I really appreciate all your help."

"I'm happy to be of assistance my Queen." He smirked at her discomfort. He took her hand and kissed it gently then he winked at her. "You are a gem. Dimitri's a lucky man."

"Oh you," she said with exasperation. "I never should have admitted how much I hate that. Now, you'll never stop." She walked with him to the door. "I hope you have a safe drive home," she turned to Ariel, "I'll see you at seven." She shut the door behind them. "Are we doing the right thing?" she asked Dimitri.

"I think so. Victor is miserable and so is Ariel. They're just too stubborn to fix things on their own. If Victor's uncomfortable with our company, he won't join us. If that happens, I'm going to excuse myself and take the opportunity to have a chat with our good friend Victor."

* * * *

The group arrived at Bojan Taverns just after nine. Ariel expected to wait in line, but Dimitri walked up to the doorman and within minutes they were being escorted to a table. Dimitri and Alex sat on one side, Thomas took a seat on the other next to Ariel. Rocky strolled over from the bar. "What's the occasion?" he asked pulling up a chair and slapping Thomas on the back. "You guys haven't been in for a while. I've missed giving you a hard time," he glanced at Ariel. "Who's your friend?" He directed his question toward Thomas. Obviously he thought they were here together, possibly a couple.

Alex interjected. "This is Ariel. She's been a close friend of Dimitri's family for years. Now she's a close friend of mine," she paused. "Ariel, this is Rocky. He's the best bartender in the universe." She gave him a huge smile. "He can make anything. I like to be creative when I come here, but so far I haven't been able to stump him."

Ariel laughed. "You be creative. I'll stick to a daiquiri, strawberry I think."

"Good choice," Rocky winked. "I can do daiquiris. In fact, that's one of my specialties. Once you experience my daiquiri, you'll never be satisfied by anyone else." He grinned as he turned to Thomas. "What's your pleasure tonight?"

Victor left his office and headed for the club. He needed a break. Maybe he'd spend a few minutes with Rocky. He was always good for a laugh. Victor rounded the corner and froze. Rocky wasn't at the bar. He was sitting at a table with Dimitri, Alex,

After Dark

Thomas and Ariel. His insides clenched. He wasn't ready for this. He was still too hurt and angry to have a casual conversation with Ariel. He spun around and headed back to his office. Luckily Ariel hadn't seen him. He thought Dimitri had though. But, Dimitri he could handle. Once inside, he pulled a bottle of Jack Daniels from the cabinet. He and Danny boy were going to have a quiet evening alone tonight.

A short time later there was a knock at the door. "Go away I'm busy," Victor barked out.

The door crept open and Dimitri slipped in. He silently shut the door and twisted the lock. "Hello Victor," Dimitri said as he slid into the chair in front of Victor's desk. As he sat, he took the bottle of Jack Daniels and gently placed it on the floor beside his chair.

"I said I was busy," Victor grumbled again. "Give me back my bottle. I have a date with Jack tonight."

Dimitri shook his head. "I have some things I want to say and for this, you are going to be sober. I want you to remember this conversation." He shifted subtly placing his foot next to the bottle to shield it from Victor.

Victor sighed. "You can tell me what to do when I'm working for you, not tonight. You gave me a few days off. I'm on vacation. This is my club so right now, I'm the boss. Give me back my whiskey."

"No," Dimitri wasn't going to budge. Victor was going to listen to what he had to say.

Victor stood. "Fine, I'll just go to the bar and get another one."

"I'd like to do this the easy way, without violence, but if you try to walk out that door you'll have to go through me to do it." Dimitri was still sitting, but he was obviously serious about the threat.

Victor was surprised. Dimitri wasn't usually this forceful or unbending. Maybe he should listen to what he had to say. Then Dimitri would leave and take Ariel with him and Victor could get back to a night of drunken bliss. He watched Dimitri for another second and then sat back down. "Fine, make it quick."

Dimitri studied Victor. He looked terrible. When was the last time he'd slept, or ate for that matter? Maybe allowing him time off had been a bad idea. "When was the last time you had something to eat?"

Victor shrugged. What did that have to do with anything?

"Guess," Dimitri pushed. "An hour ago? At breakfast? Two days ago? Give me a rough idea."

"Dimitri, why are you here?" Victor demanded. "Because I don't think it has anything to do with my eating habits."

"Actually in a roundabout way it does," Dimitri said coyly.

Victor rolled his eyes. "If I have to put up with this, give me back my Jack. A man can only endure so much."

Dimitri smiled. At least Victor hadn't lost his sense of humor. "Okay, I'm worried about you."

"Well, don't worry. I'm fine," Victor said defensively.

After Dark

"Actually you're not. I'm the leader now, remember? When you're in pain, I know and feel it. It comes with the job. With you, it's always more difficult to gage. It's easy to tell when the others are just having a bad day or they stub their toe or something. It's obvious when the pain goes deeper or it's something I need to worry about. With you, there's always a dull pain. I have to concentrate more to determine if it's the usual, or something more significant. For the past couple weeks, it's been more significant. You know you can't hide what you're going through from me, so we might as well talk about it."

Victor sighed. He didn't want to talk about it. Where would he even begin? Especially with Dimitri, Ariel was like a sister to him. This had all become so complicated.

"How about we try this for a while, I'll talk and you lose the attitude. I know you're in pain Victor. The act is just pissing me off," Dimitri said. He turned to the small fridge against the wall and pulled out a bottle of water. "Mind if I help myself?" he asked.

"It looks like you already did. If I can't have Jack, pass me one of those." Victor smiled and took the water.

Dimitri leaned back in the chair and straightened his legs. He crossed one ankle over the other. He was watching Victor, trying to decide how to start this conversation. He took another swig of water. "You and Ariel," he began.

Victor winced. He really didn't want to have this conversation, but there was no escaping it now. "Yeah, what about us," Victor asked.

"Well, I guess in a nutshell, that's my question. What about you? Are you just going to sit back and lose the best thing that ever happened to you over some sort of misunderstanding?" Dimitri asked.

"What makes you think we had a misunderstanding?" Victor questioned.

Dimitri rolled his eyes. "Oh, I don't know. Because I know you. I know her. I know how stubborn and bullheaded you both are. And I know how miserable you've been the past few weeks."

"That doesn't automatically point to a misunderstanding. Maybe we understand each other perfectly," Victor said defensively.

"Cut the crap, Victor. I want to have a serious conversation with you. If you become defensive and shut me out, it's not going to do anyone any good," Dimitri said forcefully. "Are you angry with Ariel for something?"

"Why do you automatically assume I'm the one keeping us apart? That I'm the reason things didn't work out? Maybe she's angry at me," Victor answered. A little offended.

"Don't jump to conclusions or get defensive. I'm not blaming you for anything. I'm just asking. Are you angry with her?" Dimitri pressed.

"This isn't something that simple," Victor admitted. "It's not about me being angry. To answer your question, no I don't think I'm angry. I'm mostly just confused I guess."

"Confused about what?" Dimitri asked seriously.

After Dark

Before Victor could answer there was a knock on the door. Victor walked over and opened it a crack. Alex stood there, looking apologetic.

"Sorry to interrupt. Ariel wanted to go home so Thomas offered to take her. He has an early day tomorrow. I just wanted to let Dimitri know I'll wait for him at the table, unless he wants me to catch up with Thomas and bum a ride."

Dimitri started to tell her to go home, but Victor interrupted. He pushed the door open wider and stood back. "Come on in."

"Are you sure?" she asked, watching Dimitri. She wanted him to have a chance to talk to Victor. She wasn't sure he would open up if she was there.

"Yes. Come in," Victor motioned to the chair next to Dimitri.

Ariel sat in the corner instead. Maybe if she didn't say anything they would both forget she was there.

Victor laughed at her. "Alex, move out of the corner. Go sit by Dimitri. We're all friends here. Really, it's fine. I know we haven't known each other a long time, but you are the Queen and you're one of my best friend's fiancé. You don't need to hide in the corner and hope you're forgotten."

Alex smiled. So, he figured her out. She walked over to Victor and gave him a big hug. "Did you know you are one of my favorite people in the whole world?" she asked.

Victor was surprised by that. Her words touched him. More than he could have imagined. "Thanks. I think you're pretty special too," he turned to Dimitri, "So, where were we?" He sat back down and propped his feet up on the desk.

"You were going to tell me what you are confused about. I wasn't out there with you in the forest, but I've had a few conversations with Thomas. He thought you and Ariel were hitting it off pretty well. The problem seemed to start once you got into that cave. Was he reading the situation correctly? Was something starting between you and Ariel?"

Victor paused. Did he want to admit the truth? Dimitri already knew he was suffering. He had to know Victor had feelings for Ariel. Why not? Maybe these two could help him. "I thought something was developing between us," he paused. "I'm not good at relationships but I thought things were starting out pretty well, yes."

"So, are you willing to tell me what you think happened in that cave?" Dimitri asked.

"I'm not really sure. I guess that's what has me confused," Victor admitted. "We went in and things were going smooth. We got to the door, no problem. Morrigan and I went in the small room followed by Austin. I spotted Abby chained to the wall. As I glanced around, I saw Lakeisha chained to the other wall. I was shocked. You know our history. Seeing Lakeisha chained there after five years surprised me. I always knew there was a chance I'd run into her again but still, it took me by surprise. After my initial shock, I realized how terrified she was. Regardless of our history at that moment she was just a scared, weak woman, chained to the wall of a vampire's lair.

I knew I had to help her, so I went over and tried to get her attention. At first, she was frantic. Once I calmed her down, we realized we couldn't save her unless we could get the chains off. Abby said something about shifting to get out of her chains, but that wouldn't work for Lakeisha. Lakeisha became frantic again, but this time she was vocal. I was afraid she was going to alert the other vampires and we wouldn't get out of there without trouble. One of the vamps had already let out a scream before we could kill him. The last thing we needed was more noise. I had to focus all my attention on Lakeisha just to keep her calm. Ariel was a life saver. I had no idea she could do that," Victor smiled. "She's amazing. She burned the chains off Lakeisha in seconds with that beam. I was finally relieved. All we needed to do was get out of the cave. Then suddenly, Ariel knocked Lakeisha out. No warning, nothing. She just suddenly punched this weak, defenseless woman for no reason."

"And you got angry?" Dimitri asked.

"Of course I was angry. There was no reason for her violence. Plus, now I had to carry Lakeisha. I wouldn't be free to fight if we had trouble. Ariel complicated our situation and put us all in danger. Worst of all, she did it for no reason. Then when we got back to our cave, Ariel shut us all out and went to bed," Victor shrugged. "We haven't talked since. Not really, just a brief conversation about that bear. I guess she changed her mind. She decided she wasn't interested in me anymore," he paused. "I guess I don't know if I'm interested in her either. I thought I knew her. I thought she was good and kind and amazing. Now that I've seen her violent side, I don't know what to think. I couldn't seriously consider being with someone that would victimize a person that was already a victim. Lakeisha was scared and weak and defenseless. What kind of person would attack her like that?" he asked.

Dimitri's first instinct was to defend Ariel, but he was going to cut Victor a little slack because of the situation. "Are you telling me you have decided based on this one incident that Ariel is not the good, kind amazing person you thought she was? Based on something you don't understand you have judged Ariel and decided she's a bad person? You've known her for how long now? Several months anyway. But this one incident has cancelled out all the good you've seen her do. Don't you think that's a little unfair?"

"I don't know," Victor admitted. "I just don't know."

Alex could tell Dimitri was getting upset. She had an idea. "So Victor," she interrupted. "What happened after you left that room?"

"My worst fear became a reality," he said soberly. "Hector grabbed Ariel and I wasn't available to save her. I had to pass Lakeisha off to Austin and that took time. Ariel might have been killed because I wasn't available to help. When I finally got to her, Thomas had already taken care of it."

"So, Ariel's actions made you feel helpless?" Alex asked.

Victor paused. "Yeah, I guess. Sort of."

"And you blame Ariel for that? You're angry at her for it?" she asked.

"I guess," he admitted hesitantly.

"Well get over it," she said angrily. Why did men have to be so stupid and egotistical?

After Dark

Victor raised one eyebrow. "Get over it?" he demanded. "Just get over it? I open up and tell you why I'm upset and you tell me to get over it? This has certainly been helpful."

"Yes, because you don't have a valid complaint. So you weren't right there by Ariel's side to shield and protect her. So what? Thomas helped her and if he hadn't been there, I have complete confidence in Ariel. She can handle herself, better than most men. Just because she's a woman, doesn't mean she's a helpless maiden that needs you to save her. Get over it already. I am so tired of you warriors and your chauvinistic egotism. Just because we're women, it doesn't mean we're weak."

Dimitri laughed. "You walked right into that one."

Alex shot him a look and he sobered. "Oh, sorry," he said trying to stop a smile. They all knew he really wasn't sorry.

Victor wasn't amused. He wasn't egotistical. Was he? Wanting to protect the woman he loved wasn't wrong or chauvinistic. It was being responsible and caring.

"So tell me what happened after that," Alex prodded.

"You already know, I'm sure. Thomas killed Hector," Victor told her.

"Well, it's my understanding he didn't just kill Hector. Didn't he fight him for quite some time?" Alex asked. "Didn't he block out everyone and everything else in that room while he attacked Hector?"

"Yes, Hector needed to be punished. Thomas was fighting, but he wasn't giving him a death blow. He was punishing him. He needed Hector to suffer for the pain he caused you, Luke and himself after Hector assassinated your mother. Hector also needed to be punished for Luke's death and then for abducting Abby and Lakeisha. You already know all this, why are you asking?" Victor said impatiently.

"Do you agree with what Thomas did that day?" she asked innocently.

"Sure. Hector caused a lot of people pain. He hurt not only the people he killed, but their loved ones. An easy death wouldn't have been justice. Thomas needed to get a little revenge for all the pain," Victor admitted.

"So, you agree justice was done?" she asked. "Even though he put the rest of you in danger?"

"Yeah, I'm okay with what Thomas did. It was therapeutic I guess," Victor answered.

"Thomas wasn't just being violent for no reason? Showing his dark side?" Alex asked. "He wasn't demonstrating his inability to be a good, decent person? From what I understand he was pretty ruthless. He tortured Hector as much as he could under the circumstances before he actually killed him."

"Of course not," Victor said appalled. "Thomas is one of the best men I know. He would never hurt anyone without cause. He was just punishing Hector for the pain he inflicted on his loved ones. You know that. Where are you going with this Alex?" Victor asked.

Dimitri finally understood what Alex was doing. She was making a comparison between Thomas and Ariel. He was impressed, it was a good tactic. It was a good way to make Victor understand where Ariel was coming from and why she punched Lakeisha in the cave.

"Because Ariel knocked Lakeisha out for the same reason," she paused just a second to let that sink in. "Yet you say her actions make her a bad, callous and violent person. I'm just trying to understand why. Why was it okay for Thomas to punish someone for hurting the people he cares about, but it's not okay for Ariel?" Alex asked.

"What do you mean?" Victor asked. "How was Ariel doing the same thing as Thomas? Lakeisha didn't hurt anyone Ariel knows."

"For such a smart person, you're being quite dense Victor," Alex said. "Lakeisha hurt you. She has caused you a tremendous amount of pain. When you saw her in that cave, you saw a weak defenseless woman. Ariel saw the woman that hurt you. The woman that forced an innocent man to accept a suspension he didn't deserve. A woman who walked away without consequences. So, she gave her one. She knocked her out."

"What?" Victor said incredulously. "If that's true, she shouldn't have done that. It wasn't her place to stand up for me. It wasn't up to her to get vengeance for what happened to me five years ago."

"Why not?" Dimitri asked. "Because she's not a warrior, or because she's a woman?"

"Neither. Because I didn't ask her to," Victor answered.

Alex laughed. "Like that would matter if the tables were turned. If someone hurt Ariel, would you wait for her to ask you before you went after them?"

"That's different," he said knowing he was losing this argument.

"Why? Because you're a man? I think we already covered that earlier," Alex countered. "Do you really want to go there again?"

Victor was silent. Had Ariel really knocked Lakeisha out for him? Could it really be that simple? Had he judged her so unfairly? He was going to have to think about that. If that was true, maybe she wasn't like his mother. Maybe he could trust her. Did he dare try?

Dimitri was studying Victor intently. "Victor, why are you prejudice against women?" He knew he was walking on shaky ground, but it was time for Victor to start dealing with his past. Dimitri wanted Victor to realize he was being unfair.

"I'm not," Victor argued.

"I disagree," Dimitri told him. "I think Alex just proved I'm right. You looked at Ariel's actions and saw a violent woman that couldn't be trusted. You looked at the exact same behavior in Thomas and saw justice. In fact, Thomas was more violent and brutal, but to you he was still justified. You have a double standard."

Had he really done that? Victor wondered. Did he have a double standard? Maybe. Was he tainted by the actions of his mother? Definitely. Was he really prejudice and unfair? He'd never considered that, but probably. He didn't want to be, but what could he do to change? How could he overcome this distrust and skepticism?

Alex walked over to Victor. She took his hand and studied him for a minute. "Victor, will you let us help you?" she asked him softly. "Let us be here for you."

Victor took a deep breath and lifted his legs off the desk. "I'm afraid you might be right. I might have a double standard. I probably am unfair to women. I'd never considered that and I don't want to be, but I don't know how to change it. It terrifies me when I try to trust a woman."

"You're trusting me," Alex pointed out. "Why do you feel comfortable with me?"

Victor thought about it. He didn't really know. Maybe because she was nothing like his mother. Alex was always so caring and understanding. She made it easy to talk to her. She wasn't a pushover or weak, she was just loving and caring. She came across as being sincere, almost transparent. He looked at his two friends and realized they were expecting an answer. "I don't know exactly," he confessed. Should he talk to them about his mother? He'd never talked to anyone about her. His father knew the basics, but Victor hadn't even told him how bad it really was. He didn't want his father to suffer more than he needed to. If he was ever going to talk to anyone, these were the two people to talk to. He knew he could trust both of them. Maybe it was time.

"I can't explain why I feel comfortable with you, Alex. I just do," he paused as he looked up at her. "I think maybe I can help you understand why I have a double standard though. I guess it goes back to my childhood." He looked over at Dimitri, then continued.

"I'm willing to talk to you about my past if you promise to keep everything I say here confidential. Alex you might want to go back and make yourself comfortable. This is going to take a while."

"You can trust us, Victor. We won't tell a soul anything you're willing to trust us with," Alex assured him. "Your secret is safe with us." She gave his hand a little squeeze then returned to her seat next to Dimitri.

Victor nodded and looked out the window. "I had a difficult childhood," he began. "I don't know when it started. I don't know how old I was the first time my mother locked me in the old cellar. I just always remember being locked in there when my father left. I suspect I was pretty young though. I don't remember ever not being locked in there. Does that make sense?" he asked.

"Yes," Alex said softly. She was horrified. Why would his mother lock him in the cellar?

"I think when I was little, she just put me in there and locked the door. Once I got older, it was harder to keep me inside. She started using a leather strap to secure me to the wall. That way I couldn't escape. She'd keep me there for weeks. Sometimes she would leave me food, sometimes she'd leave me there for days before she brought me something to eat. She always locked me up the day dad left and she'd let me out the night before he was scheduled to come home. She threatened to leave me in the cellar without any food at all if I told dad what was happening. It was a good way to control me. She never gave me much to eat anyway, barely enough to survive. There was no way I was going to say anything and risk getting less.

The abuse started when I was five. I remember because it was the same year dad started training me to become a warrior. It took me a while to figure it out, but the two were connected. My mother hated the warriors. She started begging dad to quit. When he wouldn't, she took her frustration out on me. I think she was mentally unstable. She became fanatical. She was constantly telling me to pray. She wanted me to pray that God would eradicate the evil warrior spirit from my soul. Each time dad left she would try different, creative ways to force the warrior out of me. Then she would test to see if her experiment worked by injuring me. Sometimes she would cut me, sometimes she would burn me. Then, she'd sit back and watch to see if I healed. When I did, she knew she had to try again.

Eventually when I was nine, she stopped trying to cure me and she started trying to kill me. The problem was, she used strange techniques. She didn't just stab me or shoot me or anything like that. I don't know why, maybe because she was crazy. She did strange things. One time she tried to drain all the blood from my body. Of course, that didn't work. I healed before I lost enough blood to do much harm. I was extremely weak, but I survived. Another time she tied me up and stripped me down to my underwear. She stuck pins all over my body. Then, she brought in a bucket of lemon juice and poured it over me one glass at a time. She'd pour a glass of juice on an area then rush to pull out all the pins hoping the lemon juice would seep into the wounds. Then she'd move to a different area and do the same. I guess she thought if she got enough lemon juice into my system it would kill me like it would a fae. It hurt like hell, but didn't do any damage. When I got older, I almost told my dad. The threat of the cellar no longer scared me. But my mother was so different when dad was home. Plus, dad loved Dannica. He would light up whenever they were together. I just couldn't take that away from him. I loved him too much to shatter his illusion."

Alex was silently crying. She couldn't help it. What a terrible thing to happen to a child. No wonder Victor had problems.

Victor took a breath and continued. "This ritual went on until I was nine or ten. That's when I talked dad into letting me walk to the end of the driveway with him any time he left. When we hit the road, dad would continue on alone or he'd hook up with the other warriors. Once he was out of sight, I would run into the woods and hide. I was getting pretty good at avoiding my mother. It really pissed her off. She became more and more frustrated with me. I learned to survive in the woods for weeks at a time. I wouldn't come back until I saw dad walking up the road, headed for home. I'd become so good at hiding from my mother there hadn't been an incident for years. I guess that's why I'm so good at survival and tracking. I learned by hiding in the woods and tracking mom while she was trying to catch me. On dad's last trip, mom talked him into letting her walk with us. He was touched that she wanted to spend that time with us. I knew better. She just wanted to stop me from hiding.

I thought I was prepared, but she took me by surprise. She acted quicker than I anticipated. As soon as dad kissed her goodbye and turned away, she knocked me out and drug me into the woods. When I woke up I was back in the cellar, tied up as usual. Mom tortured me for two full days. She'd had several years to come up with new, creative ways to cause my death. She thought she had plenty of time. Dad was supposed to be gone for a couple weeks. But dad returned early. Apparently the warriors ran into some trouble just outside of town. They had a big battle and then returned home to rest. Dannica was using salt this time. I guess she thought it would counter the healing process. She spread the salt thick across my chest. Then, she planned to stab me with a butcher knife. I don't know why she thought she needed the salt. She was aiming for my heart, which would have killed me anyway. At first, I decided to give up. I was tired of it all and was just going to let her do it and get it over with. At the last minute I realized I didn't want to die. Luckily there was enough play in the straps. I twisted to the side and she stabbed me in the upper shoulder and chest instead. The salt seeped into the wound and burned like crazy. I couldn't help it, I screamed out in pain.

Dad was just walking up the driveway at the time. He heard me scream and rushed to my aid. I still remember the horror on his face when he saw that scene and realized what my mother was doing. By the time dad got there, she had tightened the straps so I couldn't move at all. Then she came at me with the knife again. Dad tackled her and tried to get the knife away. She was out of control. She started stabbing dad. I was so afraid she was going to kill him. I knew I had to do something. I waited for my chance. When she got close to my legs, I kicked out with everything I had. She went flying across the room. Dad rushed to me and unhooked the leather strap on one hand. Mother recovered and charged us again before dad could undo the second strap. She got another good shot into my shoulder. The pain was so intense I screamed again. Dad was frantically trying to get me loose. Mom just kept coming at me, stabbing me in the legs, the ribs, the arms. She was completely mad. Dad tried to stand between us but mom started stabbing him again. Dad almost got me free, but mom barreled toward him. She shoved him hard and he flew into the wall. Then, she came at me again. Just before she plunged the knife straight into my chest, dad called her name and threw his dagger. She turned and the weapon plunged into her heart killing her instantly."

Everyone was silent for a long moment, then Victor continued. "Foster is my mother's brother. They were very close. In fact,

Foster came over and spent time with mom almost every time dad was away."

"Wait!" Dimitri interrupted. "Are you saying that Foster knew what your mother was doing to you and he didn't stop her? He never found a way to help you?"

"Help?" Victor laughed humorlessly. "He not only knew, he approved. I remember mom bringing him into the cellar one time when I was little. They thought I was sleeping. I would sometimes pretend to be asleep so my mother would leave. She always came back later, but it delayed the torture. Anyway, they were arguing. Foster was telling Dannica she was a disgrace to the family. It was the warrior's fault their family was no longer in power and she married one. Apparently she had promised the family if they gave her permission to marry dad, he would resign from the warriors. Foster was angry they had been married for years and dad was still fighting. To make matters worse, now she also had a son that was a warrior. He ordered her to do something to stop me from accepting my duty as a warrior. She couldn't bring even more disgrace to the family. Mother told him she was working on it. Then she proceeded to tell him some of the things she had done to me. She said if she couldn't force the evil out, she would make sure I would reject the warriors or die. Foster laughed and told her to keep up the good work."

Dimitri was livid. Foster knew the atrocities Victor had suffered and now he was the biggest critic when it came to Victor or Atticus' character. Foster actually went to the council and tried to convince them to expel Victor as a warrior forever. If it was the last thing he ever did, Dimitri would make sure Foster paid for everything he'd done to Victor; literally and through his inaction.

"You do know Foster should be punished for his part in this. He's an accomplice. Did he try to find you in the forest too?"

"Yes, but he's a terrible tracker. Even at ten I could outsmart him. Foster can't pay for his role in my torture unless I'm willing to testify against him," Victor answered. "I'm not. Dad spent his life protecting this secret. He gave up everything to hide it. I won't let that be for nothing. I won't do anything to throw his sacrifice away. Foster was the one that showed up at the farm and found Dannica dead. He was furious. He went to the council and demanded they charge dad with murder. He knew it wasn't murder. He knew exactly what happened. He just hated me, dad and all the warriors enough to twist the truth and demand justice for a crime dad never committed. It's been a long time, Dimitri. Let it go. Someday Foster will pay for what he's done but it won't be because I told the world what my mother really was. I won't do that to dad. He's suffered enough."

Alex stood and walked over to Victor. She knelt down so they were facing each other. Her eyes were still moist and she had a hard time talking without breaking down. "Victor," she began.

"Alex. Don't cry for me," Victor soothed, taking her hands. "It was a long time ago. I know the experience with my mother has impacted my life. That was the whole point, the reason I shared this story with you. I honestly don't think about that time in my life anymore. I had a few bad nights in the cave because of my injuries, but nothing big. I just had a couple bad dreams. That's the worst of it now. I don't want you to feel sorry for me. I only told you so you'll know why it's so hard for me to trust women. Mom was so normal and caring when dad was around. She just turned into a monster when he left. I'm not sure I can have a normal relationship. Like Dimitri said, I guess I have a double standard. When a guy does something, it seems reasonable to me. When Ariel knocked Lakeisha out, my first thought was that Ariel was hiding her true personality from me like mother hid hers from my father. I immediately wondered if she had the same violent potential my mother harbored. I wasn't sure I wanted to have a relationship with her anymore."

That was enough. Dimitri couldn't tolerate that kind of attack on Ariel's character. Ariel could never do the heinous things Victor's mother had done. "I'm going to ignore that just this once," he told him. "I realize you're not yourself tonight so you're not seeing things clearly. However if you ever imply Ariel is an evil violent person again, I might have to break your nose," Dimitri said coolly.

"You do realize that's not much of a threat for me. My nose would heal in seconds," Victor countered.

"It might be if I stuck around to break it again," he glared at Victor. "You might heal, but it would still be painful." He wasn't kidding. He was serious. The idea Ariel could be that sadistic was ridiculous. There's no way she was capable of such horror.

Alex was annoyed at both of them. Victor was an idiot if he thought Ariel could hurt anyone that way. And Dimitri was just being a typical man. His first instinct was to threaten violence to get his point across. "Both of you stop it," she demanded. "Victor, if you thought about Ariel for about half a second, you'd know she could never do any of those things your mother did to you. She is nothing like your mother. She's kind and good and caring. The only thing she's guilty of is caring too much. She couldn't sit back and do nothing when faced with the woman who had caused you so much pain. So, she punched her in the face and knocked her out.

Maybe she over reacted, maybe not. Lakeisha doesn't seem to have a problem with Ariel's behavior and neither should you. Her actions don't make her violent or evil. They make her human."

Dimitri realized Alex was right, threatening Victor wasn't helping. He knew something that would. "Victor, you told me your version of what you think happened that night in the cave. Now let me help you understand where Ariel was coming from," he glanced over at Alex. He might need her help with this.

"Fine. Go ahead," Victor was relieved. He didn't want to get into a fight with Dimitri. He wanted Dimitri to understand him.

"Ariel was involved in an incident when she was very young," Dimitri told him. "I can't tell you what happened any more than I would tell her about the things you just shared with me. Do you understand?"

"Yes," Victor admitted. "That's why I confided in you. I know you won't tell anyone, not even Ariel."

"Well, it was a very traumatic incident for her. Like you, she sometimes has nightmares or flashbacks. The night I sent you and Thomas over to the cabin she was on the verge of a panic attack," Dimitri paused.

"I knew there was something more going on that night. Can I assume whatever happened to her was pretty bad?" he asked soberly.

"It was," Dimitri answered. "Sometimes being in small dark spaces gets to her. She struggles to keep her composure. She has to work to keep the memories out."

Victor was horrified, had that happened to her in the cave? He was annoyed at himself. If she was struggling, he should have noticed. He should have been there to comfort her.

"So you all sneak into the cave," Dimitri continued. "I suspect she was doing okay until you went through that tunnel. Luckily, it opened back up into a large room and she was able to regain her composure. I doubt anyone even noticed a difference in her, but I guarantee she was shaky. When you walked into that small room where they were keeping Abby and Lakeisha, it was too much. She had to struggle to keep it together. She reached out for you, hoping you could help steady her but you were no longer there. You were across the room helping Lakeisha."

Victor was silent. He needed to hear what Dimitri had to say. No matter how much it upset him. It hurt knowing he hadn't been there for Ariel when she needed him.

"There she is, all alone while the man she thought cared about her is gone. He's across the room comforting a woman he should be angry with. He's consoling someone that has caused him years of pain and suffering. She gets angry. Maybe you have forgiven Lakeisha, but Ariel hasn't. The first opportunity she has, she punches her in the face. It might be a small consequence for Lakeisha's actions, but to Ariel it was therapeutic. Isn't that the word you used when describing why Thomas went after Hector with such violence?"

"Yes," Victor answered.

"Then instead of being understanding, even if you didn't agree with her, you got angry. To Ariel it seemed like you were choosing Lakeisha over her, again. At that point, I think Ariel gave up. She'd never be satisfied in a relationship where she didn't come first. So, she goes back to the cave and shuts everyone out. You've been back for weeks, but you've never tried to contact her. This has reinforced her belief that she's not important to you. If you want to lose her for good, continue to avoid her. But if you love her as much as I think you do, go talk to her. You are both broken," Dimitri paused. "Right now you're broken because of each other, but both of you are also broken from things in your past. This is all a misunderstanding but if you don't fix it soon, you might never be able to." He stood and held out a hand for Alex. "I think we've all said enough tonight. Think about what I've told you. You're the only one that can choose to be happy, Victor. You can take the easy way out and lose Ariel, or you can choose the hard route and tell her how you feel. No matter who he is, every man lucky enough to fall in love either has to take a risk or lose it all. I did and look how well it turned out for me," he smiled down at Alex.

She leaned in and hugged Victor. Then she stood and took Dimitri's hand. "I am so sorry for all you've been through," she said sincerely. "If you ever need anything, please let us know. Even if it's just to talk, or if you want help working things out. What your mother did to you was unforgivable. I can understand how you might avoid women and relationships after that. But by shutting out any woman you might care about, you are just letting your mother hurt you all over again. Your mother was the exception, not the rule. Don't let Ariel slip away because of your mother. You deserve a chance at happiness," she hugged him again. Then Alex and Dimitri slowly left the room.

Once they were out in the parking lot Alex turned to Dimitri. "Do you really think it was a good idea to go into what happened with Ariel in the cave? It was an extremely emotional night already. I'm not sure Victor has ever talked about his mother like that before.

Then, you added to his distress by telling him about Ariel. I'm afraid it may have been too much."

"Trust me." They had reached the car but instead of opening the door for Alex, Dimitri stopped. "I'd lay odds that Victor will be knocking on Ariel's door within 48 hours." He leaned down and kissed her softly. "I know him. Realizing that Ariel was suffering in that cave and he ignored her, especially for Lakeisha, will eat at him. He'll have to fix it. I got him to the door, now they'll have to do the rest." Alex climbed into the car and waited while Dimitri slid in beside her.

"I hope you're right," she finally said as Dimitri put the car in gear and headed home.

Chapter Eight

Victor sat alone in his office thinking about his conversation with Dimitri and Alex. His mind kept going back to the cave. He didn't know what happened in that room. He saw Lakeisha and was instantly oblivious to his surroundings. He had no idea what was going on with Ariel. He was sucked in as soon as he stepped through the door and saw Lakeisha chained to the wall. She was lying there looking so weak and alone. She had always been full of life but in that room, she looked apathetic and vulnerable. He hadn't gone to her because of their history. He'd gone in spite of it. Did Ariel really believe he had chosen Lakeisha over her?

Suddenly a memory hit him like a freight train. Ariel was crying that night. He couldn't sleep, he'd been so confused and hurt by Ariel's behavior. He laid there all night trying to figure out why she had shut him out. Why she was sleeping in the corner as far away from him as she could get. Twice that night, he thought he heard her crying but he dismissed it. He convinced himself he was wrong. She didn't have any reason to be upset. Had he been the one to hurt her? Was he the bad guy here? It tore at his heart to think she was crying because of him, to realize once again she needed comfort and he'd ignored her. At the very least, he owed her an apology. But why would she ever forgive him? Victor realized his past and all his ghosts may have ruined his future. Alex was right, he was still letting his mother hurt him. This time he may have lost the only woman he'd ever loved. How could he have been so stupid? But the bigger question was what could he do about it?

* * * *

Ariel was sitting on her couch, drinking a glass of wine and watching the fire flicker. Being in Victor's club tonight had drained her emotionally. She knew it was going to be difficult, but it was harder than she thought it would be. She used to love that club. Now, it just made her sad. From the moment she walked through the door, all she wanted to do was find Victor and work things out. The more she thought about her conversation with Dimitri earlier that week, the more she had to admit he was right. She'd been unfair to Victor. She wanted him back more than anything. But what if she wasn't strong enough to stick it out. What if she couldn't overcome the damage from his past? What if he couldn't live with hers? She would not hurt him again. He'd been hurt enough for one lifetime.

Ariel jumped at the sound of the doorbell. She looked at the clock, it was after midnight. This couldn't be good. Nobody showed up at your door after midnight unless they had bad news. She frowned. Had Radek found out about Hector and already staged an attack. She knew Radek would seek revenge, but she hoped they'd have more time. She walked to the door and checked the security monitor. It was Victor. She instantly calmed. If there was trouble Dimitri wouldn't send Victor after her. Actually, that's exactly what Dimitri would do. She tensed again and opened the door.

Victor was nervous. Would Ariel even talk to him? He knew he was pushing it, showing up after midnight like this. He couldn't wait. Dimitri's words just kept eating at him. If he had hurt Ariel, he had to make things right. Even if she couldn't forgive him. He would still apologize to her. Ariel opened the door and his whole body ached. He wanted to hold her so much it hurt. He wanted everything to be okay between them. He wanted to kiss her, make love to her and never let go. But he couldn't, he had to give her space. "Ariel, I know it's late but can I talk to you?"

"Is there something wrong? Is Radek attacking?" she asked nervously.

"No," he assured her quickly. "I'm not here on warrior business. This is personal," he waited. Wondering if she would turn him away.

"Okay," she opened the door for him to enter. "Good. I know there will be retaliation over Hector. I just hope we'll have some time. It's been so crazy lately." She was heading back to the family room. She had a sitting room just off the entrance, but that was too formal. She wanted to be comfortable.

Victor was looking around Ariel's house. It was nice. She didn't live in an extravagant mansion like Dimitri and Thomas. This was a large, comfortable home. She decorated it in a classy, but simple fashion. The neutral colors blended to create an elegant but inviting atmosphere. It suited her.

Ariel sat back down on the couch. She wasn't sure why Victor was here, but he made her nervous. She picked up her wine and took another sip. "Have a seat," she offered.

Victor sat on the couch next to Ariel. He just sat there studying her for a while. He didn't know how to start. He was nervous and afraid of rejection. "I'm sorry Ariel," he blurted.

She looked over at him in confusion. What did he have to be sorry for? "I don't understand. Why are you apologizing to me? I assumed you still wanted me to apologize to you for knocking Lakeisha out. You seemed pretty angry about that. I'm not sorry I did it. I still think she deserved it," she smiled.

"I'm not here for an apology," he grinned. "Did you really knock Lakeisha out for me? For what she did to me?" he asked. He was still having a hard time accepting that someone would do that for him.

Ariel smiled. "Well, I guess if I'm going to be honest, it was about 90% for you, 10% for me," she admitted. "To be honest it annoyed me that after everything she did to you, she was clinging to you like that. I thought she should have shown more regret for her actions. And I didn't like her jumping all over you. I was frustrated and angry and I guess I took it out on her. However, I'm not sorry I did it. I still think she deserved a little payback."

Victor took her hand in his. It was so hard to touch her and not pull her close to him and hold her. "Thank you," he said sincerely looking down at their joined hands. "Thank you for standing up for me. I'm sorry I didn't appreciate it at the time," he said quietly.

After Dark

Ariel was having a hard time breathing. Just Victor's touch sent electricity through her entire body. She missed him so much. She'd give anything to crawl into his lap right now and hold on tight. It would feel so good to have his strong arms encircling her again. She always felt safe and secure in his arms.

"But that wasn't what I was apologizing for," he continued. "I'm sorry for abandoning you when you needed me. I'm sorry that my past blinded me to what was going on in the present. I'm sorry I behaved so badly and then I was too dense to know my actions had an impact on you."

Ariel closed her eyes and took a deep breath. "I can see you've been talking to Dimitri. It looks like he hit you with a guilt trip, too," she said annoyed.

"Not exactly," Victor defended Dimitri. "He just pointed out the obvious, some things I was too caught up in my own life to notice at the time." He was still watching her.

"What did Dimitri tell you exactly?" She was being cautious. There was no way Dimitri would betray her trust and tell Victor about her past, but obviously he'd said something.

"He didn't tell me anything about your history if that's what you're worried about." Victor was so bad at this. He didn't know how to apologize to her. "Dimitri would never betray anyone's trust like that."

"I know," she assured him. "But he obviously told you I was having a hard time in the cave and now you feel guilty. What went on in that room wasn't your fault. It was mine. I'm the one that blew everything out of proportion. I'm the one that should be apologizing to you."

"Okay, I accept," Victor smiled.

Ariel had to smile back at him. "I don't think it's supposed to be that easy." She relaxed a little and started to reach for her wine. "Oh I didn't even ask, do you want something to drink? I'm such a terrible host. I always forget."

"Sure," Victor was still smiling. "Just point me in the right direction and I'll take care of it myself." He was searching around the room, looking for a bar or a tray.

"It's in the kitchen. I'll be right back." She jumped up and hurried out of the room. She had to make a decision. Did she love him enough to work things out? Could she promise him forever if he wanted it? The realization hit her hard, she wanted forever with Victor. She was miserable without him. She missed him terribly. Maybe that meant she did love him enough. If Victor still wanted her, she was going to give them a chance and hope for the best.

Ariel returned with a bottle of wine and a crystal glass. She poured the wine for Victor and then set the bottle on the table. She sat back down on the couch and turned to face him. "I..."

"Ariel..." Victor started at the same time. They both smiled. "Can I go first?" he asked.

"Okay," she conceded.

He turned so he was facing her. "I truly am sorry for everything," he hurried on when he saw Ariel was going to interrupt. "No, just let me finish. I don't know what happened to you. I suspected something that night at the cabin when we first met the shifters. Something shook you that night. I could see it. When Thomas and I arrived, you were pale and I could tell you'd been crying. That's not like you. You are strong and courageous. I saw you battling countless newborn vampires in that alley with confidence and poise. That was not the same woman I saw when I entered the safe room. I let it go, it wasn't my place to ask. Plus, I was trying to avoid you. I was trying to escape the feelings I had for you," he admitted.

"Why did you want to avoid me?" she asked seriously.

How could he answer that? How could he explain? He didn't want to go into his background again tonight but maybe he should. "I overheard Lakeisha tell you my mother tried to kill me."

"I'm sorry she did that," Ariel interrupted. "It wasn't fair to you. That's personal. She violated your confidence. It's your choice who you want to know about that. She didn't have a right to tell me your secret."

"Maybe, but she was right. We were starting to get involved and you had a right to know about my past. My mother did try to kill me, several times. I guess you could say my childhood has had a big impact on me. In a lot of ways my mother's actions have messed with my head; with my mind and my emotions," Victor admitted, glancing over at Ariel. She just sat there quiet and still, so he continued. "Because of my experience with her I've avoided all women, except for Lakeisha, my entire life. I've avoided getting to know women I knew I could care for. You asked me once why I allow the rumors and I perpetuate the facade. I do it because it makes it easier to avoid getting involved. Nice women don't fall for bad boys. I tried to avoid you. Fate wouldn't let me. We kept getting thrown together and the more I was around you, the more I cared. The more I wanted to be around you. I couldn't help it. You're just too irresistible," he smiled at her.

Ariel melted. He had such a great smile.

"Anyway, I should have been more attune that night in the cave. I should have made sure you were okay first. If I had known you were upset or struggling even a little, I never would have left you to check on Lakeisha. I'm sorry," he finished softly, obviously feeling guilt and regret. "When I walked into that cave and saw Abby and then Lakeisha chained to that wall, it shook me. It brought back memories I'd rather forget. Morrigan and Austin were tending to Abby. Lakeisha was alone and frightened. I got pulled in. I forgot my surroundings. The only thing I could think about was getting Lakeisha out of those chains. I'm ashamed to say I didn't give you, Thomas or the others a second thought. Somehow, I got tunnel vision and I reacted to the scene before me. I abandoned you when you needed me. I can never change that, but I truly am sorry. I'll never forgive myself for leaving you alone that way."

"I wasn't alone, you left me with Thomas and it was a small room. Just so I'm clear, you're apologizing because you couldn't do the impossible. You couldn't read my mind and know I was upset and needed you?" Ariel asked. Dimitri was such a manipulator. She was going to have a chat with him in the very near future. He had no right to make Victor feel this guilty and upset. This was all her fault and Dimitri knew it.

"No," Victor insisted. "I'm apologizing because I hurt you," he answered.

Ariel didn't know how to respond to that. She had been hurt. She took a deep breath. "Victor, I don't know what to say. I was hurt, but I think it was my fault. Dimitri helped me to see a few things too," she admitted.

After Dark

"How could it be your fault that I hurt you?" Victor asked, confused.

"Sometimes I have panic attacks." She was embarrassed, but had to explain this for Victor to understand. "I hate that one incident so long ago can still impact me, but sometimes it does. I started to panic in the cave so I reached for you, thinking you would give me the strength I needed to regain my composure. When I realized you were gone, you were over taking care of Lakeisha, it hurt. I watched you and her carefully. You were so loving and caring toward her. Then, she was climbing all over you like you were still lovers or something and you didn't stop her. I guess part of me was jealous." She looked over at him still embarrassed.

Victor took Ariel's hand again. He knew she was having a hard time admitting she was jealous. He really had been stupid. Lakeisha's actions were over the top, but he'd been oblivious to how they had impacted Ariel. What if the tables had been turned? If that had been Tank in that room climbing all over Ariel, he would have been jealous too. He would have knocked Tank out at the first opportunity. "I'm sorry for that, too." He ran his hand through his hair.

"Let me finish," she requested. "Lakeisha's actions made me snap out of my panic attack. She pissed me off. After everything she'd done to you, the pain she'd caused you, she was sitting there on your lap acting like nothing had ever happened. The two of you looked so cozy. I was sure you were still in love with her. That's what hurt me."

Victor got up and knelt in front of Ariel. "I am so sorry!" He said sincerely, picking her hands back up. "Ariel, it kills me to know you were hurting and I wasn't there for you. I should have been. It makes it worse that I was over with Lakeisha while you were suffering. I need you to know I'm not in love with Lakeisha. How can I prove that to you? I would never choose anyone over you, especially not Lakeisha. I am such an idiot." He sat back and put his face in his hands.

"Victor, stop. Look at me," she requested. She pulled his hands from his face and held onto them. "Please look at me," she said more forcefully. "I have something I need to tell you."

Victor was studying her. Now what?

Ariel pulled on Victor's hands. "Please, come sit back up here by me."

Victor climbed back onto the couch. He never let go of Ariel's hands. He liked the contact and didn't want to lose that connection.

"Alex and I went shopping a couple days ago. We were in Central Park and saw you."

Victor's head shot up. He looked at her in question.

"Yes. We saw you with that boy and his mother," she admitted. "I saw how loving and caring you were with her. It struck me almost immediately that you were just as loving toward that stranger in the park as you were with Lakeisha that night in the cave. I had to admit to myself I was wrong. I misread the situation totally and completely. You are so kind hearted and caring, it wouldn't have mattered who was chained up in that cave. You would have reacted the same way to anyone, even a stranger. I finally realized it didn't have anything to do with Lakeisha. It was all about you and the unbelievable goodness you have inside of you. You don't owe me an apology for that, I owe you one."

"Ariel," Victor said, emotion in his voice. If Ariel really did understand he wasn't in love with Lakeisha, maybe she could give him another chance. Dimitri's words echoed in his mind. It was time to do the hard part. "I met this stunning and fascinating woman a short time ago. She is good and kind and truly amazing," Victor moved a little closer. "I've been stubborn and stupid. I've made a lot of mistakes." He lifted Ariel's hand to his mouth and kissed it. "I've been so focused on my own little world, I've hurt the only woman I've ever loved." He looked Ariel in the eyes. "Have I lost you for good? Or would you consider giving me a second chance." He continued to stare, barely blinking. "I've fallen in love with you, Ariel. I'm miserable without you."

Ariel couldn't hold back any longer. She jumped into his lap and pressed her lips to his. After a long desperate kiss, they broke apart. "I think we still have a lot to talk about, but right now I want something else from you." She stood and held her hand out to him.

Victor took her hand and let her lead him into the bedroom.

* * * *

Ariel was lying on Victor's chest. She was tracing the dragon with her index finger. "I think it's wonderful." She lifted her head and kissed his lips. "It's a symbol showing you have slain the dragons from your past."

Victor ran his hand over her head and down her back. "I'm not sure I've overcome anything. The mistakes I made with you clearly demonstrates I have a long way to go. I'm just grateful you're willing to forgive me. It terrifies me, but I need you Ariel."

She lifted her head and pressed a long and loving kiss to his lips.

"I love you," he said softly, pulling her closer and smiling. "I never thought I would say that to any woman, but I truly love you Ariel."

Ariel ran her fingers through his hair. She looked into his eyes. "I love you too," she admitted smiling. "Victor, I need you as much as you need me. Before that night at the cabin, that night when you kissed me, I was content. My life wasn't all joy and happiness, but it was okay. I didn't feel like I was missing out on anything. I had my friends and my family. I really was content with my life. Then I met you. It was like something inside of me opened up. I was finally happy. Then, it was instantly gone again. I've been miserable since we got back from the forest. Well, actually I've been miserable since that night in the cave. My life is empty without you."

"Me too," Victor said quietly. He sat up and pulled her with him. He kissed her temple and studied her. "I think it's time I confessed my history to you," he said soberly. "Sorry to ruin the mood, but you have a right to know what you're getting into. I am going to do my best to make you happy. I'm working on my baggage. But you need to know, I might have some bad moments. I might make more mistakes. I'll apologize in advance for my stupidity."

Ariel didn't know what to say. She thought back to her conversation with Lakeisha. Victor might push her away. Ariel knew she wouldn't allow that again though. As long as they loved each other, they could work through this together. She'd just have to be strong. If she knew Victor accepted her for who she really was, she could be patient with him. She was going to have to tell him about her past, too. But, she'd let him go first. She wouldn't interrupt him. If he was willing to tell her about his mother, she was going to listen quietly. "Well, I'm not going to accept your apology in advance. If you're stupid in the future, you'll have to apologize for it then. I like diamonds," Ariel smiled.

Victor laughed, then sobered. He proceeded to tell Ariel the same story he had shared with Alex and Dimitri. When he was finished Ariel didn't speak for a long time. She reached out and ran her finger along the scar on his chest. Then, she traced the entire dragon. Victor was waiting for a response. She was driving him crazy. He needed to know what she was thinking. Ariel never did react the way he thought she would. Was she still willing to give them a chance? Or was his history too much for her to deal with?

Ariel finally spoke. "I think you've dealt with the horrors in your past better than you think you have." She looked into his eyes. "This dragon is just a symbol representing all the tangible things you've done to overcome the atrocities of your childhood."

"What do you mean?" He wasn't sure he understood.

"Your life was horrific until you were twelve years old. Sure, your father loved and protected you when he was home. I think he would have done anything for you. Technically, I guess he has. But your mother was a monster. She was definitely mentally unstable. I suspect her family knew that. Foster fueled her insanity for his own evil and sadistic purposes. Maybe the rest of them did too. I don't know. But you have overcome it all."

"I don't feel like I've overcome any of it. Like Dimitri pointed out, I'm unfair to women. I was unfair to you. I avoid them and mistrust them just because of their gender. That's not overcoming anything," Victor said, ashamed of what he'd become.

"The first step was becoming a warrior. You grew up and accepted your destiny. All the torture and death attempts couldn't stop you. You were a warrior. You didn't turn your back on that even after your father was unjustly punished for your mother's death. You beat them. Your mother, your uncle, her whole family."

"That's not why I became a warrior," Victor began.

"Exactly!" Ariel said. "That's my point. You did it because that's who you are. I doubt you could have experienced anything worse as a child and lived through it. Yet, you are a warrior. Nothing she did could change that. She couldn't change your character. You are what you are. Does that make sense?"

"I guess," Victor said pondering what she was saying. "I've never thought of it that way before, but I guess you're right."

"I suspect you are now taking care of your father. Not physically, but emotionally. I knew he was a recluse. I think I heard he lives in Pennsylvania. It makes sense to me now. He was in love with your mother and she tried to kill his only son. How do you get over that? How do you get over killing the woman you loved? He must be a very strong and special man. I assume you got your strength and compassion from him."

Victor was touched. He was afraid of Ariel's reaction when he told her his father was shut off from the world. He was afraid she wouldn't understand. Once again, she surprised him. He didn't have to explain anything. "I'd like you to meet dad someday. He is a recluse, but he's a great guy. He just won't leave the farm much. He was always a great father to me. No matter how bad things got with mom, I always knew dad loved me. I always had that. Knowing he loved me and would always be there for me was huge. It's what got me through a lot of very bad days. Then he gave up everything for me. He's always been proud of me. I only hope he knows how proud I am to be his son."

"I'd love to meet your father. It would truly be an honor to meet the man that raised you and helped you become the person you are today." Ariel was a little surprised at the offer, but she was also thrilled. She couldn't wait to meet Victor's father.

"I'm planning on going down in the next couple weeks. If you're free, maybe you could join me. I'm past due for a visit," Victor said. He missed his dad and wished he could talk him into visiting New York. They'd be able to see each other more often if he would just leave that farm.

"Anyway back to my point," Ariel continued. "Then, you opened Lavena Tèarmann. You were a helpless child when you were abused. You were victimized over and over again. People knew what was happening to you, but nobody stepped in to help. You've made up for that by opening a world class shelter to help others. Countless women and children have you to thank for rescuing them from their horrible situations. You've created a sanctuary for those who can't help themselves. I know it sounds corny and a little condescending, but I am so proud of you. I only wish I had half the character you have."

Victor was embarrassed. He wasn't used to this kind of praise. He was also surprised at how good it felt to know Ariel was proud of him. She approved of who and what he was. He'd never experienced that before. Lakeisha had never understood him and she certainly never approved of his life. That was part of their problem. She wanted him to change to make her happy. She didn't understand he couldn't change who he was. She didn't realize that if he tried, he would be unhappy which in turn would make her unhappy. His mother had done the same thing to his father. Mother wanted father to give up being a warrior. If he had done that for her, he would have resented her for it. Victor realized he had been lost in thought and hadn't responded to Ariel. "I'm not sure what I've done is something to be proud of. It was just something I needed to do. It's funny you would refer to it as a sanctuary. Do you know how I came up with the name Lavena Tèarmann?"

"No," Ariel admitted. "What does it mean?"

"Lavena is Celtic for joy and Tèarmann is Gaelic for Sanctuary. I know it doesn't exactly go together, but I wanted the shelter to be a joyous place for the kids and a sanctuary for those in need."

"I should have known," Ariel commented. "After the way you came up with Bojan Taverns. You are clever aren't you?"

He smiled at her. "It feels good to have someone understand me. I think maybe you really do accept me for who I am. I don't feel like you want to change me like my mother and then Lakeisha did."

"Absolutely not," Ariel exclaimed. "I would never try to change you, Victor. I'm disappointed in myself for what happened in that cave. I thought I wanted you to be angry with Lakeisha. At the time, I wished you had rejected her. I wanted you to somehow demonstrate your anger for what she did to you. It took Dimitri's meddling to make me understand I really didn't want that. That's not who you are. I respect you for who you are. If you had done things my way, I would have lost some of that respect. I would have been disappointed. I love you because of who you are. I could never try to change that."

"Thank you," Victor said humbly. He really did love her. He was beginning to think maybe she loved him, too. Maybe it was possible to have an open relationship with her. He was still terrified and trusting her completely was going to take work. But he never wanted to lose Ariel again.

"Back to my original point," Ariel continued. "There's one more thing you've done that demonstrates you have overcome your past. You've simply tried. You've had a couple relationships with women. First with Lakeisha and then again with me. Lakeisha's actions could have damaged you forever, but they didn't. Even though you tried to avoid me at first, eventually we got together. I almost ruined things, but you wouldn't let me. You showed up on my doorstep tonight so we could talk things out. You're further along than you give yourself credit for, Victor. I only wish I could cope with my past as well as you have yours. If you're willing to listen, I would like to tell you my story now," she said solemnly.

"I know how difficult it is for me to talk about what happened with my mother," Victor told her. "In fact, I haven't told anyone besides you, Alex and Dimitri. I hid most of the details from my father my entire life. I don't want him to suffer any more than he already has," Victor admitted. "You can tell me your story later or not tell me at all if you want. I guess what I'm trying to say is you should only tell me what happened if you want me to know. Not because you feel obligated." He kissed the top of her head. They sat silent for a minute. Victor was thinking about the things Ariel had said. "I'm not sure I've overcome my history, but for the first time in my life, I'm actively trying. I want to overcome my past. I want to be the best man I can be for you. I want to deserve your love, Ariel. Right now, I don't feel like I do. But I promise you I will try," Victor said softly.

"The feeling is mutual. I want to deserve your love too," Ariel admitted sincerely. "I'm so far behind you in dealing with my past. I feel inadequate next to you. Knowing what you've been through and what you've done to overcome everything motivates me to overcome my issues. I want to tell you what happened to me. But first, can I ask you a question?"

"Of course," Victor was surprised she hadn't had more questions.

"It's about that night in the cave. The night you went out alone searching for the location of the vampire's hideout. The night you discovered where they were holding Abby," she paused.

"Yeah," Victor prodded.

"Did you have a nightmare that night about your mother and your childhood?" she asked hesitantly.

"Yes," Victor admitted. "That's not typical for me. Once my mother was dead, I pretty much left the past in the past. In the beginning, I would periodically have nightmares. I guess that's what you would call them. Basically, I would have dreams about the past. Dad always helped me get through them. I honestly believe his love is what healed me so quickly. He loved me so much, he gave up everything for me. I couldn't dwell on my history, it felt like a betrayal. It seemed almost too easy to put the past behind me. Unfortunately, Alex and Dimitri have helped me realize I didn't really put it behind me. I'm still overcoming it."

After Dark

Victor continued. "That night in the cave I was so tired and my blood level was low. My hands were burning like they were on fire. I hadn't felt pain like that for a very long time. As a warrior, I typically heal quickly. I don't even require as much blood as the other warriors. I think that is a result of my childhood, too. Mom never gave me blood to heal my wounds. She didn't want them to heal. Anyway, the extensive burning brought back a memory I haven't thought about since my childhood. I had a dream about an incident that happened when I was six." Victor proceeded to tell her about his dream.

Ariel was horrified. How could a mother do that to a six year old child? How could anyone be that demented? Victor had been through so much. It was amazing he didn't have more issues than he did. "I'm so sorry, Victor. I know you don't want my pity and that's not what I'm feeling right now. I'm just sad and horrified. I feel bad for the child and amazed at the man he has become." She kissed him, hoping to convey her emotions through affection. They were silent for a long moment. "What happened when she got you back into the cellar? The part you didn't have to relive because you woke up?" she asked.

"She beat me severely," he said flatly. "It was one of the worst beatings of my life. I think she broke a couple ribs. I don't know what else. I just remember lying there wishing I was dead. I hurt everywhere. The beating was so severe, I'm actually surprised she didn't kill me that night. If I hadn't been a warrior, I think she would have. Fortunately, or unfortunately depending how you look at it, I healed fairly quickly and the wounds weren't fatal."

"I'd say it was fortunate. Otherwise, I never would have met you." She smiled at him. "So, it's definitely fortunate for me."

Victor kissed her this time. It was good to have someone who understood him. Victor knew the only reason she understood was because she had experienced something terrible herself. He wondered if she was still going to tell him what happened to her. He wasn't going to ask. She'd reveal her story when she was ready. "I'm sorry I'm so much trouble. I know I'm not easy to love."

"You're not that much trouble. You're good and strong. I'm weak and vulnerable. Once you hear my story you might change your mind about me. Underneath it all, I'm just a coward." Ariel said, she really was worried he'd be disappointed in how she'd handled herself during and after the incident. It seemed so trivial compared to what Victor had lived through.

"I don't believe that. I've seen you fight. You're not a coward, Ariel. It's not fair to judge yourself because of the way you dealt with the worst situation of your life. You have more courage than most men when it comes to fighting vampires. Don't discount that." He wished he could take her pain away. He knew what it was like to be victimized. It angered him to know she had been a victim sometime in her past.

Ariel took a deep breath and began her story. "I was nineteen at the time. I had just left a friend's house and was headed home. It was dark outside and I was late. I didn't want to worry my parents so I decided to cut across a field and take a shortcut. But I got lost. My family hadn't lived in New York very long and I was still trying to find my way around. I somehow ended up in a dark alley in the more seedy part of town. I was nervous, but still confident I could find my way home. That's when I realized someone was following me.

After Dark

I came around a corner and my path was blocked by a man. He was dirty and smelled of alcohol. I knew he was drunk and I was in trouble. I immediately turned to run and collided with the man who had been following me. They were together. They both grabbed me and threw me to the ground. One of them held me down while the other went for the buggy. They drove me to a rundown house on the outskirts of town. It was cold and musty and unkempt. I was shoved into a small room and chained to a metal ring secured into the wall," she paused and took a deep breath. Then she climbed out of bed and walked to the closet. She pulled on a robe and headed back to the bed. Victor was watching her intently. Ariel felt a little self-conscious. "What?" she demanded.

"I just like to watch you," he said pulling her back onto the bed. "You are so beautiful. I could look at you for hours. It's kind of like watching a beautiful sunset, or studying a painting. I never tire of seeing your beauty, that's all."

Ariel rolled her eyes. She didn't believe him. "Okay whatever," she narrowed her eyes at him. "Are you trying to distract me? Now that I've started, I want to get through this."

Victor tipped her head back and kissed her gently. "Okay, finish telling me your story." He was sitting up, leaning against the headboard. He pulled her onto his lap so he could hold her while she talked. He thought he knew what was coming. Nothing good could come out of this situation. Ariel relaxed against his chest and continued.

"The two men kept talking about Robert. They needed to wait for Robert. I figured he must be their leader or something. I was scared, but I was trying to find a way to escape. If they were waiting for Robert, maybe I had time to come up with something before he got there. Time passed so slowly. No matter what I tried, I couldn't get out of my chains. I don't know how long I'd been sitting there when the door opened and one of the men quietly slipped into the room. He sat down next to me and put his hand up my shirt. I immediately understood what he had planned. At first I fought him off. He laughed at me. That seemed to encourage him. He hiked up my skirt and climbed on top of me. Then, he started to take off his pants. I don't know what happened. It was like a light switch went off inside of me. I shut down completely. I knew he was going to rape me. I kept telling myself to fight, but I couldn't make myself move. I was frozen, it was like I was in a trance.

The guy got angry. He wanted me to fight him. It excited him to victimize a frightened, scared woman who fought him off. I wouldn't fight. I just laid there quietly, cold and limp. He became so angry he started to beat me. Ironically, my weakness saved me. He couldn't rape a woman that didn't fight him off. He wasn't excited anymore. He was furious. He was straddling my legs and he just kept hitting me in the face, the ribs and the stomach. He was out of control with his rage. Eventually, the door flew open and the other man pulled him off me.

They left the room, but I could hear them arguing. Again they brought up Robert, that's the only name they ever said. He was going to be furious with them. Robert was going to be there the following day. It was clear these two were frightened of Robert. I worried all night what I was in for in the morning.

The next day Robert and another man showed up. One look at me and he became angry. My face was swollen and I couldn't open one eye. I'd been beaten pretty severely. He'd broken several ribs and my abdomen was so bruised and sore. This was after I started to heal, but the process was slow without the aid of our tea. Robert

267

yelled at the two men for a long time before the four of them carried me from the room. They took me to another small, dark room. They stripped me naked and chained my hands to a metal table or bench type thing. I was terrified. I knew this time nobody would stop them. They all smelled like whiskey and they were so gross and dirty.

The Robert guy looked me over and then ran his hand across my stomach, I cringed. It made my skin crawl to be touched by someone so disgusting. He turned back to the other three and they all started arguing. Robert kept telling them they were going to have to kill me. The fourth man that had shown up with Robert didn't want to. He said they had accidentally killed the last girl, but he wasn't willing to kill me on purpose. The argument went on for a while. Neither man would give in. Robert finally walked back over to me. He touched my breast and then trailed his finger down to my stomach over the bruising. I wanted to throw up. I was so scared and I was sure nobody would ever find me in time to save me.

That's when Dimitri stormed in. He was like an avenging angel. You know what he's like. Three of the men froze. I could tell they were afraid of him. Robert tried to act tough. He had a gun and he started to go for me. Dimitri was too quick. He grabbed Robert and threw him across the room. Robert dropped the gun at my feet. The guy that assaulted me the night before picked it up. He was laughing again and staring at me. I was terrified of what he was going to do with that gun. Was he just threatening me, or was he going to shoot me or shoot Dimitri? I just didn't know, so I started to kick him. I went crazy just kicking and screaming. I was trying to kick the gun out of his hand, but I couldn't get to it. He pulled the trigger and shot me in the upper right hip. The bullet traveled all the way through and exited through my groin area. I was in so much pain and the blood was dripping down that awful metal table. The bullet had struck a main artery. I think I must have passed out. The next thing I remember was Dimitri carrying me to his carriage. He rushed me home and Tianna nursed me back to health."

"What happened to the four men?" Victor asked a little too controlled.

Ariel looked up at him. His face was hard and grim. She could tell he was angry and trying to hide it. "I'm confident Dimitri took care of them. He never would tell me what he did. I suspect it was really awful. That was enough for me. I guess that's why I understood Thomas so well. I stood there in that cave watching Thomas brutalize Hector. I just kept thinking I hope Dimitri did the same thing to those men that abducted and abused me."

Victor sighed. He was furious. He wanted to punish those men himself. Knowing Dimitri had taken care of them made it a little better. But he wanted to hunt them down and kill them right now. Knowing they were dead and he couldn't do anything to avenge Ariel for their abuse, made him feel cheated somehow. He held her a little tighter. At least he could be there for her now. He would never let her feel scared and alone again. He would never let what happened in that cave happen again. He was going to be there for Ariel, forever if she'd let him.

"I didn't deal with it well. I was shattered inside so my physical healing took longer than it should have. Tianna and my mother fussed for over a month. I finally forced myself to get out of bed, but I wouldn't go outside. Once I was able to go outside, I wouldn't leave the yard. After several months my parents talked me into moving to France with my aunt. She lived in Paris and they thought maybe the change would do me good. Very few fae live in that region. I stayed in France most of my life. That's why nobody here really knows me. I came back to visit on occasion, but I still didn't venture out into town much. I either spent the time with my parents and Dimitri, or Breena and I would take a trip.

I found this house for sale on one of my trips back home and fell in love with it. I thought maybe if I had a place of my own here, I'd be able to cope with the past. I didn't stay long. It was just another place to hide out. I think I understand your dad better than most. I'm sure that farm has become his comfort zone. Somewhere he feels safe and shut off from the rest of the world. Anyway, I left soon after I bought this house and decided to travel. I lived all over, but never really settled. Finally, about six years ago I moved back here. I was determined to fight my demons and get on with my life.

For the first year or so I didn't really socialize much. Then I met Tank. And you know the rest. Once he left, I stayed for another year mostly to deal with the council and make sure they didn't find him. Then I decided to go visit my aunt in Paris again. I've only been back about six months now. I get out a lot more, but I still don't like to socialize much. I think I'm getting better at that, too. I like being close to my parents and I'm determined to make a life for myself here in New York."

Victor was at a loss for words. He was angry that Ariel had been attacked that way, but he was also proud of her. She didn't think she'd dealt with her past, but she had. "So when are you going to get to the cowardly weak part?" he asked.

"Very funny," she looked up at him. It was nice to have his support, but she knew she was weak. "For starters, I bet you've never had a panic attack in your life."

"Actually, no. I've never had a full-blown panic attack," he began.

"See," she interrupted.

"But when I walked into that cave and saw Lakeisha and Abby chained to the wall. It did impact me. I was shocked and I was desperate to get them free. I'd say that's pretty close to the same thing. I shut everyone and everything out around me. I remembered what it was like to be imprisoned that way and I had to do something. Does that make me weak?" he asked.

"No, of course not. The difference is, you react. I just freeze," Ariel countered.

Victor tipped her head back so he could look into her eyes. "That doesn't make you weak."

"Well you have to admit it was pretty cowardly to run away from home," she replied.

"I think you're looking at this all wrong." Victor twisted so they were looking at each other. "When you said you went to live with your aunt in Paris, I didn't look at that as running away. It was a small step you needed to take to heal from the horror you experienced in that rundown house. That's not being weak. It's being proactive. I bet you didn't have any problems going out into the streets of Paris, did you?"

"Well, no. Not really," Ariel admitted.

"That's not being weak, it's doing what you had to do to heal. I don't know why you think you're a coward. First you fought off your attackers. There were too many and they were stronger and bigger than you but you still tried to fight. So you shut down when that asshole tried to rape you. It saved you, didn't it? So that wasn't weak, it was smart. Then you were kicking and screaming when the guy pointed a gun at you. That's not cowardly, either.

Now, you're back here in New York determined to face your demons and make a life for yourself. You also sat in that cabin for over an hour, fighting the fear when you didn't know what was in the woods rather than call for help. By the way, if you ever do anything like that again, I'll strangle you myself. That was stupid and dangerous, but courageous. You are not a coward Ariel and it pisses me off to hear you call yourself one."

"Well I certainly wouldn't want to piss you off," she smiled at him.

Victor cradled his hand around the back of her neck. He pulled her in for a long, meaningful kiss. "I love you and I will always be here for you. I'll help you slay your dragons if you'll let me. I think you're pretty close already." He reached down and untied her robe. Ariel laid down next to Victor on the bed. He ran his hand over her right hip. "Where did he shoot you?" he asked as he slowly circled her hip area with his fingers.

"Right there," she said pressing her hand over the top of his. "I don't have visible scars, but I'll never forget where the scar should be. Maybe I'll get a miniature tattoo right there to remind me what I've done to slay my dragons," she said watching him. She liked the idea but wondered if he would think she was copying him or something.

"It's a very painful process," Victor said as he continued to circle the spot where Ariel had been shot. "But if you want a tattoo, I'll go with you to get one."

Ariel sat up. "I feel sort of like I'm copying you, but I really like the idea. What do you think about it? Would it bother you if I had a dragon tattoo? Would you feel strange if we had matching body art?"

"Not at all. I guess you're kind of right. My dragon is a constant reminder of what I've done to overcome my past. When I look in the mirror, I always see it. When I got it, I thought I was just hiding that scar. I was tired of the constant reminder of what my mother did. So, I decided to turn something ugly into art. But now I don't think of it that way. I guess in a way it gives me the strength I need to move forward, not backwards. If getting a dragon tattooed on your hip would do the same for you, I think it's a good idea. But it really is painful. For me, the pain was also part of the healing process. If that's what you want to do, I support you and I will be there for you if you'll let me." He slowly moved his hand up the curve of her body and slid the robe off her shoulders. Then he leaned down and kissed her gently. "I will always try to be there for you Ariel."

Ariel leaned in and kissed Victor. "I love you," she said softly. "I'm here for you, too. I hope you remember that."

"I know," Victor smiled. It had been a long, stressful night and he was getting tired. "So, does that mean I can stay here tonight or do you want me to head home?" He pressed his mouth to hers before she could answer. His kiss was seductive and enchanting.

"Stay," she said as she pulled him on top of her and returned the kiss.

After Dark

The following afternoon, Victor was sitting in Dimitri's library sipping on a Coke and waiting for Dimitri to arrive. Alex walked back in with a deck of cards. "You up for a friendly game while we wait?" she asked.

Victor smiled. "Are we betting or just playing? Betting's always more fun."

"Okay," Alex agreed. "We'll play for money, but no credit. Collecting is so messy on credit. I like you. I'd hate to have to track you down and break your legs," she smiled.

Victor laughed. "I'll deal this round." He took the cards and started to shuffle.

Dimitri walked through the front door and heard laughter in the library. He headed that way. As he stepped into the room, he realized Alex was playing poker with Victor. She laid down her cards triumphantly. Dimitri saw she had a good hand, three kings. Victor was in trouble. Victor smiled and laid down a flush. He counted out his winnings and glanced back at Dimitri.

"Your girlfriend is killing me." He grinned and checked the memo pad. Victor slowly pulled out his wallet. "Here you go." He laid down three one hundred dollar bills. "Promise me you'll use it to get your hair done or something. I'll be crushed if you spend it on the gorilla over there." He pointed to Dimitri and laughed.

"Don't you have a woman of your own to spend time with? I was sure you'd get your act together by now." He walked over and kissed Alex lightly.

Victor winked at Alex. "Sorry, sweetheart. The fun's over. Grumpy's home." He glanced at Dimitri again as he stood. "Give me a call next time he's away, maybe we'll play strip poker for variety." He leaned over and kissed her cheek.

Dimitri scowled at Victor. "Not funny. Why are you here?"

"I need to talk to you," he sobered as he glanced back at Alex.

"I'll be in the kitchen. I need to finish dinner," Alex took the hint. "There's plenty, do you want to stay Victor?" She smiled, amused at Dimitri. He was still scowling.

"I'd love to, but I have plans. I won't stay long. I just need a few minutes." He moved to the couch and sat down.

Dimitri walked over and sat in the chair across from him. "What's on your mind?"

Victor studied him for a minute. "I need to know what you did to the men that abducted Ariel," he said flatly.

"So, you and Ariel did talk. Did the two of you work things out?" Dimitri asked.

"Yes, but you already knew we would. Don't be too proud of yourself. I'm still annoyed at you for putting her on a guilt trip," Victor glared at Dimitri.

"Yeah, and I'm sure I'll hear the same from her," Dimitri smiled. "I knew you were perfect for each other."

"The four men?" Victor asked.

"I took care of them," Dimitri shrugged.

"I realize that. I need to know how. Be specific," he countered.

"It doesn't matter how. All you need to know is they're all dead," Dimitri answered.

"Actually, I need to know more than that. I need to know everything. The evasive stuff might work with Ariel, it's not going to work with me." Victor studied Dimitri, he wasn't going to back down. He needed to know the truth.

Dimitri took a deep breath. He understood why Victor needed this. He just didn't like to talk about it. Victor needed assurance that those men had suffered and paid for their crimes. They had. "Okay," he got up and shut the door. "I'll fill you in but I'll need you to keep it to yourself. If possible, I'd prefer Ariel didn't know the details."

"If she asks I won't keep it from her," Victor answered.

"I'm not asking you to lie. I'm just saying she's been okay without the details until now. I'd like to keep it that way if possible. If she needs to know, I'll understand. However, I need your promise you won't talk about this with anyone else. I did what I had to do. I don't regret my actions, but I'm not proud of them either. It's not something I want people to know. Do you understand?" Dimitri asked.

"I understand," Victor assured him. So, they had paid for their actions. Good.

Dimitri went through the deaths one by one. Each of the men had died in a terrible and painful manner. Robert and the one that shot Ariel received the worst punishment by far. Robert because he was the ring leader, the other man because he shot Ariel. If Dimitri had known about the attack the previous night, the torture would have been much worse. Dimitri didn't have any regrets. As far as he was concerned justice had been served. He did it for Ariel, but those monsters also needed to pay a high price for the other women they had victimized.

Victor sat back, watching Dimitri. He was satisfied with the punishment Dimitri had dealt out. He still felt cheated and helpless. He wished he had been the one to protect and avenge Ariel. He had to admit Dimitri took care of things appropriately. He also understood why Dimitri kept the details to himself. His tactics were not for the weak. "Thank you," Victor said quietly. "For what it's worth I approve of everything you did," he paused. "I don't know if that matters, but I do and I just wanted you to know."

"Thank you," Dimitri said sincerely. "It does matter. I've had more than a few bad moments thinking about my actions that day. I've questioned my right to take things into my own hands," he studied Victor. "Maybe I didn't have that right, but I wouldn't change anything either. I couldn't trust human laws to handle those four. They'd gone unpunished far too long. Nobody hurts one of mine and gets away with it."

"I agree," Victor stated. "You shouldn't question what you did. It had to be done. You're a good leader because you're willing to make the hard decisions. You are personally willing to make sure justice is served, regardless of the personal sacrifice. Instead of questioning your right to dish out that justice yourself, you should think about all the additional victims there would have been if you didn't. Those men never would have stopped. My shelter is full of women and children that have been victimized by evil men. Thanks to you, there were fewer victims in the world. Be proud of what you did. Don't ever question whether you had the right to do it," Victor stood.

Dimitri also stood. He put a hand on Victor's shoulder. "I know it's none of my business, but can I assume everything is okay between you and Ariel?"

"Yeah," Victor placed his hand on Dimitri's opposite shoulder. "We're fine, don't worry about us. Thanks for being honest with me, tonight and last night. I needed both." He held out his hand for Dimitri to shake.

Dimitri took his hand and pulled Victor in for a quick hug. "I'm always here for you, Victor. I hope you'll remember that."

"I know. The offer is mutual. I don't have many close friends. You've been there for me most of my life. When I told Alex you were one of my best friends, I meant it. If there's ever anything I can do for you, all you have to do is ask," Victor offered.

"Thanks," Dimitri grinned. "It's a good thing I like you so much. Otherwise you'd have to pay for spending so much time with my future wife," they both smiled. Dimitri would never tolerate anybody else flirting with Alex the way Victor did and they both knew it.

"Well, she's all yours. I've got to go," Victor admitted. "I have plans with Ariel tonight."

* * * *

A couple weeks later, Victor and Ariel were sitting in her living room relaxing. Things had been going extremely well between them. Ariel already knew she wanted to spend the rest of her life with this man. Every day she loved Victor a little more. She knew he loved her, but they hadn't talked about their future at all. She didn't know how he felt about marriage or children. After more than five hundred years, he didn't even own a home. He was still living in an apartment. Did that say something about his feelings toward commitment? She didn't want to scare him, but she wished she knew the answers to some of those questions. If she had her way, Victor would be living here already. What if he didn't want to live in this house? Was she willing to move? Maybe, but not into his apartment. She needed a home.

They were lounging on the couch. Ariel was sitting in front of Victor while he massaged her neck and shoulders. They had spent every night together. Mostly they stayed here, but she did stay at Victor's one night when he worked late at the club. He had a nice place. Dimitri made it sound like a cheap apartment with no security. That wasn't the case at all. Victor lived on the top floor of the apartment building, kind of like the penthouse. There was security, it wasn't as high tech as her system but it wasn't bad. He'd done wonders with his place, she just liked her place better.

Victor wrapped his arms around Ariel and pulled her back against his chest. He brushed her hair aside and began to trace gentle kisses down her neck. Ariel closed her eyes. She loved spending time with Victor. When they were like this, she could forget everything else and relax. She could get lost for hours with

Victor. The problems and concerns of the real world somehow disappeared completely.

"So," Victor said softly, "I was thinking about visiting dad this weekend. I know its short notice but if you're free, I'd love to have you join me."

Ariel looked up at him. "How long? When did you plan to leave and when are you coming back?" she asked. She wanted to go, but she might have to reschedule a couple things.

"I need to go into Tèarmann Friday morning. When I get finished there, I thought I'd stop in and check on the club. Jack's pretty good at handling things while I'm gone so that shouldn't take long. I was hoping to be on the road by noon Friday. I want to stay as long as I can, so I planned on coming back Sunday evening sometime." Victor was now playing with Ariel's hair.

"I can probably swing that. Are you sure it won't upset your dad to have me there?" She was concerned about his father. Did he have the same aversion to women that Victor struggled with?

"Dad's going to love you. He doesn't leave the farm much, but he's not as antisocial as he used to be. For years I had to hire someone to do the shopping, the laundry, everything for him. Now he drives into town himself to shop and drop his clothes off to be laundered. I know that doesn't sound like much, but for him it was a big step. I'm proud of him. He'll be fine with the company. If you're sure you can make it I'll call him and let him know. I don't want to say anything if there's a chance you can't make it though. Dad will get nervous and fuss over having company. He'll probably overdo it with the cleaning and the shopping. I don't want him to bother if you aren't going to go."

"I'll make it," Ariel promised then paused before she continued. "Do you need me to meet you at your place, or are you going to pick me up here?"

Victor turned her head so he could look at her. There was something in her tone. He'd heard it there before, but it was so slight he'd ignored it. He was studying her for a clue. He knew she didn't like his apartment, was that what this was about? Or was there something else going on?

"What?" she asked casually.

Victor watched her for a few more seconds. He didn't know what. How could he ask her about that tone if he didn't know what to ask?

Ariel sat up and turned to face Victor. "What's wrong?" she asked furrowing her brows.

"I don't know," he answered honestly sitting up and leaning back against the couch. "That's what I was going to ask you. You always have this tone when you talk about my place. Do you really hate it that bad?" He didn't plan on living there forever, but it was part of him. If Ariel hated the apartment, what did that say about him?

"No," Ariel answered. "I don't hate your apartment."

"But?" he asked. "I can tell there's something going on, Ariel. What is it?"

How did Victor read her so well? She couldn't hide anything from him. She stood up and walked over to the window. She wasn't ready to have this conversation. She was so worried that Victor wasn't ready for this conversation. She didn't realize it, but she was pacing in front of the window.

Victor stood up and walked over to her. He placed his hands on her shoulders and forced her to stop. He was confused. What was going on here? "Baby, talk to me," he soothed. He was studying her face, trying to get some clue what she was upset about.

Ariel closed her eyes. "I didn't plan on having this conversation tonight. I just don't know what you want and I don't know if it's too soon to ask," she confessed.

"Come back over here and sit down." He took her hand and guided her to the couch. Once they sat down he held her face between his hands. Didn't she know she could talk to him about anything? He leaned in and kissed her. "Talk to me," he said softly. "If you're worried about something, tell me. What do you mean you don't know what I want?" He pulled her in and hugged her. "I want you, Ariel. Everything else is just gravy." He brushed her hair away from her face. "Whatever it is, it's not too soon to ask."

"I really don't hate your apartment," she said. "I thought I would. Dimitri constantly dogs it. I expected something run down in a dangerous part of town with no security," Ariel began.

Victor laughed. "He's just upset because I won't pay him to redo the whole system. I don't need it. The system is fine. It fits the area and the apartment. Anyway, so you don't hate my apartment but you don't like it either."

"Actually, I really do like the way you've decorated it. I think our taste is very similar," Ariel countered.

"I'm still confused here. What is it you don't like? That night you stayed with me, I got the impression you were uncomfortable there," Victor stated. "That's why I haven't asked you back."

"I'm sorry," Ariel apologized. "It's not that I was uncomfortable, I guess I just don't understand. You are more than five hundred years old. Why do you still rent an apartment? It seems like such a waste," she asked.

Victor smiled. "Well for starters, I don't rent that place. I own it."

"I don't understand. You can't own an apartment," Ariel said confused.

"I own the whole building. It's my complex," Victor admitted.

"Oh," Ariel said, wide eyed. That changed things. Maybe Victor wasn't against commitment.

Victor smiled. "I have a manager that lives on the first floor. She handles everything. I also have a handyman that does all the repairs. For me the building is really low maintenance, those two take care of everything. I live there out of convenience. It's centrally located between my other two businesses. I moved in as soon as I purchased the building and converted the top floor into my home. At the time I was managing everything myself. Living there made sense, the tenants could always find me if they had a problem."

"So, do you have any other businesses you want to confess to owning?" she asked. "Wait, let me change that. Do you own any other businesses? There could be some you don't want to admit to," she stated narrowing her eyes at him.

After Dark

Victor smiled. "No. I only have the three. That's enough for me. I've never been as ambitious as Luke was. Thomas and Alex run an empire and I think they both love it. I'm content with my little world. Like I said, the apartment building doesn't take much of my time anymore. It was my first business venture. When I moved onto the club, I just couldn't sell it. It grew on me and I was fond of my tenants. I couldn't sell to a stranger and hope they'd be taken care of by the new owner. I decided to keep it and hire a manager. Opening a new club was going to take most of my time. I was able to find a way to focus my energy on the club and keep the complex. I have managers at Bojan and Tèarmann now too, but they still take quite a bit of my time. Then add in the warrior stuff and I have enough on my plate."

"No wonder you're so busy," Ariel commented. "Do you plan to live there forever?" she asked, trying to sound casual.

So, maybe they would finally get to the point. "No," he answered honestly.

Ariel waited, but he didn't elaborate. Of course he wasn't going to make this easy on her. Ariel sat back and pulled her legs up. She wrapped her arms around them for comfort.

Victor watched her. What was she so worried about? Did she want to talk about their living arrangements? Or was that just wishful thinking? He wanted them to start their lives together immediately, but after her story about Tank there was no way he was going to bring that up this early in their relationship. He thought he'd know when the time was right.

Ariel took a deep breath. She'd stalled long enough. She couldn't drag this on any longer, it was just making things worse. "Victor, I know we haven't been together for very long, only a few weeks. But, I love you. I love you more than I have ever loved anyone. One year, ten years, a hundred years won't change how I feel. Well, actually I know I will love you even more as time goes by. Knowing that makes me anxious to start our lives together. I haven't said anything because you already told me I terrify you. I don't want to push things. I don't want to scare you away," she paused.

"Ariel, you could never scare me away," he answered. "I love you. I'm not sure you realize just how big that is for me." He slid his fingers through her hair to cup her face and brushed his thumb across her cheek bone. "I love you," he said kissing her forehead.

"I didn't realize I had a tone when I talked about your place, but if I do it's only because I don't want to have your place and my place. I want our place. I've just been too scared to bring it up. We've never talked about what you want. I don't know how you feel about marriage or children. If I asked you to move into my home, would you run away because I'm moving too fast? That's what I meant when I said I don't know what you want. I don't know if for you, it's too soon to talk about us." She sat there, looking directly into his eyes, not moving an inch. She needed to watch for a reaction. She needed to know if she was scaring him away. At first, he didn't move.

Finally Victor gently picked up one of her legs and straightened it, then the other one. He leaned in, placing one arm on the couch beside her thigh and the other on the back of the couch next to her head. He slowly moved forward until his lips were up against her ear. "I'm not running Ariel," he whispered. Then he nipped gently at her earlobe. He started trailing kisses down her neck, across her collarbone and then back up and across her cheek until he reached her mouth. He pressed his lips to hers, gentle at

After Dark

first then hard and possessive. They shared a long, intimate kiss then Victor moved back slightly to look into her eyes. "So, diamonds then?" he asked.

Ariel was confused. What was he talking about?

"My apology for being stupid again," he said when he saw her confusion. "You said you wanted diamonds. Do you like those by themselves, or with rubies or sapphires or something with them?" he asked.

"Oh," she got it now. But what did he have to apologize for? She was the one that was being stupid this time. "I do like diamonds, but I think this one's on me. You didn't say what you wanted when I did something over the top," she asked.

"That's easy. I'm a guy. I want sex." He grinned at her then swept her into his arms and settled her on his lap. "I'm sorry you've been stressing about our future. I guess I was just as hesitant to bring it up as you have been." He kissed her lightly. "I hate it when you compare us to my relationship with Lakeisha, like that situation was some kind of roadmap you need to follow. Our relationship is nothing like the situation with Lakeisha. It's so much more. Nothing that happened there applies to us. Do you understand what I'm saying? I wasn't sure what I wanted with her. That's why after almost a year, we still weren't living together officially. I didn't love Lakeisha. I'm madly in love with you, Ariel."

Ariel's smile widened. "Me too."

"That's why I owe you an apology. I hate it when you do that with Lakeisha but then I did the same thing with Tank," he confessed.

"What do you mean?" she asked.

"Tank told you he loved you and wanted to move in together. The two of you hadn't known each other very long, and you sent him packing. You weren't ready for something like that with him. I know you told me you didn't love him, but I avoided talking about us living together because I didn't want to blind side you like Tank did."

Ariel understood now. She leaned back a little so she could get a good look at Victor's face. "Our relationship is nothing like the situation with Tank, either. I love you, I didn't love Tank. I cared for him. We had some good times together, but I didn't love him. I didn't want to spend my life with him. I want to spend my life with you, Victor."

"I was stupid enough to think I'd know when you were ready to take things to the next level," Victor confessed. "I should have known better. I don't know anything about relationships."

"So you do want to live together?" she asked hopefully.

"I've wanted to start my life with you since the first night I spent here," Victor told her. "I know what I want. I want you, Ariel. I want to fall asleep holding you every night and wake up next to you every morning. After five hundred years of isolation and casual sex, I finally found a woman that I love. A woman I can actually trust. I don't need time to think about what I want with you. I know I'm going to love you forever. I have issues and I'm trying to overcome them, but that doesn't change the fact that I can't live without you. I would absolutely love it if we could begin our lives together. Moving in together seems like a very good first step," he paused. "So, I assume you don't want to move to my place." He laughed at the horrified look she was trying to hide.

"Uh, I kind of like my place better," she said hesitantly. "Do you think you could be happy here?"

Victor kissed her hard and fast. "I am happy here," he answered gleefully. "Are you sure you can put up with me on a full time basis?" he questioned. This felt too good to be true.

"I'm sure," Ariel answered immediately. "How about you? Are you sure you can handle the makeup and blow dryer lying around in the bathroom? And all the rest of that women stuff?"

"Absolutely. When can I move in?" he asked.

"How about tomorrow. I have plans for you tonight," she said seductively. "I think I owe you that apology."

Victor stood and carried her into the bedroom. Tonight he realized he still had a long way to go when it came to trust. He trusted Ariel with his life, but when it came to trusting her with his heart he was still struggling. It was comforting to know she was struggling with the same thing. Maybe the vulnerability he was feeling was normal. Maybe it wasn't a result of his past and his baggage. He gently placed Ariel on the bed. She was so beautiful. His heart swelled with the love he had for her. She was his. That fact still amazed and delighted him. He would cherish her forever. And, tomorrow he was going to buy her some diamonds.

Chapter Nine

Victor woke early the following morning. He silently slid from the bed, grabbed his jeans and headed for the kitchen. He stood leaning against the counter while he waited for his coffee. This was actually going to be his home. He was really going to begin his life with Ariel. Victor didn't think life could be any better. He'd move his stuff over this morning. There wasn't much, so it shouldn't take long. He'd need his clothes and a few incidentals, but he wanted to keep the apartment furnished. Most of the furniture and dishes would stay there. Ariel's house was perfect already. He wouldn't need most of that stuff anyway. Plus, he wanted a place available if he ever convinced his father to visit New York. Victor opened the fridge. Ariel had eggs and half a package of bacon. Maybe he'd fix her breakfast in bed.

Victor entered the darkened room and placed the tray on the dresser. Ariel was still out cold. He stood there, watching her sleep. He didn't know how he had gotten so lucky. Why did this amazing woman choose him to fall in love with? He'd probably never know why, he was just grateful she had. He gently sat on the edge of the bed and brushed her hair away from her face. She looked like an angel lying there so peacefully. He leaned down and placed a soft kiss on her lips. Ariel stirred, but didn't wake up. Victor smiled and tried again. This time the kiss was more forceful. He knew the instant she woke up. He pulled back and smiled at her. "Morning, beautiful."

Ariel sat up and brushed her hair away from her face. "Probably not right now. Unless of course you're into tasseled hair and smeared mascara." She glanced around the room looking for a robe.

"I'm into you," he said softly. "And I think you're beautiful in the morning." He stood and walked to the closet. He shuffled around for a minute and then pulled out a silk robe. "Here," he watched as she slid the robe over her sexy body and tied the sash around her waist.

"What is that smell?" she said as she headed for the bathroom. An amazing aroma hit her and she stopped in the doorway. "I know I smell coffee, but is that bacon and eggs?"

"Yep," he answered. "Better hurry if you want me to share, I'm starved."

Ariel smiled as she entered the bathroom. Nobody had made her breakfast before. She was thinking about last night and remembered Victor said he would move in today. She couldn't wait. She felt like this was the first step in the right direction for them. Eventually she wanted to marry him, maybe have kids. Then it struck her, what if she couldn't have children. Would Victor be disappointed, or did he even want kids? He had that vasectomy, did that mean he wasn't interested in being a father. She hoped not. He would be such a wonderful dad. But that brought her back to her original thought, what if she was incapable of having a child? Orin had been such a trouper before Alex healed Breena. But Ariel could see it had been devastating for him. They were so much happier now that Breena was healed and they both knew there was hope. How could she do that to Victor? Alex might be able to help, but that felt wrong. She wouldn't use her friend's powers that way. She wouldn't use her friend that way. Ariel jumped at the knock on the door. She turned to see Victor standing in the doorway.

Victor was smiling until he saw Ariel's face. She looked so sad and disappointed. Was she having second thoughts about their living arrangements? No, she was the one that brought that up. It had to be something else. He rushed to her side and turned her so he could wrap his arms around her. "What's wrong?" he asked.

Ariel was surprised at the tears that gathered in her eyes. Victor's arms felt so good wrapped around her in comfort. He'd made her breakfast and she was ruining everything. What was wrong with her?

Victor leaned back and gently lifted Ariel's head. It broke his heart to see she was crying. "Sweetheart, what's wrong?" He gently wiped the tears away with his thumbs. "My cooking can't be that bad. You haven't even tried it yet." He ushered her out of the bathroom and back onto the bed. He sat there, cradling her in his arms, trying to comfort her.

"Sorry," Ariel finally sniffed out. "I was in the bathroom thinking how wonderful it was that we were going to start our lives together," she paused.

"And the thought made you cry?" he asked.

"No," she laughed. "I was touched that you went to the trouble of making me breakfast. You really are wonderful, did you know that?"

Victor leaned down and kissed her. "I wish I could believe those were happy tears, but I know better. When I opened that door you looked so sad, it broke my heart." He brushed away another tear.

"I'm sorry. I guess I owe you more sex now," she gave him a weak smile.

"I'm not going to turn you down, but that can wait for later. Right now, I wish you'd tell me what has you so upset," he kissed her gently.

"I will, but I'm just sorry I ruined the mood. You went to so much work for me and I've ruined everything." She looked over at the tray. "Do you think maybe I could get a cup of that coffee?"

Victor stood and carried the tray back to the bed. "You can have anything you want if you will just tell me why you're so sad this morning." He poured her a cup of coffee and then climbed back onto the bed.

Ariel took a sip of the hot liquid then smiled at Victor. "It's delicious. Maybe I'll christen you the official coffee maker of the family now that you're moving in," she smiled at him. "Can you cook as well as you do everything else?" she asked.

"Try it and see," he pushed a plate toward her. He'd already learned that with Ariel, he had to be patient. She needed time to work up to talking about the big stuff. He sat there quietly waiting for her to continue.

"This is great," she said as she took a bite of bacon. "I really was thinking happy thoughts at first in the bathroom. I am so excited that we're going to move your stuff in today. I want to start our life together."

"Me too," he agreed. "So how did that lead to this?" he asked.

"Because I was standing there glowing with happiness thinking this was the first step to something wonderful. Then I realized I didn't know how you felt about the rest. I didn't know if you wanted marriage someday…and children," she said hesitantly.

Awe, so that's what this was all about. She didn't know if she could have children. Was she upset because she wanted them or because she was worried he did? Maybe both.

"Last night when you asked me if I wanted to move in with you, it was the happiest day of my life," Victor began. "It's a big step for me but I'm ready for it. I would eventually like for us to get married, but I'm not ready for that step yet. I hope that doesn't upset you, but I'm not. I don't know why. I can't even explain it to myself. I know I love you. That's never going to change. I also know I want to spend my whole life with you, that's not going to change either. But for some reason, I'm just not ready to take that step and ask you to marry me." He paused, waiting for a reaction.

Ariel took his hand in hers. "I understand. And you might be surprised to know I feel the same way," she smiled at him. "I know without a doubt that one day I want to be your wife. I'm just not ready for that yet. Maybe because this has all happened so quickly. Maybe because we both have things we need to work through before we can be the kind of spouse both of us wants to be. I can't explain it either. All I know is that I do want to marry you someday. I'm just not ready for that yet. Right now, I want more than anything for you to move in here with me. I want this to be our home. I want to start my life with you. I know that doesn't make any sense, it's just the way I feel."

"It makes sense to me." Victor moved the food away and pulled her into his arms. "I feel the same way. One day you will be my wife. And I promise I will do everything in my power to be a good husband," he paused. The other part was going to be tricky. "As far as children go, sure I'd be open to having children. I had the vasectomy because I didn't want to have a child with just anyone. I would not marry someone just because we had created a child together. To be honest, at the time I never really believed I would get married. You changed that. I would be honored to create a child with you and the vasectomy is easy to reverse if we decide that's what we want." He kissed her lips. "But I would also be perfectly happy for the rest of my life if I couldn't have a child. Loving you and knowing that you love me too is more than I ever hoped for in my life. If we can't have kids Ariel, it won't matter. You are enough for me."

"Is that true?" she asked skeptically. "I've watched Orin. He has suffered so much trying to be strong for Breena. He tried to pretend it didn't matter but you know as well as I do, it did. He was disappointed when he found out she couldn't have children and then he was upset at himself for being disappointed. I don't want you to go through that. Orin was unhappy but tried to make the best of his circumstances. I never want you to be unhappy, Victor."

"You can't compare me to Orin, it's not the same. Orin grew up believing he would have the dream. The whole dream. He always thought he would find the perfect woman, get married and have the perfect family. I guess that's what normal people do. I think Breena had the same dream," Victor surmised.

"She did," Ariel admitted.

"I on the other hand had a terrible childhood. I never once dreamt about growing up and finding the perfect woman or having a family. I honestly didn't believe she existed. I like children. I interact with them almost every day at the shelter. For me, that's fulfilling enough. Those kids bring plenty of joy into my life. Ariel I told you all I want is you, everything else is extra. My life is complete now that I have you." He brushed his fingers across her cheek. "You are my perfect woman, my miracle. I can't ask for anything more. I certainly wouldn't feel disappointed if I didn't get more. If we eventually have kids, great. If not, that's fine too as long as I have you. What we have is more than I ever imagined for myself. Unlike Orin, I haven't lost my childhood dream. With you, I have the dream I never dared to hope for."

Ariel looked up at Victor. This time she had tears of gratitude in her eyes. She smiled at him. "I don't know how I got so lucky. I don't think I deserve you. But I plan to spend the rest of my life trying." She shifted her body so she was straddling him then kissed him long and hard. "I think right now I'm the luckiest, happiest woman in the world."

"If you give me a few minutes, I think I can add to that joy." He pressed her back onto the bed and untied her robe.

* * * *

Victor and Ariel were just finishing up at the apartment. "I forgot to ask, do you mind if I take over that old garage in the backyard?" Victor asked casually.

"No," she said a little perplexed. "What do you want to use that for?"

"My cars," he answered.

Ariel narrowed her eyes. More secrets? "We have that three car garage. I only use one spot so the truck and the bike will fit in there perfectly."

"Yeah, you already offered that. Thanks." He was walking the apartment, making one last sweep just to make sure he hadn't missed anything.

"So, what are you planning on putting in that old garage?" she asked. "It looks pretty unstable. That's why I haven't done anything with it. At one point I considered tearing it down, but I just couldn't do it. That garage is old and I think it adds to the charm of the place."

"I have a couple extra cars. I'll leave them here for now. I want to fix up that garage before I use it. You're right, it is a little unstable. But I don't want to leave them here forever. A short period of time is okay, but it would make me nervous to leave them here permanently if I'm not around to check on them every day. It's a good neighborhood, but I'd feel better if we took them home."

"What cars?" Ariel asked. "And will there ever come a time when I'm not blindsided by all your secrets? Maybe someday you'll share information just because you love me and think I should know."

"I don't have that many secrets. In fact, I think you are now up to speed. Grab that box. We'll take a couple things to the truck and then I'll show you my cars. I was planning on taking one of them to Lancaster tomorrow. Dad loves to drive the Ferrari," Victor headed for the door.

"The Ferrari?" Ariel gaped at him. She shouldn't be surprised. He did ride a Harley. Fast cars and bikes fit his image. Victor loaded the boxes in the back of the truck, then he took her hand and walked toward the corner of the parking garage. There were three cars parked together. They were all hidden under custom covers. Victor slid the cover off a sleek, black Enzo Ferrari.

"Wow!" Ariel gasped. "So, do I get to drive tomorrow?" she grinned.

Victor studied her. "Sorry, I'll trust you with my heart but not my Ferrari." He laughed at the annoyed look she gave him. "Once we're out of the city you can drive." He pulled her into his arms. "If we're going to make this work, we have to be partners right? Just remember how accommodating I am next time I want something from you." He leaned in and kissed her. "I'll drive this home tomorrow when I come to pick you up." He carefully placed the cover back over the car.

"So, what are the other two?" she asked curious now.

"That one is a dark grey Pagoni Zonda C12-S and the other one is my baby. It's a 1961 Ferrari 250 GT California Spyder." He smiled at the confused look on Ariel's face. "It's old. I don't drive that one much."

"These are all expensive cars. Don't you think we should move them over to our place right away? We could park them in the garage and leave the car and truck outside until you get that old building fixed up."

After Dark

"Thanks for the offer, but they'll be okay here for a month or so while I repair the garage. I'll come by and check on them periodically. Nobody will mess with them. Contrary to Dimitri's assessment of my security system, I'm confident the cars will be safe here. If I wasn't, they wouldn't be here now." He took her hand and led her back up to the apartment. "Once we load these last few things and drop them at the house, I'll need to take off. I have a couple problems I have to take care of tonight if we're going to get out of here by noon tomorrow." Victor took a hard look around the place. He'd lived here a long time. It was kind of sad to be moving.

"What are you going to do with it?" She wrapped her arms around his waist. She sensed he was feeling a little nostalgic about the apartment. She was sure it had been his first home.

"I thought I'd leave it the way it is," he admitted.

Ariel was surprised. Was he making sure he had an escape just in case things didn't work out between them? Was he afraid he wouldn't like it at her house?

Victor took her chin in his hand. "Don't worry. I'm not leaving it this way for me. I'm totally committed to our relationship. I don't plan on living here ever again."

"Then why?" she asked.

"I'm hoping that someday dad will feel comfortable enough to visit me here in the city. I need to have a nice, well-furnished place for him to stay if he's ever willing to take that step. I want him to feel like he has his own place here. If he thinks he's intruding on us, he'll never come. If he knows I have an apartment just for him,

someday I think he might. I hope you don't mind, but I have to try."
He took her hand and headed for the truck.

Ariel was surprised at Victor's generosity. She shouldn't have
been. She knew him well enough by now, but somehow he always
seemed to amaze her. "I don't mind at all. I think it's a great idea.
I'm looking forward to meeting your father. I hope he likes me. I'm
sure no woman will ever be good enough for his son, but I'll be
crushed if he hates me."

"Dad is going to love you," he promised. "It's your parents
I'm worried about. The village screw up and the council leader's
daughter. How disappointed are they?" he asked dreading the
answer. "Be honest. I'll know if you lie to me."

"My parents are not at all disappointed. Dad thinks you're
great and mom is looking forward to getting to know you better. I
don't like it when you talk about yourself that way. You are not a
screw up and nobody in my family thinks you are," she said irritated.

"Hey," he stopped and pulled her into his arms. "I'm sorry,"
he kissed her forehead. "I'm just used to joking about my reputation
in this community. I didn't mean to upset you. I really am worried
about your parents though. I have a lot of respect for your father. I
don't want him to be disappointed in his daughter's choice for a
mate. I don't know your mother well, but she seems like a great
lady. I look forward to spending time with her too. I'm sure your
parents had high hopes for their only daughter. I don't want them
to be upset at your choice. I know I'm not an aristocrat and I don't
come from a highly respected family. I just hope they can
eventually accept me. They're going to take a great deal of heat
from the other fae. You need to be prepared for the fact that some

people are not going to approve of us. I can promise you one thing though."

"What's that?" she asked. She didn't care what anyone else thought about their relationship.

"Nobody could ever love you as much as I do. I am going to devote my entire life to making sure you are happy. I almost lost you once, I never want to go through that again."

"Victor, I don't care what other people think is appropriate. Neither do my parents. I only care about us. I only care about making you happy. You already make me happy. Stop worrying about my parents. But, once we get back in town mom wants us to come over for dinner. Will you look at your calendar and see when you can fit that in.?"

"Sure," he kissed her again and then opened the truck door. "I might be busy for a couple days, but we'll get over there as soon as it's physically possible. Deal?"

"Deal," she smiled at him. He smiled back and shut her door.

Victor headed home. He had just left Dimitri's. He felt guilty about leaving even with Dimitri's blessing. Things had been too quiet. They should have heard something by now. Radek had to be furious when he heard Hector was dead. So far he hadn't retaliated. It wasn't like him. Something big was coming. He could feel it. He'd never forgive himself if anything happened while he was so far away. He pulled into the garage and shut off the truck. He was still surprised at how good it felt to call this home. Victor walked through the back door smiling. A wonderful aroma hit him immediately. He glanced at the clock as he entered the kitchen and realized it was already dinner time. Ariel was standing at the stove.

He quietly slipped behind her and slid his arms around her waist. "What smells so good?" he whispered as he moved her hair and kissed her neck.

"I don't know who you are, but Victor's going to be home soon. If he catches you nibbling on my neck, you'll regret it." She turned into his arms. "Oh! It's you," she said feigning surprise.

Victor pressed his lips to hers and lifted her off her feet. Ariel wrapped her legs around his waist as he carried her across the room and rested her on the counter. "I brought you something," he said sliding his hands under her shirt and rubbing her back. He loved the feel of her skin.

"What did you bring me?" she said a little surprised.

Victor reached one hand into his pocket and pulled out a small box. He held it out for her to take.

"What's this for?" she asked. "I know I haven't missed a special occasion. What gives?" She asked as she opened the box. Inside was a beautiful set of diamond earrings, princess cut. "Victor!" She exclaimed. "I wasn't serious."

"I was. Does that mean you like them?" He asked sliding his hands down her back, over her hips and resting them on the tops of her thighs.

Ariel slid her legs open and pulled Victor in close. Then she pressed her mouth to his and savored the moment. "I love them, but you shouldn't have. They look expensive."

"You're worth it," he kissed her again. "Is dinner ready? I'm starved."

After Dark

Ariel jumped off the counter and ran to the stove. She stirred whatever was in the pot and then flicked off the heat. "That was close. You can always distract me so completely. I think that could be dangerous," she smiled back at him. "Dinner is ready. Wash up and I'll put it on the table. It's nothing fancy. I just made spaghetti." She opened the oven and pulled out hot buttered bread.

Victor smiled. He was already glad he'd moved in. This all seemed so perfect, so right. He headed out to change and wash up. He didn't want to, but he was going to have to stop in at the club tonight. It made him a little nervous knowing he had to bring that up. Ariel was always so understanding, but he was still concerned. He'd already been gone most of the day. Would she get upset when he told her he had to go to the club tonight? They still had so much to do here at home, all his stuff had made the house a complete mess and they didn't have much time before they headed out of town tomorrow. Victor sighed, he'd put off that unpleasant conversation until later. Right now he wanted to enjoy their first official meal together in his new home.

Dinner was delicious. Ariel had put on her new earrings. They looked great on her. Victor usually hated shopping, but he found buying things for Ariel made him happy. He liked hunting for the perfect gift. He was going to have to do that more often. "I'll do the dishes," he offered. You cooked.

"Okay," she agreed. "I'm almost finished cleaning out the dresser for you. I'll be in the bedroom finishing that up when you're done." Victor watched as she walked casually out the door, headed for the other room.

A short time later, Victor stepped into Ariel's bedroom with an arm full of clothes. Most of them needed to be hung in the closet. "Where do you want these?" he asked.

"I cleaned that half for you," she pointed to the walk-in closet.

Victor laid the clothes out on the bed. "Are you sure?" he asked. "I could use one of the spare bedrooms to store my things."

Ariel stopped what she was doing and stood. She walked to Victor and took his hand then led him into the closet. "This closet was made for two, his and hers. I don't mind sharing. This way it feels like our home, not my home. I want you to be comfortable here. I want you to feel like it's your place too. Yes, I'm sure."

Victor pressed her up against the wall and kissed her. Then he sighed. "I have bad news," he said hesitantly. "I have to go back to the club tonight. There's a problem I have to deal with in person. I'm sorry."

Ariel looked at him amused. "Why are you apologizing to me? Did you think I wouldn't understand? I know there are always unexpected problems when you run a business. You're the owner, of course you need to take care of them personally."

"I guess I feel guilty. I spent half the day trying to take care of things so we can leave tomorrow, but I got tied up at Tèarmann. Then, I finally made it over to the club and found out there were problems over there I'm going to have to deal with tonight. I've left you here by yourself with a big mess most of the day and now I have to leave again. When I get home I still need to pack for our trip. I'm not sure I'll have time to clean everything up before we head out."

After Dark

"We'll just move the boxes into one of the spare bedrooms and take care of them when we get back. Don't worry about it, Victor. I understand. Is the stuff at the club something you have to deal with alone, or could I join you? Maybe I could hang out with Rocky and have a drink while you take care of business."

"No, I don't need to go alone. Are you sure you feel up to it? You spent all that time helping clean out the apartment and then you fixed dinner and rearranged things here for me. I'm sure you have to be beat." Victor took her hand and led her out of the closet.

"Actually, I'm not that tired. A drink sounds kind of nice. I'll just relax at the bar with Rocky and you can work the night away." She picked up a stack of his clothes and headed for the closet.

Victor grabbed the rest and followed. "You really are okay with this, aren't you?" he said a little amazed. "I've been stressing for hours. I wanted to come home, put my stuff away and relax a little before we headed to dads. Dealing with the club ruined my plans for the evening. I assumed you would be upset, too. You never do react the way I think you will."

"Good," Ariel smiled. "I like to keep you guessing. If you want to finish this up," she pointed to another stack of clothes on the bed, "I'll change and then we can head to the club. Anyway, how could I complain tonight? You bought me diamonds?"

"You're easy to please." He gave her one more kiss before he grabbed another arm full of clothes and headed back to the closet.

The club was packed and loud. Ariel really did love it here. Everyone seemed to be having such a good time. She sat at the bar and chatted with Rocky while she sipped on a mango daiquiri. Rocky was a hoot. She could have sat there for hours. She was just finishing the last of her drink when Victor walked up behind her. He sat on a stool and pulled her into his arms. "I'm beat. You ready to go home?" he asked as he slipped Rocky a fifty-dollar bill. He thought he was being sneaky, but Ariel caught it. She smiled inwardly, no wonder his employees were so loyal.

"I'm ready if you are," she turned to Rocky. "Thanks for the company. I hope I wasn't too distracting. Don't worry though, your boss has a soft spot for me. I don't think he'll fire you."

Victor laughed as he pulled her toward the door.

* * * *

Victor glanced at Ariel as they merged onto I-78. "You still want to drive?" he asked. He was finally starting to relax. It had been a hectic morning. After the long day yesterday, they still hadn't gotten on the road until after one o'clock.

"I do, but I wanted to talk to you about something first. I wouldn't want to crash your sleek sports car or give you a heart attack, so I'll take over in a while if that's okay," Ariel teased.

"Sure, what did you want to talk about?" He briefly looked her way then returned his attention to the roadway. She didn't look stressed this time. Good. Lately it seemed like all their serious conversations were also emotionally draining.

"Well, I was wondering how you would feel about me helping out with some of your business stuff," she asked. "Before you panic, I do know a lot about business. I don't have a regular job so to speak. However, I have been helping dad out with projects at his company for years. In fact, I'm just finishing up with a large project now. It should be finished in a couple weeks. Once that's done I'll be pretty free for a while. I thought if you'd let me, I could start getting to know how things worked at your companies."

Victor was a little surprised. Nobody had ever offered to help him before. If Ariel helped run the businesses, maybe they'd have more free time together. He glanced back over at her. "Are you sure that's what you want to do?" he asked. "Sometimes it can be pretty time consuming."

"I would love to help you but if it makes you uncomfortable I understand," she put in.

"It doesn't make me uncomfortable. I would love to have you help me with my work. I just don't want you to feel obligated, or chained to a business just because it's mine. The club and the shelter bring me pleasure. That's why I keep them. The apartment complex takes very little time, but helps fund the shelter. I don't want you to get stuck doing something you don't enjoy, that's all."

"I won't. We've both said we want this thing between us to become permanent. I want to be involved in your life if you're willing to let me. I can help at Bojan Taverns, but I'll be out of my element there. I don't know the first thing about running a club but I guess you could teach me," Ariel continued.

"I will teach you anything you want to learn," he offered.

"I was thinking I would be better equipped to help at the shelter," Ariel stated.

Victor looked at her. "Do you think you'd be okay there? Almost all of those women have experienced trauma in their lives.

That's why they're living there. It might bring back bad memories. I know I've had a few bad moments listening to some of their stories."

"I know it's not going to be easy but I think it might help me deal with my ghosts. Plus, I was wondering if we could expand a little," Ariel said shyly.

"Expand?" he asked. "You don't think it's challenging enough right now?"

Ariel laughed. "Yes, I do. Actually, that day Alex and I sat across the street at the coffee shop waiting for you to come out, I noticed there's a vacant building next door. The architecture is pretty similar to your building."

"Yes it is," Victor answered. He had considered buying that place, but hadn't gotten serious about it because the price was too high. It had been on the market over a year now. Victor was toying with making an offer if the price ever dropped.

"Well, I was thinking if we bought that place, we could expand the shelter and turn the upper floors into a counseling center for rape victims or victims of other tragic events. Obviously we'd have to hire trained counselors, but I think there's a need for that service." Ariel was starting to get excited.

Victor watched her. He thought this might help her heal. The same way the shelter had helped him through his healing process. He thought it was a great idea. "That building's been on the market a long time. They should be dropping the price here any day. Once they do, let's look into it. Dimitri set up the security on the shelter. I'm sure he could easily expand it to include the building next door.

After Dark

It's going to take a lot of work and a lot of money to renovate though. It's been vacant for more than a year now."

"I have my trust fund. I'm willing to spend my own money to make this happen," she offered.

"That's an option, but we'll keep that in reserve. I have enough money to renovate, too. I know we've never discussed our finances, but I have a comfortable nest egg. How do you think I can afford my cars?" he asked.

"Only comfortable?" she teased. "I assumed you were loaded. I might have to rethink this arrangement. You might be after me for my money," she joked, pretending to be deep in thought.

Victor took her hand. "I don't think we'll starve babe. But I have money because I invest wisely and talk other wealthy saps into giving me the cash I need for my projects. I'm confident we can find enough investors to make this happen. Let's sit down and develop a plan as soon as we get back home."

"Really? Just like that?" she asked. "You are really willing to do this just because I asked?"

"Of course," Victor answered. "We're now building our life together. Not just my life. I think it's a good idea and I can see it's important to you. It's just money. We can always make more."

"Well, I'm glad you see it that way because now I'm ready to drive this fancy sports car and see what it can do. Pull over at the next turn out," she ordered.

Victor laughed. "Wow, bossy already and we're not even married. I heard women can be bossy. I always thought those men were exaggerating. Apparently I was wrong." He continued laughing when Ariel slugged him in the arm.

"You're adorable when you're angry," he said as he pulled onto the exit ramp and came to a stop on the shoulder. "She's all yours. But please, remember you have me in the car. Don't forget how much you love me and how important my safety is to you." Victor watched Ariel as he settled into the passenger seat. "Have you ever driven a sports car before?" he queried skeptically.

"Is this the brake or the gas?" she asked absently.

Victor placed his head in his hands. "What have I done?"

Ariel laughed. "Just sit back and relax. I know what I'm doing here. I lived in France most of my life but I moved around a lot, remember? I spent several years in Germany. You can't live in Germany and not own a sports car. Autobahn baby! Mine wasn't as fancy as this one, but it was still a lot of fun. I owned a Porsche while I was there and all my passengers survived."

Victor relaxed. He trusted Ariel, but it made him feel better to know she had experience with a fancy sports car. A lot of people didn't. He sat back and enjoyed the rest of the ride.

* * * *

Atticus watched as Victor and Ariel washed the dishes. It was obvious they were in love. He was thrilled for his son. After everything that had happened to him, it was nice to see Victor happy and content. He had finally found a good woman. Atticus didn't know anything about her, but she seemed like a kind and loving

After Dark

person. He continued to sip on his beer as he observed their interaction. Even menial tasks like doing the dishes seemed intimate between them. He thought about his relationship with Dannica. He had been so infatuated with her. He thought what they shared was love but in reality, she had never loved him. What he felt for her wasn't love either.

A few years ago Victor had brought another girl to meet him, that shifter Lakeisha. Watching them together is what really brought things home to him. He had been obsessed with Dannica the same way Lakeisha had been obsessed with Victor. The feelings they had for each other were unhealthy and destructive. He'd known for a long time Dannica wasn't stable. He just refused to admit it because of his obsession. He had been blind to her defects. His inability to accept what she was had caused so much pain for his son. It almost cost him his life. Maybe now Victor could be truly happy. Atticus was cautiously optimistic this time, but in a way he was also a little jealous. Things would have been so much different if he had found the kind of love Victor shared with Ariel. A love that could last a lifetime.

Once the dishes were done, the two kids joined Atticus in the living room. They sat there catching up and getting to know each other well into the night. Ariel finally stood. "I'm beat. Sorry to be a party pooper, but I can't keep my eyes open any longer. See you two in the morning." She headed toward the guest room. She stepped through the door and realized Victor was following her. "You didn't have to come to bed too," she smiled at him.

"Actually, I'm not. I'm going to stay up a little longer with dad. I just wanted to tuck you in. I won't be up too late and I'll try not to wake you when I do come to bed. Goodnight, baby." Victor pulled Ariel to him and kissed her softly. "By the way, I can already tell dad likes you. I knew he would, but you were so nervous about it." He kissed her goodnight. "I love you. Thank you for coming. It really means a lot to me."

"Goodnight. And, you're going to make it up to me when we have dinner with my parents. No backing out. You owe me," she smiled and climbed into bed.

Victor walked back into the living room and sat in the lounge chair adjacent to his father. "So, is there anything new here I should know about?" he asked.

"Nothing worth talking about," Atticus said. He had been having problems for about a month now, but he didn't want to worry Victor. He was always so protective. It was kind of ironic, Atticus was supposed to protect Victor not the other way around. But Victor had been protective of Atticus since he was a child. "I can see you love Ariel. I'm happy for you. It looks like this time might be the real thing."

"What do you mean by that?" Victor asked.

Atticus smiled. "You never loved the last girl you brought here. Oh, I think you cared about her but you didn't love her. This one you love. Lucky for you, she loves you too."

"Yes, I do," Victor answered. "I just hope I can make her happy. You know I have a lot of baggage. She's great, but sometimes I feel like it's unfair to her. Like fate was much kinder to me than it was to her when it put us in each other's path."

"Nonsense," Atticus objected. "You never have seen yourself clearly, Victor. You can do anything you put your mind to. If you want to make this girl happy, she'll be the happiest woman alive."

After Dark

"I think you're a little bias, dad. You always have been," he hesitated, but now was as good a time as any. "We've decided to move in together. In fact, we did move in together. I moved to her house yesterday. It's a nice place. I think you would like it." He pulled the apartment key out of his pants pocket and set it on the coffee table. "The apartment's free now if you ever want to visit. I have the only other key. Think about it. I'd love to show you around the city," Victor finished hopefully.

Atticus looked at the key. Maybe he would go visit his son in New York. It was probably time. He'd never live in a city again. He enjoyed the solitude he had out here on the farm. But he did miss his boy. He'd been doing his own shopping for years now and that wasn't too bad. If he had a place to himself in the city, somewhere he could go to get away from it all if things became too difficult for him, maybe he would give it a try. "I'm not making any promises, but I'll think about it. Did you tell her about your past yet?" he asked.

"Yes," Victor said watching his father. He didn't want to upset him but he wouldn't lie to him.

"Good," Atticus surprised Victor. "She needs to know." Atticus stood and walked to his son. "I'm a little tired, too. I think I'll call it a night. See you in the morning."

Victor stood and hugged his father. "Goodnight dad," he watched as Atticus left the room. He missed his father every day when he was in New York, but he couldn't run his businesses from Pennsylvania. He walked slowly down the hall and quietly slipped into the bedroom. He stripped off his clothes and climbed into bed. He'd just have to make the most of the time he had here. It was all he could do for now.

* * * *

Ariel woke early Sunday morning. It had been a good weekend. She loved Victor's father. He was funny and obviously loved his son very much. She'd expected an introvert. Instead, she'd met a great man that enjoyed living on a farm unencumbered by the rat race of the city. He had a wonderful garden and four amazing horses. It was a simple life, but Atticus obviously enjoyed it. They'd gone horseback riding through the countryside yesterday. It was a beautiful place; peaceful and quaint. She hoped they'd be able to come back here soon.

She climbed out of bed, dressed and silently found her way to the kitchen. She'd make coffee, then sit on the front porch and watch the sunrise. It would be a perfect start to their last day here. Ariel opened the front door and froze. She stopped herself just before she burnt the large snake to a crisp. It was already dead. Who would hang something like that on Atticus' front door? It was hooked to a fishing line and tied to the roof of the porch. She took a step back and let out a scream as she collided with Atticus.

"Easy," he soothed. "Let me take care of this." He gently maneuvered her to the side so he could deal with the snake.

Victor burst into the room. "What's wrong?" he asked Ariel, then he saw the snake and frowned. "Dad, what's going on here?"

"Nothing to worry about. Just another prank. I'll have it down in no time." He cut the fishing line with a pocket knife and the snake fell to the ground.

Victor was by his side in an instant. "What do you mean another prank? How many have there been?"

Atticus sighed. He had hoped Victor would be gone before the culprit struck again. "A few," he admitted.

"Dad," Victor said exasperated. "How many and for how long?"

"Like I said a few," he glanced up at Victor. "It's no big deal. Nothing dangerous, just inconvenient and annoying. There's nothing to worry about. Let me take care of this and I'll join you in the kitchen for a cup of coffee." Atticus picked up the dead snake and headed for the garbage can.

Victor didn't like it. Someone was trying to frighten his father. Who would harass him that way? Why would they do that? He didn't bother anyone. He rarely left the farm. Atticus stepped back into the house and began to pour himself a cup of coffee. "Dad, I need to know what's been going on out here. How many incidents and for how long?" he asked again.

"Okay fine," Atticus sighed. "There have been four prior to this one. It's been once a week, but so far there's no pattern. I never know when I'm going to wake up to find a new present. It seems pretty random."

"Once a week, so over a month now? Why didn't you say something?" Victor asked.

"Because I knew you'd overreact like you are right now. I'm your father, but you are so overprotective of me. I didn't want you to worry. I know you already worry more than you should. I'm not helpless, Victor. I was a warrior once too you know. I can take care of myself. I chose to quit, I didn't get fired because I'm helpless," he added with defiance.

"So, to prove your independence you've kept this a secret from me?" Victor shot back. "That's how you prove you can take care of yourself, by being stubborn and stupid?"

Ariel felt out of place. These two needed some time. She silently slipped out the back door. She'd have her coffee on the porch while Victor and his father worked this out.

"I'm not stupid," Atticus shot back. "And I'm no more stubborn than you are. So I've had a few dead animals on my front porch. I don't think that's a sign a major attack is eminent. I don't need you or anyone else to protect me Victor."

They sat in silence for a long time. "Why did you quit?" Victor finally asked. "Why didn't you go back after your suspension was over?"

Atticus studied his son. "I couldn't," he said quietly. "I know by the time my sentence was over you were an adult. But my stubborn hold on being a warrior is what caused you so much pain in the first place. It's what almost got you killed that night. I couldn't go back. Everything that happened to you was my fault. It was my fault for leaving on that job. My fault for refusing to see what Dannica was. My fault because I wouldn't give up the warriors." Atticus rubbed his hands over his face and then up through his hair. "I'm sorry," he croaked. His voice was tight with emotion.

"That's not true and you know it," Victor argued. "Everything that happened to me was mom's fault and her stupid family that twisted her mind and encouraged her behavior."

After Dark

Atticus studied Victor for a long time. "I know you think my refusal to leave the farm is an indication that I'm weak. I'm not. I don't feel like I've ever been weak. I just have a hard time facing the guilt. Facing other people when I feel so responsible. I've had to learn to accept and deal with my part in what happened to you as a child," Atticus paused.

"You didn't have any part in what happened to me as a child," Victor interrupted adamantly.

"From the moment you were born, you've been the joy of my life. You are the best thing that ever happened to me. I have always been so proud of you. When Dannica begged me to quit the warriors, I considered it for her. But I couldn't do it. I thought I was staying for you. I wanted you to grow up with values, with a goal. I wanted you to be strong and learn humility. I thought if I sacrificed what I wanted for the good of the community, it would make me a better man and a better example to you.

When I walked into that cellar and saw what your mother was doing to you, it broke me. All I cared about was you. I saved your life that night, but until this weekend I wasn't sure I saved you. All this time you've been just as lost as I have been. I shut myself off on this farm. You shut yourself off inside. I know I failed you in so many ways, but seeing you with Ariel gives me hope. Maybe now you are finally starting to heal."

"Dad. You were never a failure and I don't think you're weak," Victor began. "I never knew you blamed yourself for what happened with mom. That was foolish of me. Of course you would take that on yourself. It wasn't your fault any more than it was mine. Mom was what she was."

"True, but she was my weakness," Atticus insisted. "I refused to see what she was because I was too obsessed with her. If I had been paying attention, I would have seen the way she acted around you. Instead I was too caught up in my own life to notice the signs. My weakness almost got you killed. You're still trying to protect me by not sharing the details of your childhood with me. Sometimes, I'm grateful I don't know. Other times I go crazy imagining the horrors you must have faced at your mother's hand. All of it is my fault. I know you didn't say anything all those years ago because you were protecting me. Even as a child you thought I was too weak to handle the truth. Maybe I was weak back then, but only when it came to Dannica. I'm not weak now. Whatever this is, I can handle it. I've come a long way in five hundred years. A few dead animals on my doorstep is not going to push me over the edge."

"I wasn't protecting you because I thought you were weak. How could you even think that?" Victor said incredulously. "I worshiped you. To me you were a strong, invincible warrior. You were everything I wanted to be. I knew I could get through anything mother did to me because I had some of you inside me." Victor paused to look at his father. Atticus was staring out the window. "Look at me dad," Victor waited for his father to turn back to face him. "I didn't tell you what mom was doing because I loved you. I wanted you to be happy. I wanted to be strong and courageous and self-sacrificing like you. I do not believed you are weak." Victor stood and paced the room. "I have never considered you weak."

"If you need to know what mom did, I'll tell you everything. I haven't kept it from you because I thought you were too weak to handle it. I kept it from you because I didn't want to hurt you any more than I already have." Victor paused to blink back the moisture forming in his eyes.

After Dark

"You have never hurt me, son. What are you talking about?" Atticus stood and walked across the kitchen to stand in front of Victor.

Victor turned and placed his hands on the countertop, bracing himself as he hung his head in sorrow. "You gave up everything for me. You are out here because of me. You won't even come visit me in the city. I know how much losing mom hurt you. I know how much you were in love with her. You killed her because of me. Then, you didn't defend yourself to protect me. You didn't have to give up the warriors, you didn't have to be punished at all. You did that for me. Did you think I wouldn't figure it out? You gave up everything because you didn't want people to think I was weak. You have sacrificed your entire life. You gave up everything you loved to protect me. You lost mom, hell you had to kill mom, because of me. You were so proud of being a warrior, but you gave that up for me. I know that still hurts you. You're not happy, dad. I wish I could make you happy, but I don't know how. I have often wondered how much better your life might have been if you hadn't come home early that night. If mom had killed me and made some excuse then the two of you might still be together. You might still be happy."

Atticus was floored. Did Victor really believe that? He stepped back and stumbled into his chair. What had he done? "Do you really think I could ever be happy without you, Victor?" Atticus finally spoke. "I didn't give up everything I loved for you. I gave up everything for the only one I loved," Atticus took a deep breath. "Victor, will you please come back over here and sit down. I have some things I need to tell you. I want to be able to look you in the eye when I do."

318

Victor turned to his father. Atticus looked so miserable. Why had he brought this up today? He rarely got to see his father and on the last day of his visit, Victor had ruined everything. He slowly walked over and sat back down at the table.

Atticus held his coffee cup between his two big hands. This conversation was obviously past due. "I'm not really sure where to start with this or the best way to explain things so you can understand. I guess I'll just start at the beginning. I thought I fell in love with your mother the first time I saw her. She was so beautiful and energetic. It was intoxicating to be around her. We had what is referred to as a whirlwind courtship. I asked her to marry me before I really knew her. I wasn't myself when I was around her. I wasn't in control of who I was anymore. I thought that was love. After we got married, your mother immediately started to nag me about quitting the warriors. Her family was putting pressure on her. They blamed the warriors for removing their bloodline from power. I almost quit for her. I didn't want to, but I wanted her to be happy. Then she told me she was pregnant.

I was ecstatic. I was going to have a child. I didn't care if it was a boy or a girl. I was just thrilled we were going to be parents. I refused to quit the warriors. Dannica didn't understand, but I knew there was a good chance we would have a son. I had to continue to be a warrior. I had to be a good example to my son. I decided if we had a girl, I would quit. I would find something else to do so I could make Dannica happy. I knew I would miss it terribly. I would be miserable every time I saw a group of warriors leaving to go fight or returning from battle. But I was willing to give up my happiness for Dannica.

Then you were born. I was so proud. I loved you immediately. I guess my attention shifted the moment I saw you. I now realize that was part of the problem. Before you, Dannica was my world. We'd been married a while now and I was starting to notice little problems. I was still so obsessed with her, I refused to acknowledge the signs. As the years went by, the little problems became bigger and my excuses for her became more frequent. The last couple years got really bad. We were fighting more than we got along. She wouldn't stop nagging me about the warriors. I had finally realized Dannica was unstable. Our marriage was crumbling. By that time, my focus had completely shifted to you. I realized I didn't have anything in common with Dannica.

The time I spent with you is the only thing that brought me happiness. I was concerned about you when I left on those trips, but I believed you were old enough to tell me if there was a problem. I didn't realize you would hide something so important from me. I was devastated when I learned such terrible things were happening and you didn't trust me enough to confide in me," Atticus said clearly upset.

"I did trust you, dad. That's not why I kept it from you." Victor paused, how much should he admit. "Do you remember how old I was when things got bad between you and mom?"

"I believe you were about eight or nine. Probably nine, why?" Atticus questioned.

"That makes sense," Victor replied.

"I can see that filled in some blank spot for you, what is it?" Atticus asked.

"It seems that mom's behavior was directly impacted by changes in her life. I knew what the first milestone was, I wasn't aware of the second. I guess I was too young to notice you two were having problems. You had such a glint in your eyes when you came home. I just assumed it was still for mom," he paused. "She always locked me in that cellar when you left," Victor began.

"What do you mean always? When did it start?" Atticus asked.

"I don't know. I can't remember, always. I can't remember a time she didn't lock me in there. She'd put me in the day you left and let me out the day she expected you home. I don't ever remember a time she didn't do that."

"Always!" Atticus was horrified.

"Yes," Victor confirmed. "That's why it never felt like a secret or something to tell. It was just the way things were. It wasn't that bad until I was five. That was the first milestone. It took me a while to figure it out, but that's when you started training me to become a warrior."

"What happened when you were five?" Atticus asked, dreading the answer.

"That's when mom started trying to cure me of my disease. That's how she put it anyway. It started when I was five and continued until I was nine; another milestone. It was just one I didn't know about. At that point she stopped trying to cure me and started trying to kill me," Victor said hesitantly.

"Your mother was trying to kill you for three years and you never said anything!" Atticus was horrified by this knowledge. "Why didn't you trust me? How did I not see that?"

"Dad, it wasn't about trust. I have always trusted you. Once I was five and she tried her demented cures on me, she threatened to leave me in the cellar without food if I said anything to anyone, even you. She barely gave me enough as it was, I didn't want to lose my food supply so I didn't tell you. It was about survival, not trust. Later, when I got older, I didn't care about the food. I almost told you several times, but you were so happy when you came home. Mom was completely different when you were there. I couldn't tell you what was happening and take that joy and happiness away. I couldn't shatter your illusion of her. I thought you were in love. How could I take that away? It didn't have anything to do with trusting or not trusting you."

"How much did you suffer over those three years?" Atticus swallowed hard. "Did she come close to killing you before that night?" Atticus asked, not sure he really wanted to know.

"No. Not really," Victor answered. "She made a couple attempts on my life. They were strange things though. She tried to drain my blood once. Obviously that wouldn't work on a warrior. We heal too fast. It was always stupid stuff like that. If you remember, it was about that time I started walking with you to the end of the road when you left."

"I remember," Atticus confirmed. "I wanted to take you with me, but I was worried you were too young and I would be putting you in danger. I had no idea I was putting you in more danger by leaving you home."

"Well actually, once I started walking with you, the death attempts stopped until that last trip," Victor admitted.

"Why?" Atticus asked, confused.

"She didn't have a chance. I would walk with you to the end of the road, then I'd run into the woods and hide until you got back. Mom was furious, but neither her nor Foster could ever track me down," Victor smiled.

"You spent weeks alone in the woods at the age of nine? You hid out, hunted for food and avoided two adults and never got caught?" Atticus was amazed. "I always knew you were a clever boy. I just didn't know how clever," Atticus said, proud of his son.

"Remember, that last trip mom walked with us? She pretended to be supportive of you, but really she just wanted to be there to stop me from escaping into the woods again. You know the rest. I'm sorry you had to kill the woman you loved to save me. I've always felt guilty about that," Victor finished quietly.

"Victor, by the time you were twelve I wasn't in love with your mother anymore. I still cared about her, but I knew she was sick. I knew what we had wasn't love. It never had been. I just didn't know what to do about it. Every time I left, I worried about you. But you never said a word about the abuse. Being a warrior, you healed before I got home. There wasn't any physical evidence to alert me. I feel like I should have known, but I honestly didn't. I just didn't trust your mother anymore because of her illness. I was frantic when I left you that morning. Dannica never liked to walk up to the road. I wasn't buying her excuse, but I couldn't come up with an explanation. You have no idea how close I came to taking you with me that day. I just couldn't get past the danger I would be putting you in if we came across a group of vampires. You were too young to fight. We were all thrilled to be home early, but I was desperate to get home. The other warriors thought I wanted to get home to my wife. Really, I wanted to get home to you. Everything became a lot more clear a few years back when you brought Lakeisha out to meet me," Atticus admitted.

"What does Lakeisha have to do with this?" Victor asked, confused.

"I watched her with you. She was just as obsessed with you as I was with your mother. Like me, Lakeisha thought what she felt was love but it wasn't. The relationship was unhealthy and couldn't last forever. I was married to Dannica for more than thirteen years. Our relationship was unhealthy and destructive. Dannica didn't love me, she loved the idea of marriage. She loved being the center of my world. Being mentally unstable made that need even worse. She fought against anything that occupied my time. First it was the warriors, then it was you. She may have had issues even without her illness, I don't know. I do know that I've never once regretted what I did that night. If your mother had killed you and said you died in an accident, I would not have been happy. First of all, I wouldn't have believed her. But more to the point without you, your mother and I would not have lasted one more day together. Don't ever think differently. Nothing could be further from the truth."

"I wish I could believe that was true," Victor said watching his father. "It's hard to wrap my mind around this new information though. I've believed your misery was my fault for so long. It's hard to imagine everything was so different than I thought it was. It seemed like you were so unhappy because you had to kill the woman you loved for me. I thought you shut yourself off from everyone because you couldn't handle life without mom. In my heart, I've always felt your unhappiness was all my fault."

"Victor, you were a child. You were the victim. None of this is your fault. I know it's been hard on you to have a father that won't leave his home. It's just been so hard for me to live with the knowledge I wasn't there for you. I've felt like I didn't deserve to have a life. I'm your father, it was my responsibility to protect you and I didn't. I'm grateful you survived in spite of my failure. I'm dealing with my guilt better now. You know I occasionally go into town. I'm not the recluse I once was. I'm comfortable on this farm, I'm not a prisoner of it anymore. I can't make any promises, but I'll try to visit you in New York. Someday I'll make use of that apartment. I need to see your new home and your businesses. Just give me a little more time. I'm so proud of you and everything you've accomplished."

"I'm sorry we had to do this today," Victor apologized. "I've never brought any of this up in the past because our visits seem so short. But, I'm glad we finally talked about things. I think we both understand the situation a little better. Maybe now both of us can heal and put the past behind us. I'm proud of you too dad. I hope you know that. I love you more than you know. I don't try to protect you because I think you're unable to do it yourself. I'm overprotective because I couldn't stand it if I lost you," Victor paused. "I'm going to talk to Dimitri about what's going on out here. I don't think it's a human problem. Do you think it could be Foster?"

"I've wondered the same thing. He also has a brother. Either one of them could be the culprit. Unless it escalates, I'm not too worried about it. I have to be honest, I suspected Foster immediately. I don't think he likes that I've started to go out and about again. I think he's viewed my refusal to leave as a punishment. Maybe like a prison sentence. If I start living a normal life my sentence is over," Atticus surmised.

"Are you starting to live a normal life, dad?" Victor asked.

After Dark

"Yes, I am. Don't worry about me, Victor. I am happy here. I have the garden and the horses. Look around. I bet your back yard isn't as stunning as mine is," Atticus smiled. "I truly am happy here. I just miss my son. I've recently realized that's my fault, too. Trust me, I will come visit." He pushed his chair back and stood. "Now, go outside and rescue that wonderful woman. She's been alone out there long enough."

Victor stood and hugged his father. "I love you dad and I miss you too. I wish I could get out here more often but running three businesses keeps me tied down. Plus, all the trouble we've been having with the vampires lately. I'm grateful we've had a short break. I'm afraid that might be over soon though. I can't say why, but I have a feeling something big is coming. Something bad is headed our way."

"Just promise me you'll be careful out there. I know you can handle yourself but I worry about you, too. Especially now that the treaty has been broken," Atticus pled.

"I'm always careful," Victor smiled a cocky grin and headed for the door.

Atticus watched as Victor walked outside. He was so proud of his son. He was also grateful Victor was finally starting to heal. It was strange how such a short time in their lives had impacted them both so profoundly.

* * * *

Lilith sat on the uncomfortable bar stool waiting for the man to arrive. She'd eaten twice already, then had a small snack before she left the cave. She was meeting a fae and needed to be in control. She couldn't lose it and attack him, that would ruin everything. She was counting on his skills. Rumor had it this guy was the best. Lilith casually gazed around the room again, still no fae. Too bad Hector wasn't here. He was so much better at self-control than she was. Lilith personally witnessed Hector meet with members of the fae before. She knew him well enough to see he was struggling with the bloodlust, but the casual observer never would have noticed. She couldn't be as nonchalant as Hector, but she was confident she would resist. That was the point of the snack. Lilith groaned inwardly. She was becoming restless. He was late. She shifted uncomfortably in her chair, she really had eaten too much.

Lawson entered the small bar. He disliked doing business in this setting, but the woman had insisted. Did she really think he didn't know who she was? He knew he was taking his life into his hands this time but he needed the money. After years of dealing with the underworld, he'd grown confident. Clients never harmed him, they needed his services. He doubled checked the room to make sure there were no fae in the building. His family already had enough problems. He would not do anything to bring more scrutiny on them.

Lawson casually strolled to the bar and sat down next to Lilith. She was beautiful, but he noticed a large scar trailing down her neck and under her shirt. He wondered what happened to the other party. Had they survived or was Lilith the victor of that fight? Maybe that's why she was after Alex. Had she been the one to cause the scar? He didn't care. What was that saying? The enemy of my enemy is my friend. Something like that. If this woman was after Alex Deveraux, he was on her side. He didn't care that she was a vampire. He casually turned toward Lilith and began negotiations.

Chapter Ten

Ariel and Victor sat in the large family room at her parents' home. They'd been playing games all evening. It was obvious her parents loved him. That made things so much easier.

"The two of you are planning on attending the festival Saturday, right?" Mara asked.

Victor and Ariel groaned in unison. Oberon laughed. Those two really were made for each other.

Victor shook the dice and then smiled triumphantly. "Am I good or what?" he asked as he moved his game piece to the finish. "What's my prize?" he asked Mara. "I know, a get out of jail free card. Or more to the point, a stay home from the festival without backlash pass," he said hopefully.

"Come on," Mara said exasperated with both of them. She couldn't understand their aversion to socializing. "Alex has put so much work into this event. She'll be crushed if you don't at least make an appearance. That morning is the official ceremony to crown Alexandria as our new queen. You couldn't miss such an important event. Then there's the parade, which of course you might as well stay for since you'll already be there. It's going to be a wonderful day of fun." Mara was clearly excited about the entire event. "Alex is being so secretive about her float. I don't suppose you know anything about that do you?" she smiled questioningly at Victor.

"Actually, she doesn't want it to get out yet but she's not using the old float," Victor answered absently glancing over at Ariel.

"What? She's not using the float? She has to be in the parade!" Mara exclaimed.

Victor looked back at Mara. "Calm down," he grinned. "She's going to be in the parade. Ty offered up a couple of his best horses and an old carriage he had at his farm. They're going to use his two jet black mustangs. They've done a great job cleaning the carriage up, too. It almost looks brand new. Dimitri's going to drive while Alex works on her parade wave. It's an elegant Landau and combined with Ty's mustangs it has an air of royalty about it. His horses look majestic and wild, but they're perfect because they won't spook in crowds. They wouldn't dare. I don't know how he does it but Ty's mustangs are like professionally trained dogs. They are so eager to please their master," Victor mused. "It'll be perfect. They're going to fold back the bellows top so everyone will get a good look at their new queen in her elegant, royal gown. I think it's going to be a huge hit with the community," Victor predicted.

"It sounds wonderful," Mara admitted. "I can't wait to see it. You two are coming, aren't you?" she pressed.

"We'll talk about it," Victor relented. "If I don't win a pass this go-around, I'd settle for another piece of that delicious cake," he suggested hopefully.

Mara laughed. She really did like Victor. She was thrilled Ariel had finally met someone so perfect for her. After all these years, maybe her daughter would finally start the next chapter in her life. Mara hoped Ariel could have a family of her own. She looked over at Oberon. She was still so in love with her husband. Mara felt blessed to have such a special man and a wonderful daughter in her life. Soon, she hoped she'd have this terrific warrior for a son.

Victor's cell phone rang. He pulled it from his pocket and quickly answered with a puzzled look on his face. "Hello."

"Victor," Lakeisha said, obviously relieved. "I need your help!" She said in a panic. "I tried to call Ariel, but she didn't answer. I'm sorry to ask but I don't know what else to do," she went on almost hysterical now.

"Ariel's with me. What's going on?" he asked.

The entire room was on alert. Who was he talking to?

"There's been an explosion," she sobbed. "My father's injured. I don't know if he's going to make it. Ryker left immediately to check on his pack and took my mother with him. There are so many of us hurt. I know a couple of the men have died. I don't know what to do, everything is out of control. Dad is in so much pain and I don't know how to help him. He's not conscious, but he's moaning." She was crying now and becoming difficult to understand.

"Lakeisha, take a deep breath and be more specific. What kind of explosion?" Victor asked. "I need to know the details. Is there any danger of another one?"

"Oh!" Lakeisha exclaimed. "I don't know. I hadn't thought of that." She took a deep breath, trying to calm down. "Maybe."

Ariel was by Victor's side. "What do you need?" she asked.

Victor placed his hand over the mouthpiece. "Call Dimitri. Lakeisha's father is injured. We need Alex. There's been some kind of explosion. Tell Dimitri I'm going to need Ty." He lifted his hand from the mouthpiece. "Lakeisha, I'm coming out there and I'm bringing help. I need you to remain calm and take care of your dad. If he's bleeding, get pressure on the wounds..." Victor looked up as Mara slid a small piece of paper with a number written on it into his hand. He didn't understand.

"It's Tianna's phone number. I just called her. She's waiting for Lakeisha's call. She can walk her through whatever needs to be done," Mara answered.

"Thanks," he smiled at Mara. "Lakeisha, do you have something to write with? I'm going to give you a phone number. I need you to call Tianna. She's a nurse. She can stay on the phone with you and help stabilize your father until I can get there. Do you understand?"

"Yes," Lakeisha answered. "I have a pen, go ahead."

Victor read off the number and then made Lakeisha read it back to him. "Okay, I'm going to hang up now. Call Tianna immediately. I'll be there as soon as I can with help." He hung up and turned to Oberon.

After Dark

Before he could say anything Ariel interrupted. "Dimitri and Alex are on their way. They should be here any minute. I think we need to call Morrigan. Actually dad, maybe you should call Mason."

Oberon and Victor looked to her in question. "Why?" Oberon asked.

"I've been worried about retaliation from the vampires since we got back. Tonight, as soon as Lakeisha called it hit me. The vampires don't know we were involved. How would they? They are retaliating. They're retaliating against the shifters. If they hit Lakeisha's pack, they probably hit Abby's too. Or they will. Mason needs to be warned. They need to be prepared. If they've already been hit, they might need help."

Oberon was across the room and dialing Mason immediately. He explained the situation and warned him to be on alert. He hung up and turned to Victor. "So far, everything's quiet in his community but he's going to get the word out." The doorbell rang and they all headed toward the front of the house. Dimitri didn't waste time. Once the door opened, he headed back to the car. "You riding with us?" he asked Victor.

"Sure," Victor grabbed Ariel's hand and pulled her to the truck. "Oberon," Victor called back over his shoulder. "You might want to contact the council. I think Ariel's right, but they should be on alert just in case." He opened the door and helped Ariel inside. "Hey Alex," Victor said as he pulled the door shut. "Thanks for coming. You might be busy tonight. I have no idea how many people have been injured. Lakeisha wasn't communicating very well. She was pretty upset. I didn't get a lot of information," he turned to Dimitri. "Is Ty coming?"

"Yep," Dimitri confirmed. "He was further out, but I told him to hurry. We should meet up with him once we hit the highway." Dimitri started the truck and sped up the drive.

They were speeding down the highway, passing traffic left and right when Ariel noticed a vehicle approaching from the rear. She knew they were speeding, so the approaching car was flying. As it began to close in, Ariel realized it was Bastian. Ty must be with him. The car slowed and pulled in behind them. It continued to tail them all the way to the panther community.

"Where to?" Dimitri asked once they entered the main road.

"Up there on the left," Victor pointed.

Ariel saw a big group of people gathering on the front lawn of a large home. Dimitri pulled into the drive. Once the truck stopped, Alex was out the door. She ran for the house; Victor, Ariel and Dimitri on her heals. Ty and Bastian were right behind them. Lakeisha was on the floor kneeling over her father. She was still on the phone.

Alex knelt down next to Lakeisha and placed a hand on her shoulder. "Can you give the phone to Dimitri? I need to get some information from you." She waited while Dimitri took the phone. "Okay, I know there was an explosion. Can you be more specific about his injuries?"

"His leg is bad," Lakeisha sniffed. A small boy approached and climbed into her lap. Lakeisha pulled him in tight against her body. This must be her son, Trae. "He's been unconscious so I can't ask him where he hurts the worst. He also has a serious burn on his side." Lakeisha pulled the blanket away to reveal a large, deep burn.

After Dark

Alex decided to start with that one. She took a deep breath and concentrated on Lakeisha's father. Her hands glowed as she gently pressed them to Cayden's side. The wounds were serious. Alex visualized his anatomy and the damage as she healed Cayden's numerous injuries. He had a lot of internal wounds. She stopped the bleeding and healed the surrounding area. Once she was confident the damage was repaired, she moved to his leg. Lakeisha was right, his leg was bad. Once she took care of that, she slowly surveyed the rest of his body. He had a few additional injuries, but nothing too serious. She'd done all she could do. The rest was up to him. She stood and stepped back to Dimitri.

"I think he'll be okay. He had a lot of damage and probably wouldn't have made it, but he should be fine now. He'll need rest and it might be awhile before he regains consciousness. Are there other people that are seriously injured?" she asked.

Dimitri took her hand. "His injuries were really bad. Are you sure you're okay?" he was studying her for any weakness.

Alex smiled. "I'm fine," she pulled the locket he gave her out from under her shirt. "I think it works. You're brilliant." She gave him a quick kiss then turned toward the door. "Now, lead me to anyone else that needs help. I saw the damage to those homes, there has to be additional victims."

They walked outside and saw Ty talking with a couple men. Ariel, Victor and Bastian were with them as well. Alex hadn't even noticed them slip outside. The conversation looked serious. She followed Dimitri to the group.

"Hey," Ty said as they approached. "Dimitri, they need someone to take charge and give them direction. I can't do it. I've got to search for additional devices. We need to keep all these

334

people away from the structures that haven't been cleared. They also need to know where to take the injured. They've moved two members who have passed away into that barn." Ty pointed across the street. "I checked it already. It's clear. I suggest we keep that as the morgue so to speak, but we need to find a large building to direct the wounded." They all glanced up as they heard a vehicle approach.

Thomas climbed out of the car. "The rest of the warriors should be here any minute. We're at your disposal. Just tell me what you need. Oberon and Mara are also on their way. Oberon said he talked to all the council members. They started the phone tree so the entire community should be on alert in no time." He looked to Dimitri in question. "Where do you need me?"

"You go with Ty and Victor. He's going to start checking for additional devices." He turned to Ty. "How many of these buildings have you cleared?"

"The barn, Lakeisha's parents' house and that house over there. I was going to systematically work that way." He pointed down the main street.

"Good idea," Dimitri agreed. "You guys get started." He turned to Bastian as they walked away. "I need you to take control of these people. We'll move the injured into Lakeisha's parents' house and the house next door. Both of them have been cleared. As Ty moves down the street, we can start relocating the uninjured women and children to the homes that are safe." He looked at Bastian apologetically, "Sorry. Once Oberon gets here, he'll help. I need to stay with Alex. She's going to eventually wear herself out. I need to be there for her."

"Where do you want me?" Ariel asked.

After Dark

"You come with me," Dimitri answered. "As they bring in the wounded, you evaluate them and get the worst cases to Alex first. Once Mara gets here, she can help. I also need you to see if there's anything you can use to make Alex some tea. She's never healed this many people before. I know she's going to need some before the night is over."

"I'll look but if I know mom, she'll bring plenty with her." They all headed for Cayden's house. Once inside Ariel approached Lakeisha. "We know it's safe here. Is it all right if we use this house for the injured?" she asked.

Lakeisha looked up. "Sure. What do you need from me?" she asked.

"Dimitri will take your father to his bed if you tell him where it is," she looked around. "We'll need somewhere to lay the other wounded. Do you mind bringing us all the sheets and blankets you can find? As the rest of the homes are cleared, we can send members of your pack to gather additional bedding as needed," Ariel guided.

"Okay," Lakeisha stood. "Follow me," she left the room. Dimitri followed carrying her father. When they returned they were both holding bedding.

Ariel had moved the furniture to create a large open space to lay the wounded. Lakeisha noticed several pack members lying on the floor already. Alex was crouched down leaning over a friend of her mothers. Trae was holding the woman's hand in comfort. Lakeisha was worried about her mother and Ryker. They should have been back by now.

Oberon stood in the roadway directing activity. He looked up and saw a flock of blue jays coming their way. He was surprised when they began to descend. It appeared they were coming in for a landing. Just before each bird hit the ground, it shifted into a person. Oberon smiled, he didn't think he'd ever get used to the wonder of watching the shifters transform. They were so graceful. "Hello Mason," he held out his hand in greeting.

"Oberon," Mason answered reaching his hand out to his new friend. "Thank you for the warning," he said soberly putting his arm around his wife, Jackie. "Without it, our community would be dealing with the same horrors the panthers are experiencing tonight." He glanced down at his wife. "You saved us. We barely had enough time to warn our people and get into the air when the explosions started."

"I'm sorry for that," Oberon said sincerely. "Do you know how much damage?"

"No," Mason answered. "Nothing we can't deal with though. We're just grateful none of our people were injured or killed. Without your warning, the casualties would have been high."

"Actually, Ariel is the one that saved you. She's the one that put it all together. Our community was expecting an attack on us. We never thought the vampires would retaliate against the shifters. I'm sorry it took so long to figure it out," Oberon apologized.

"Nonsense," Mason answered. "None of us thought of it either. We certainly didn't expect a surprise attack using explosives. That's not the vampire's typical MO," he paused. "How can we help here?"

Oberon looked around. "It still looks pretty chaotic, but there is a method to our madness. Ty found three additional devices that were still hot. He's working on locating any remaining bombs then defusing them, but it's taking time. I think we have everything else under control. Mara and Ariel are inside helping to care for the wounded. Abby and Jackie could help in there if they are willing."

"Absolutely!" Jackie answered as she put an arm around her daughter. She turned to the large group. "Anyone that has medical knowledge of any kind, follow me. We need to assist with the wounded. Everyone else stay here. Mason will give the rest of you assignments soon." She turned and headed for the house. Several members of the group followed.

"They'll be grateful for the help," Oberon said sincerely.

"Direct me to Ty. I have an idea," Mason requested.

"Follow me, what do you have in mind?" Oberon asked as he started up the roadway.

"If Ty has a device that we can get a scent off of, I think we can shift into search dogs and help locate devices. I'll direct the men to leave the building if they even get a hint of that scent. With this group we should be able to narrow it down pretty quickly," he shrugged, "It's worth a shot."

Oberon nodded. "It's a good idea, but the men need to know it's going to be dangerous. One of the bombs almost went off before Ty could neutralize it. This area still isn't safe. Once we get finished here, we'll head over to your place and start over again. At least we won't have to set up the triage there. We'll try to save as much property as we can, I promise," Oberon said soberly.

"I'm not worried about that right now. Let's do what we can for these guys. Their community has suffered far more than we have. Looking around makes me even more grateful our members escaped when we did. I can never repay you or your daughter completely. Thank you my friend. I hope you'll let us return the favor someday."

Oberon understood Mason's gratitude. "Thank you. Let's get through tonight. Then, we'll need to re-evaluate the situation and formulate a strategy to deal with this new development." Oberon led the group of shifters to Ty.

Alex was worn out. There were too many wounded. At least the worst healing was behind her. She'd been so relieved when she learned there were no more life threatening cases for her to handle. Now she was working on the less severe wounds. Healing this many people was taking a toll. Mara had already forced three cups of tea into her. She felt waterlogged, but her energy was fading fast. She was going to need another cup. Alex stood and looked around, Dimitri must have stepped outside for some air. She walked into the kitchen and collapsed into a chair.

Ariel studied Alex. She looked exhausted. "How's it going out there?"

"I think the worst of it's over," she said, unable to keep the relief out of her voice. "Now that the most crucial wounds are healed, I thought I'd have one more cup of tea. I feel sloshy, but I need the energy," Alex confessed.

"Why don't you take a break? There's nothing out there that's pressing. You need to rest. I'll get Dimitri. The two of you can relax in here for a while." Ariel slid out the back door. Dimitri needed to know how tired Alex was. If she kept this up, she'd wear herself out. Ariel knew Dimitri was the only one that could make Alex take a break.

After Dark

Ariel walked down the deserted roadway. She was saddened by the destruction surrounding her. The warriors had paired off with the shifters to locate and neutralize the bombs. They were scattered everywhere. It was relatively quiet now. There hadn't been any more explosions. The pack members were either helping with the wounded, tending to the children, or helping the warriors. She spotted a group at the end of the lane. Dimitri was talking to her father. As she approached, she also recognized Ryker and his parents, Numair and Felina. Ryker had checked in with Lakeisha once he returned, but then immediately left to assist with cleanup. The shifters not helping Ty locate devices, were working on cleaning up the damage and debris. Ariel paused. Just a few weeks ago she never would have believed it was possible for these three groups to work so well together. None of the usual conflicts existed tonight. It was just a cohesive group working toward the same goal.

"Dimitri," Ariel called as she approached.

"Yeah?" he turned and headed her way.

"Alex is in the kitchen. I'm heating her another cup of tea, but she's beat and needs a break. I think you're the only one that can make her stop for a while. She's dealt with the life threatening injuries, but there are still a lot of wounded in there."

"I'll take care of it," he assured her as he turned and headed for the house.

* * * *

Lilith was furious. She had watched from a safe distance when the first explosions went off. It was beautiful. There was no doubt

340

the panther leader had sustained fatal injuries. If he wasn't dead, he would be soon. Things were right on schedule. The explosives were better than she had hoped. She'd quietly slipped away and headed to the other shifter's location. She wanted to see the initial explosion and witness the damage as the first blast went off. Seconds before her pyrotechnic display began, the entire community shifted into a flock of birds and flew to safety. How had they known? This was unacceptable. The shifters needed to pay. Hector had to be avenged. She responded back to her first target and almost screamed in frustration.

The warriors were ruining her plans. Some of the bombs hadn't gone off yet, but the men were working together to neutralize them. She wanted more damage. She wanted more death. Was Alex here tonight? Lilith had seen the warrior leader, but there was no sign of the queen. She was probably holed up in her mansion watching TV. Lilith watched as the shifter pack approached the area, landed and shifted into people. So, that's how they'd known. One of the panthers must have warned them. Maybe that panther and the shifter became friends during captivity. Lilith watched as all three groups worked together. She surveyed the area for over an hour, but the warriors were ruining her bombs. They were ruining her plans. Then a possibility occurred to her. Had the warriors helped the shifters escape? Were they responsible for Hector's death? There had to be a connection somewhere or they wouldn't be here tonight. Alex was at the top of her list, but maybe the warriors needed a little payback as well.

Lilith narrowed her eyes. The shifters got lucky tonight, but next time there would be no warning. Next time all of them were going to pay, including the warriors. She slid into the cover of night and headed home. She had another attack to plan.

After Dark

* * * *

Victor was watching Ty work on what they hoped was the last device. He was impressed as he watched Ty defuse bomb after bomb. Ty was a master with explosives and he definitely had magic fingers. Not one of the bombs had gone off since they arrived. Ty deserved the credit for that. They'd had a couple close calls, but none of them had been this close. Ty had ordered everyone far away from the building, but Victor wouldn't leave him alone. Victor glanced down and checked the display, only three seconds left. Ty cut the last wire and breathed a sigh of relief. He slid the cord away from the detonator and stood. "That was too close, bro," Victor said as he slapped Ty on the back.

"Piece of cake," Ty smiled. "I think that takes care of everything here. Now we need to head over to Morrigan's place and start all over again. We're in for a long night boys," Ty joked as he walked passed the warriors. "These were all made by the same person. If we get lucky, the ones at the other target will be the same. The shifters seem to have the hang of it now." He paused as he passed Morrigan, Austin and a couple other shifters. "Ready for another round?" He asked as he continued to the vehicles.

"I don't know how you do this," Thomas admitted. "I can't count how many times tonight I've thought my life was over. You've been so calm the entire night. How do you do it?" Thomas was truly amazed. Ty was good, but the amazing part was his controlled demeanor when he knew he could die.

Ty shrugged. "You have your strengths, I have mine." They were now back at the vehicles. "Let's rock. The longer we take, the fewer houses we're going to save." He climbed into Thomas' car, laid his head back and closed his eyes. He needed to relax before he started another round.

* * * *

Victor and Ariel stumbled into the house. It had been a long night. Ty found three bombs that still hadn't gone off in the shifters' community, but the property damage over there was extensive. Most of the targets had been destroyed before they arrived. The only comfort was the fact none of the shifters had been injured. Nobody complained. They were grateful for the blessing and worked together to salvage what they could. The shifters were going to be rebuilding for a very long time.

Ariel overheard Alex talking to Thomas about donating supplies to the effort. Ariel promised a large donation as well. Ty called his father and got a commitment for a full construction crew. They couldn't work full time for the shifters, but they would do what they could to get people back into their homes as soon as possible. It was amazing what the community could accomplish when they all pulled together. Once Ty was certain there were no additional devices, everyone headed home. There was still a lot to resolve, but they were all too beat to think straight. Thomas and Alex had arranged hotel suites for all the displaced families. They would be able to stay at the hotel as long as they needed to.

Ariel and Victor climbed into bed and immediately fell into a deep, dreamless sleep.

After Dark

* * * *

Victor woke early and realized Ariel was still sleeping. He snuggled in close and relaxed. It was amazing how comfortable he was here, how easy it had been to slide into his new life in a new home. He loved waking up next to Ariel. He loved falling asleep with her in his arms. Ariel shifted groggily. Victor kissed her temple and watched as she slowly woke for the day.

Ariel groaned. "Is it morning already?" she asked.

"It is," Victor smiled. "But you can sleep as long as you want."

"I need coffee," she grumbled and started to get up.

Victor pulled her back down. "You stay here, I'll make it." He slipped out of bed and pulled on his jeans. He liked to take care of Ariel. He looked forward to pampering her for the rest of their lives. Once the coffee had brewed, he carried a mug into the bedroom and set it on the nightstand. He gently settled on the edge of the bed and brushed Ariel's hair back from her face. "Morning baby," he smiled as she slowly opened her eyes.

Ariel sat up and sipped her coffee. "Why are you so happy? Your night was just as long as mine."

Victor smiled. "Waking up next to a beautiful woman always makes me happy." He laughed as Ariel rolled her eyes. "Awake yet?" he asked.

"Mostly," she admitted. "What's up?" She could tell he had something on his mind.

"I've decided to go to the festival tomorrow," he admitted. "I know you don't like social events any more than I do, so if you'd like I can make your excuses. You can stay home, veg in front of the TV and visualize me suffering all night."

Ariel narrowed her eyes. What was he up to? "Why?"

"Why am I going?" he asked.

"Yeah. You don't want to go any more than I do," she pressed.

Victor paused. "I think all the warriors should be there. After last night, I think we need to be on alert. The festival is big. All the fae are going to be in one place. I just think the warriors should attend and make sure we're close in case anything happens. I'm going to talk to Ty later today and have him conduct a sweep first thing in the morning. I talked to Dimitri last night, he agrees. We all need to attend the event and keep a close watch on our people. But like I said, there's no reason for you to attend. I'll tell everyone you got sick last night or something."

"You're trying to protect me," she accused. "Sorry pal, no dice. If you're going, I'm going. I'm not sitting home alone all night wondering if you and everyone else I care about are okay. We're a package deal now. Get used to it."

Victor smiled and studied her for a long time. "Well, when you put it that way, it's hard to argue. I like the sound of the package deal part," he paused. "I really don't want you there. If there's an explosion, I want you as far away as you can get. But I guess I have to get used to compromising," he smiled. "Partners?" he asked as he leaned down and kissed her.

"Partners," she agreed.

After Dark

Ariel and Victor were standing in the large ballroom. The festival had been wonderful so far. Alex had outdone herself. After the royal inauguration, the new queen led the parade in her horse and buggy affair. Ariel had to admit she really did look like royalty. Once the parade was over everyone went to the park for a carnival and food. That had lasted all day. Most of the kids were now completely worn out, or sick from all the junk food. That worked out perfect for the adults who were beginning to arrive for the formal ball. There would be a night of dancing and then Alex would give a small speech and the festivities would be over for another year. Ariel glanced at Victor. He was stunning in a tux. She felt honored to be his date tonight.

So far, there hadn't been any problems. Ty had been busy all day. He swept the parade route for explosives early this morning. Then, he'd spent the day double checking all the buildings and roaming the park. He'd performed one more sweep of the ball room about an hour ago. The warriors had all slipped home to change and then planned to come back and keep an eye out all night. Victor would be extremely happy when this day was over. He'd had about all the socializing he could handle.

"Mom and dad just arrived," Ariel said, relieved. She hated these things. Oberon and Mara spotted the kids and headed their way.

"Any problems?" Oberon asked.

"Not so far," Victor answered. "Maybe I'm jumping at shadows that aren't there. It just feels like something's coming. But maybe it came the other night. We all know that was big enough. Both packs are going to be dealing with the cleanup for months. A lot of their members were displaced and the panthers lost a couple good men. They were lucky to have Alex, otherwise the casualties would have been higher." He glanced around the room. The fae were starting to arrive. Pretty soon the room would be packed.

"Why don't you two go dance," Mara suggested. "Nobody can approach you while you're out on the floor. You won't have to socialize for a while."

"Good idea," Victor looked at Ariel and held out a hand. "Shall we?" he smiled.

"Love to," Ariel smiled back.

Mara stood watching Victor and Ariel for several minutes. She was happy for her daughter. The two of them looked so content in each other's arms. She looked across the room to see where Oberon had gone and realized he was off talking to Dimitri. She turned, hoping to find a place to sit down and almost collided with Charlotte Walker. "Wonderful," Mara thought. What now?

"Mara!" Charlotte said enthusiastically. "I'm so glad I caught you alone. I need to talk to you." She looked around like she was about to share a big secret or something.

"What can I do for you?" Mara asked, trying to sound polite.

Charlotte looked to the dance floor and studied Victor and Ariel for a moment. "Do you really think that's a good idea?" she asked.

"What's that?" Mara inquired.

After Dark

"Well, after that scandal a few years back with the criminal drifter and your daughter, I would think you'd be more careful. We all thought you would control Ariel a little better. She can't afford another scandal. How could you allow her to show up in public with that man?"

Mara narrowed her eyes and took a deep breath. Sometimes it was so difficult being the council leader's wife. Right now all she wanted to do was punch Charlotte Walker in the face. But that would not be proper behavior and it would cause problems for Oberon. Before she could respond, Charlotte continued.

"There are so many proper young men in this community, men from good, dignified families. Men that are worthy of a council leader's daughter. You really must put an end to this and arrange a proper marriage for Ariel. We all realized long ago she had poor judgment, but you mustn't let her continue to date these men," Charlotte said, sounding concerned. "If you don't step in and arrange a proper wedding, people will start to question your judgment as well. Heaven forbid they question Oberon's. You simply must stop this immediately."

Mara turned to study Charlotte's son-in-law, the town drunk. The music stopped and he let out a large hick-up and almost fell off his chair. Mara let her gaze rest there until she was sure Charlotte got the point. She turned back to Charlotte, her eyes cold and challenging. "I suppose I should arrange a marriage for my daughter with someone as dignified as your illustrious son-in-law. Doesn't he have an older brother that's addicted to drugs? Would that be considered a good match?" Mara shot back. "Or maybe I could hook her up with Avery's son. There's a dignified man for you. I forget how many women have made formal complaints against him this past year? Your daughter seems so happy with the man her

348

mother chose for her. I just don't know what my hang-up could be," Mara finished sarcastically.

"Well," Charlotte huffed. "There's no need to be rude about it. I was just trying to save you from disaster. I'd think you'd be grateful. If you're going to be so obstinate, never mind." She turned and stalked away, clearly offended.

"Good," Mara thought. How dare she judge Victor? You'd think she'd be embarrassed enough about the deadbeat she forced her daughter to marry, that she'd leave the rest of the community alone. That woman had nerve. She was still fuming when Victor and Ariel returned.

"I need a drink. You two want anything?" he asked.

"I'd love one," Ariel answered. "What do you want, mom?" she asked.

"Orange juice would be great. Thanks Victor." She watched as he quickly walked to the refreshment table.

"So, what was that about?" Ariel asked as soon as Victor was out of earshot.

"What?" Mara asked.

"Come on mom, I saw you talking to Charlotte Walker. I also saw the look on your face. If the two of you were in a dark alley, Charlotte wouldn't be walking out on her own," Ariel pressed.

Mara glanced at Victor then back to Ariel.

"Oh," Ariel said, extremely annoyed now. "What did she say?"

"Nothing worth repeating," Mara answered. "Just forget it. She's a small person and her opinion is insignificant. Let's just be grateful for what we have. I'm certainly glad I'm not that small minded and petty, it must be exhausting."

Victor returned with the drinks. He knew something was up. The two women looked annoyed. Victor smiled and handed Mara an orange juice. He turned and handed Ariel a slightly doctored OJ. He studied Ariel for a moment, then leaned in and whispered in her ear. "I'm sorry," he gently kissed her temple and moved back.

"For what?" Ariel asked.

Victor turned to Mara. "I guess I should actually be apologizing to you," he kissed her cheek. "I'm sorry you had to deal with that, whatever it was, from Mrs. Walker." He had watched Mara from a distance, the conversation hadn't been a pleasant one. Mrs. Walker stalked off angry, glaring in Victor's direction. He was certain Mara had taken some criticism over the fact that Ariel was dating him. It bothered him. Ariel and her family should not be hassled by the community because of him. Maybe he was being selfish. He was so happy with Ariel, but maybe it wasn't fair to her or her family. Maybe he should disappear for a while.

"You can just wipe that thought right out of your head this instant," Mara demanded.

Victor jumped a little. He was surprised, what did Mara mean by that? "What thought would that be?" he asked giving her his most charming smile.

"It's written all over your face, Victor. You somehow feel responsible for other people's actions. You were thinking of running, weren't you? You're feeling guilty for something out of your control. You want to take the criticism back onto yourself and spare our family the hassle. Am I right?" Mara demanded.

She was. How did she know that? "I wouldn't call it running," he said defensively. "I'd call it being responsible. You shouldn't be subjected to this kind of public scrutiny. It's not fair to force you to deal with my baggage," Victor answered.

"What!" Ariel said angrily. "You would throw away what we have for someone like Charlotte Walker? Do I mean that little to you?" she was hurt.

"No, you mean that much to me. I feel like I'm being selfish. You make me happy, Ariel. I'm not sure I have a right to be this happy. I know I don't have a right to make your family suffer for my happiness. I was just wondering if all this was fair to you. I know it's not fair to your parents," Victor answered solemnly.

"Victor Keisser," Ariel tried to calm herself. She would not lose Victor over these people. "I love you and you love me, that's all that matters. Who cares if those people..." Ariel swept her hand across the room, "understand anything? It would be unfair to me and selfish if you threw it all away to appease them."

"I guess," Victor said hesitantly. He wasn't sure she was right, but he didn't want to lose her.

Mara stepped forward. "Victor, if Charlotte wasn't complaining about you, she'd be harassing someone else. Think of it that way. You're saving the community from that stuffy old bat. Don't give her a second thought," she took Ariel's drink. "Why don't you two go back out and dance? I want you to be seen. I'm proud of the man my daughter is dating and I want the whole town to know it." She pushed the two of them toward the dance floor.

After Dark

Mara stood watching the two kids dance. Sometimes she was so ashamed of her people. How could anyone look at Victor and see anything but a courageous and honorable man? She didn't understand it. She saw movement out of the corner of her eye and spotted Agnes Jackson headed her way. It was too late to escape. She'd just have to deal with it. She took a deep breath and tried to prepare herself for another battle.

"Mara," Agnes said immediately as she slid in next to her.

"Hello Agnes," Mara answered. "It's a lovely party, isn't it? Alex has done such a wonderful job. We're lucky to have her."

"Yes, yes. Alex is settling in quite nicely but that's not what I wanted to talk to you about," she said undeterred. "You really must do something about your daughter," Agnes demanded. "She's ruining your family name. The council leader must have the respect of the community. If Ariel continues to see that Keisser fellow, Oberon will be ruined." She paused for effect.

"We all overlooked the scandal with that thief, but she's out of control? You're lucky Maryann was so successful in chasing that Tank scoundrel away. Otherwise things might have been different. He showed his true colors in the end. Mark my words, Ariel is following a course that is not only going to prove disastrous for her, but it will ruin your entire family. Before you know it she'll be dating Radek himself," Agnes predicted.

"Don't you think your being a bit melodramatic?" Mara said calmly. "I hardly think you can compare Victor to Radek. I happen to think it's wonderful that Ariel and Victor found each other. They both deserve a little happiness in their lives," Mara added.

"Wonderful?" Agnes exclaimed, eyes wide. "What could possibly be wonderful about the council leader's daughter dating the son of a man who has been ostracized by his entire community? Please tell me you have more sense than that. You can't honestly think they would make a good match," Agnes was horrified.

"I certainly do," Mara said defiantly. "Oh I know, there are a few small-minded halfwits in this community that have turned their backs on Atticus Keisser." Mara smiled inwardly at Agnes's sharp intake of breath. It wasn't every day someone called her a halfwit and got away with it. "But all of that is nonsense. Atticus is a good man. His lineage is stronger than my own. I am absolutely thrilled that Victor has taken an interest in my Ariel. Look around you, the entire community is packed into this room tonight. In my opinion you couldn't find a more dignified or honorable man than Victor Keisser in the group," she glanced at Agnes. "The fae have always admired the warriors. A woman lucky enough to gain a warriors' attention has always been envied by those less fortunate. I doubt that will ever change. Of course Oberon and I approve of this match and since she's our daughter we're the only ones that matter," Mara said with finality.

"But..." Agnes began.

"I'm sorry Agnes but you'll have to excuse me," Mara hurried away. She had spotted Foster moving towards Victor. He had a confrontational air about him that Mara didn't care for. She quickly moved to Victor's side and linked an arm through his in support. "Foster," she greeted before he could start something. "How are you this evening?" she said politely.

Foster was taken aback, he hadn't noticed Mara move in next to Victor. Well, that wasn't going to stop him. Victor had to be put in his place. It was bad enough Atticus was starting to leave that farm and wander around town. They couldn't tolerate Victor dating the council leader's daughter. Foster nodded to Mara then turned back to Victor. "I think you should leave," he demanded.

Ariel stepped forward. "Unfortunately, this isn't your party Foster. You don't have the right to ask Victor to leave."

Victor wrapped his arm around her shoulder, securing her tightly against him. He was not going to allow a scene between Foster and Ariel over him. "I'm sorry you feel that way, Foster. However, I'm here on warrior business. I won't be leaving until the party is over."

"Warrior business!" Foster shrieked, the sound echoed throughout the ballroom. Everyone had become extremely quiet. "You have no right to be a warrior. You are a disgrace just like your father. Both of you should have been dealt with long ago. I don't know how you can show your face at a fae celebration like this after abandoning your own child the way you did. If my family was still in power, you and your sorry excuse for a father would be long gone."

"Lucky for all of us you're not still in power," Thomas said coldly as he moved forward to stand beside Victor. "If you were, we would all be long gone. The entire community would be extinct."

"Be careful, Thomas. I don't have a beef with you yet but that could easily change," Foster warned.

"Let me help you out there, Foster. If you have a problem with Victor, you have a problem with me." Thomas stood firm.

Maryann and Frank Saunders joined the group. "Young lady," Maryann interrupted, directing her words at Ariel. "You should be ashamed of yourself. Look at the spectacle you've created tonight. Have you ever once stopped to consider what your actions are doing to your parents?" she criticized. "You have become such an embarrassment," she shook her head. "And Oberon is such a great man. It's shameful."

"I tried to talk to Mara myself," Agnes Jackson put in. "She's besotted with this young man and can't see beneath the charm to the monster he really is."

Ariel stepped forward clearly angry. "You might want to be careful Mrs. Jackson," she threatened. "I have one word for you," Ariel narrowed her eyes. "Sticky," she smiled when Agnes went ghostly white. Everyone in the room started looking around in confusion. Nobody knew what was going on between the two women, but it was clear the word Sticky held some significance to Agnes.

"How do you know about Sticky?" she stuttered.

"Oh, me and Sticky are great pals," Ariel said casually. "I first met him while I was living in Paris. In fact, that's when I did my first favor for good ol' Sticky. I ran into him again in Amsterdam. He owes me quite a debt. So while we're discussing individual virtues, we might as well discuss Tank. You have about five minutes to publically clear up that mess to my satisfaction, or I am going to file formal charges against you. I only need one witness, Sticky." Ariel smiled wickedly. "He assured me he'd be happy to clear things up if I wanted him to. You amuse him but not enough to jeopardize our friendship," she finished coldly. "It's up to you. Time's a ticking," she finished, tapping her finger on her wrist.

After Dark

Once she realized Sticky was Mrs. Jackson's bookie, she had known the information would come in handy someday. Now seemed like as good a time as any to challenge the dishonest thief. If she didn't clear Tank to Ariel's satisfaction, she would use the information to humiliate both Agnes and her husband.

Mr. Jackson stepped forward. "I can clear this up. We were mistaken. Tank did not take that money. We misplaced it. About a month after he left, I went into town and made a deposit. There was an extra two thousand dollars in our safe. One of us must have cleared out the till and forgotten. We considered bringing it to the attention of the council, but what would have been the point?"

Ariel raised one eyebrow. "What would have been the point? Oh, I don't know. Maybe the point would have been clearing an innocent man's name for starters," Ariel said exasperated.

"So many dignified and highly respected members of the community stood up for us. Maryann saw through that man as soon as he arrived. She was very vocal at the time. I couldn't do anything that might make her look bad. I still believe she was correct in her assessment. Maybe he didn't steal money from us, but he was still bad news. We are all grateful he moved on when he did."

Ariel glared at Mr. Jackson. "I'm not sure I'm satisfied with that. Maybe you could clarify a few things for me," Agnes cringed. She was still visibly worried her secret was going to be revealed. "You're willing to clear Tank's name by admitting he didn't steal from you, but he's still bad news and the community is better off without him? Is that correct?"

"I guess," Mr. Jackson admitted a little hesitantly. "Ask Maryann and Frank. They clearly demonstrated that Tank fellow must be a criminal, or he comes from despicable blood lines.

Otherwise, he would have told us his real name. He was hiding something bad, we all knew it," Mr. Jackson finished defensively.

"He told me his real name," Ariel answered. "I am fully aware of his lineage. He is not a criminal nor does he come from undesirable blood lines," Ariel laughed. "If you only knew the truth, every one of you would be embarrassed and ashamed of your actions. Think about that for a while."

Mr. and Mrs. Jackson sank back into the crowd. They both hoped Ariel was finished. For the first time, they realized their dark family secret was vulnerable. They were going to have to be more careful in the future. The rest of the group could fight this battle. They wanted no part of it.

"So, you didn't disgrace your family by dating Tank. What does that have to do with anything?" Foster demanded. "You are disgracing them now by dating Victor. I formally demand his resignation as a warrior and order him banished to Pennsylvania to live with his father," Foster declared.

"I'm not sure what fantasy world you're living in Foster," Oberon said humorlessly as he slid in next to his daughter. "But you don't have the authority to demand anything. You certainly don't have the right to order Victor, or anyone else for that matter, out of this community. This ridiculous display is over. We all know you're after power. Your family failed. It's time for you to accept that and move on with your life. Stop living in the past and what might have been. We have enough problems to deal with from the outside. We don't need this contention from within."

Victor was stunned. He had accepted his fate long ago. He knew anytime he went to social events there would be talk. He also knew if Foster was around, there would be a confrontation. Victor usually took the higher ground and walked away. He was going to do the same tonight. It surprised him that Thomas, Ariel, Mara and now Oberon were publically shielding him from scrutiny. He was touched at the display of support, but this couldn't go on. He was about to leave when he spotted Alex and Dimitri walking toward them. Dimitri was furious. His hands were clenched tightly into fists and he was barely containing his anger. Alex didn't look any happier. Not them, too. Alex was still trying to gain support. She couldn't stand up for him now.

* * * *

Alex was thrilled with the festival's success so far. A couple more hours and the ball would be over. At the end of the evening she would be giving her first speech as queen. She couldn't wait. She was going to use that opportunity to clear Victor's name. All the paperwork was finally in order. She'd spent hours planning everything out with Dimitri and Oberon. They all thought it would be the perfect ending to a wonderful day. She was smiling as Dimitri opened the large door leading to the ballroom and placed his arm around her waist. Once inside, he suddenly stopped. It took her about half a second to discover the reason for his mood change. His face had grown cold and angry. A few members of the crowd were verbally assaulting Victor. Ariel's family and Thomas were standing by Victor, demonstrating their support. Dimitri took two long strides forward before Alex stopped him.

"Wait," she pled knowing this wasn't going to be easy for him. "I think this is a good opportunity for me to establish some rules of conduct in the community. I need to demonstrate to my people I'm willing to take control as their queen. This behavior is unacceptable and I will not tolerate it," Alex said angrily. "Come with me, we need to show solidarity. But please let me handle it." They continued forward and stood next to Victor. Thomas, Mara and Oberon stepped aside to make room for the Queen and Dimitri.

Alex took a deep breath and began to address her people. "The last several months have been difficult in so many ways. The community has lost one of its long-standing council members, a good man and leader, to violence. The rest of the council has continued to function under the most trying of circumstances. The council, the warriors and I have done our best to shelter and protect this community the best we can.

I am the first to admit times have not been easy. Over the past couple years you have lost your queen, lost a great warrior leader and lost a council member. In addition, we have lost countless fathers, mothers and children to this war. I realize it may be difficult for you to accept me. Until recently, you had never met me. I can assure you, from the moment I discovered I was your queen, I have done my best to be worthy of that honor. My mother was so proud of her people. She believed they were good hearted and decent. She believed in this community, in your goodness and your strength. For the past few months, I have been operating on the assumption my mother was correct. I believed the pain and sacrifices my family, the warriors and the council have made for you was worth it. I accepted my position with pride and have always felt honored to call you my people," Alex paused.

"Tonight, when I walked through that door and observed your cruelty to someone I consider a member of my family, someone who has sacrificed so much for your safety and happiness, I was truly ashamed. For the first time, I find myself wondering why we have given so much for such a cruel, disrespectful and ungrateful society.

This man has not only given his time and money to ensure your protection, but he's come very close to giving his life for you. He has shed his blood for you. He has gone home numerous times battered and bruised protecting you. Yet, he's never asked for anything in return. Apparently not even respect," Alex glanced at Victor. "He's performed his duties with grace and dignity and this is how you repay him?"

Foster stepped forward and addressed Alex. "With all due respect, ma'am, you haven't been part of this community long enough to understand this man's history. You don't know of the atrocity his father committed against one of us, his very own wife, the woman he swore to love and protect. We are all trying to accept you. Over the past few months, many have come to respect you. We are grateful for the sacrifices you have made on our behalf. But if you stand by this man; a man whose past actions have demonstrated he is as dishonorable as his father, a man who refused to accept responsibility for his own child, many of us will be forced to question your judgment."

Oberon was furious. This had gone far enough. He stepped forward and addressed the crowd. "Our queen may be new to this community. She may not know the history of Victor's family, but I do. I sat on the council after the incident with Atticus. I also sat on the council when Victor's actions were reviewed. It's easy for you to claim Alexandria is acting in ignorance, to claim she is trusting and respecting this man because she doesn't know any better. What about me? I have more knowledge on this particular subject than anyone else in this room. Do you question my judgment?" he demanded. "If so, now is the time to vocalize your concerns. I am the chairman of the council. If this community questions my ability, my character and my judgment, you have a responsibility to step forth immediately. If this community does not have complete confidence in my abilities, it's time for me to step down."

The room was silent. Oberon was one of the oldest members of the community. He was well respected by everyone. Nobody had ever questioned him before. No one was willing to question him now. Most of the fae were intimidated by him and unwilling to take him on. But more important was the fact that nobody wanted to. They believed in him, they trusted him, they felt honored to have him on their council.

"In light of what's happened here tonight I don't feel I can simply take your silence as acceptance," Alex announced. "Foster has openly questioned my judgment as well as Oberon's. In response, Oberon has issued a challenge. He is asking for a vote of confidence from his community, or in reverse a vote of no confidence. As queen, I believe it is essential for the community to have faith in their leaders. It is even more essential they believe in the judgment and abilities of the council chair," Alex looked around the crowd. "Breena, would you please assist me?" Breena moved forward. "I need to know if we have a majority present here tonight. If so, we will conduct a vote. You will need to document these proceedings to create an official record."

Breena conducted a count and verified attendance. The entire community was present except for the other council members and their immediate families. They had agreed to remain in their safe houses as a precaution. The vampires had been unusually quiet for too long. Nobody was willing to take any chances tonight.

"Good," Alex said as Breena announced the count. "We will now vote." Everyone seemed uncomfortable. A casual evening out had just become serious and confrontational.

After Dark

"Before we get started, I need Bastian, Ty, Dante, Nicholas and Jake to come forward." Alex paused while the five warriors moved in to stand next to Victor, Thomas and Dimitri. They were clearly demonstrating their solidarity and support. "Now, let me tell you how this is going to work. We are going to have a vote to determine not only if Oberon should remain on the council, but also if he should continue as council chair. Are there any questions?" Alex was silent for several minutes. So was the rest of the room.

"Fine. I will now give the community an opportunity to voice any concerns regarding Oberon's ability. If you have any doubts, any concern whatsoever regarding this man, his judgment, his ability to lead, anything, you need to voice them now. Once the vote has been cast, I will not tolerate dissension. If you do not officially voice your concerns publically in this procedure, you give up any right to voice them in the future. Are there any questions regarding my position on this?"

Nobody spoke so Alex continued. "I'm going to repeat myself to make sure you are crystal clear. If you do not speak up in this procedure and it is brought to my attention Oberon's judgment or ability is questioned in the future, you will be subject to sanction."

"Look," Foster stepped forward again. "This is getting out of control. Nobody has ever, or is currently questioning Oberon, his judgment, or his ability to lead the council. Victor's character is the one in question. We all have complete confidence and trust in Oberon. I'm not clear on how this got turned around to the point we are having a vote to determine Oberon's qualifications. Maybe we should be voting on Victor, deciding if we have confidence in his ability to protect us as a warrior. I for one am not sure he's qualified to continue in that capacity."

Alex wanted to lash out at this man. She wanted to walk over and pummel him until he shut up for good. She was doing her best to control her temper and had almost regained her composure when Oberon stepped forward.

"Foster, I would like to address your question personally. First, we are having a vote regarding my qualifications as you put it, because you have not only insulted the queen tonight by questioning her judgment, but you have indirectly questioned mine. Alexandria has already explained her position in regards to Victor. She was very clear that she not only respects the man, but has the utmost confidence in him as a warrior. My position is much the same. I however will go one step further. I will publically announce, before we vote, that I too have complete confidence in Victor's ability as a warrior. In addition, I would literally trust him with my life, the life of my wonderful wife and the life of my daughter. Unlike many of you, I do not have any questions regarding Victor's character. He is the most honorable and selfless individual I have ever had the pleasure of knowing.

Not only is a vote unnecessary with regard to Victor's position as a warrior, it would be inappropriate. The community does not get to choose their warriors any more than a warrior chooses his destiny. It is his birthright. Only the council or the queen can take that right away. Tonight, the council and the queen have publicly given their support and gratitude to this man for his dedication and service to his community. Like our great Queen, I too am disappointed in the members of this society. I've been around a long time. I know you are better than this. I've seen the best in each and every one of you. Unfortunately, tonight I have also seen the worst. I want to say this again, I am the only person in this room with complete knowledge regarding Victor and his father's previous actions. Therefore, anyone who questions Victor's character or his

363

position as a warrior is essentially questioning my judgment and my ability." He turned to look at Foster. "That is why a formal vote is required."

Victor didn't know how to respond to what was going on here. He had gotten used to being shunned. He expected it. He was overwhelmed by the support he was being given not only from his fellow warriors, but his queen and the chairman of the council. He wasn't sure he deserved this. True, he hadn't shirked his responsibilities. He had been unfairly punished for a crime he hadn't committed. Still, he was humbled by Oberon's words and by his unconditional support. Alex too for that matter. She was still trying to gain the communities respect. Yet here she was, putting her very reputation on the line for him. How could he ever repay them for their kindness, for their trust and support? He didn't know, but he would spend every day for the rest of his life trying.

Alex stepped forward. "Now that Oberon has cleared that up. Does anyone have anything to say regarding Oberon, his character, his judgment or his qualifications to remain on the council or to continue as council chair?" Alex swept the area with her gaze. The room was completely quiet. She waited three full minutes before she continued. "Breena, will you document for the record, no one in this crowd has voiced any objection or concerns regarding Oberon or his ability to serve on the council and help lead our people."

Breena wrote quickly, trying to document the proceedings as completely as possible.

"We will now vote. There will be two votes. The first will determine if Oberon remains a member of the council. The second will decide if he continues as Council Chair. Are there any questions?" Again, there was silence. Alex led the community through the voting process. Both votes were unanimous in favor of Oberon.

Once again Alex addressed the crowd. "Tonight, as a community, you have unanimously accepted Oberon as a council member and as chairman of the council," she announced. "By doing so, you have also unanimously agreed that you trust his judgment. Oberon was very clear in his support for, and confidence in, Victor as a warrior. I believe I was also clear earlier when I told you I have the utmost confidence and respect for Victor Keisser. I believe he is a great warrior and an asset to this team. Foster is correct when he says I don't know all the history of my people. I may not know every detail of Victor's family history. However, I do know this man. I know his heart. I know some of the sacrifices he has made for your benefit. As far as I'm concerned, each of these men standing before you today are members of my family." She motioned to the warriors. "When you disrespect one of them, you disrespect me." Alex paused to look at the warriors. Her gaze stopped and held on Dimitri for an extra moment. Then she turned back to her people. "I will not tolerate anyone disrespecting my family." Alex shifted her gaze back to Victor. She turned and walked toward him, then linked her arm through his and pulled him forward.

"As your Queen, I have the authority to offer a pardon if I am convinced any person was wrongfully convicted of committing a crime; or to any individual who has demonstrated to me they have fulfilled their debt to society. I have personally determined Victor Keisser meets both requirements. Effective today, I Queen Alexandria Deveraux, grant Victor Keisser a full pardon. I fully exonerate him of all charges and order the expungement of any council records pertaining to the Victor Keisser incident brought before them by the were-panther leadership. In other words, no record will exist regarding this incident. It will be as if the incident never occurred. I expect my people to accept my decision on this. I also expect my people to treat this man with respect, something he has been denied for the last five years.

Foster was wrong about one crucial matter. Victor did not fail to accept responsibility for his actions or his child. He did not prove himself dishonorable in any way. In fact, he did just the opposite. He stood trial for a crime he did not commit. He accepted his punishment without complaint, served his time and returned a year later to protect and defend the very community that wronged him. A great injustice was done that day. A good man was hurt and has been rejected by his community ever since. It stops today," Alex declared. She turned to face Victor. "I personally want to apologize on behalf of our people for the pain you have suffered over the past five years. I thank you for your service and dedication," she smiled at him. "I also expect it to continue as long as I'm your queen."

Victor smiled. "You have my word on it." Alex turned, her arm still linked with Victor's and together they silently walked out of the room.

The rest of the warriors followed. As soon as they were out the door, Dimitri maneuvered in front of them and stopped. "Can I have my woman back now?" He was glowing with pride. "I need to take her home and show her just how proud she's made me tonight."

Victor laughed. He pulled Alex into a hug, lifting her off her feet. "Thank you," he said setting her back down. "I can never repay you for what you just did for me but I promise to spend the rest of my life trying," he said sincerely. He paused as he glanced at Dimitri. "Now, you better go to your man before he gets the wrong idea and punches me in the nose." He smiled at Dimitri and then wrapped an arm around Ariel's waist pulling her in close. "I think I'm going home to show my woman just how much I appreciate her coming to my defense." He leaned in and gave Ariel a gentle kiss, then turned to the rest of the warriors. "Thanks," he said looking each warrior in the eye. "Over the past five years I have never once felt like any of you believed, even for an instant, that I was guilty. Your support has meant a lot to me. I won't forget it." They'd reached the parking lot and Victor's truck. The warriors were about to disburse when a large explosion rocked the night.

* * * *

The entire group immediately turned and ran back towards the large ballroom. As they reached the entrance, they realized most of the congregation had followed them out of the building. They were now scattered around the parking lot and on the lawn in front of the damaged building. Ty grabbed Thomas and the two of them began searching for additional devices. "Keep these people together and away from any buildings," Ty called back. "There could be other bombs."

Dimitri gathered the warriors. "We need to get the rest of those people out of that building. I'm not going to order anyone to go in there. Even if Ty neutralizes any additional devices, that structure's not stable. The north side could collapse at any moment. I'm going to leave it up to you, but I need to search for the wounded. If you want to join me, step forward. If you don't feel comfortable going in there, don't hesitate to say so. I could use a couple good men out here to organize this crowd." Every warrior stepped forward.

After Dark

"Looks like you'll have to ask for volunteers to handle the crowd," Bastian observed. "We're all going with you."

Oberon and Mara approached. Ariel was relieved. She hadn't seen her parents leave the building. She rushed over and hugged them both. "I'm so glad you made it out before that blast. Any idea how many are still left inside?"

"We got lucky, most of the crowd had already left. I don't think there were very many people still inside. Foster's escapades ruined the celebration. Once the queen, the warriors and I left most of the crowd disbursed as well," Oberon supplied. "We parked at the back of the lot thinking it would be easier to get out once the party was over. A few people already left. Sorry it took us so long to get back," he turned to Dimitri. "Do you have a plan?"

"Yes," Dimitri said soberly. "The warriors are going back inside. We need to see if there are any injured that need rescuing. Ty and Thomas are already around back searching for additional devices. You can coordinate the people if you don't mind. They need to stay in a group and avoid any buildings until we are certain they are safe. For now, keep them away from the parking lot too. It would be easy to plant bombs underneath cars." He turned to the warriors. "Pair up. Let's go in. No matter what, do not lose your partner." He pulled Alex in for a long kiss. "I have to do this. I hope you understand."

"I understand but I don't like it," she admitted. "Bring the wounded to me. I'll take care of them." Alex watched as the warriors headed for the building then she turned toward Ariel. She was going to suggest they set things up the same way they did at the panther base, but Ariel was focused on something out in the field. Suddenly, Ariel took off running. Alex turned to Mara. "I need you to coordinate the wounded until we get back. Whatever's out there I can't let Ariel face it alone." Alex took off at a dead run behind her friend.

Ariel surveyed her surroundings wondering who could have done this to her people. As she glanced around the nearby buildings, she saw Samantha. "What was wrong with that human?" She thought, exasperated. Sam was on top of a building, again. It was the building furthest from the ballroom and the one closest to the enormous field that led to the woods. She was shooting arrows into the field. Ariel surveyed the large expanse and finally saw movement. Was that Lilith? It had to be. She started to run.

Alex spotted Sam the moment Ariel took off running. She watched as Sam climbed from the building and sprinted at a dead run into the field, toward the woods. What was she doing? Alex followed Ariel across the opening. They collided with Sam just before she disappeared into the thick trees.

"What are you doing?" Ariel yelled. "Are you crazy? You can't win Lilith in a one on one attack." Ariel was flabbergasted. Sam had guts, that was for sure, but Ariel wasn't sure she had any common sense.

"Lilith?" Alex repeated. She looked toward the woods but couldn't see movement. "Lilith was here?" she asked.

Sam looked at her watch. "Lilith is still here. She's hiding just inside those woods, watching us I'm sure. Let me go, I want her dead once and for all. She's caused enough damage."

Ariel and Alex turned toward the woods. They subconsciously maneuvered to shield Sam. They were both concentrating on the darkness, watching for movement.

After Dark

Moments later Sam spoke up. "We might as well go back to the building and see what we can do to help," she sounded deflated. "Lilith left. I'm sure she's long gone now."

Alex turned back to her. "How do you know that?" she asked.

Sam looked at her watch then showed it to Alex. "The light's gone. That means she's at least 250 yards away. No signal."

"You're tracking Lilith?" Alex said alarmed. "You have a lot of explaining to do. Start now."

"Hey, I'm off duty. I'm on my own time. I'm pretty sure I don't have to answer that," Sam said defensively.

"Actually, now that you're in charge of D-Tech you're always on duty. You are a salaried employee. When you accepted the raise, you accepted my authority 24/7. Spill it. How did Lilith come to have a tracking device on her person and why are you interested in tracking her in the first place?"

"I planted it that night on the roof. The night in the alley when she killed John. I thought it might come in handy. Plus, I decided that night she was one of my prime targets. That's why I'm tracking her. I can't kill her until I find her. She's a tricky one though. She's been a bigger challenge than I expected," Sam admitted. "Sorry, I didn't know what she was up to tonight. If I'd known she had explosives I could have warned you before anyone got hurt."

"We have to get back," Alex turned and headed toward the building. "I need to help the wounded. Do you happen to know how many bombs she planted?" Alex asked.

"Two for sure, maybe three. I think she was about to plant a third one or was just finishing with it when I hit her with the first arrow. I'm proud to say I got her really good. She's definitely wounded. I couldn't get to her heart, but she's got a few holes in her. She won't be back tonight. I used the holy water again. It seemed to work pretty well last time."

Ariel surveyed the building and saw Ty working on a device. She knew he was good. She just hoped they found both the bombs before another one went off. She was almost back to the front of the building when a second explosion erupted. Ariel panicked. Victor was still in the building. She darted for the door without a second thought.

Alex saw Ariel enter the building and started for the front door. She paused when she saw Dimitri exit the side of the building with someone slung over his shoulder. Alex relaxed. Dimitri was okay. The sound of that blast had terrified her, Dimitri was inside. She instantly froze, wondering if Dimitri had been seriously wounded or killed in the explosion. She knew that was why Ariel darted inside so quickly. She needed to find Victor. Alex met Dimitri half way across the expanse. "Ariel just ran into the building. I'm sure she's looking for Victor. The building's not stable and she's alone." Bastian exited the door and headed toward Dimitri. They must have been partnered inside.

Dimitri scowled. "Great! Just what I need, another complication." He walked over to a tree and laid the injured man on the ground. It was Mr. Jackson.

Alex inhaled. He was wounded fairly badly. "What happened to his wife?" she asked, worried she wouldn't like the answer.

"Relax, she's fine. Well, she has injuries, but they're not as severe as Earl's are." He looked back at Bastian who had joined them. "Where's Agnes?"

"She's over there," Bastian pointed. "Once we got out of the building, she wouldn't move another inch. She just collapsed outside the door. Should I physically carry her over here or is she okay where she is? She might eventually make her way over on her own," Bastian surmised.

Alex looked where Bastian was pointing then back to Mr. Jackson. "Bastian, will you go tell her I want to heal her husband, but I can't do it without her help. That should get her away from that building."

"Good idea," Bastian said as he headed back toward the door.

"What are you going to do about Ariel?" Alex asked, then saw his face. "What's wrong?" She asked concerned now.

"Victor," he answered solemnly.

"How bad?" she asked.

"It's bad. I'm having a hard time sensing any of the other warriors through his pain," he said quietly. "Promise me you won't go anywhere," he winced. "I've got to get to Victor and bring him out here to you. It's serious, you can't move from this spot. I won't have time to search for you. I need to know you'll be right here when we come out." He closed his eyes. "Where is Bastian, I can't wait much longer?"

Alex was worried. Victor had to be in a lot of pain. Dimitri could feel all the warriors' injuries as the warrior leader. It helped him protect his men. If he could only feel Victor, he had to be seriously wounded. She glanced back at the building and saw Bastian speaking to Agnes. "I promise, I'll be right here. Hurry, Dimitri. Go save Victor and find Ariel."

"As soon as Bastian gets back, we'll go in. Which door did she enter?" Dimitri asked looking around. He relaxed a little, Bastian was heading back their way.

"The front door," Alex answered. She knelt down and surveyed Earl. "I haven't seen a lot of injured out here. What's it like inside? Do I have a lot of injuries to deal with tonight?" she asked.

"Not many. Most of the crowd left before the explosion. Nick, Dante, Victor and Jake were looking for Maryann and Frank. The Jackson's were sure they were still in there when the bomb exploded. Foster's also in the building somewhere. We haven't located him either. Between the six of us, I think we can clear things out rather quickly. I just hope there aren't any more explosions before we can get out," he confided.

"Oh, I didn't tell you." She looked around, trying to find Sam. "Sam was up on the roof of that building shooting arrows at Lilith. She saw her plant the bombs. Sam's pretty confident Lilith only had time to get three bomb's in place before she shot her with an arrow. Then, Lilith escaped into the woods. We're going to have to do something about her and this vampire hunting kick she's on, but that's a problem for another day. Anyway, Ty was working on a device when that second one went off so all three of them are accounted for. I think we should be okay now."

"Well at least that's good news," Dimitri responded. "If you see Ty and Thomas, have them clear the parking lot first and then start on the surrounding buildings. Once they're certain the parking lot is safe, Oberon can start directing people to their vehicles. I'd like to get everyone out of here as soon as we can." He turned as Bastian approached.

"I'll take care of it. Go find Victor and Ariel. I'm worried." Alex took Agnes Jackson's hand and led her to her husband. She was obviously in shock. Alex would take care of that once she'd finished with Earl. She silently watched as the two warriors hurried back into the building. They had to find Victor in time. She couldn't bear the thought of losing him. She was surprised at how close she had become to all the warriors in such a short amount of time. Apparently adversity did create strong bonds.

Sam sat back and watched the group from a distance. She had been shocked when she saw Alex with that injured man. Once her hand started glowing, Sam knew Alex was something other than human. The injuries were completely gone in seconds. Sam wondered what Alex was. She must be whatever her friend Ariel was. Sam remembered watching in amazement that night in the alley. Ariel had created fireballs from her fingertips and threw them into the vampire's chests, destroying them instantly. These people were strange. It was funny, she had always thought Luke was too normal. She'd told him many times he needed a good hobby, or an adventurous vacation. Little had she known, Luke had more adventure than twenty men. Thomas appeared from the side of the building with a sexy blond guy. She could say one thing about Alex and Thomas, all their friends were hot. The blond was in a tux, but he'd lost the coat and had the white shirt sleeves rolled up to his elbows. He strolled casually like a Texas cowboy. Thomas and the blond seemed to be looking for bombs. Sam wondered who he was. She'd never seen him before, but that didn't mean he wasn't employed by the Deveraux's. Maybe he was some kind of explosives expert. She settled in against a nearby tree for a long night of people watching.

* * * *

Victor and Jake circled the room searching for anyone that remained in the building. Dante and Nick just left to escort Maryann and Frank outside. Luckily, they hadn't been injured severely. They had a few bruises, but mostly they were just afraid. When the debris settled they hid in a corner, too scared to find the way out on their own. Bastian and Dimitri left seconds earlier with the Jackson's. Mrs. Jackson was okay, but Earl looked pretty bad. Victor saw a slight movement. "Jake, I think I found something over there. I'm going to investigate. Don't move out of my sight. We need to stick together." Victor pushed aside a large piece of wood, it looked like it had once been part of a beam. The ceiling had collapsed in this part of the room. The bomb must have been planted right on the corner of the building. It was a good tactic. Both walls were now compromised.

Jake continued to search the room, making sure he didn't venture too far from Victor. They needed to stick together. They were the only ones left in the building now. If anything happened, they would need to be there for each other.

Victor slowly made his way through the debris. He was sure he'd seen something move over here. He was carefully searching through the rubble when he heard someone moaning. "Jake, I think I found someone." Victor pushed away a large section of wall and found Foster. He was bleeding from his head and his leg was obviously broken. He had a compound fracture. They would have to be careful when they carried him out, but if they could get him to Alex he'd survive. Right now, he looked like he was in a lot of pain.

Victor quickly started moving the rubble in an attempt to free Foster. A lot of debris had fallen on him. Victor wasn't sure exactly how extensive Foster's injuries were. Right now he could only see the two, but there could be more. "Foster, can you tell me where you're wounded?" Victor asked.

"Of all the people in the world that could have found me, it had to be you," Foster grumbled.

"Yeah, that's my dumb luck. Now I have to do something nice for you. Where are you injured?" Victor demanded.

"That piece of ceiling landed on my head and I can't move my leg. I also have something stuck in my side," Foster answered. "I don't think I can walk out of here, so you might as well leave. I doubt you're going to carry me," he said angrily.

"Do you know how many people were still in here when the explosion went off?" Victor asked. "We know about the Jackson's and the Saunders. Can you think of anyone else?" Victor questioned.

"No. I think everyone else left once the spectacle was over. The five of us were furious with the queen for giving you a pardon. My family's going to be pissed. Lawson is going to go berserk," Foster froze. "Did you say an explosion did this? Like a bomb?" he asked.

"Yeah," Victor answered. He thought if he could keep Foster talking, maybe he wouldn't go into shock. They might actually make it out of here alive. He studied Foster, he was obviously upset.

What had he just asked? He was saying something about Lawson, then asked if a bomb did this. Were the two connected? Had Lawson bombed the festival ball? But he wouldn't do anything to injure his own brother. Or would he? Victor didn't know Lawson, but he'd heard rumors over the years. He always wondered if Lawson had some of the same mental deficiencies his mother had.

Just then a second explosion rocked the night. Victor threw himself on top of Foster in an attempt to protect him from the brick and wood falling all around the area. He looked up and saw a large ceiling beam crashing toward them. Victor shoved Foster out of the way, but couldn't move fast enough. Foster was clear, but the beam landed directly on top of Victor. He let out a gasp as the force of it knocked him across the floor and trapped him underneath. Once the dust began to settle Victor remembered Jake. "Hey Jake, you okay?" he gasped. He could barely breathe, the weight of the ceiling beam was pressing on his chest and his lungs. No answer. "Jake!" Victor yelled. "Answer me, are you okay?" Silence continued to loom throughout the room. Finally, Victor heard coughing. "Jake? Is that you?" he called again.

"Yeah," Jake answered. "It's me. I'm afraid I'm stuck though. There's a large piece of ceiling teetering above me. If I move too quickly, I'm sure it's going to fall. I'll try to ease my way out in the other direction. Are you okay? You sound a little off," he asked.

"I'm fine. I found Foster, but now I've lost him again. Foster?" Victor called, it was getting harder to talk. He tried to pivot around to look behind him and winced. There was a jagged piece of wood protruding from his thigh. It was not his lucky night. The rubble started to move beside him and he saw Foster emerge from the pile. He couldn't stand, he was kind of dragging himself into the clearing. Foster took one look at Victor and immediately looked confused. "Why did you do that?" he asked, clearly perplexed.

"Do what?" Victor croaked. The beam was starting to cut off his air and he was sure he'd lost a lot of blood from the leg wound.

"Why would you risk your own life to save me?" Foster said silently. "I don't understand. After everything I've done to you, everything I helped my sister do, why would you save me? If the tables were turned, I would have gladly let you die."

"I'm not you Foster," Victor closed his eyes. Tonight was proof that no good turn goes unpunished.

"Victor," Jake called. "Are you sure you're okay? I can tell someone is having a hard time breathing. Is that you or Foster?"

"It's not me old man," Foster answered. "Victor is okay if you call having a large piece of wood protruding out of your leg okay. Oh yeah, the fact that his chest is supporting a seriously huge ceiling beam might also be a problem. Other than that, I think he's peachy."

"That's not helping Foster," Victor chastened. "Jake, any luck getting out of that mess you're in? I could really use some help over here." Victor took a jagged breath. "Foster has a compound fracture to his leg, a large gash on his head and he has a large piece of wood protruding out of his side. I'm afraid without help we'll both be doomed," Victor admitted.

"I'm trying, but I can't make any promises. If I move too quickly, I'm going to be as trapped as you are. I just hope the other warriors return to check on us. We could really use the backup."

Just then Victor thought he heard Ariel calling his name. She better not be in this building. It wasn't safe.

Ariel pushed her way into the ballroom. It was a mess. There was no longer a room discernable. It was all just a big pile of rubble. "Victor!" She called again. "Are you in here?" She yelled.

"Ariel?" Jake exclaimed. "What are you doing here?"

"Jake? Is that you?" she asked.

"Yes, it's me. I'm in a bit of a bind but not as bad as Victor and Foster," he admitted.

"Victor," Ariel called. She was starting to panic now. What did Jake mean not as bad as Victor and Foster?

"Ariel," Victor croaked. He was trying to sound normal, but he knew he failed miserably. "Can you go get the rest of the warriors? Jake's trapped in a cavern created by the debris and I have a large beam on my chest. I can't move. Foster's also injured and can't get out of here himself."

Ariel took a deep breath. She had to be careful, but she thought she could slowly make her way toward the sound of Victor's voice. If she could get to him, maybe she could help him get free. "Victor?" she called. "Is Foster with you then?"

"I don't think he should talk," Foster answered. "We're together, but Victor is having a hard time breathing. We really could use some help to get this beam off him. I think you should try to get the other warriors," Foster sounded worried. He was surprised at himself. He was actually concerned about Victor and didn't want him to die this way. Victor couldn't die because he'd saved Foster's life.

"I'm sure they're on their way," Ariel assured him. "I'm not leaving without Victor," she said stubbornly. She shoved another pile of debris away and finally spotted someone, maybe Foster. Ariel methodically made her way to Victor. She was moving too slow, but she didn't want to disrupt anything. It might cause a domino effect and she wouldn't make things worse for him. As she climbed over a massive section of ceiling, she saw him. Victor was so white. He was trapped beneath a huge ceiling beam and covered in rubble. There was a large piece of jagged wood protruding from his thigh. Foster didn't look much better. His head was bleeding and he had a broken leg and an equally large piece of wood protruding from his side. "Where are you Jake?" she called. Maybe she could help him and the two of them could figure something out to free Victor.

"I'm over here, probably about six or seven feet from your location. There's a big section of the ceiling dangling precariously above me. One wrong move and I'll be crushed like a bug," Jake admitted. "I'm doing my best, but alone this is going to take forever."

"Ariel!" Dimitri bellowed as he entered the room, Bastian at his heels. "What do you think you're doing? It's not safe in here. Get back outside at once."

Ariel rolled her eyes. Dimitri was always so bossy. "I'm not leaving without Victor. He's injured, so is Foster. Jake's somewhere over there afraid to move an inch for fear a large piece of ceiling will fall and crush him. I don't think this is the time to argue about safety," she countered. "All three of these guys need help immediately."

"Jake, I realize you're trapped but are you okay?" Dimitri asked. He was new at sensing his warriors and he was still having trouble sensing anything other than Victor's pain.

"I'm fine. Just a few superficial wounds. It's Victor I'm worried about. It sounded like he was having a hard time breathing. He needs help fast," Jake answered. "I'm working my way free, it's just going to take time."

"Victor," Dimitri called. "How bad are you?"

"He's pretty bad," Foster supplied. "He has a large beam crushing his chest. He's wheezing and having a hard time breathing."

Ariel moved in beside Victor. "You better not give up on me," she ordered, tears running down her cheek. "I need you," she cried.

Victor raised his hand and wiped away a tear. "Don't cry babe," he wheezed and gave her a pitiful smile. "I love you."

Ariel lunged to her feet. "Dimitri, you and Bastian get over here right now. We need to get this beam off his chest or he's not going to make it."

The two warriors were making their way to Ariel's location as quickly as they could. They finally reached her and stopped in horror at the sight of Victor trapped under that beam. Dimitri looked up just in time to see Dante and Nick enter the room. "Good," Dimitri called. "You two get over here, quick! I need your help to free Victor. He's in bad shape," Dimitri looked at Foster. "You're going to have to hang on for a while. We need to help Victor before we can get you out of here."

Foster slid backwards, trying to give the warriors as much room as he could. He had such conflicted feelings. Why had Victor risked his own life to protect him? Victor had to hate him. He'd spent the last several centuries causing problems for Victor at every turn. Now he might die all because he shoved Foster to safety when that beam fell. Fosters thoughts shifted back to Lawson. He'd come home with a large bundle of cash a few days ago. Did he build those bombs? If so, his own brother had almost killed him while the nephew he had tried to ruin had saved his life.

Ariel felt helpless. Her gift was no good here. The laser beam wouldn't even work. She could probably get through eventually, but it would take too long. The beam was too thick. Plus, it was resting on Victor's chest. The chance of added injury was too great. She couldn't do anything to help Victor. If Alex were here, she could heal his wounds. At least he wouldn't be losing all that blood. How were they going to move that beam? They had to get some of the pressure off. She knew Victor was going to die if they couldn't find a way to get him out soon. Tears continued to run down her face. They had to get Victor free, she couldn't lose him now.

The warriors were doing their best to lift the beam, but even with four of them it wouldn't budge. They were getting discouraged when they heard a noise. Dimitri glanced up to see Morrigan and Austin shift from birds into men.

"How can we help?" Morrigan called out.

"Morrigan!" Ariel exclaimed. "Victor needs help. Can you get over here and see what you can do?" she begged.

Austin and Morrigan shifted back and flew over the debris. They shifted again as they landed next to Ariel.

"Show off," she accused.

Morrigan sobered. Victor was in trouble. He looked at Austin. "Any suggestions?"

"If we can move this guy, Ariel and two of the warriors out of the area, I think there might be enough room for the two of us to shift into elephants." Austin was studying the space. "If you get on one end and I get on the other, we might be able to lift that thing off him. We should at least be able to lift it enough for the other two warriors to pull him clear."

Ariel immediately began climbing away from the area. It sounded like a good plan.

Dimitri turned to Nick. "Can you and Bastian carry Foster into that clearing over there? You need to be far away from us in case we shift the wrong pile and everything comes tumbling down," he turned to Dante. "Are you okay with that? I'm putting you in danger, but I can't move Victor myself."

"I don't mind. I can't count how many times Victor has saved me over the years. I owe him. I'm not leaving without him," Dante answered. He looked down at Victor, worried. He wasn't sure he was still conscious or even breathing.

Morrigan and Austin shifted. They used their trunks to slowly lift the beam off Victor's chest. Dante and Dimitri immediately pulled Victor to safety. The elephants gently laid the beam on the ground then shifted back. "Is he okay?" Morrigan asked. "He doesn't look good."

"We need to get him to Alex," Dimitri answered. "She's his only hope," Dimitri was worried. Victor was unconscious and Dimitri was positive he'd stopped breathing, or worse. Now that Victor had passed out, Dimitri couldn't feel his pain anymore. Was that because he was unconscious, or was he dead? Dimitri couldn't bear to think about that.

"Jake?" Dimitri called. "How you doing?"

"I've reached an impasse," Jake admitted. "Don't worry about me. It's tight in here, but I'm not hurt that bad. As long as this concoction doesn't cave in on me, I'll be fine. Get Foster and Victor out of here. Get Victor to Alex."

Dimitri gently lifted Victor into his arms. "Dante, try to clear the way as much as you can. Let's get out of here. We need to get to Alex."

Nick picked Foster up and followed Dimitri out of the room.

Bastian turned to Morrigan. "Any chance you can shift into something small and find a way to Jake? I realize he's not seriously injured, but we have to get him out of there. The building's extremely unstable."

Morrigan looked to Austin. "How about a mouse?"

"That should work," Austin agreed. They both shifted and went in search of Jake.

* * * *

Ariel lay on the bed next to Victor. He was still unconscious. Alex assured her he was going to be okay. She said she healed all his injuries and he just needed time. Ariel watched the blood slowly drip from the bag. He was so still. She just wanted him to wake up. She wanted to feel his touch again. She needed to know for sure he was going to be okay. She brushed his hair away from his forehead and gently pressed her lips to his. As she leaned back, she realized Victor was watching her.

Ariel smiled. She couldn't help it. He was finally awake! Victor had been out for more than two days. She wanted to celebrate. He really would be okay. The last sixty three hours had been awful. Ariel had been so worried he still might die.

Victor smiled back at Ariel. He tried to lift his hand and stopped. He was connected to an IV pole. "Can you unhook that?" he asked. "I'm kind of tied up in knots here," his voice was raspy and dry.

Ariel shook her head. "Dimitri said you need at least one more bag." She stood and brought him a glass of water. "Drink up. Your throat sounds dry."

Victor sat up and drank the entire glass. His mouth felt like sand. He smiled sheepishly at Ariel. "Can I have another one? My mouth and throat feel like sandpaper."

Ariel brought the large container over and poured another glass of water. She set the picture on the nightstand and stood, watching him. She loved him so much. Almost losing him had made her realize how much she wanted a life with him. A very long life. She studied his face. He still looked tired and weak. She hated to see him this way. Victor had always seemed invincible to her. But that was just an illusion. He had almost died, just a few more seconds and Alex wouldn't have been able to save him. Her eyes started to moisten. She blinked several times, forcing herself to hold back the tears.

Victor was watching Ariel. She looked upset. "Come back over here by me," he said holding out his hand. "I want to hold you."

Ariel grinned and climbed back onto the bed. "I would love for you to hold me," she said as she settled in next to him. She rested her head on his chest and took a deep breath. He really was going to be okay.

"Hey," he lifted her chin so he could see her face. "What's going on? Why are you upset?"

"Not upset, relieved," she corrected. "Just relieved." Ariel sat up straight and studied him. He looked confused. She realized he didn't know how long he'd been out. He probably didn't know how close he'd come to dying. "You almost didn't make it out of that stupid building," she told him.

"Is Jake okay? I know he was trapped. He said he wasn't hurt but I was worried about him," Victor asked.

"Jake's fine. He wasn't hurt, not bad. He had a couple scrapes and bruises but he was pretty lucky. When the roof caved in, it kind of cocooned him into a small protected space. He couldn't get out on his own, but as long as he stayed there, he wasn't in any danger either. It took a while, but they got him out." She leaned in and kissed him. She meant for it to be light and gentle but Victor deepened the kiss into a long, passionate embrace.

"I'm sorry I worried you," he said as he brushed his palm across her cheek.

"I was worried, Victor. You have no idea." She took a deep breath. "When that second explosion went off, I panicked. I just went running into the building. I had to find you. When I did, when I saw you lying there with that huge beam pinning you to the ground, I felt so helpless. There was nothing I could do. You were so pale and weak. I'd never seen you that way before. You weren't even that bad in the cave when you were suffering from poison. Morrigan and Austin are the ones that saved your life. If they hadn't come along, you would have died in there. You would have died protecting Foster of all people. I don't think I would have ever forgiven you for that," she stated.

Victor smiled. "Dead and in trouble. I'm glad Morrigan and Austin showed up. How did they know anyway?"

"Mason sent them," Ariel supplied. "After the trouble the shifters and the panthers had, he wasn't convinced the fae community was safe. Dad told him we were having our annual festival Saturday, so he sent Morrigan and Austin to do flyovers. Apparently they were checking periodically throughout the day to make sure there wasn't trouble. When they didn't come back right away, Mason got worried and flew over himself. I think the shifters are going to be good friends with the fae for a very long time," Ariel commented.

"I'm glad," Victor told her. "I like the shifters. I think they are truly good people," he paused for a moment. "How's Foster? It

387

didn't look like his injuries were life threatening as long as he got to Alex in time."

"He's fine too," Ariel said scowling.

Victor slid a finger across her brow. "Why the long face?" he asked.

Ariel smiled. "I was just thinking about Foster. You almost lost your life for him after everything he's done to you. The sacrifice wouldn't have been worth it. Not for me. He's still amazed and confused. He can't understand why you did it," she smiled at him.

"Are you?" he asked.

"No," Ariel answered. "You did it because you're you. It didn't matter who was in trouble, you had to help him because that's the kind of person you are. I don't think you could have lived with yourself if you hadn't pushed Foster out of the way and took the beam yourself. I don't like it but I understand," Ariel admitted.

"I'll try not to be so much trouble in the future," he promised as he lifted her hand to his lips and kissed her knuckles softly.

"I don't think you realize it, but you've been out for days. By the time Dimitri got you to Alex I was frantic. You had stopped breathing and you'd lost so much blood. Alex said you crushed your sternum and broke eight of your ribs. The wood stuck in your thigh hit a major artery. You bled a lot from that wound, but if the wood hadn't been lodged in place, you would have bled out in seconds. Your lungs were damaged and you had a lot of internal bleeding. Basically you were a mess," she told him, tears were starting to gather in her eyes again.

"Days?" he asked. No wonder Ariel was upset. If she'd been out for days, he would have gone insane. "I really am sorry I worried you," he kissed her forehead. "I know it made it worse that I was injured saving Foster. I just had to do it. He was lying there, so sure I was going to leave him to suffer and die alone. I couldn't do it. The thought never even crossed my mind. He's not the most honorable guy in the community, but it's still my job to protect him. He still deserved to be saved and it was my job at the time to save him. I don't think he'll ever understand why I did it, but I hope you can. I hope you can forgive me for all the pain I've caused you."

"There's nothing to forgive Victor," Ariel admitted. "I have been worried. I couldn't live without you. If I lost you, I'd never recover. It didn't have anything to do with who you were saving. I guess I'm even more proud of you because it was Foster. I still don't think he deserved it, but I totally and completely understand. You are a good, caring person. That's part of why I love you so much," she grinned. "There are other parts I love more though."

"If you'd unhook this annoying IV, I could show you some of the parts I love about you." He smiled wickedly.

"Oh, I forgot. Dimitri said you needed at least one more bag. I better hook it up." She jumped out of bed and walked to a small portable fridge. Once the bag was hooked up, she climbed back onto the bed and sat before Victor. "Can I talk to you about something?" she asked.

"Sure," he studied her. Was she still upset?

"Almost losing you made me realize how much I need you," she began. "We both said we weren't ready to start our lives together for a while, as a married couple that is. At the time I honestly believed that was true," she paused.

After Dark

"But you changed your mind?" he asked hesitantly. Lying under that beam, thinking he was going to die had shaken him too. He wasn't ready to leave Ariel. They hadn't really begun to live. Marriage had also crossed his mind. He wasn't quite ready to propose and start planning the wedding, but he was closer than he had been. He wanted a little more time, maybe a year, to finish working things out. He knew he wanted Ariel to be his wife. He wanted to be a family. He wanted to try to have babies with her. He realized he wanted it all. For the first time in his life, he wanted it all.

"Not tomorrow or anything," Ariel continued. "I'm not saying let's run to Vegas. I'm just saying it hit me how much I want that. How much I want to start my life with you, as your wife. Before, I was thinking we'd move in together and maybe five or ten years from now we'd talk about marriage. I don't want to wait that long anymore. I still need a little time, but I want to be your wife Victor. I want you to be my husband," she confessed. She worried he wasn't ready for this, but she thought he needed to know how she felt.

"I love you baby," Victor said softly. "I want you to be my wife, too. I will always try to be a good husband to you," he smiled at her. "I won't do Vegas, but once I can get up and around again maybe we could go ring shopping. I've heard some people have long engagements. Would that be okay? Maybe we could set a date a year or so from now and work toward that goal?"

"Really?" she said enthusiastically, beaming. "You would really be okay with that?"

"I'd be more than okay with that," Victor assured her. "I still think we have a few things to work out from our past, but being with you has helped me work through most of my issues already. You make me a better person, Ariel." He leaned over and kissed her again. "So," he paused looking at her seriously. "I love you with every molecule of my soul. If I promise to take you ring shopping in the next couple days, will you marry me? A year should give you plenty of time to plan a wedding, won't it?" He smiled at her questioningly.

"Of course!" She exclaimed. Then she cupped his face between her hands and kissed him. Ariel was still reeling. They were actually going to get married. She didn't know anything about planning a wedding. She'd have to talk to Alex. She was already planning her wedding, maybe she'd have some pointers. Plus, her mother would be good with the details. Her thoughts were interrupted by a soft knock on the door. Victor looked at her in question. He thought they were alone.

"The warriors have been checking on you every few hours for the past couple days. It must be one of them," she told him as she got up and walked over to greet their visitor. Ariel slid the door open a crack to peak out. She smiled and moved further into the hallway. "He'll be so happy to see you!" She said enthusiastically as she pulled Atticus in for a big hug. Then she took his hand and drug him into the room.

Victor was stunned. His father had come to New York? His father had left the comfort of his Pennsylvania farm and traveled to New York City. Victor felt weak and joyous all at once. It was a good thing he was lying down. He probably would have passed out if he'd been standing.

"I'm going to go downstairs and make some tea," Ariel said as she slipped out the door. Victor needed time alone with his father.

After Dark

"So, this is how you take care of yourself?" Atticus asked pulling a chair up next to the bed. "You promised you would be careful."

Victor smiled. "I survived didn't I?" he asked.

"From what I hear, barely. If Alex hadn't been right there..." Atticus couldn't finish. The thought of losing his son was too painful to think about.

Victor reached over and took his father's hand. "Thank you for coming," he said, emotion in his voice and moisture filling his eyes. He just couldn't believe his father was really here.

Atticus placed his other hand on top of Victor's. "You scared me," he admitted quietly. "When I heard you were seriously injured, it shook me. You almost died. I realized I've been stupid. I realized I've been letting the past and my guilt control my life. There have been so many times I've sat out there on that huge farm and missed you terribly. Instead of climbing into the truck and coming to you, I just sat out there alone wishing you would visit me more often. I should have been visiting you all this time. Oh, there was a time or two that I briefly considered coming here, but I always came up with a good excuse to avoid it. I'm so sorry, son. I promise I will visit you here in that fancy apartment of yours on a regular basis."

"You like the place?" Victor asked.

"It's great," Atticus admitted. "The city really isn't that bad either. There are a lot of people, but they just ignore you. It's like being alone in a large crowd. I think I have more solitude here in New York City than I do when I go into town in Lancaster. Being here is not as difficult as I always imagined it would be," Atticus confessed.

Victor glanced up at the IV, he wanted to take the annoying thing off but it wasn't quite finished yet. "So I have some news," he said softly.

"Oh?" Atticus answered. "What's that?"

"Ariel and I have just decided to set a date to get married." Victor hurried on when he saw the huge smile on his father's face. "We still need some time. I'm still working through a few things, so is she. We decided to have a long engagement. As soon as I'm up and around, in a day or two, we're going shopping for a ring. Then we thought we'd set a date around this time next year. What do you think?" Victor asked.

"I think you're a lucky man and she's a lucky woman. It's obvious the two of you are in love. I was wondering what was taking you so long. How do her parents feel about all this?" He asked.

"I don't know why but they seem to like me," Victor confessed. He proceeded to tell his father about the festival, the ball and Alex exonerating his record. It was so nice to have his father back. Victor truly believed he was back. Getting away from that farm and coming to the city was huge. His father didn't seem at all stressed. He appeared comfortable and content to sit here and visit with his son.

Ariel quietly entered the room awhile later. "You have company," she told the two men. Today was the happiest day of her life. Victor was okay and they were going to get married. On top of that, his father came to visit. That was huge! She couldn't hide her happiness, she didn't even try.

Victor pulled the blankets off and started to get up. "Oh, I'm still hooked up." He began to pull on the IV in his arm.

"Let me do that," his father said swiping Victor's hand away. Atticus quickly removed the IV and stood. "Take a quick shower and meet us downstairs. I'll entertain your company until you arrive," he offered an arm to Ariel. "Shall we?" he asked.

Ariel took his arm and then glanced back at Victor. "Hurry. Everyone is anxious to see you," then Atticus and Ariel walked out the door.

Victor sat on the edge of the bed watching them. Today was definitely a day of miracles. He still couldn't believe his father had come for a visit. He grabbed some clean clothes and headed for the shower. Life was good. Better than he had ever imagined it could be.

Once he showered and dressed, Victor quickly headed for the living room. He heard voices and laughter echoing throughout the house. As he stepped through the door, he saw his father, Alex, all the warriors, Ariel and her parents. The house was full of all the people he loved. They were telling stories, laughing and joking. His father looked comfortable. He was actually enjoying himself. Tears welled in Victor's eyes. He was so proud of his dad. Today was a big day. Today was the start of a new beginning. His father was back and Victor actually had a plan to marry the most wonderful woman in the world. He walked across the room and settled on the couch next to Ariel. She grinned as he took her hand in his. "Life couldn't get any better than this," Victor thought. He smiled to himself as he settled in for a wonderful evening at home surrounded by family and his closest friends.

THE END